The Remarkable Adventures of
TOM SCATTERHORN

THE FORGOTTEN ECHO

THE MUSEUM'S SECRET

THE HIDDEN WORLD

The Remarkable Adventures of
TOM SCATTERHORN

THE FORGOTTEN ECHO

Henry Chancellor

OXFORD
UNIVERSITY PRESS

OXFORD

UNIVERSITY PRESS

Great Clarendon Street, Oxford OX2 6DP
Oxford University Press is a department of the University of Oxford.
It furthers the University's objective of excellence in research, scholarship,
and education by publishing worldwide in

Oxford   New York

Auckland   Cape Town   Dar es Salaam   Hong Kong   Karachi
Kuala Lumpur   Madrid   Melbourne   Mexico City   Nairobi
New Delhi   Shanghai   Taipei   Toronto

With offices in

Argentina   Austria   Brazil   Chile   Czech Republic   France   Greece
Guatemala   Hungary   Italy   Japan   Poland   Portugal   Singapore
South Korea   Switzerland   Thailand   Turkey   Ukraine   Vietnam

Oxford is a registered trade mark of Oxford University Press
in the UK and in certain other countries

Database right Oxford University Press (maker)

First published 2012

British Library Cataloguing in Publication Data

Data available

ISBN: 978-0-19-272744-2

1 3 5 7 9 10 8 6 4 2

Printed in Great Britain by the CPI Group (UK) Ltd, Croydon, CR0 4YY

Paper used in the production of this book is a natural,
recyclable product made from wood grown in sustainable forests.
The manufacturing process conforms to the environmental
regulations of the country of origin.

FOR CHLOË.

CONTENTS

CHAPTER 1

THE VISIONS OF BETILDA MARCHMONT

The mist had been collecting in the bottom of the valley for some time now. It puddled in the dips, laid siege to the trees, and nestled around the walls like an unwanted guest. Miriam Marchmont was not happy. Not about the mist, but about the car headlights moving up the long drive towards her. She glanced at her watch: it was 4.20 p.m. Already the staff had gone home; the teashop was closed, as this was 31st October, the last day before they shut the castle up for the winter. Though they did not technically close until 5 p.m., and last admissions were at 4.30 p.m., Miriam had hoped, this being Friday, *and* the last day, that she might be able to wrap things up a little earlier. It was not to be.

'What is it?' asked her brother Edward, who was just cashing up the day's meagre takings in the shop.

'Someone's arrived,' Miriam replied tersely, wiping a line of dust off the window frame.

'What, now? But we're closing.'

'I know we're closing.'

'Then you'll just have to send them away, Midge.'

'But I can't just send them away.'

1

'Yes you can. Tell them they're too late. We've already shut for the winter, and they'll have to come back next year. That's the truth,' he added, closing the door and hastily scurrying down a passage. Miriam watched him go. The truth was Edward was a coward when it came to this sort of thing. How typical.

'Oh dear.'

With a sigh Miriam descended the great oak stairway towards the hall. This was going to be unpleasant. Visitors to Marchmont Castle had often made a great effort to get there. Even though they were in central Scotland and far from any main road, tourists from Texas and even New Zealand were not uncommon.

There was a crunch of footsteps across the gravel followed by a loud rap on the door. Miriam pretended she hadn't heard it.

'Hello?'

Another rap. Louder.

'Hello?'

Miriam steeled herself for a polite but firm rebuttal and reached for the latch.

'Excellent. Then I'm not too late.' A long, dark silhouette strode purposefully out of the gloom and into the hall. 'Last entry is four thirty, which by my watch is in three minutes, is it not?'

'I'm afraid we've already—'

'I would hate to have missed it. I have come rather a long way, you see. All the way from Peru, as it happens.'

Peru? Already Miriam was in retreat. The man took off his gloves and looked around. He was extremely tall, high shouldered and narrow framed, and he wore an immaculate long grey coat. His forehead bulged a little beneath a dome of thickly oiled hair, and Miriam could not help noticing that he seemed to be standing on tiptoes.

'I'm really very sorry but—'

'Don't worry, Miss Marchmont, I have no interest in your extensive collection of Scottish thimbles, fishing rods, stags' heads, tartan teddy-bears, nor do I want to see the pathetic collection of wooden rakes that passes for Bygones in the shed.'

The man grinned and Miriam bristled visibly. She and her brother may have been down on their luck and forced against their will to open the crumbling castle to the public, on the promise of some rather gloomy staterooms, a homemade scone, and the remote possibility of seeing the family ghost walking through a wall (which in truth had last 'appeared' to a drunken servant over a hundred years ago), nevertheless, she was still the Lady of the House. Had anyone else dared to speak to her like that she would have turned them straight out of the door . . . but there was something oddly commanding about the visitor. She could almost feel his yellowish eyes boring into her as he spoke.

'So what exactly *have* you come to see?' she snapped. 'Is it something specific?'

'As a matter of fact, it is,' he rumbled. 'The room of remarkable paintings made by your great-aunt, Betilda Marchmont. She was an artist, I believe?'

Miriam Marchmont was rather caught off guard. This was a rare request, and one that she found hard to turn down. That Betilda's oeuvre had been overlooked by history was a wrong that she was determined to right.

'So you've heard about them?' she murmured, her frostiness melting by the second.

'Indeed I have,' smiled the man, sensing that he had pushed the right button. 'In fact, ever since I found out about her curious life seeing these pictures has become something of an obsession. I do hope that will be possible, Miss Marchmont?'

Miriam wavered.

'And that is really all you want to see?'

'More than anything else in the world.'

The man was smiling strangely in anticipation. He happened to be telling the truth.

'Very well. How can I refuse?'

The visitor bowed graciously, disguising his excitement. Miriam took the stranger's money and led the way up the great staircase to the top floor.

'I suppose you've read that Betilda was an eccentric recluse, a madwoman whose family kept her locked up in the attics?'

'Something like that.'

'Well it is true she occupied the north wing for many years, and she was eventually committed to an asylum by her own brother. But in my humble opinion Betilda was far from mad. She merely had an overheated imagination, which she found far more interesting than the real world. That was why she chose to spend every waking moment lost inside it.'

'But she never left this house?'

'Never. Barely even left her room. Which makes it all the more remarkable.' Miriam paused and caught the visitor by the sleeve. 'Would I had a tenth of her imagination. What things *I* would have done.' The tall stranger stared down at his host, who was wearing a scarf and three separate jackets to keep out the cold. She seemed to be winking at him. 'Knot garden.'

4

He glanced through the mullioned window into the small courtyard below, where a symmetrical pattern of low box hedges was cut into curiously spiky shapes.

'Insects?'

'Beetles. Betilda had a fascination with them. She planted and clipped them herself. She liked to go walking down there in the evenings.'

The visitor stared at the dark forms appreciatively. All of this was making a great deal of sense . . . but he must be patient. On they went through a warren of narrow corridors lined with gloomy portraits.

'And this is where she lived.' Miriam paused before a small panelled door. '*Nunquam minus sola—quam cum sola.*'

'What?'

Miriam pointed at the inscription painted in gold on the lintel.

'"Never less a lonely lady—than when a lady alone." Do you read Latin?'

The tall man shook his head vaguely.

'My daughter does. I don't have much use for it.'

'Shame. Betilda read it fluently of course.'

With a small smile Miriam led the way into a small square room that was panelled on all sides. In the corner stood a narrow bed, and next to it, a simple writing desk and chair. A few odd sketches lined the walls. There was nothing else here.

'It's like a prison.'

'Blank page,' corrected Miriam. 'Betilda hated contact with other people. She found it violently distracting. She even installed that.' Miriam pointed to a small panel on which there was a painting of a waiter riding a bicycle. He hadn't any mouth.

'What is it?'

'It's a dumb waiter.'

The visitor seemed bewildered.

'Perhaps you don't have them in Peru. It's a little lift—for food. She had her meals sent up from the kitchen, along with letters and quite a lot else I suspect. Dumb—waiter? It's a joke.'

'How amusing.'

'Yes. I suppose not everyone understands it.'

The tall man grunted impatiently. He was beginning to find this bossy little woman mildly irritating. He glanced out of the window at the remains of the day.

'So where are the paintings then?'

Miriam smiled and moved towards a small door in the panelling, turning the key in the lock.

'Mind your head,' she said, ushering him inside. The room was unexpectedly long and large, and as the tall man's eyes adjusted to the light he was surprised to find himself in the midst of a deep forest. On every surface were great trees, their branches snaking up onto the ceiling overhead.

'Light?'

Miriam drew a pair of torches from her pocket and handed him one. The visitor took it gratefully and switched it on. Through the endless forests he began to pick out castles, rivers, villages, and people—but of course, they weren't quite people, they were fantastical goblins, fairies, elves, dwarves, knights—

'All the usual flimflam.'

'Excuse me?'

'Aha.'

The visitor peered closer and saw he had been too quick to pass judgement. Here and there among the trees were other, much more sinister creatures, insects that he recognized . . . flame-coloured spiders, vast brown centipedes, burnt-headed ghouls holding gangs of savage red beetles straining at the leash . . .

'Quite something, isn't it?'

The stranger coughed to disguise his excitement. He picked out a line of heavily-laden beetles with his torch beam. They were all roped together and herded by a hollow-eyed drover wearing a distinctive black beret.

'Even old Rainbird,' he murmured, inspecting that grinning, gargoyle-like face. 'Extraordinario.'

'Yes he's a funny little fellow isn't he?' said Miriam, somewhat puzzled by the stranger's reaction. 'The whole thing's a story, you know. A fantasy that took Betilda many years to imagine. This is where it all begins.'

Miriam walked across the room and flashed her torch at a dark column of rock rising up in the centre of a vast cave. Clinging to its upper reaches were roofs and balconies, and slender stone causeways sprang from its sides. The whole edifice teemed with outlandish insects of every shape and colour.

'It's called Scarazand,' she said confidently. 'Odd name, isn't it?'

The visitor nodded: he knew exactly where this was. It was his home.

Miriam flashed her torch at the Latin banner fluttering above.

'Out of the darkness of Scarazand there came a great light,' she translated. 'The kingdom of the devil is also the birth place of the hero.'

'The hero?'

'We assume that is what he is. You really can't miss him. He's everywhere.' Miriam darted her torchlight around the room, picking out a knight clad in a magnificent suit of black armour. 'There, there, there, over there . . .'

The visitor seemed genuinely surprised. Stalking forward, he fixed his beam on an image of the knight galloping through the forest. For a long moment he stood in silence, studying his armour—the swirling layers of gleaming chitin that formed the breastplate, the intricate tangle of dark spikes around the collar, and that extraordinary helmet, half-wolf, half-beetle.

'Scaramoor,' he muttered to himself, as if he had just remembered the name. 'Scaramoor.'

'I'm sorry?'

'Who is that knight?'

'Nobody knows precisely. But there is a family tradition that he was someone that she knew.'

'Oh?'

'The servants used to overhear Betilda talking to herself as she worked. They thought he might have been someone she was secretly in love with. Either that or a ghost.'

'A ghost?' The visitor snorted. 'How quaint.'

Miriam bristled. As the self-appointed keeper of Betilda Marchmont's flame, she took a very dim view of such mockery.

'Actually, I happen to believe that he was a real person.'

'And why is that?'

'Somewhere in this room Betilda secretly painted his portrait beneath the helmet. She recorded doing so in her diary.' The visitor turned to stare at her. 'And now I suppose you are going to ask me where it is. But I'm afraid I can't help you.'

'Why not?'

'Because I don't know,' Miriam said flatly. 'I would like to know, we all would. But Betilda disguised it very well. It could be anywhere. Anywhere at all.'

The tall man glowered at all the paintings of the knight in the endless forests. There were certainly a lot of them.

'A secret hero. How conveniently mysterious.'

Miriam Marchmont shrugged.

'Artists do things like that, don't they? Indulge their own private fantasies, make little jokes.' With her torch she picked out a small woman dancing arm in arm through the trees with a fat golden man. 'Who knows who any of these people are supposed to be, are they real, or not?'

The visitor had his suspicions. And there was something disconcertingly familiar about that golden man, even though he seemed to be covered in blue butterflies. Betilda Marchmont was plainly as mad as a snake.

'I read about some great battle with serpents?' he rumbled, disguising his curiosity. 'Is that here too?'

Miriam sighed.

'Ah yes. You would have done.'

Unfortunately, this was the most famous image Betilda had ever painted—but in Miriam's eyes for all the wrong reasons. An Austrian psychologist had once visited the house and described it as the finest vision of the future ever painted by a madwoman, and ever since a steady stream of local schoolchildren had come to snigger and gawp. She walked around the corner and flashed her torch at the large scene that dominated the entire wall.

'There you are. "The death of the colony."'

'What did you say?'

Miriam pointed at the large Latin inscription fluttering across the top.

'I see.'

The visitor moved forward uneasily, his torch sweeping across the picture. It certainly was impressive. On each side the forest gave way to a wide snowbound valley, upon which hordes of silvery serpents were hurling themselves at squares of grim-faced men and beetles and every other kind of insect. The battle was vast and bloody and intricately painted, but none of these details interested the visitor. His eye was immediately drawn to the events in the foreground. Here Betilda had painted a stockade of dark towers, inside which there was a giant serpent rearing up above the chaos. It was something like a cobra, with a flaring hood and flashing yellow eyes, and it was about to strike at a dark cloaked figure lying on the ground before it. But at that very moment the mysterious knight had galloped in and buried his spear deep into its white underbelly.

'George and the Dragon,' said Miriam. 'That's what I've always thought, anyway. Betilda's knight rides in and saves the day.' She smiled and turned to the visitor. He wasn't smiling at all. In fact in the half-light he looked positively grey. 'Obviously it's the end.'

'The end?'

'*Ut moreris vives.*' Miriam pointed at the inscription fluttering across the debris below. 'You will die the way you lived.'

The man pondered the words a moment.

'What does that mean?' There was an urgency in his voice that he could not disguise.

'It's a riddle. Or a prophecy. Both, probably. If this is the death of the colony, then something, or someone, will die.'

'But who?'

Miriam shrugged. The visitor stared hard at the knight killing the serpent, saving the cloaked figure lying on the ground. On closer examination he was not entirely human, either. He had a large black beetle's head and jaws perched on his slender shoulders.

'I'm finding this all very hard to understand, Miss Marchmont.'

'Perhaps that's the point.'

'What?'

'Nec habet victoria laudem.'

'CARAMBA!' The tall man screwed up his eyes in rage. 'Will you just stop spouting the Latin!'

'I'm simply—'

'Translation. Just give me the translation, Miss Marchmont.'

Miriam was unnerved at the stranger's violent reaction. Her torchbeam flitted towards a bird standing at the edge of the valley with its bill stuck in an oyster shell.

'Although a victor, he may not have praise.'

'At last. A clear, simple fact. The winner of this battle is unpopular, then?'

Miriam nodded.

'That is one interpretation.'

Oddly, this seemed to calm the visitor.

'And are there any more?'

'This was the last panel Betilda painted before she was taken to the asylum,' Miriam replied, briskly checking her watch. It was long past closing time and she had lost patience with this peculiar gentleman some time ago. 'I appreciate the meaning isn't straightforward, but Betilda's weaving a rich tapestry, using riddles that can be read in many different ways. These are not photographs, you know.'

The tall man scowled. Unfortunately he suspected that was precisely what they were.

'Have you seen enough now?'

His eyes swivelled from the battling insects to his host, rattling her keys in her pocket impatiently.

'Miss Marchmont, I need to know something.'

Miriam's lips tightened with frustration.

'You can ask, but as I have been trying to explain—'

'Be quiet. You see, like you, I too want to discover the identity of that mysterious knight. It is very important to me. More important than you can possibly realize.'

At first Miriam did not understand. Then the stranger stepped forward and ran his hands around the edge of a panel. Suddenly a very unpleasant idea came into her head.

'You'll find each of these paintings is securely fastened to the wall.'

'I don't doubt it.'

Deftly the visitor flicked a small black blade out of his cuff. Miriam's pulse quickened: what was he going to do with that? Was he a thief? He didn't look like a thief, but . . .

'I'm warning you, before you go any further, we are directly connected to the police station.'

The stranger ignored her and approached the great battle scene, knife in hand.

'One call from me and they will be here in a matter of minutes!'

The man smirked: he could have told her that he had already cut the telephone lines from the house but he didn't bother. With calm intent he raised the flat of the blade and began to scrape violently. Miriam gasped.

'Now look here, stop that! Stop that! That is a work of art!'

The visitor ignored her, razoring hard into the knight's intricately painted helmet . . . large flecks of black paint began cascading to the floor.

'Stop it! I command you to stop it this instant!'

Miriam Marchmont paced up and down frantically, watching the delicate flakes fly. How on earth could she stop this maniac, this vandal? Punch him in the head? Kick him in the shins? But she couldn't help noticing that the more he scraped the more he revealed something hidden underneath . . . Half an ear, part of an eye . . .

'This is going to take far too long.'

Turning, the stranger spotted a fire bucket in the corner, next to a large bottle of bleach . . .

'Oh no. Absolutely not.' Miriam stepped valiantly before it. 'Don't think you can just just march in here and—'

Miriam found herself unceremoniously knocked aside.

SLAP! On went the bleach, splashing all over the painting, burning into its surface. Rivulets of colour ran in lines down onto the floor. Miriam Marchmont stared at him open-mouthed, then scrambled to her feet.

'That's it! I'm going to find Edward and . . . and . . .'

SPLASH!

On went the water. Miriam shrieked.

'By George, you've done it now!'

The tall man barely heard the door slam behind him. Wiping away the black paint with his sleeve he stepped back to admire his handiwork. His eyes betrayed only the merest flicker of emotion as he stared at the image. This was not what he had expected at all.

'Betilda Marchmont, how did you slip through my net?' he growled, then with bleach and knife set to work on the cloaked black beetle figure lying on the ground. A fur hat, a tight fitting coat . . . red and gold insignia . . . the true image did not take long to reveal itself. With one final angry splat of water, the tall man revealed it for what it was. The face was contorted and dripping with pink paint, but it was a portrait—unmistakably.

'You see!'

The small wooden door banged open and in strode Miriam Marchmont in high dudgeon, reluctantly followed by her brother.

'Look what he's done! I insist you stop him! Edward?'

It took the best part of two seconds to take in the image before them. There was the great painting, scarred and dripping wet, and yet it was different, somehow. The mysterious beetle-headed figure lying on the ground had gone, replaced by a hideous, twisted portrait of a man in black. His face was bloodied, and there was a look of sheer terror in his eyes as the serpent bore down on him. But that was not all. The hero knight's elaborate helmet had also been scraped away to reveal a face underneath. And he was not a man, but a boy, with a determined set jaw and dark piercing eyes, quite at odds with his thatch of blond hair. He looked a little terrifying, too.

'That is s-s-sheer, unadulterated, v-v-vandalism, that is what

14

that is,' stammered Miriam, unable to disguise her curiosity at Betilda's hero revealed at last.

'But who . . . I mean, who is he?'

It was Edward who asked the question, to no one in particular.

'His name is Tom Scatterhorn,' rumbled a low voice from the darkness. Such was the shock of seeing the changed picture that Miriam and her brother had almost forgotten about the person who had revealed it. There he was, leaning against the forest in the corner, his sleeves covered in black and pink paint.

'Tom *Scatterhorn?*' repeated Edward, who had never heard the name. 'And what about . . . '

It took just about a second for Edward's brain to catch up with what he saw. The small chin, large forehead . . . and those extraordinary lizard-like eyes that seemed to stare right into your very skull . . . he gasped and took an involuntary step backwards. Even cowering and defenceless beneath that great snake thing, it was him. The visitor. They were one and the same.

'That's right,' growled the man, walking right out of Betilda Marchmont's visions and into the room. Miriam shivered; the air seemed to have suddenly grown colder. There was a lazy, predatory smirk on the stranger's face.

'So you knew B-B-Betilda, erm . . . did you?'

'As a matter of fact I didn't, Miriam. Which makes this even more remarkable, don't you think?' He turned to admire his glowering portrait. 'How did she achieve such a likeness without once meeting her sitter?'

'Who are you?' snorted Edward. He noticed that the tall man had shaken something like a clear rubber ball from his cuff and his fingers were skimming over its intricately decorated surface.

'My name is Don Gervase Askary,' said the visitor. 'I doubt you have ever heard of me.' With a curl of his long fingers he took in the entire room. 'This is my world.'

'I'll bet it jolly well is,' snorted Edward shortly. Obviously this was some loony from the loony bin—*that* was who he was—one of Betilda's cronies got loose, it was all becoming very clear now—only . . . Edward, who had never been much good at maths, suddenly remembered that Betilda was his great-aunt, and had died rather a long time ago, before his father was born, in fact. Which meant that this man must be at least a hundred and . . . and—oh. Oh dear. Erm—

'And are you . . . the king of this world?' asked Miriam, keen to humour the madman. She had to admit she could not account for the portrait, but she'd tripped the burglar alarm so the police would be here pretty soon to take him away. Distract him, that was the thing to do, with madmen.

'King?' The visitor seemed a little put out. 'Something more, Miriam, than a mere *"king"*.'

'Emperor?'

Don Gervase grinned wolfishly, revealing a line of broken teeth.

'Supreme lord of the endless forests, ruler of the night?'

'No, not even that, Miriam. Though I am very special. Almost unique. I can change form from man to beetle and back again. Metamorphose. At will.'

'How exciting. What fun.'

Miriam began to edge backwards. He really was a fruitcake. Quite doolally. That was the police now, she could hear movement out in the corridor . . . probably the dog section. Here come the boys in blue, and not a moment too soon . . .

The visitor stiffened oddly, his fingers sliding across that curious ball.

'I'm very sorry about this. It's really too bad, seeing as we were getting on so well. But there it is.'

Suddenly something red and shiny burst into the room. Two somethings . . . like dogs, only—

Don Gervase Askary whispered low and before Miriam and Edward could utter a word the bombardier beetles' metallic jaws closed around their chests, crushing them like paper.

'DOWN!' he screamed.

Instantly the insects let go. Miriam and Edward Marchmont fell to the ground, their bodies twisting horribly. The pair of yellow-eyed beetles clattered to their master's heel and awaited the next command.

'You just saw too much, I am afraid. Pity.'

Miriam stared at the creatures in terror. She recognized them from the paintings all around.

'So you . . . you really are . . . '

'Who I said I am? Yes, Miriam. I am as real as Scarazand, a place in the distant future to which your beloved Betilda has obviously strayed. How she did it, I don't know, but she was extremely lucky not to get caught. I would have had her ripped to pieces.'

Miriam's eyes widened.

'And that boy . . . '

'Tom Scatterhorn? He is another traveller, and he is alive right now in fact. Why Betilda decided to paint him I have no idea. But it doesn't matter, because he won't be alive for much longer.'

Edward stared up at the tall stranger, his life draining away.

'You mean, you're going to murder him?'

Don Gervase smiled hideously.

'But you can't do that.'

'Can't I?'

Miriam gasped and pointed at the vast bleach splattered canvas.

'Isn't he going to save your life?'

Don Gervase Askary scowled darkly. He had never believed he would find the truth so uncomfortable.

'Miriam, do you think I am going to be held hostage to fortune by the visions of a madwoman?'

'But you—'

'Enough! That battle is pure fantasy, along with the rest of this flim-flam. It hasn't happened yet, and I shall see that it never will.'

With a snap of his fingers, he led his beetles away towards the door. Miriam did not understand.

'But supposing it's the truth,' she persisted, 'supposing Betilda didn't make it up?'

Don Gervase Askary winced at the suggestion. He turned and stared at his victims coldly.

'Don't kill him. Please . . . '

'I hardly think you are in a position to tell me what I can and cannot do.'

With a grimace he took one last look at that great painting. Even in the half darkness, that boy's blond hair was glowing like a lamp, taunting him. How could this possibly be true? How could it?

'*Ut moreris vives,*' whispered Miriam, her life slipping away.

Don Gervase Askary said nothing. He spun on his heel and walked out.

CHAPTER 2

Beginning, Middle . . .

'Tom?'

'I'm coming!'

'Well please get a move on! You've been up there for hours!'

Tom Scatterhorn knelt in the middle of the chaos of his bedroom floor staring angrily at his half-empty bag. He had already packed it and pulled everything out twice.

'I can't understand how it can take you so long. You're only going for two weeks.'

'I just don't know what to take.'

'How can you not know what to take? Isn't it obvious?'

But that was precisely the problem. It wasn't obvious at all. Last time Tom had been to stay at the Scatterhorn Museum he had narrowly avoided a tidal wave in Polynesia. The time before that he had found himself on a tiger hunt in India, by way of an Edwardian ice fair a hundred years ago. The Scatterhorn Museum was an old, gloomy, and decidedly peculiar place in Dragonport, a small town on the other side of the country. Tom owned it, loved it, had paid for its restoration, but felt so embarrassed about that he preferred to keep it separate from his own normal life.

The Scatterhorn Museum was his own strange, secret world, and it was also the gateway to many other strange and secret worlds . . .

'Taxi's here,' said his mother, opening the front door as a car turned into Middlesuch Close. 'Taxi's *here*, Tom.'

'OK OK.'

Tom scanned the mess in hope rather than inspiration. What to take? It was a Scatterhorn trait to hoard unwanted stuff, and Tom seemed to have caught the bug particularly early. Somehow his room was full of everything from elk horns to dried puffer fish . . . there were ammonites, sand dollars, stuffed spiders, broken clocks, sweet wrappers, an ostrich egg . . . how did all this stuff get in here?

'Tom, you really will miss this train!'

'I'm coming!' he shouted, staring at the mess desperately. Balaclava? Flip-flops? He glanced at a postcard of a girl with dark hair and deeply tanned skin, laughing as a blue parrot stood on her head. 'Marquesas, Sweet, Sweet,' it said. This was Tom's friend Pearl Smoot, whom he hadn't seen since the last time he went to Dragonport. What would she take? Something practical, like a compass or a penknife or—no, of course . . . Tom scrambled forward and, lifting a loose floorboard, pulled out a dog-eared exercise book entitled 'Scarazand'. Scarazand could not be found on any map or internet site, and only very few people knew it existed. Tom was one of them—Pearl Smoot was another—they had been there together, last summer, to rescue Pearl's father, Arlo. Scarazand was an underground colony of insects in the distant future, ruled by a certain Don Gervase Askary, a man who haunted Tom's dreams . . . Tom flicked through the scribbled pages, the diagrams . . . this book contained everything he could remember about that place, and Pearl's memories too . . . this was precious, unique . . . supposing he lost it?

'Right, I'll get him.'

Footsteps thundered up the stairs and Tom quickly replaced the book under the floorboard and shoved a handful of socks into his bag.

'Bloody hell.'

Tom's father, a tall, spare man with a mop of blond hair, appeared at the door and stared down at the chaos.

'Not a good moment to have a clear out, Tom.'

'I'm not. I was just . . . packing.'

Tom thrust his feet into his trainers and picked up a thick jumper from the floor.

'You're seriously leaving your room like this?'

'Well if I tidied it up now I'd miss the train. And I thought we were in a hurry?'

Sam Scatterhorn briefly considered saying something but decided now was not the moment. He surveyed the sea of stuff and shook his head.

'Just don't tell your mother,' he whispered.

Tom took one last look at his room. He glanced at the floorboard, with its precious book hidden below. Suddenly he had an overwhelming sensation that he would never see this room ever again.

'Sure you've got everything?' said his father.

'I think so.'

'Good. Let's go.'

He pulled the door tight shut and ran down the stairs. Tom's mother emerged from the kitchen in a fluster.

'You can't do this, Tom, it's too stressful. The train's in twenty minutes. Have you got your ticket?'

'Yes.'

'Both of them? Because there are two?' she said, stuffing some sandwiches into his bag.

'I know. I checked.'

'He'll be fine, Poppy,' said his father leading the way past the old camper van on bricks down to the rusting gate.

'And you have Jos and Melba's number in case you miss them? Because you know how hare-brained they are. They've probably forgotten you're even coming. Probably—'

'Relax, Mum, really. It's OK. I've got everything.'

'I'm sorry, I know, you're old enough now and all that. But—'

Tom's mother took a deep breath, then another, but it didn't work. She stared at her son and brushed his tangle of blond hair out of his eyes. He looked so like his father.

'I just worry about you, my darling. I can't help it.'

She hugged him tight.

'Me too,' said Tom, holding her tight. In fact, he was far more concerned about his parents going to Ecuador to collect moths than about any trip they had ever been on before.

'So we'll see you after New Year then,' said his dad cheerfully, slapping Tom round the shoulders and chucking his bag into the waiting cab.

'Dad?'

'Yes?'

Tom looked up into his father's wide, weather-beaten face, wrinkled by years of collecting insects in all weathers on every continent on earth.

'You will be . . . you will be careful up that river. I mean, like . . . you won't do anything crazy, will you?'

'Careful is my middle name,' he grinned. 'Anyway, when do I not do something crazy?'

'Exactly.'

Sam Scatterhorn's eyes twinkled, surprised at his son's concern.

'It's moths we're collecting, Tom, not venomous, fire-breathing snakes. Moths.' Sam Scatterhorn could tell his son was not convinced. 'But we are going to do something exciting. The night we get back we've been invited to a birthday party in London. A very interesting birthday party indeed.'

'Go go go,' said his mother, planting another kiss on his forehead and pushing him into the car.

'I'll tell you all about it when we get back,' Sam winked. 'But don't you worry about us. You have a good time—promise?'

'Bye!'

Sam and Poppy Scatterhorn stood at the gate of the scruffiest house in Middlesuch Close, waving, and Tom turned and waved back, and kept right on waving until the taxi turned the corner and the two silhouettes were gone. Tom stared at the grey pavements flashing past, the bare trees, the rows of identical houses . . . suddenly he was overwhelmed by a feeling that a door was shutting on this old life. Perhaps he would never return to Middlesuch Close, go back to school, see his friends . . . he was never coming back . . .

'You're a bit young to be running away, aren't you, son?'

Tom looked up and saw the cab driver grinning at him in the mirror.

'Sorry?'

'You said you ain't never coming back.'

'Oh I was . . . nothing. Just talking to myself.'

'Oh.'

Tom's throat tightened, and he was surprised to find his eyes had filled with hot tears. He blinked them away angrily.

Later, on the train, Tom stared out of the window at his own half-reflection above the flooded fields. Perhaps he should have told them. Maybe that would have made it easier. But the problem was, during the course of Tom's remarkable adventures he had collected so many secrets they had become remarkably easy to keep. He took out a crumpled piece of paper from his back pocket and stared at it. He had read and re-read it so many times that it was starting to fall apart.

'Oh my . . . good god . . . what's that?'

Another crash. Scream. (Is that an animal?)

'Who are you?'

Pause. Scratching. Digging?

'What do you want from us?'

DG laughter. Vicious.

'You really don't know who I am, do you?'

'No.'

'Are you the parents of this boy?'

Deafening silence.

'I'll take that as a yes.'

'He's got nothing to do with this! Nothing at all!'

(Brave speech, Sam.)

'You really never guessed, did you?'

'What?' Poppy uncertain. Nervous. 'Guessed what?'

'Young Tom is the reason why you are here. And he is the reason why we are here, too.'

Silence.

'He has set you up. He has betrayed you.'

'What? What are you talking about?' Sam shouts.

'Oh I know, it's hard to take. Why would he do a thing like that?' DG sniggers. 'So trusting. So foolish. Its tragic.'

Click of fingers. Screams—a fight. Heavy thump. Silence. Sam and Poppy Scatterhorn dead? Hard to know. Much insect noise.

'Remove them. Destroy the evidence. See that they are taken down to join the rest of the riff-raff.'

Tom knew the words so well he hardly needed to read them any more. They were scribbled out by his friend Pearl, copied from her father's secret notebook. Arlo Smoot was a radio spy: he could tune in to voices from the past, present, and future— and this scene he had heard in his headphones and copied down. It was not a prediction—it was a fact. Arlo Smoot did not make mistakes. One day, somewhere, somehow, Don Gervase Askary, the ruler of that vast empire of insects, would either kidnap or kill his parents, and it would be all Tom's fault. How, why—he did not know. The only question was, when?

But the probability of somehow betraying his parents wasn't Tom's biggest secret. There was travelling through time, finding an elixir of life . . . all that, and then—there was what was going on inside his head. Which in a way was the most precious secret of all.

To put it briefly, Tom Scatterhorn's mind had become beetlized. It had happened last year, down a hole on a remote island, where an unremarkable grey insect had laid its egg in his ear. When it hatched, the tiny grub had burrowed down through the soft cartilage and out into his brain, its blind meanderings creating a storm of new connections in the forgotten recesses of his mind . . . Luckily Tom had been forced to take an antidote—killing the grub and stopping the conversion instantly—but nevertheless, damage had been done.

What did this mean? On the outside—nothing. Tom looked the same. But inside, like millions and millions of others, he could hear the heartbeat of Scarazand. These pulses came from the Queen, a beetle the size of a nuclear submarine, who lay at the centre of that vast underground colony hidden in the future. Sometimes it was just a dull thud in the distance; sometimes it was like a hot wire passing through his skull. He might be walking down a corridor at school, riding his bicycle, waiting for a bus, or even about to cross the finish line in a running race when he closed his eyes to find a red wave rushing through the darkness towards him, a roaring screaming message booming out across the universe. What could he do?

Pretend to faint. That was usually the best idea. Tom dropped instantly to the ground, keeping his eyes tight shut and concentrating hard on something else, anything—as the wall of sound engulfed him.

'Look, Scatty Scatterhorn's having another fit!'

Anxious voices, shakes, prods, a few kicks—Tom would ignore them all till the wave broke and rumbled away. And when he opened his eyes, his head was fizzing and the sound was gone. He had no idea what it meant. But he had no doubt where it had come from. Don Gervase Askary possessed a small rubbery ball named the mesmerion, with which he could broadcast instructions, orders, even his own voice straight into the minds of each subject, using the vast power of the Queen. It was like a radio inside Tom's head, permanently switched to full volume that he could never turn off.

It took a while for doctors to explain these strange fainting fits. First they thought it was epilepsy, then diabetes, then rabies, bubonic plague—Tom traipsed from surgery to surgery, and the questions became more and more exotic . . . have you ever eaten a thousand-year-old egg? No. Have you ever shared a meal with an ape? No . . . What colour do you see when you close your eyes? Erm . . . Tom's worst nightmare was finding himself in a brain scanner and being told that a small insect had burrowed from his ear into his brain and that he had a head like a maggoty apple. He would probably never be allowed to leave hospital again. But somehow that never happened, and eventually the doctors were forced to admit they could find nothing wrong: Tom was just a completely normal thirteen-year-old boy, and his curious fainting fits were nothing more than 'growing pains'—a mysteriously convenient expression that Tom did not quite understand. But it turned out that everyone who was growing had them. Simply, blood not moving round his narrow body swiftly enough. Growing pains. Growing pains. His parents sighed with relief and took him out for a pizza to celebrate.

'Well that's something. You're officially normal,' giggled his mother.

'Ish,' added his father, his eyes smiling. 'Not too many thirteen-year-old boys I know were given a sapphire by a one-hundred-and-fifty-year-old man to buy a museum.'

'Well yes, apart from that.'

Had Sam Scatterhorn known about his son's visit to Scarazand he might have mentioned that too, but he didn't. Because the fact was Tom hadn't told anyone what had really happened to him. He didn't want anyone to think he was some weird, half-insect alien from a film: definitely not. And anyway, it was not a complete conversion. He was not, and he never would be, Askary's slave. And thankfully, ever since last year when he had visited the museum, Don Gervase Askary had not chosen to speak to him directly. Amongst the millions of other converts, he obviously wasn't very important. Tom even began to wonder if he had forgotten about him . . .

It was because of this that, despite his predicament, Tom felt happy. He was looking forward to going back to the museum, seeing Uncle Jos and Aunt Melba, perhaps meeting August and Sir Henry again in some unexpected way and finding himself on some new adventure, far away from the tentacles of Scarazand . . . if that was possible.

Tom glanced around the busy train, packed with tired commuters silently reading the evening paper. 'Prime Minister's daughter sick from mystery insect bite,' ran the headline. Tom picked up a grubby paper from the floor and opened it. Someone had discovered the tracks of a giant centipede in the desert in

Australia. There was a photograph of eight identical weightlifters from Bulgaria. A man leaving a lonely pub in Scotland swore he saw two beetles the size of bloodhounds running away across the moor . . .

'We are now approaching Waterloo station, your final station stop . . . '

Tom shook his muddled head, picked up his bag and joined the scramble out onto the great concourse. The problem was, the more you looked for signs of Scarazand the more you found them. Even now, all these people rushing in all directions, dodging out of shops, through barriers, down escalators, just like so many . . . Tom closed his eyes and took a deep breath.

You've got to stop this. You're going nuts. It's just your imagination. Ignore it.

Doggedly he made his way towards the large notice board and stared up at the flashing numbers. This was where he was to wait for Jos and Melba, and then they were all going to travel back up to Dragonport together. But Tom's mother was right, it was more than likely that they would have forgotten this arrangement, and Tom would probably have to make his own way there. Tom walked over to the entrance of the underground and looked down at the queue of disgruntled passengers standing around the barriers.

'Stand back, ladies and gents! Stand back please! The platforms are temporarily closed . . . severe overcrowding . . . we ask for your patience please . . . ' Garbled words echoed above the growing hubbub of angry voices.

'I wouldn't bother going down there if I were you.'

Tom looked up to see a man shuffle up next to him. He appeared slightly lopsided, and he was carrying a large white box.

'Mayhem, innit? Mayhem.'

'Is it broken?' asked Tom, clutching his piece of paper with the scribbled train times.

'Is it broken!' The man guffawed loudly. 'Everything's broken round here, mate. And where's all these people come from? Someone's called the cavalry.'

Tom was aware that suddenly there seemed to be hundreds of people behind him, jostling to go down the steps. In fact the whole concourse was a seething mass of people. He glanced down at his watch. Jos and Melba would almost certainly be late now, and they had less than an hour to make the connection—perhaps he should forget the underground and take a bus instead . . .

'So there you are.'

Tom turned round and the lopsided man had melted away into the crowd.

'I've been looking for you.'

Tom felt the hairs stand up on the back of his neck. That voice . . . little more than a growl . . . he knew it only too well . . . like distant thunder inside his head. He closed his eyes and saw fire licking along the dark horizon . . .

'Over here.'

Tom turned and turned again, past blurring angry faces . . .

'Mind where you're going!' shouted a man as Tom's bag hit him in the back.

'Sorry I'm . . . '

'In a daze are you?' said another, ostentatiously wiping his suit.

'This way.'

Tom's skin began to crawl.

'Leave me alone,' he breathed.

'Leave you alone? But you haven't heard what I have to say.'

'I don't care . . . I don't—'

The next moment a burst of energy slammed Tom onto his back sending stars dancing before his eyes.

'Let's not have a scene, shall we?' hissed the voice inside his head. 'I only want to talk to you.'

'I'm not listening,' gasped Tom.

'Oh but you are.'

Another pulse of electricity crashed through him, burning every nerve.

'And I know that you can hear me even if no one else can. So I suggest that you cooperate.' Through the thickening air Tom was aware of anxious voices all around.

'Is he sick?'

'Someone should phone an ambulance.'

'Is there a doctor—?'

'Get up—' barked the voice inside his head. 'NOW!' it shrieked.

Tom was shaking uncontrollably as he staggered to his feet.

'Are you all right, love?' A women in a red overcoat put her arm around his shoulder. 'You don't look at all well. Have you lost your pills?'

'No I'm . . . f-f-fine,' stumbled Tom, trying to ignore the burning pain in his head. 'Please . . . '

And then he saw a dark shadow emerge from behind a pillar at the far end of the concourse. A silhouette he could not fail to recognize . . . narrow shoulders and a large domed head, a man who almost appeared to be standing on tiptoes. In his hand he held a clear ball the size of an egg. His thin fingers caressed it restlessly.

'That's right. You see I haven't forgotten you, Tom. *Au contraire*, you have suddenly become uppermost in my thoughts.'

'What do you want?' murmured Tom, making his way through the puzzled crowds.

'Who's he talking to?'

'Are you *sure* you're OK, mate?'

Tom ignored the voices and approached the pillar where the slender silhouette stood. Despite the fizzing pain he was concentrating hard on what he would do next. Tom stared up into Don Gervase's heavily lidded yellow eyes, his bisected forehead, his strangely small, almost lipless mouth. He really was hideous, in a suave kind of way.

'Well?'

Don Gervase Askary looked Tom up and down with a sneer. To think this ragamuffin, this scruffy, scrawny, unkempt—

'Like I said, just a tiny *tête-à-tête*—nothing more. Gosh you've grown, Tom. Quite the young gentleman.'

'Get on with it. I've got a train to catch.'

In any other circumstances the Glorious Leader would have punished such insolence violently and instantly. Instead he chose to bottle his anger with a smile.

'You see, I have a problem, or should I say, a conundrum, to deal with.' Don Gervase met those dark, angry eyes head on. 'I need to know how far I can trust you. I need to know if you can be relied upon, when the time comes.'

Tom glared at the tall man murderously.

'Relied upon to do what?'

'To defend what is yours to defend, and to protect . . . your leader.'

It was a most unexpected question.

'You mean, me protect you?' Tom snorted. 'Why should I protect you?'

'Because . . . *if* you don't, I shall make your life a misery. With this,' he said, raising the mesmerion. 'Every single day of your life.'

Tom shrugged as nonchalantly as he could. He knew this was possible.

'I don't care.'

'You don't care?'

'I'm not going to defend Scarazand. You've got millions of other brainless slaves to do that. Forget it.'

Tom's answer was barely a whisper, but it had the desired effect. The tall man glared at the boy viciously, and his fingers spun across the ball. Tom felt as if a bomb had gone off in his brain. His knees seemed to give way and, staggering a little, he slumped against the pillar, his eyes screwed tight shut. Sweat poured down his cheeks. He tried desperately to concentrate on something else—anything—something happy—like—

'Listen to me when I'm talking to you!' screamed the voice. Tom obediently opened his eyes and saw the tall man white with anger before him. It irked Don Gervase more than he could say that he couldn't just be done with this snivelling scarecrow right now, but he somehow held himself in check. That picture . . . just remember that picture. And then the most curious idea floated up into his head.

'Supposing we went about this another way. Supposing I were to make you an offer.'

Tom wasn't sure he had heard correctly. He raised his head and stared at the dark shadow.

'Supposing you were to become a knight. My knight. Learn the arts of war—become an expert at fighting, make something of yourself.'

'Why?'

'Why not? Become something more than what you are—an ordinary, snivelling boy, who will grow up to be an ordinary, snivelling man, live a brief and boring life, and die a premature death. Because that's the alternative.'

Don Gervase was going far far beyond what he had intended, his words somehow taking him there. But the thrill, the danger of it, excited him.

'You could become a hero, Tom Scatterhorn. *The* hero. Defender of the people,' he grinned, writing out imaginary words in the air. 'Defender of Scarazand.' For a short while—he might have added. Until after the battle, when I will kill you. Because I *will* kill you—boy. There is no doubt about that.

Despite the roaring pain in his head Tom's mind was galloping. He felt strangely light-headed. Don Gervase needed him: he must do—why else would he be talking like this?

'You're not serious?'

'Actually, I think I might be.' He grinned wolfishly. 'It would be . . . could be . . . much more convenient.'

'Convenient—'

'Are you sure you are all right, love?'

The woman in the red overcoat had elbowed her way through

the crowds and crouched down beside him. She glanced up at Don Gervase standing there and withered a little before his piercing stare.

'Has this man been hurting you?'

Tom pulled himself shakily to his feet, meeting Don Gervase full square. He shook his head.

'No. He hasn't. He can't.'

Don Gervase curled his lip.

'Tom!'

Tom turned round to see a familiar figure in a flat cap standing beneath the notice board. Beside him stood a thin rake-like woman with a medieval haircut and glasses. It was Uncle Jos and Aunt Melba.

'Halloo!' called Jos raising his stick.

'Coo-ee!' chimed Melba.

Don Gervase glowered angrily in their direction, then slipped back into the shadow of the pillar. The voice echoed in Tom's ears.

'You are making a very big mistake, boy. Defy me and you will regret it for the rest of your little life.'

'Will I?' he gasped.

'Will you what, love?'

Don Gervase smiled thinly, and Tom felt another blow right between the temples, causing him to fall onto the woman's shoulder. She grabbed him for support.

'There you go, take it easy. That's it.'

Using every ounce of his willpower, Tom stood up again shakily, then turned away, ignoring the thudding in his head. Already Jos and Melba were crossing the busy concourse towards him, their expressions changing as they saw his face screwed up with pain.

'I am warning you, this is just the beginning,' hissed the voice. 'Don't think you can just walk away and forget.'

But Tom did keep walking, slowly putting one foot in front of the other, and with every step his confidence began to grow . . . somehow he was able to defy Don Gervase Askary, and somehow, for whatever reason, he had become far more important to him than he had ever imagined.

Later, Don Gervase sat in the back of the Bentley scowling. He watched the evening traffic flashing past. The sense of venom was palpable.

'I should have known, the first time I set eyes on him, I should have known,' he muttered.

The sandy-faced driver glanced back in the rear view mirror.

'My lord?'

'That Scatterhorn boy. How is it that that miserable scarecrow has caused me more trouble than practically anyone else I have ever known?'

Ern Rainbird chewed thoughtfully. He wasn't quite sure if he was supposed to find an answer to this question, but he was desperate to please his master.

'He has had *some* uses,' replied Ern Rainbird carefully. 'He gave you the elixir, and then brought you the mesmerion. That's not bad.'

The tall man stared at the rubbery ball in his hand. His fingers manipulated it restlessly.

'But he is not to be trusted, Rainbird. He is only a half-convert. And he's stubborn, and he's arrogant.'

Ern Rainbird nodded. He had already had some dealings with Tom Scatterhorn and he could vouch for all of that.

'It don't precisely square away—do it?'

The glorious leader shook his head. The truth was painful—almost as painful as having to agree with Ern Rainbird. Should he really set so much store by the paintings of a madwoman?

'I could kill him for you, my lord. Be done with it, like. Break his scrawny neck—one snap. Gone. Problem solved.'

Don Gervase said nothing. He had no intention of playing fast and loose with the future, neither would he be held hostage to fortune by such an unreliable witness as Betilda Marchmont. If there was going to be any great battle in the future he was going to win it. And if that miserable Tom Scatterhorn was apparently going to save his life . . . *if* . . . Don Gervase Askary cracked his fingers irritably. He needed more evidence, obviously, but in the meantime . . . he stared at the dark wet streets flashing past, the raindrops sliding across his cruel, hard features. That offer he had made to the boy: just an off the cuff remark, a ruse . . . but there was something in it. Wouldn't *that* be the prudent thing to do? The glorious leader smiled as the beginnings of a labyrinthine plan began to form in his mind. Of course . . . of course . . . and the irony would be delicious . . .

'Send him where, my lord?'

Don Gervase was unaware he had spoken out loud.

'What?'

'You said something about making absolutely sure and removing him permanently.'

'I said nothing of the kind, Rainbird. You are here to drive— not eavesdrop, do you understand?'

Rainbird lowered his eyes furtively and swung the great black car into the square. Don Gervase Askary watched as the tall grey building loomed into view, the letters IMPAI emblazoned above the door. This was his headquarters: he had hundreds of workers here—millions more in Scarazand . . . dealing with that delinquent boy could be done quickly—instantly, but he could hardly have this inconvenience become general knowledge . . . so—

The car slowed and he saw that freckled, deeply lined face watching him in the mirror. Rainbird possessed a certain low cunning . . . perhaps that wasn't such a bad idea after all . . .

'Keep driving, Rainbird.'

'My lord?'

'Drive on, man. Once more round the square.'

Rainbird, did as he was told, leaving the reception committee waiting on the rain lashed steps.

'Rainbird, I have a little task for you.'

'Oh yes.'

'It's not difficult, but it must be kept entirely between ourselves. Just you and me.'

'Oh. I see.' Ern Rainbird's rubbery face split into a wide grin. He sensed this was an extraordinary privilege. 'On the QT, is it?'

'Exactly. As you say. An absolute secret. You will tell no one. No one at all.'

'And will Miss Askary also be involved, your grace?'

'Absolutely not.'

Ern Rainbird was unable to conceal a smirk. The animosity between him and Don Gervase's teenage daughter was legendary.

'In fact if everything goes to plan Lotus is going to find herself in very unfamiliar surroundings.'

'Oh indeed?'

'Yes, Rainbird. Everyone's time comes to an end. Even Lotus Askary's.'

Rainbird grinned from ear to ear, and Don Gervase found himself smiling in sympathy. There was something about Ern Rainbird's simple pleasure in the misfortunes of others he found strangely comforting.

'When do we begin, my lord?'

'Right now, Rainbird. Right now.'

CHAPTER 3

WHEN THE LAZY WIND BLOWS

'Now that's what they call a lazy wind.'

'A what?'

'A lazy wind,' rasped Uncle Jos, a small ball of a man who had just found himself buffeted all the way up the wide stone steps to the museum door. 'It doesn't bother going round you—just straight through.'

'Come on, let's get inside,' shivered Aunt Melba, who was as thin as Jos was round and had been blown up the steps behind him. Tom followed as they huddled in the freezing grey dawn before the great wooden door.

'Hagfish on a houseboat,' muttered Jos, turning out one pocket then another. 'I could have sworn—'

'Jos, you haven't.'

'I'm afraid I have, my peach.'

'You can't have!'

Aunt Melba looked as if she was about to explode.

'Have you forgotten your key?' asked Tom.

'Appearances would suggest that unfortunately—' Jos stopped as Tom delved inside his jacket and drew out a large ornate key, fitting it into the heavy lock.

'Now look at that,' Jos beamed. 'Where on earth would we be without this lad?'

'Still standing here like idiots locked out of our own museum.'

'Thank you, Melba.'

The door creaked open on its hinges and they squeezed gratefully inside, slamming out the wind. Uncle Jos paced off into the brown gloom and flicked on the lights. 'Now, how about a spot of breakfast to cheer us all up?'

Soon they were sitting in a circle at the bottom of the stairs over bacon sandwiches and steaming cups of tea. All around the high vaulted hall were glass cases filled with taxidermy of every size and shape: a dodo, a mammoth, a gorilla in a tree, South American jungles and African dioramas, models of lost islands and frozen rivers . . . to anyone else, this musty, eccentric collection might have appeared creepy and even a little weird, but to Tom Scatterhorn it felt familiar: so familiar that it was almost like a photograph album of his own remarkable adventures . . . And though he was embarrassed to admit it, the museum belonged to him.

Every single specimen had been collected by his great-great-great-uncle, Sir Henry Scatterhorn, over a hundred years ago, who at that time was the greatest hunter in the world, and each and every one was stuffed by his best friend, August Catcher, the greatest taxidermist in the world. Together they had created this extraordinary museum that Jos's father had looked after, then passed on to Jos and Melba, who had steered it through the high winds and storms of fifty years until at last it was ready to sink beneath the waves . . . and at that moment, two years ago, Tom

Scatterhorn walked through the door, and everything began to change. With the help of the sale of a lost sapphire, the Scatterhorn Museum had been restored, inherited some very fancy displays, and become popular again . . . well, *almost* popular . . . it was still, at its heart, a dark and mysterious place caught in a time warp, and not everyone's cup of tea . . .

'So does anyone know what happened to Ern Rainbird then?' asked Tom, munching on the last of his sandwiches. He had leapt up and punched the air when he had heard that the old janitor had disappeared. But that was almost a year ago . . .

'Ern Rainbird?' wheezed Jos, knitting his thick eyebrows together into a single hedge. 'I don't believe anyone has seen or heard from him since that day the Deluge collapsed. I made a few enquiries but his landlady had no idea where he'd got to. Something funny going on there, I believe. Old Ern was always very tidy and particular. Forever shining his shoes, ironing his underwear—but he seemed to have just vanished into thin air.'

'I heard he'd become a tramp,' sniffed Melba. 'And that he was living in a skip.'

'Hmm, well if he is I'm sure he's got it all ship-shape and tickety boo,' said Jos. 'He wasn't *that* bad—good cleaner, Ern—forever brassing and tatting about, rotas, lists, locks, his little den in the cellar with his biscuits numbered and stowed away—'

'Quite,' sniffed Melba, 'I felt like I'd joined the navy.'

Uncle Jos harrumphed loudly.

'Ern won't have gone far, Tom, unfortunately,' she continued. 'He'll be lurking somewhere. There's always been Rainbirds in Dragonport.'

'That is true,' echoed Jos, polishing his glasses on his cuff. 'But we don't need him any more, because there's nothing to do. It's all fixed. Hooray!'

Tom stretched and looked around. Yes it was all strangely quiet and clean. There were no buckets on the floor catching the raindrops, no rotten cabinets, disintegrating animals, clanking pipes, wheezing boilers, missing banisters. The whole place smelt of polish.

'I think I'll have a wander,' he said.

'Survey the fleet, very good idea,' murmured Jos, shambling over to the foyer. 'In which case I'll run out the cannons to repel boarders. Never know, we might get ten people today.'

'In your dreams,' muttered Melba. She stood up and looked at Tom kindly. 'And if you need to have a little sit down—you know, put your feet up for a bit, the office is very quiet.'

'I feel fine now. Thanks.'

'I'm sure you do. But it's there, anyway, if you fancy.'

Tom nodded: he was well aware that his mother had warned Melba about his strange fainting fits, and he couldn't pretend nothing had happened at the station. But the last thing he wanted was to be treated like an invalid.

'The Deluge has scrubbed up a treat,' she added, gratefully retreating to the foyer. 'Why don't you have a look?'

Tom smiled: yes, he had almost forgotten about that little escapade. Climbing the stairs, he passed memory after memory: the model of frozen Dragonport where had learned to skate, the Bengal tiger lurking in the undergrowth, about to spring . . . the model of Tithona, that tropical island that had led him down to Scarazand . . . even the heron battling with an eel that he had first seen frozen stiff in August Catcher's workshop . . . this was his life, all of it. He hovered in the doorway of the West Wing and stared at the tumble of shadows against the far wall. There was what appeared to be the contents of a zoo tipped over a cliff before a vast glassy wave . . . vultures, lions, monkeys, snakes, even a rhinoceros . . . a snapshot of fifty animals caught in mid-air as they plunged headlong into a chasm. The Deluge—'The showiest piece of taxidermy August Catcher ever made' according to Uncle Jos, an absolute flight of fancy. And yet Tom knew that even this fantastic scene was real, too. He had seen it happen, right in front of his very eyes . . .

A shudder ran down Tom's spine as he walked up to the vast construction. Until yesterday, this was also the last place he had seen Don Gervase Askary. That had been last summer, and then he had tried to kill him in revenge for entering Scarazand and presuming to escape . . . so what had changed?

'Defender of the people . . . Defender of Scarazand.'

The words swirled and eddied around his head. It didn't make sense. Why would Don Gervase say that? What did he really want?

Tom had been so lost in thought he hardly noticed that the museum was now full of voices. Walking out to the balcony he saw a party of children running around excitedly with torches.

'Whoops!'

Two girls ran past, shining a torch right up into his face.

'Gotcha!'

'What are you doing?'

'It's him,' one whispered to the other. 'You know. Him. Come on!' They giggled and ran off. Confused, Tom made his way down to the main hall.

'St Denis's Christmas outing,' explained Jos, shuffling out from behind the case of mandrills. 'I'd clean forgotten they were coming. Thought we'd keep the lights off and give 'em torches for a bit for fun. Spookier is better,' he grinned. 'Oh and there's a letter for you just arrived. Melba's put it in the office.'

'A letter?'

Tom was surprised. Who could have written to him? Hardly anyone knew he was even here.

'Fan mail probably,' grinned Jos, squeezing his arm. 'Don't forget, lad, you're not a nothing when you come to Dragonport. Far from it. Everybody's heard of Tom Scatterhorn round here. Get away, you blighters!' he roared as three small boys ambushed him from behind the dodo. With a chuckle he shambled off into the gloom.

Tom turned and made his way through the jumble of cases towards the African diorama and went through the small wooden door in the corner. The office was a narrow room overflowing with boxes, dominated by a wide desk before the window. It was so dark he barely noticed Melba until she sprang up from behind the desk and guiltily tucked her newspaper away.

'Oh just tidying up,' she volunteered, apropos of nothing. 'Gosh what a mess.'

'Hi. Am I—'

'No, no, not interrupting anything. Erm . . . yes there's a letter for you. Hand delivered this morning. Erm . . . so yes. Yes . . .' Melba looked up at him above her half-rimmed spectacles. She seemed strangely concerned. 'Listen, Tom, I know you don't want to talk about what happened at the station but—'

'Honestly I really am completely fine. There's nothing wrong with me.'

Melba smiled weakly. She was obviously finding that hard to believe.

'OK—sometimes, like yesterday, I just pass out, and then I wake up again. It's not a problem.'

'Well as long as you're sure about that.'

'I am. Quite sure.'

There was an awkward silence. Melba's fingers scratched at the desk.

'And you are quite sure that your condition—'

'It's not a condition.'

'No of course it's not, dear. I understand that, but . . . I mean, is it possible that you could have accidentally been somewhere, in some way, and erm . . . not remembered it?'

Tom felt the colour rise in his cheeks.

'What do you mean?'

Melba seemed to be struggling with something.

'Scotland, perhaps?'

'*Scotland?*'

'It's all probably some colossal coincidence I know but . . . you see—' Melba pulled out the copy of that morning's *Dragonport Mercury* she had hidden under a box and slid it across the desk towards Tom. 'Page five, I think.'

Tom flipped through the newspaper until his eyes halted at the headline: '*Bleach Murders reveal all.*'

Beneath it was a photograph of a grand old painting, which at first sight seemed to be of some enormous battle scene. Great splatters of white chemical had been hurled at it and burnt away the paint. Tom began to read.

'Detectives in Stirlingshire are investigating the mysterious murders of Miriam and Edward Marchmont, the late owners of Marchmont Castle. The vicious attack was carried out by dogs "or some other unidentified animal." Bleach was also used to reveal the face of the knight whose secret identity has long been a source of speculation. The boy, who wears a distinctive suit of armour, is present in many of the paintings of Betilda Marchmont, an artist born over a hundred years ago. She spent her life decorating the old attics of the castle with fantastical scenes until she was committed to an asylum, and her work is still considered by experts to be "the greatest work of art ever made by a madwoman".'

Tom looked at the photograph again. In the centre was what appeared to be St George slaying the dragon. The knight was riding a beetle, but his face, his eyes . . . his expression. Tom put down the paper, stunned. He did not know what to say.

'Strange, isn't it?'

Tom nodded helplessly.

'But it's just a coincidence. It must be.'

Melba raised her eyebrows.

'It was a terrible murder. They were crushed to death, and for what? Why vandalize the picture, kill the owners, and then just leave?' Melba peered at Tom again curiously. 'Unless of course, revealing the identity of the mysterious knight *was* the motive.'

'What do you mean?'

Melba smiled awkwardly.

'As you know, dear, life in this place can get crushingly dull and I have probably read far more detective stories than is good for me. I couldn't help noticing that another person in the picture seemed a little familiar too.'

And with that she disappeared into the gloom. Tom stood staring at the newspaper guiltily. Who was this Betilda Marchmont? Where had she been, what had she seen?

He leant down and peered at the busy scene. It was a riot of insects, misshapen men, beetles, cannons, towers collapsing and strange silvery serpents everywhere . . . so who? Below the rearing knight, half cut off by the photograph, was another man, his features smudged and burnt by acid . . . but there were those yellow eyes, that bisected forehead, the small dark mouth . . .

Tom felt as if he was going to be sick.

'It can't be,' he murmured. 'It can't be.'

Wasn't this just some crazy fantasy? Deep in his heart Tom longed for it to be so. But he had a terrible feeling it wasn't. Defender of Scarazand . . . the phrase ricocheted around Tom's brain like a stray bullet. Had Don Gervase Askary murdered these people to reveal this? Is this what he had discovered?

The letter. Tom picked up the envelope, unable to control his trembling hands. There was his name, spelt out in neat capitals with today's date. It was not writing he recognized. As so many times before, Tom had a sense that if he opened this letter, right now, everything was going to change, and not necessarily for the better . . . ripping it open, he unfolded the scrap of paper and stared at it dizzily. It was written in capitals with a pencil, pressed very hard into the surface.

'DEAR TOM SCATTERHORN,

I AM GLAD TO SEE YOU'S BACK. I HAVE BEEN WAITING FOR YOUR RETURN FOR A LONG TIME. YOU SEE, I HAVE SOME IMPORTANT INFORMATION TO GIVE YOU. IT CONCERNS A CERTAIN GENTLEMAN WHOSE PICTURE IS IN TODAY'S MERCURY—TOGETHER WITH YOUR OWN. I'M SURE YOU KNOW WHO. COME AND MEET ME AT SUNSET AND I SHALL TELL YOU EVERYTHING. YOU MAY NOT BELIEVE IT, BUT

WE ARE IN THE SAME BOAT, YOU AND ME. YOUR LIFE MAY DEPEND
ON WHAT I HAVE TO SAY.

YOURS MOST RESPECTFULLY,

ERN RAINBIRD.
THE GARAGES, SPONG BOTTOM.

PS. DON'T FORGET, WALLS HAVE EARS. BEST NOT TELL ANYONE,
ESPECIALLY THE POLICE. WE DON'T WANT THEM TO KNOW OUR
LITTLE SECRETS, DO WE?

Tom had to read the letter several times before he could catch
its sense. That Ern Rainbird was still alive and living in Dragonport he could just about believe. But was he really hiding from
Don Gervase Askary, and could he *really* offer Tom some life-
saving advice? It didn't sound very likely. In fact the longer Tom
thought about Ern Rainbird the less likely it seemed. Ern Rainbird was probably the least trustworthy man he had ever met,
and yet: 'your life may depend on what I have to say' . . . was that
a threat?

'Oh yes, Mrs Scatterhorn. But it's Inspector now.'

Tom looked up from the letter. There in the foyer stood two
policemen talking to Aunt Melba.

'Inspector Moon? How very grand.'

'Fast tracking, Mrs Scatterhorn. Moon is one of the best and
brightest we have and you can't keep a good man down. We did
try, mind.'

Inspector Moon laughed nervously. Tom watched them approach, their radios echoing into the darkness. He had a dim
memory of these two policemen from his very first visit to the

Museum. Could it be that they were looking for him? But what could he possibly tell them?

'I never forget a face, Mrs Scatterhorn. Everything registers up here.'

'Encyclopaedic, Mrs Scatterhorn. Positively elephantine.'

'But surely it's just a coincidence?' fretted Melba. 'Surely you don't think Tom's—'

'Of course not. But you never know how useful a little chat could be.'

Tom stood pressed behind the dome of hummingbirds as Melba led the two policemen into the office.

'How odd,' she murmured, peering into the empty room. 'He was here a moment ago. Perhaps he's gone upstairs.'

Tom hugged the shadows as the search party threaded its way through the cases and up to the landing. Why he had done that he could not explain. It had just happened. Perhaps it was just the merest grain of doubt that Ern Rainbird might—*might*—have something useful to say. And Tom wanted to hear him say it.

Tom waited until they had safely disappeared into the bird galleries then silently wrapped his coat around him and slipped out through the great front door. Pulling his hat down low, he skirted around the side of the police car and was buffeted away down the grey street. Spong Bottom . . . how was he ever going to find that? It sounded very much like the end of the road.

'I suppose it's the funny name that's attracted you, has it—eh?'

Tom smiled charmingly. Luckily the librarian was very short sighted and did not seem to recognize Tom with his hat on. He squinted at the town map spread out on the table before him.

'There's plenty of Spong this and Spong that up that way. Street, drive, crescent . . . bottom, is it?'

Spong Bottom turned out to be a row of condemned houses teetering on the very edge of the town. Beyond was nothing but the marching forest of the Hellkiss estate. A perfect place to hide out, thought Tom, as he raced down the library steps and out into the street busy with Christmas shoppers leaning into the wind. Perhaps Melba was right, Ern was living in a skip after all. Half an hour later Tom found himself shivering on the edge of a stretch of wasteland at the outskirts of town. Below lay Dragonport huddling on the edge of the wide grey estuary. Tom checked his watch: it was barely half past two and already the streetlights were coming on. He glanced again at his crumpled instructions, then back at a row of houses set in a dip away from the road. Beyond was nothing but scrub and woods. Spong Bottom—that must be it . . .

As Tom drew closer he saw the sign, 'ong bot'—the rest had been graffitied out. Every house was either boarded up or empty. The only signs of life were a couple of crows sitting on a burnt out car, which cawed then clattered away angrily as he approached. At the last house a broken concrete track led on down to a small huddle of garages arranged in a horseshoe. Black smoke was rising from behind one of them. Was Ern Rainbird down there? He must be. Tom steeled himself. Did he really want to do this? Yes, he really did. And what if something happened? Then he would take his chances. Rainbird might be fit, but Tom felt confident he wouldn't catch him. Running was about was the only thing Tom was good at.

Picking his way down the muddy track Tom stood at the entrance to the cul-de-sac. At the end two steel garage doors stood ajar. Outside one of them was a small trailer on which there was a heap of old radios. Tom walked towards them.

'You're early.'

Tom almost jumped out of his skin. Between two garages appeared a small stocky man wearing an old green coat covered in dirt. His thick black bobble hat was pulled down low over his deeply lined, freckled face, and his lizard-like eyes watched Tom suspiciously. Clamped between his lips was a match that rolled from one side to the other.

'Nice to see yer, lad. You ain't changed.'

Ern walked forward and, with one boot, lifted the corner of the garage door. Inside was a small stove on which a kettle was steaming merrily.

'Come in and have a brew. Don't worry, I won't bite yer.'

Ern shuffled in and took down two mugs from the windowsill, then drew a large pack of ginger nuts from his pocket.

'I just got you these, an' all. Cos I'm partial to them myself—remember?'

Ern set about making the tea and Tom glanced around inside the garage. It certainly looked as if Ern Rainbird had been here a long time. Whatever possessions he had were wrapped up in plastic bags and hung from the ceiling in rows. In one corner was a small sleeping bag, neatly rolled up as if ready for an inspection.

'How did you know I was here?'

'Oh . . . you know, grapevine,' rasped Ern, sitting down and squeezing out the teabags. 'Not many secrets in a place like Dragonport are there?'

'Aren't there?'

Ern looked out at him and grinned.

'Come on in and pull that door to behind yer. Lord knows it's cold enough.'

'I'm fine here, thank you.'

Ern Rainbird added the milk and shoved a biscuit in his mouth. He shrugged nonchalantly.

'Suit yerself. But the way I sees it there'd be no point you running away now. Not now you've come this far. And how could I hurt you? I'm not armed. My knees are shot. I'm an old man.'

Tom watched him ladle four large spoons of sugar into his tea and stir it briskly.

'Sugar?'

Tom nodded. Ern heaped in four generous measures and stirred.

'I really would appreciate you closing that door. It's perishing. Come in and I'll tell you what you want to know.'

Still Tom didn't move.

'What *do* I want to know?'

'How to get rid of Don Gervase Askary. Up here.' Ern tapped his forehead. 'Cos that's where he's lurking isn't it? That's where he's got into you, isn't it?'

Tom shifted uncomfortably.

'First a little grub in the ear, then these waves coming over, screaming voices telling you to do this, do that, fetch and carry— oh, I know all about it. Like a little bloody robot I was. Until I got rid of him.'

Tom stared at Ern as he blew on his tea and slurped it loudly.

'*You* got rid of him?'

'That's right. It can be done.'

This was not at all what Tom had expected. Ern's face split into a grin.

'You didn't know that did you?'

'No.'

'Neither does he. But it's something us travellers have learned to do. And we help each other out. It's sort of an unwritten code. Betilda Marchmont told me how to do it.'

'Betilda Marchmont?'

Ern nodded wisely.

'The artist who painted them pictures. She was infected an' all. I knew her, see. But if you don't want to know then that's no skin off my nose. Suit yerself. Just thought you might be interested.'

Ern looked like a little gnome in his bobble hat and greasy coat, sitting in the dark chewing his biscuits solemnly. What could he possibly do to hurt him? Tom decided to trust his instincts. Carefully he stepped into the garage, pulling the door down but not quite shut.

'That's better. More civilized. Cos that's a lazy wind that is. Here, have a pew.'

Tom sat down cautiously and Ern handed him the scalding cup.

'How did you know I was a traveller?'

'Two and two, mate. I always suspected. You don't go to bed and get up the next day with a suntan by accident. Plus there's a look, isn't there? Sort of secretive, like you've been to places that you can't tell people about. Sort of confusion, not quite sure where you are.'

Tom said nothing. Was it really that obvious? He hoped not.

'And Scarazand is a hell of a place, after all.'

'You've been there?'

'Lived there, son, for two years. Had a shop selling military memorabilia to the tourists. Quite a profitable little business it was, too. Rainbird's Collectibles. But that was before I met Betilda and she saw me right.'

Tom blew on his hot tea, then took a small sip. It was incredibly sweet, like honey. Ern watched him out of the corner of his eye.

'So how do you do it, then?'

'Chinese bush medicine. You make up a paste and then drink it. Every day for a week. It's disgusting.'

'What's in it?'

'What's not in it!' Ern guffawed. 'Beetles, nettles, worms, fish heads, dried maggots, but worse than all that is who—' Ern coughed violently. 'Who . . . who do.'

'Who do?'

'Whoodoo flies,' croaked Ern. 'Taste like mouse guts. Biscuit?'

'Thanks,' said Tom, taking two. He bit into one nervously. 'And where can I get this Chinese medicine?'

Ern Rainbird had got his breath back and he seemed to be counting to himself.

'Oh erm . . . well it's dead simple. There's this chemist in London. Backstairs business, you know. I'll give you the address. Mister . . . Wong. Behind Leicester Square. Tell 'em you've got verrucas—or corns, any complaints of the feet, and he'll give it you. It's the code, see.'

Tom finished his biscuit and glanced down at his steaming mug. Mr Wong's medicine was sounding less likely by the second.

'Why should I believe you?'

Ern Rainbird levelled his yellow eyes upon him. Tom couldn't read his expression, but his lips still seemed to be counting.

'You'll just have to take my word for it, son. Beggars can't be choosers. I'm all you've got.'

Rainbird stood up and moved towards the mattress. When he turned round there was a length of rope and a blanket in his hand.

'What are you doing with that?'

'Oh I've just got a bit of business to get out of the way, you know.'

'Business?'

'That's right. Later.'

Tom stared up at Ern's smiling face. Ern seemed to be waiting expectantly. Tom was dimly aware that his fingers were going numb, and so were his feet. A tingling feeling began creeping up his body . . .

'It's very cold in here.'

Ern glanced at the garage door, then down at his watch.

'Yes. Funny how that wind just gets through anything.'

Tom shivered violently. The garage seemed to have gone cloudy. Suddenly he began to panic.

'What was in that tea, Rainbird?'

'The tea? Nothing, son. The tea was in the tea, 'cos it's tea, innit?' he smiled, finishing his cup. 'Oh, I don't think it's the tea you should be worried about. Have another biscuit.'

Tom was dimly aware of Ern Rainbird moving off into the shadows and starting a motor. He tried to turn round, but found that none of his muscles would move. He tried to speak but his lips just tingled strangely. Then the teacup clattered from his frozen hand and smashed on the floor. Tom looked down in horror. Not the tea, the biscuits, numbered—he'd poisoned . . . and then there was nothing.

CHAPTER 4

WELCOME STRANGERS ALL

'Ladies and gentlemen, we shall soon be approaching Dragonport. Dragonport, your final station stop . . . '

There was a sound of a bell somewhere. The floor was rattling.

'This is Dragonport. All change, all change.'

Tom blinked and blinked again. He seemed to be lying in the guards' van of a train. Two crates and a jumble of parcels filled his view. When he tried to roll over onto his back he found that his hands and feet were tied, and he was bundled up in a grey blanket. The brakes squealed and the train juddered to a halt. Footsteps marched up the platform.

'In here, is he?'

'That's it.'

Suddenly there was a clank and the door opened.

'Aha.'

Tom immediately decided to close his eyes and feign sleep as two men grabbed each end and slung him roughly onto a trolley. Soon the rest of the parcels were loaded on and they were trundling down the platform. Tom dared to open one eye. Fog, shadows, and people, muffled against the cold. Gradually he realized his neck was stiff and he had a blinding headache. How long had he been lying there? Maybe all night—he had no idea. Somehow his mind was completely empty. But this blanket was familiar, and it smelt of wet leaves . . .

'Where'd they find this one?'

'Ticket doesn't say. Special delivery—so picked up in the forest I'd guess. Vee's on his way now.'

'He'd better be. I don't want to be stuck with one of these all day.'

The men trundled through the station arch, and Tom saw shimmering holograms of what looked like a ship capsized in heavy seas. **'MERICAN FERI SASTER L8TEST—NYNE TWENI TOWSAN FURD DRUYND.'** Something about this was familiar . . . but what? Tom racked his brains; a vague memory was floating up through his mind, a newspaper, from long ago . . . Out they went into the thick white mist. There were no cars or vehicles of any kind. The station seemed deserted.

'Speak of the devil,' muttered one of the men as a single headlight loomed up out of the gloom. A moment later a battered three-wheeled van rattled to a halt in front of them. It looked like a loaf of bread on wheels. The door slid open and a short swarthy man stepped out wearing a scarf wrapped around his head. He rubbed his tired face violently.

'Apologies apologies. Engine not happy this morning. Too cold. Like me.'

The men grunted.

'You have him, a Mr Tom Scatterhorn?'

'That's it.'

'Is he asleep?'

Tom instantly closed his eyes. The clammy dawn was rapidly sharpening his senses and he had an idea what was going to happen next.

'Straight in then; before he wakes is better.'

Tom heard the back door of the van slide open, and the next moment the two men hefted Tom off the trolley and sat him upright in the seat.

'Very dozy still. We untie now I think.'

'Now?'

'I think now is good.'

Tom let his head flop forward and felt the knots at his ankles and wrists being undone. Looking back, that would have been the perfect moment to escape . . . but he was still too confused, too surprised . . . in a second the door slammed shut and Tom opened his eyes. He was sitting on an old brown leather bench. There were two slit windows on either side and a grille separating him from the driver. The whole contraption smelt vaguely of gas. The baggy-eyed man climbed into the cab and glanced back at him in the mirror.

'Ah. You wake. Hello. I am Mr Vee.'

The Russian accent was familiar. Tom had a vague memory that this man, or someone like him, used to run the internet café next to the station. Mr Vee wiped the steamed up windscreen with an old rag and the engine squealed to life. It was some sort of gas-powered motorbike.

'Where am I?'

'This is Dragonport. Dragonport new town. Welcome to you.'

'Where are we going?'

'Now we go Museum. I am coming to pick you up.'

They bumped at speed over the cobblestones. Tom cast an anxious glance at the filthy buildings looming up on either side of them.

'So you knew I was coming?'

'Yes yes. You are expected.'

'And this is definitely Dragonport?'

'New town. Old town, far side causeway. We go there.'

The van rattled round a corner and suddenly they were speeding across a long, low bridge towards a small island cut off by a wide expanse of grey water. Beyond it, Tom could just make out a forest of steel tubes rising up out of the estuary. The lazy swoop of the blades up above told him they were wind turbines. Tom's heart began to beat faster.

'So . . . has there has been a flood?'

Mr Vee waved his hand ahead cheerily.

'No no. Old town is island since many years ago. Is special place—much history there.'

Tom's eyes widened as he stared ahead. There was the unmistakable silhouette of the Scatterhorn Museum, its towers and pinnacles rising up above a higgledy-piggledy pattern of roofs tumbling down to the waterline. Beyond it was the grey shape of Catcher Hall looming through the mist . . . no, this was a dream, it couldn't be real . . . and then to the left he heard a long low mournful note. Peering out through the tiny window he saw a church tower rising directly out of the grey water. On its battlements stood a man ringing a bell.

'You've got to stop!'

'Stop? No no—'

'There's been a mistake! Stop!'

Mr Vee glanced back in his mirror as the boy tried to force the handle of the door. He had been warned that this might happen. Actually he was surprised to have got this far without trouble.

'No stopping on the causeway, sir. Is not possible for us.'

Tom ignored him and began thumping on the roof and pushing at the small windows.

'Please, Mr Scatterhorn. Stay calm now.'

'LET ME OUT!'

The whole van began rocking as Tom threw himself from one side to the other.

'Please . . . it's not helpful this way. Please—'

The boy in the back seemed to be going mad, and Mr Vee knew that if he carried on they might well tip over. That was probably his intention . . . suddenly Mr Vee screeched to a halt.

'No good, sir,' he said sadly. 'It won't work. Me sorry you.'

Tom ignored him and carried on. A long line of small figures loomed up out of the fog and stared at the rocking van curiously. Each was wearing a thick black woollen cloak, decorated with droplets of mist, and wooden clogs. They were children.

''Nuther nutter, is it, Mr Vee?' said one of the boys in a sing-song voice.

'Not nutter. Very special case. Go on, you go home.'

But the children ignored him and crowded closer, pressing their faces to the windows. The inside of the van grew darker and Tom looked up, breathless, to find a row of filthy faces staring down at him.

'Proper weirdee, in'ee?' said one girl, with a snarl.

'Oi, doolally-boy!' shouted a boy, banging on the glass with his fist. 'What's your problem, doolal!'

'Go back, please,' instructed Mr Vee, climbing out of his cab and trying to shoo them away. But the children pressed closer to get a better look at the stranger.

'Woz 'e done 'en?'

'Must be somethin' villainous. Look at him.'

'Most unscrumptious.'

There was a cackle of laughter all around the van and Tom stared about him wildly. He felt like an animal in a zoo.

'Right scrawny one, 'en he?'

'I'd give him a week.'

'If that.'

'Please! Go away! Shoo!' Mr Vee pulled the children away roughly and climbed back in his seat. Starting the motor, he revved hard.

'See yer later, nutter!' shouted the children, thumping on the sides of the van as it moved off. Tom looked back through the tiny window at the shadows disappearing into the mist.

'Who were they?'

'You no worry about them,' said Mr Vee, glad to see that the boy seemed to have calmed down. 'They only workers.'

'What do they do?'

'Factory,' said Mr Vee vaguely indicating with his hand. 'You'll see.'

The small van left the causeway and entered the narrow streets around the wharfs. Everything was so blackened with oil and filth that Tom struggled to make out anything he recognized.

'Not far now, Mr Scatterhorn,' said Mr Vee. With a cheery grin he swung the small van round a perimeter wall and in through a pair of high steel gates that mysteriously opened then closed behind them. Hopping out of the cab, Mr Vee ceremoniously slid open the door.

'Please.'

For a moment Tom hesitated: somehow he still believed that he could escape from this . . . but where to? Nervously he stepped out into the damp air. The narrow courtyard was entirely encircled by a high concrete wall bristling with broken glass. Several guards loitered idly by the gate. Before him stood the Scatterhorn Museum, its façade black and wet and ancient. Above the great door stood the two once fierce looking gryphons, but both were now missing their heads and the mottled tablet between them was barely legible:**THE SCATTERHORN MUSEUM**, was all it said.

A tatty white sign had been slung across the middle:

WELCOME STRANGERS ALL

Below that, barely visible beneath the lichen and streaked with grime:

funds provided by Mr Tom Scatterhorn

Tom stared at the cracked tablet and felt a lump rise in his throat. Suddenly seeing his own name almost obscured by time somehow confirmed that he really was in some far, far distant place, well beyond anything he knew. Was this a hundred years into the future, five hundred, a thousand, even? A wave of hopelessness swept over him. But *why*—why had he been sent here? Tom looked up at the barred windows and saw curious white faces staring down at him. They looked like ghosts. Nutter . . . Doolal . . . it must be some kind of asylum.

'Mr Scatterhorn?'

Mr Vee was watching him expectantly. Tom felt the cold wind licking hungrily around his collar. Whatever else might have changed—that hadn't.

'Shall we go in?'

Tom took one last look at the miserable yard, the high walls, and the heavy locked gate, then obediently followed Mr Vee into the gloom.

'Nice trip?'

It was the nurse who asked the question, or at least Tom presumed she was something like that—given her white uniform.

'Well?'

The amply proportioned woman with small, quick eyes peered at Tom over her thin spectacles. Tom sat on the other side of a wide mahogany desk and stared back at her in surly silence. She looked the sort of person who did not suffer fools gladly, but he felt not the slightest inclination to be cooperative.

'I want to know why I am here.'

The nurse put down her spectacles and glanced at the rumpled-looking man sitting next to her. He had a long, swarthy face that Tom was sure he had seen before, and he was wearing a curiously old-fashioned double-breasted suit. From the few bookcases lining the peeling white walls Tom assumed that this was his office.

'Of course you do,' he said, in a not unfriendly way. 'And I'll bet you also want to know what this place is. It must all be very strange indeed.' The man smiled cheerily. 'My name is Doctor Logan. I'm in charge here. This is Nurse Manners, and Mr Grimal you have, I believe, already met.'

Tom did not need to turn round to know that the large warder was standing behind him at the door. He had met him at the foyer, a man with a lazy eye and skin like crumbling cheese, who made very clear to him that he should do exactly what he was told. Perhaps some of the other inmates got rowdy and needed restraining. Tom could easily imagine that Mr Grimal was rather good at that.

'So, why *am* I here?'

Dr Logan stiffened a little, preparing to deliver a lecture that he had practised many times before.

'You are here because you are not who you think you are.'

'I'm not?' Tom snorted. 'So who do I think I am then?'

'You *think* you are Tom Scatterhorn. But unfortunately that is an illusion. What you actually are is an accidental *duplicate* of Tom Scatterhorn. What we here call an echo copy. Which is also a fine thing to be, in its way.'

Tom's eyes widened. He had imagined many strange excuses, but not this.

'I know it's hard to believe, but it's the uncomfortable truth, I'm afraid. One little echo beetle bites someone in the middle of the night, flies back to Scarazand to lay a few dozen eggs and before you know it there's lots of little echoes wandering around, and who knows what might happen then? Unfortunate conse-quences, that's what happens then. So, it has been decided that you should be sent here, far away from the hustle and bustle, to be safe. Which is all rather good, isn't it?'

Tom stared at Dr Logan in amazement, wondering if this was some sort of joke. His smile told him nothing.

'But I *am* Tom Scatterhorn. I am not an echo copy.'

There was silence as they stared at him.

'I am Tom Scatterhorn. That's my name out there above the door. I was here yesterday, in Dragonport, staying with my uncle and aunt.'

Nurse Manners's lip curled up a fraction.

'Look, it's very simple. I've been abducted. Ern Rainbird sent me this letter, telling me to come and meet him in this garage where he was living because he had something important—' Tom checked himself. 'It doesn't matter what, it was just a lure to draw me up there and drink his tea and eat his biscuits—which he'd poisoned. And then he must have wrapped me in a blanket, tied me up and put me on that train which brought me here—somehow. That's the truth.'

Nurse Manners took a deep breath and her lip curled up a fraction more. Tom had a very strong sense that his explanation had made his predicament a lot worse.

'Why don't you believe me?'

Dr Logan smiled.

'Because it is not true. You merely *think* it is. That story is just an accidental memory that has nothing to do with you. You've never been here before.'

Tom stared at the doctor hard.

'Do you know what year this is?'

'What's that got to do with anything?'

Dr Logan swivelled around the curiously old-fashioned desk calendar. The numbers read thirteen, twelve, sixty-eight.

'Thirteenth of December, 2168.' A small triumphant smile crept around his mouth as Tom tried and failed to conceal his shock. He had guessed this was the future, but somehow seeing those numbers confirm it made it seem an awful lot worse. How had Rainbird done it? A portal, hidden in those garages, or somewhere up in the forest—

'Show me your left wrist.'

'What?'

Dr Logan smiled kindly.

'There is something written on it. Show me.'

'Why should I?'

With a flicker of his eyes Dr Logan indicated to Mr Grimal to come forward. The burly warder unceremoniously pulled up Tom's left hand and slapped it on the table.

'You see, Tom?'

Tom looked down and felt a lump rise in his throat. There was the tiny red weal of an insect bite. Above it ran a line of small blue-black numbers, stamped into the skin like a tattoo.

'But . . . but someone's put this on me somehow,' gasped Tom, his voice rising. 'You've . . . it's fake it's—'

'Not fake, Tom,' interrupted Dr Logan evenly. 'It's the mark of an echo beetle. Each and every one is stamped in the hatchery before being sent out into the world. You are no different.'

Tom scratched at the numbers, his nails ripping into his skin. How had they done this? And what was that bite . . .

'You were born in Scarazand, Tom, and that number is your length of life.' Dr Logan consulted the notes in front of him, reading the file. 'Twenty-nine days, three hours, and forty-one minutes, to be precise. Which is about average. Not a bad span.'

Tom looked at the numbers tattooed to his wrist. 29, 3, 41 . . . his heart was beating so fast he could barely think.

'I suppose this is starting to make sense to you now?' Tom stared at Nurse Manners angrily. There was something about her he had already taken a severe dislike to. 'You are an echo, a copy, and the sooner you accept that fact, the better. We have no time for troublemakers, do we, Mr Grimal?'

There was a grunt behind Tom.

'Believe me, Tom, every one of our patients is under the delusion that they are indeed important,' said Dr Logan smoothly. 'Many arrive full of anger, but after a few days of vigorous activity they all settle into the swing. It's one big happy family, is it not, Nurse Manners?'

Nurse Manners smiled thinly. Happy families was stretching it a little far. This was a loony bin—not a holiday camp.

'But what's the point?'

The boy had spoken, spitting out each syllable as if it were poison.

'If I am an unwanted copy, why don't you just kill me? I am hardly useful—am I?'

There was an uncomfortable silence as Dr Logan fidgeted with his pen, and Nurse Manners suddenly found a fascinating mark on her cuff. Actually she agreed with the young tyke—killing every man jack of them would be a lot easier in her book. But Dr Logan looked very serious.

'You will discover you *are* useful, young man. And as for murder, that is out of the question. The Glorious Leader would never consider such a thing.'

'Ha!' Tom stifled a snort, knowing nothing could be further

from the truth. That was exactly what Don Gervase Askary would consider—instantly. 'Why don't you just tell me the real reason I am here. The truth.'

Dr Logan stared at the angry looking boy. Normally he would not bother to explain such things to a mere echo, but this one seemed to show more intelligence than most.

'But that *is* the truth. Significant echoes cannot be killed because killing an echo weakens the original. Don't ask me why, or how, but it is a proven fact. Many wiser heads than mine have spent years studying this phenomenon. And as for letting you fend for yourself,' Dr Logan emitted a little chuckle. 'My boy, that would cause utter chaos and confusion. We can't have lots of Tom Scatterhorns just wandering around. Imagine that!'

'So there are others, then?'

'Scatterhorns? No. Not at this moment. You are the first.'

Tom said nothing. Somehow, that was a relief.

'And what is so significant about Tom Scatterhorn?'

'Even if I knew the answer, I couldn't tell you,' said Dr Logan firmly, screwing the top back onto his pen. 'As far as I am concerned, you are here because you are here, and you shall remain here until your time comes to a natural end. Twenty-nine days, three hours . . . now slightly less.'

Dr Logan shuffled Tom's papers into a brown file, rather amazed to be having this conversation with a mere echo copy. That tiny beetle's duplication technique must be improving rapidly.

'Mr Grimal will show you to your room.'

Tom sat staring at the numbers on his wrist. Should he really go along with this charade? What if he ran, right now, back down the short corridor and out into the yard? Maybe he could make it over the wall—avoiding the broken glass somehow—or through the gate, sprint back across the causeway, and then . . . then he was over a hundred and fifty years into some nightmarish future, in a time of beetles and floods . . . the bubbles of inspiration floated for a second then popped almost as soon as they formed in his mind.

'Tom Scatterhorn?'

They were all standing, looking at him expectantly.

'I am not an echo,' Tom growled. 'And I know that—even if you don't.'

Dr Logan smiled generously.

'Of course you are. Mr Grimal, if you please.'

The bulky warder picked up Tom and the chair he sat on as if it were made of air, and led the way down a dark corridor to a small spiral staircase. From somewhere further on into the gloom came the sound of voices and a thrashing of pans.

'I can walk, you know. I'm not an invalid.'

'Very good sir,' chuckled Grimal, setting the chair down.

Tom recognized this narrow staircase as once being at the back of the museum. Up they trudged, and here and there Tom could see parts of the old structure poking through. The cornicing, the mahogany panelling, but little else. It was as if a wasps' nest had been built inside a doll's house.

'What happened to all the taxidermy?'

Mr Grimal smirked.

'Stuffed animals, you mean? All long gone, son. This ain't been a museum for years an' years. Before my great-grandfather's time—cos he worked here too. I imagine it was all very fancy.'

'It was. Very.'

'You would know.'

With a roll of his eyes Mr Grimal led the way down the rows of cells towards a large mullioned window that Tom recognized as once being high up above the Deluge. Now the window was at floor level, which meant that the old west wing had been divided in half and two floors were crammed into the space of one. They must have needed the space. Perhaps Dr Logan had hundreds of unwanted echoes in here waiting to die. It was not a happy thought.

'That's where I sit,' said Mr Grimal, indicating the desk before the window. 'And this is where you are, in the special cell. So we'll be neighbours.' He nudged open the nearest cell door with his foot. 'We'll be getting to know each other rather well over the next few weeks, eh?'

Tom peered in at the small room. White walls, a narrow bed, and a portion of a window, high up. Nothing else. It smelt of chemicals.

'What's special about it?'

'It's nice and close to me. I like to keep an eye on things in case there's trouble.'

'Is there much trouble?' asked Tom hopefully. In his mind he pictured all manner of unruliness amongst the fellow inmates.

'It all depends, don't it? The echo might look the same—but his mind can be ever so unpredictable. Almost the opposite of what you might think.' Mr Grimal sniggered to himself. 'It's an interesting job.'

It was fast dawning on Tom that perhaps his best strategy was

to appear as echo-like as possible. The problem was, he didn't
exactly know how . . . He sat down on the edge of the hard bed
and swung his feet idly.

'So what happens now?'

'Now is rest time. I would suggest that as you have had a long
journey, you might like a little sleep, and then after that we shall
see about a spot of dinner. How does that sound?'

'Sounds great.'

'Good good.'

Tom was quite aware that Mr Grimal was treating him as if
he was three years old, but that was fine. The warder was on
the point of closing the door when Tom thought of one last
question.

'Supposing I stay asleep—will you wake me up?'

'You need have no fear of that,' he smiled, his cheesy white
face floating out of the door like a balloon. There was a heavy
click as the door shut, and Tom was quick to notice that there
was no handle on the inside. He was obviously not intended
to let himself out. The silence barely lasted a few seconds,
whereupon there was a scrabbling sound, and something began descending from the ceiling. Glancing up and around, Tom
saw vertical black lines emerging from holes in the ceiling like
ink drawn on a blank page. What was this? Jumping off the
bed he stood in the middle of the room, his heart thumping.
They were beetles . . . soon others began to emerge from the
corners, travelling in horizontal lines, equally spaced . . . in a
minute the living grid was complete. Silence. The creatures
stood stock still, as immobile as stones.

Was it some sort of security device? Could they see him?

For some reason Tom did not want to move. But he did. He took one small step towards the wall. Nothing happened. Then another . . . and another until he was so close that he could see each and every insect in a line. A thin black thorax, red abdomen, and glowing pink eyes on stalks. What was their purpose? There was only one way to find out. Deliberately Tom flicked one out of line. Instantly a buzzer sounded in the corridor and the door hatch flashed open.

'Best leave them alone, Mr Scatterhorn. They don't like any monkey business, and neither do I.'

Tom looked at Mr Grimal's angry eye in the hatch. He gave his best smile.

'Sorry. Accident. Sorry.'

The eye watched him.

'Now, Mr Scatterhorn, how about you have that nice little rest.'

Tom meekly walked over to the narrow bed and obediently lay down, turning his face to the wall. So this was the special cell . . . the hatch snapped shut behind him and he closed his eyes. For the second time that morning Tom felt a great weariness sweep over him. In the last twenty-four hours he had been drugged, abducted, sent on a train two hundred years into the future and then locked up in some sort of jail for unwanted echoes, which just so happened to be housed in the Scatterhorn Museum, Dragonport, now a deserted island off the coast of England . . . Tom smiled grimly—he might have burst out laughing if it didn't happen to be true. Obviously all this had something to do with his refusal to help Don Gervase Askary. Perhaps it had everything to do with it. Perhaps this was Don Gervase's bizarre idea of a punishment. And perhaps Dr Logan and his gang really did believe that he was just an echo, nothing more. Whatever the truth, Tom was determined to find it out . . .

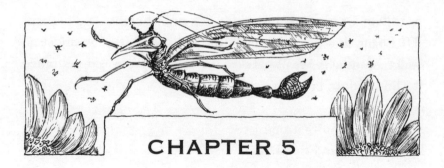

CHAPTER 5

FIGHT THE POWER

'Up and out! Up and out! Let's be having you, ladies and gents!'

Tom sat bolt upright in bed and opened his eyes groggily. He felt as if he had been asleep for days. He had dreamt he was in prison for a crime he knew he had not committed, and just as he was about to escape using a rope conveniently dangling down from the ceiling Mr Grimal appeared banging a saucepan . . .

'And you too, Mr Scatterhorn!'

Mr Grimal banged the saucepan on the door.

'Up!'

Rubbing his head, Tom swung himself off the narrow bed and watched the grid of black insects retreat into their holes, leaving the white walls blank. Yes he was in prison. It was not a dream.

'Aha—if it isn't the owner. Feeling better are we?'

Tom watched Mr Grimal march towards him as a line of inmates shuffled down the stairs.

'How long have I been asleep?'

'Twenty-four hours, which is more than enough, young man,' boomed Grimal. 'I was going to wake you up but seems you have some friends in high places. Can't think why.'

And neither for a moment could Tom.

'Perhaps they were hoping that if I slept for long enough I might forget who I really am.'

The warder's eyes narrowed and he stared at his dishevelled new charge.

'Still stuck on that one I see.' Mr Grimal's peeling pink face loomed down and Tom noticed that he looked very clean indeed. In fact, even his breath seemed to smell of soap. 'A word of advice, young Scatterhorn. Don't go thinking that your name makes you special. Because it doesn't. Not in here.'

Tom shrugged innocently.

'I don't.'

'Good. You'll find breakfast that way.' Mr Grimal extended a large pink forearm towards the spiral staircase at the far end of the corridor. 'But I suggest you put your new clothes on first. *If* you don't want to look daft, that is. Or maybe you do?'

Mr Grimal nodded inside and, turning round, Tom saw a heavy brown cotton shirt and trousers folded up neatly on the chair. Beneath them was a pair of plastic clogs and a small round hat. It looked like someone's idea of a uniform.

'Correct.'

Tom sighed deeply. He felt very hungry and even though Mr Grimal was hardly pleasant, he could see no point in making an enemy of him on his very first morning. Who knew what sort of power he held in this place.

'Now that's much more like it,' grinned Mr Grimal, as five minutes later Tom emerged from his cell in his ill-fitting uniform. Tom held up the small round hat.

'This as well?'

'If you please, Mr Scatterhorn, if you please. So you're just the same as everyone else.'

Tom jammed the hat onto his mop of blond hair then walked nonchalantly down the corridor. He felt slightly taller in his clogs, but his swagger was only skin deep. At the end there was a girl mopping the floor who glanced up at him as he passed.

'Ignore him, Evie,' bellowed Mr Grimal from his desk. 'His name's Tom Scatterhorn and he thinks he owns the place. He'll be telling you what to do in a minute.'

Evie smiled to herself and went back to her mopping with a peculiarly determined expression. She must have been a couple of years younger than him, her elfin face half hidden beneath a large orange cap. Tom did not feel inclined to explain. In fact, he had no idea how he was expected to behave. Like an unwanted echo, however that might be . . . At the bottom of the stairs Tom followed the sounds down a narrow corridor and, steeling himself, pushed open the heavy swing door to find himself in the main hall of the museum. The cases of animals had all gone, replaced by a rowdy eating hall that reminded him of a school canteen. The room was full of inmates all dressed in the standard brown uniform eating at long refectory tables. In the centre stood a small pulpit, where a grizzled warder kept order with a beady eye. The air was thick with a sickly, sweet smell, but this was not enough to stop Tom from walking straight over to where a line of cooks was busy and join the back of the queue. The closer he got the hungrier he felt and the cooks barely glanced up at him as they piled his plate high with shining heaps of what might have been beans and chips and peas, each coated in a different colour. Finding the quiet end of a bench, Tom had just taken his first mouthful when a man sat down opposite.

'Surprising, isn't it?'

Tom's shock was so great that the spoon clattered down onto his plate.

'Like chocolate on the outside—but on the inside—'

'Do I detect notes of cabbage? I think I do. Hmm, I rather like them.'

Another man had sat down next to the first, equally unkempt, but in a different way. He wore a beard, and his cap was set back at a jaunty angle.

'So much easier when you realize that whatever you get it will all taste of chocolate. So much easier, that.' The man crunched his food noisily and smiled at Tom. 'You're new here, aren't you?'

'Of course he's new. What's that supposed to mean?'

Tom stared at the two men who in any other circumstances would have brought a chill to his heart.

'Don Gervase Askary?'

'I am he,' rumbled the man on the left.

'That is true. But so am I,' rumbled the man on the right.

'And so are they over there.'

Tom looked around and saw that it was true—there were Don Gervases everywhere. Some had moustaches, some sported thick sideburns, some had shaved heads and some had ponytails . . . There must have been fifty of them amongst the crowd.

'Finders of the elixir.'

'Masters of the mesmerion—'

'Saviours of Scarazand.'

'Except of course, we're not, are we?' said one with a wink.

'So you . . .' Tom struggled to find the right words for this delicate question. 'You know . . . that you aren't—'

'The original? Of course we do,' said the man on the left without blinking. 'We are echoes. Echoes, echoes, one and all.'

'And . . . don't you mind?'

Both men looked at Tom curiously.

'You really are new, aren't you?'

'How could we *not* mind?'

'But they think we don't. They think all us echoes are daft as
brushes, ignorant as bricks, but they are very much mistaken. We
know tutti.'

'Tutti?'

'Tutti di frutti. But we are just too lazy to do anything about
it,' said the twirly moustache, crunching up the last of his beans.
'That's what all the chocolate's for.'

Tom didn't understand.

'To keep us happy,' he grinned, and fixed Tom with his large,
milky green eyes. 'Has that effect doesn't it?'

'There'd be a lot more trouble in here if it didn't,' agreed the
other Don Gervase, withdrawing a handkerchief from his cuff
and delicately dabbing the corners of his mouth. 'Why bother to
fight the powers that be when you get a full chocolate breakfast
like this every day of your life?'

'Not to mention the beetle juice,' chimed his friend, slurping
from his cup. 'Made on the premises of course.'

'What's your span, amigo?'

'My span?' Tom looked at these two strangely similar men and
decided that Mr Grimal was right: they might look exactly like
Don Gervase but somehow they were his exact opposite. 'I don't

have a span,' he whispered, glancing up at the warder.

'Of course you do! Everybody has a span.'

'I'm not an echo,' he pressed on. 'And I shouldn't be in here, either. I was abducted.'

The two Don Gervases rolled their eyes simultaneously.

'You'll have to do better than that, compadre.'

'Honestly. I'm Tom Scatterhorn. The real one.'

'But you *do* have one of these?' said the man on the left, pointing at the numbers on his wrist.

'It's fake,' protested Tom, unconsciously concealing his arm below the table. 'They put it on me, it hasn't always been there.'

The two Don Gervases looked at him steadily, then at each other.

'Delusional?'

'Definato. Totalicos.'

'It's the truth,' hissed Tom, struggling to control his anger.

'And why would *they* do that?'

The note of sarcasm was unmistakable. Tom looked from one to the other helplessly.

'This is it—I don't know. It's like . . . obviously I'm being hidden here, because . . .' Tom thought about mentioning his meeting with Don Gervase at the station but decided against it. 'I don't know why. Maybe even Dr Logan doesn't know why. But he knows.'

'Who knows?'

'Your original. He knows I'm not a real echo.'

The Don Gervase on the left raised his eyebrows quizzically.

'So it's like a vendetta, between us—I mean him—and you. Is that what you are saying?'

'Yes. Sort of. Only—'

'Did I hear the word vendetta?'

Another Don Gervase with a particularly wild look in his eye slid up along the bench. He had a ponytail and long sideburns and he smelt terrible. 'What he do what he do—burn your house, murder your family?'

'No. But actually I think he might—'

'And then what? Lock you in jail with a bunch of madmen?'

'Kind of.'

'Throw away the key?'

'Yes.'

'Yes? Then what—feed you food you wouldn't give a dog?'

Tom smiled.

'Caramba!'

'Tom Scatterhorn, this is The Soap,' said the moustache by way of introduction.

'Pleased to meet you, boy,' said The Soap, violently shaking his hand. 'So who is this guy?'

'Actually it's you,' said his friend.

'Me?'

'No! Old fishface, the cat's mother—'

'You mean the devil king of the insects—'

'He means the ruler of all things couth and uncouth—'

'Tweedledum? OK OK! I get the picture. Perfetto.' The Soap rubbed his stubbly chin excitedly. 'So how are you going to get even with this hombre? What can you do?'

'I erm . . . ' Tom smiled awkwardly: he had never really been asked this question before. 'First I'd have to get out of here.'

'Of course you would. And then?'

'And then . . . if anything were possible?'

'Why not anything?' smiled The Soap.

Without even thinking Tom knew the answer.

'I would destroy Scarazand,' he whispered. 'Get rid of it for ever. And him too—if I could.'

The Soap slapped the table and grinned madly.

'CARAMBA! Fighting talk! I like this boy!'

Tom sat grinning inanely. There, he had said it, and expressing his deepest wish to these three strange men had made him feel relieved, somehow. The warder in the pulpit swivelled round to stare at them.

'But if you destroyed Scarazand you would destroy us,' whispered the Don Gervase in the middle. 'Is that a good idea?'

Tom shrugged awkwardly. The truth was brutal.

'It's not your fault. But he's poisoning the world, killing everything, destroying everything.' Even me, Tom might have added. But he didn't. 'It doesn't have to be like this.'

'Doesn't it?'

'No. Not at all.'

The three Don Gervases sat for a moment in thoughtful silence. Tom watched them. Could these echoes really help him plot the downfall of Scarazand, the place where they had been created? The idea of it made his heart beat faster. Tom felt breathless, almost light-headed.

'It would be totally crazy!' giggled The Soap at last, drumming his long fingers on the table. 'And not as hard as you might think.'

'I have spotted a snag,' said the Don Gervase on the left.

'What's that?' asked Tom.

'No more chocolate!'

A great gong clanged out across the room, and Mr Grimal strode out through the tables.

'Right everyone, form two orderly lines *if* you would be so kind!'

There was a general murmur of discontent as everyone reluctantly stood up and began to wander towards the double doors in the corner.

'What happens now?' asked Tom, following the three men as they shuffled into the nearest line.

'The other bit, Mr Tom Scatterhorn. That's what happens now,' groaned a Don Gervase.

'The bit in between the chocolate,' added his friend.

'So we have to work, then?'

'And how!' howled The Soap. 'I'm insane! I should be locked up! Work is too good for me—I don't deserve it. I demand to be put in a straitjacket this instant!'

'Smallest at the front, tallest behind!' roared Mr Grimal, thrusting The Soap into a shambolic line that began to vaguely form across the hall. 'Hurry along otherwise we will all still be here at lunchtime!'

'With any luck,' muttered a Don Gervase under his breath.

'Not there, Mr Scatterhorn, if you please.' Nurse Manners hauled Tom out of the line by the shoulder and frogmarched him down towards the front. 'Now, do exactly as he does and keep that trap of yours shut,' she barked, slotting him in behind a gaunt looking boy with dark hair.

'Hi,' said Tom.

'Shut!' she bawled.

The boy turned and formally offered his hand for Tom to shake.

'How do you do. I'm Francis. Francis Catchpole.'

The boy's skin was so pale it was almost green. He didn't look well at all.

'And your name is?'

'Tom Scatterhorn.'

'Oh. Like the name above the front door.' Francis looked at him without interest. 'Why are you here?'

'Erm . . . ' For some reason Tom did not feel like sharing his secret again. 'I just am.'

'What's your span?'

'Right, people, let's be having you!'

A large steel grille opened, revealing a long tunnel with wires and pipes snaking along its roof.

'Quick march!'

The two lines jerked forward in a disorderly fashion, and the thunder of clogs filled the darkness.

'Where are we going?' asked Tom above the din. This wasn't any part of the museum he remembered.

'To the factory,' Francis replied.

'And what do we have to do?'

Francis shrugged absently.

'You'll see.'

Tom was vaguely wondering if it was the same work Mr Vee had mentioned as they eventually reached some steps, trudged over a bridge, and then in through the side of another building towards the sound of machinery clanking somewhere ahead. Blasts of hot air greeted them as they crossed over a wide hexagonal space several storeys high, in the centre of which hung a fat chimney suspended above three large open fires.

'That's purification,' said Francis, pointing down at the men sitting on the edge of the embers sprinkling long cotton tubes with water and scraping away a thick black glistening treacle that oozed out of the sides. Others were squeezing the ends of the tubes like enormous rolls of toothpaste.

'Purifying what?'

'Lac beetles,' Francis replied, suddenly sounding a little more enthusiastic.

'Lac beetles?'

'*Tachardia lacca*. They live on twigs, millions of them, and they excrete that stuff. It's collected in the Far East and sent over here to Dragonport. Where we make it into shellac.'

By now Tom was feeling very ignorant, and he could tell Francis was more than happy to explain. In fact he seemed almost proud of the importance of this work.

'Shellac. You know—it's in everything—varnish, polish, dye, fireworks, food, juice—'

'Juice?'

'Beetle juice. What you had for breakfast. And this is Spongs: the greatest handmade shellac factory in the world.'

Just as Tom was beginning to wonder if everything he had eaten had been coated in shellac, a sweaty-faced foreman began directing the echoes into various doorways according to their size.

'With him, son,' grunted the man, turning Tom by his head and shoving him after Francis into Nine A, a long low room overlooking the chimney. A group of boys and girls were already there, lounging on the ground. They looked both bored and hostile.

'Welcome, nutters all,' said a thin, sharp-faced boy at the front, breaking the surly silence.

'Hi, Slim,' murmured Francis, sitting down meekly in the corner. He seemed very uneasy.

'Who's yer friend, nutter?'

'Oh this is—'

'Tom,' said Tom, looking round at the weary faces. 'Hi.'

'It speaks,' tittered a girl.

'Tom who?' demanded Slim.

'Tom Ssk—' Francis touched Tom's arm and shook his head violently. There was a giggle at the back. At that moment the burly foreman rolled in.

Approaching the wall on which a sign was written: 'Room 9A. Today's quota:' he switched on the oily machine and set the mechanical numbers to seven, zero, three.

'Seven hundred! Seven hundred and three!'

The room erupted into a chorus of howls and indignation.

'But we've got two of them doolalls!' protested a short girl at the front. 'How's that ever gonna square?'

'Yeah!'

'That's impossible!'

'Shut it, you lot!' rasped the foreman, dropping open several hatches to reveal machinery behind. 'There's nineteen of yous, so that's thirty-seven a piece, by my reckoning.'

'But they's never gonna do that!' the girl spat back, pointing at Tom. 'Not him! He's never done nothing! Ten more like!'

'Well then you's gonna have to make up the difference, aren't you, sweetheart?' snarled the foreman. 'You know the rules; no quota—no pay!' and with that he slammed the door and locked it.

The children swore and protested as the heavy boots marched away down the corridor, then glared murderously at Tom and

Francis in the corner as if it was all their fault.

'What we gonna do, Slim?'

'See these doolally-boys pull their weight, or else,' said Slim marching towards them belligerently.

'Is it difficult?' asked Tom. Slim was a full head shorter than he was, and he didn't feel intimidated.

'No it ain't, nutter. So don't you go pretendin' it is.'

'I won't.' Tom held his gaze steadily. 'Maybe you could show me what to do.'

Slim glared at Tom. He was obviously the self-appointed leader of this bunch, and he seemed surprised that Tom had answered back. And so did Francis Catchpole.

'He'll show yer,' he snarled, looking disdainfully at Francis sitting quietly on the floor. 'Won't you, Francis?' he added, giving the boy a swift kick. Those large milky blue eyes looked up at him blankly.

'I will, Slim.'

'All right then.'

Somewhere in the distance an alarm sounded, and there was a great clanking of wheels as the machinery in the hatches began to turn.

'This shift has begun!' declared a loudspeaker out in the corridor. 'You're late already!'

The children wearily hauled themselves to their feet and gathered beside the hatches. A series of wooden compartments began moving vertically upwards and soon small metal trays began to appear, each one heaped with a pile of that strange treacle-like substance Tom had seen being prepared below, together with a long flat piece of wood.

'What do we do with this?' Tom whispered to Francis as they took a tray in turn and walked over to the corner. Francis pointed at the hatch on the other side of the room, where children were hefting steel cylinders off a horizontal conveyer belt and rolling them to an empty spot on the floor.

'Spread it on one of those,' he said.

'Spread it?'

Tom was mystified, but he followed the rest, grabbing a jar and finding it was surprisingly warm and heavy.

'But it's full of water,' he murmured, placing it carefully on the floor. He was about to ask what next when he saw the girl in front of him was already using her long flat stick to spread the golden treacle-like substance over the curved surface in long deliberate strokes.

'That's right, Tomsk—use your stick,' she said, expertly evening it out to the corners, 'then do this.'

Standing up, she took a corner of the flat square and carefully peeled it off the side of the cylinder and held it out in front of her like a dishcloth.

'Now for the hard part,' she said, slipping off her clogs. 'Watch carefully, doolally boy, cos I'm only showing you once.'

The girl crouched down and slipped the bottom side of the square beneath her toes, gripped the top side between her teeth, and moved her hands around either side of the shellac. Then with one violent motion she began to pull at the material. Incredibly, it began to stretch—not much—but a little. And the girl did it again, then again, then again, each time pushing her legs up a little further, spreading her arms out a little more.

'See?' she gasped. 'It's not difficult.'

Looking around Tom saw that all the children were at it now, crouching and stretching in a strange, bird-like dance, holding their teeth clenched while working their legs and arms wider and wider apart until the shellac was a floppy translucent sheet of gold stretched between their outstretched limbs like a kite. Some of the taller boys had already stretched their first sheets as far as they could and were now onto the next phase, carefully spreading them out on star shaped boards and setting them down on a conveyer belt. Ding! A bell rang as each sheet shot down into the darkness—and so the mechanical numbers began to turn: eleven, twelve, thirteen . . .

'Get a move on, nutter!' shouted Slim as he walked across the room with his stretched sheet. 'Shellac don't spread itself!'

Tom took a deep breath. Whatever work he might have imagined them being forced to do, it was nothing like this. He peeled off the shellac and, slipping off his clogs, crouched down and sank his teeth into the top and curled the bottom under his toes. He began to pull. It moved a little. The second time he tried a little harder but promptly lost his balance and fell over. Scrambling to his feet he expected howls of derision from the other children but there was nothing—just hard-bitten scowls. They all knew that if he fell short it would be them making up the difference.

'Try lots of small pulls, not one big one,' said Francis, stretching out his sheet. 'You've got to coax it.'

'OK.'

Tom wiped his brow and crouching down grabbed the shellac between his teeth. Coax it—be patient. Slowly.

After half an hour of pulling, stretching, falling over, dropping the shellac into a sticky mess and starting again Tom proudly laid out his first floppy sheet on a board. His neck burned, his fingers ached and his thighs felt as if they had been pulverized into jelly, but he had done it. Ding! The bell rang and it shot down into the darkness beyond. One down, only thirty-six to go . . . Thirty-six . . .

Tom glanced around at the other children, all bending and stretching mechanically like robots. Even Francis, pale and vacant, had already finished his third. This was slave labour: how could they possibly keep this up all day? Seven hundred and three . . . it was impossible.

By the time he staggered into his cell that evening Tom felt more dead than alive. Just about every muscle in his body was burning and he could barely lie down on the bed without feeling himself seize up.

'Nighty night, my friends!' shouted Mr Grimal cheerily slamming one cell door after another. In the half-light Tom was dimly aware of those curious black beetles descending all around him to form their living, watching grid. Tom was so tired he didn't care any more. He closed his eyes and a blizzard of conveyor belts, sheets of shellac and snarling young faces danced before him. Strangely, he almost envied his fellow prisoners now: at least their short life span meant that they did not have to put up with this torment for long. But what was he going to do? He couldn't live in this cell and work in that infernal factory for the rest of his life, which for him meant not weeks but years, maybe decades— it would kill him, wouldn't it?

It would. Tom knew it would. That must be Don Gervase's intention. His words at Waterloo station floated back . . .

Become something more than what you are—an ordinary, snivelling boy, who will grow up to be an ordinary, snivelling man, live a brief and boring life, and die a premature death.

Tom stared at the tiny pink-eyed insects glowing in the quickening light. This was that life. It had begun. Eventually he would become nothing more than an empty stretching machine: an insect. A worker. An echo. Tom closed his eyes. Last night he felt like laughing at his predicament—tonight he felt very much like crying. But even as the waves of desperation welled up inside him another emotion began to surface. Tom felt an anger so fierce that it began to burn through him like electricity, tingling his fingers and swelling in his heart till it felt tight enough to explode. He stared at the beetles, centimetres from his face.

Don Gervase Askary has put me here to die. He has hidden me away with all the other forgotten echoes. But I am going to survive. And I am going to escape. And then I am going to destroy Scarazand. He won't stop me. Never. There will be a way . . . somehow.

CHAPTER 6

THE IRIDESCENT FEATHER

Despite the fierce spark of rebellion burning inside him that Tom guarded as jealously as a candle flame in a storm, it was almost a week before he had another thought. During that time, he was living in a waking dream. Every day was the same: Tom got up in the grey dawn, pulled on his rough uniform, crunched through a chocolate bean and beetle juice breakfast, trudged to the factory to stretch his daily quota of shellac, and then ten hours later came back again, to eat more chocolate and sleep. It was the life of a machine: monotonous, punishing, and very, very boring. As Tom's legs and shoulders hardened to the constant stretching the work became easier, but he couldn't ever pretend to enjoy it. Like the rest of the children in room Nine A, his life revolved around the number the foreman set the clock to—the rest of it meant nothing.

And so it was with a certain grim satisfaction that at the end of the first week Tom found himself laying his final stretched sheet at the same time as Slim was laying his.

'Finished already, Tomsk?' he snorted, as one after another they placed the boards onto the conveyor belt.

'Yep,' said Tom, wearily wiping the sweat off his brow, 'that's me done.'

Slim snorted grudgingly and Tom stifled a smile; he knew that this was a small victory.

'Better help little boy blue then,' spat Slim, watching Francis bending and stretching, bending and stretching, so slowly that it was almost painful to watch. 'Cos it's all for one and one for all in here, isn't it?'

Occasionally, after work, the inmates were allowed out into the narrow yard at the back of the building. The walls were so high that the sun never shone in this place—in fact it was like being in the bottom of a well, but at least it was somewhere else. Tom would take his place in the slow shuffling line around the cobblestones, and there was a certain odd camaraderie between them all. Just about everyone was an echo of some prominent person in the regime at Scarazand: generals, spies, poisoners, Don Gervases and a few odd children . . . they came and went with alarming speed but somehow the strange doggedly cheerful at- mosphere remained. Maybe it *was* all the chocolate, maybe it was the echoes' natural state of mind—and it certainly had something to do with being stuck in this asylum twenty-four hours a day. Tom had barely been here a week and already he knew he was becoming a little peculiar.

It was to do with missing things: normal, boring things that he had always taken for granted. Smells for instance. Like every- one else, Tom had become addicted to the constant diet of sweet chocolate and beetle juice, but found himself hanging around the kitchen stairwell just to catch a sniff of old cabbage that was oc- casionally flung into the mix. Even the acrid stench of boiling clothes became as exotic and interesting as bacon and eggs . . . it was the same with sounds, too. Tom found himself straining to hear the distant boom of a foghorn out in the estuary, or the rattle of an engine somewhere beyond the high walls. These small snatches of life took on an extraordinary significance: they were the only signs that this cloud-hidden island of old Dragonport had not been abandoned by the world altogether.

Then on the morning of the seventh day, Tom had a surprise. The alarm rang as usual, and with a wide yawn Tom rolled over and stared at the wall. In the grey light he watched the grids of small, pink-eyed insects retreating in an orderly fashion, just as they did every morning.

'UP! UP! UP, YOU LAZY SODS!'

The clanging continued, but the high voice was not Mr Grimal's. There was a chorus of coughs and shuffling of feet, and Tom wandered out into the long narrow corridor to see the square shape of Nurse Manners swinging a steel rattle with gusto.

'Aha, if it's not the owner,' she said, finally stopping her racket. 'I hear you've taken to shellac like a duck to water. The foreman is very impressed. Quite the model worker.'

There was a rather nasty smile on Nurse Manners's small red lips that Tom could not fail to recognize. But he refused to take the bait.

'How are you?'

'Oh very well—for a Sunday. Which is Mr Grimal's day off, of course. And yours, too.'

'Mine?'

'Certainly! Factory's shut on Sunday, so you can sit in the canteen eating chocolate beans all morning. Now isn't that just what you want to do?' She ruffled his hair like a dog. 'I'll bet it is.'

Tom almost replied that he would rather eat mud, but decided against it.

'Trot along now,' she said, waving him down the stairs. 'That's it. There you go.'

Tom ambled obediently away, feeling more and more like making a serious enemy of Nurse Manners, but knowing it would do him no good at all. Sauntering into the main hall, he did notice that the atmosphere was different: it was not quite carefree, but almost.

'A very good morning to you,' said a Don Gervase, sliding onto the bench opposite Tom. Even though they all looked the same, Tom recognized this echo from his first day, as he had long greasy hair and a hat jammed squarely on the back of his head.

'Hi,' said Tom, wincing a little as he crunched his first spoonful of shellac coated beans.

'How's asylum life treating you?'

Tom chewed thoughtfully. He really wasn't sure if he could eat this.

'There's a lot of chocolate.'

'Isn't there just.'

'And there's a lot of shellac.'

'And the less said about *that* the better,' rumbled the Don Gervase, popping a chocolate ball into his mouth. He sucked it hard for a while, then carefully withdrew a wet orange cube and placed it in his bowl.

'What are you doing?' asked Tom.

'I am fishing. That, my friend, is a genuine cube of carrot.'

'Really?'

'They hide them on purpose. Appalling, isn't it?'

Tom looked at the meagre vegetable longingly. And then he remembered where it had been.

'You can only do this on Sundays,' said the Don Gervase, placing another ball in his mouth and sucking hard. 'Takes too long otherwise. But with dedication and luck you could get yourself a respectable portion of something. Once I even managed to reconstruct an entire banana.'

Tom stared at his own heap of shining beans with vague interest.

'Where's your friend?' asked Tom. 'The one with the ponytail.'

'The Soap?' The Don Gervase delicately wiped his mouth. 'Well, no one lives for ever, do they? And who wants to indeed, stuck in this place?'

Tom was rather taken aback.

'So . . . he's dead, then?'

'He was very near the end of his span so it was to be expected. And there's such a high turnover, I expect half of this lot are new.' The echo glanced around the busy room. 'Strange, isn't it, to be so old when your life is already so short,' he winked. 'Come to think of it, he was looking forward to talking to you. Because he had it all worked out.'

'All what worked out?'

'Oh you know, that idea of yours. Escape, destruction of Scarazand, etcetera, etcetera. All that. Shame, because he's dead now.' The Don Gervase crunched up a carrot with gusto. 'I'm feeling lucky this morning. Are you eating that?' he said, eyeing Tom's untouched breakfast.

'Erm . . . no.'

'Excellent.'

The Don Gervase slid the bowl across and greedily popped something round and shiny into his mouth. He began sucking on it noisily. Tom could not contain his disappointment.

'I don't suppose he told you about this plan he'd worked out?'

'Tell me? Erm . . . I'm not sure he did. But then he didn't need to.'

The Don Gervase pulled what might have been a single green pea out of his mouth and looked at it thoughtfully.

'Why not?'

'Because he drew it all out. In the dust, under his bed. I suppose it's still there.' The echo savoured the pea carefully, as if it was the finest caviar, and when he finished he smiled. Tom sensed he was enjoying the suspense. 'Would you like to see it?'

Five minutes later they had clattered up the back stairs and into a grey room not much bigger than Tom's with two bunk beds against either wall. It felt far more like a prison in here, and the slice of window was even meaner.

'Here,' said the Don Gervase, carefully pulling the bed away from the wall. Underneath was an elaborate series of squiggles and doodles, connected by arrows and lines. 'Not bad—eh?'

Tom scratched his head, trying to make sense of it. There were chimneys, gates, trees, mountains, arrows, stick men . . .

'Getting out of this place was fiendishly complex, but then all you need is to put a bomb down that vent hole then . . . kaboom! Lovely explosion.'

'The vent hole?' repeated Tom. 'You mean the chimney—'

'Taking all that noxious gas out of the Queen's chamber: absolutely. It's Scarazand's weakest spot, isn't it? The only place where the colony makes direct contact with the ground.'

Tom tried to hide his excitement. This was the greatest secret of Scarazand, the place the beetles had successfully concealed for thousands of years . . . a small hole no bigger than a well directly above the heart of the colony . . .

'So . . . but did he know where the vent hole was?' asked Tom, searching the doodles for a hole, or anything like it.

'Oh yes. He knew.'

'Is it here?'

'Erm . . . what?'

'Did he draw it?'

The Don Gervase stared at the strange doodles and rubbed his chin.

'Now that is a very good question. Isn't that it over there?'

He pointed at what might have been a long thin chimney. There was something like an explosion at the top, surrounded by a mass of squiggles and arrows. That probably was the vent hole. But were all those swiggles plumes of gas . . . or birds . . . maybe even trees . . . a jungle?

'And how am I supposed to find that place?'

The Don Gervase took a chocolate bean out of his pocket and chewed on it thoughtfully. He knew that Tom was hanging on his every word.

'It's not going to be easy.'

'Why not?'

'Because it's a secret. The greatest secret of all.' The Don Gervase studied the doodles hard, then glanced back at Tom.

'The Soap told me a lot of things about his plan. Problem is, I just can't remember them all.'

'No?'

The echo shook his head. Tom stared at the doodles on the floor desperately.

'But how could he know all this, and you can't?'

'The Soap was a little different to us. He seemed to know a lot more things, about a lot more things. Apologies, amigo. Maybe there'll be another who—'

At that moment the door swung open and a warder with a large bag and a brush came in.

'That's very thoughtful of you, gentlemen. Thank you.' In one movement he swept the doodles in the dust away. 'Nice to see you over this side, Mr Scatterhorn. Finding new friends, that's what we like to see.' With a gloved hand he threw The Soap's old hat into the bag. 'Any more rubbish?'

They sat in glum silence until the warder bustled out of the door. Tom didn't know whether to be angry or disappointed that such an opportunity had slipped through his fingers.

'I will try to remember,' said the echo, when the warder had gone. 'It will come back. I just need to remember the right words.'

Tom spent the rest of the day in a daze. The more he brooded on this great lost opportunity the lower he felt. If only he had made friends with that wild-eyed Don Gervase straight away— he should have seized the opportunity . . . but somehow it had all been too distracting, the factory, the asylum, the future . . . and perhaps, had he admitted it, he never really believed that these echoes could be different from each other, or that they might have been able to help him. It seemed so unlikely. How could they know how to destroy Scarazand, the place that had created them—

'Watch out!'

Tom's mind was racing so far ahead he barely saw Evie kneeling in the gloom, sweeping the corners of the dark twisting staircase. Her angry elfin face appeared beneath her orange beret, then she scrabbled down the stairs to retrieve the brush Tom had kicked out of her hand.

'Sorry. I . . . didn't see you.'

Evie grunted something in return.

'Sorry.'

There was a brief awkward silence.

'Working on a Sunday can't be much fun,' Tom said, lamely searching for something to say.

'It's better than what you have to do. I was lucky to get this,' Evie murmured, going back to her sweeping. 'My brother hates that place. Says he'd burn it down if he could.'

'Your brother works in the factory?'

Evie nodded.

'And he thinks you's all right—for a nutter,' she smiled to herself.

Tom was surprised: he had hardly exchanged more than a word with Evie since he had been here, but he was aware she had been watching him. Now for the first time she seemed happy to talk. Perhaps it was because Mr Grimal wasn't here.

'So who—'

'Slim. That's right. Slim Spry.'

It was only when she said the words that Tom immediately saw the family resemblance: the wide apart eyes, the razor sharp cheekbones. He smiled; so Slim thought he was all right, did he?

'I'm not a nutter, by the way.'

'That's just what I told him.'

Tom looked at Evie curiously.

'So you can tell?'

'I seen enough of them. I should know.' She looked up at him. 'Something about their eyes, ain't it? Something that shows they's not quite all there?'

Tom considered this for a moment: should he tell her more, could he trust her? He wasn't sure . . . Evie moved her sweeping up a step.

'So what did they bang you up in here for then? Must be something bad. You done a murder or summat?'

'Murder? Of course not.'

'Well it must be somethin' serious, cos that's the special cell you're in. Grade one doolally's cell, that.'

Tom nodded grimly—he had suspected as much.

'An' Slim says you're the type'n'all. Violent.'

'Evie, I haven't murdered anyone,' replied Tom shortly. 'I'm here because they want me out of the way for some reason.'

'Who's they?'

'You know, Don Gervase Askary and all his cronies from Scarazand. Dr Logan's boss. The beetle people.'

Evie emptied her sweepings into the bucket and eyed him suspiciously.

'Beetle people?' she repeated, as if this was some sort of confirmation that Tom was indeed a nutter.

'Yes. Beetle people. Like everyone else in this place. They're copies. Duplicates. Echo beetles.'

Evie stared at Tom.

'That's why they're here. That's the reason they all have tattoos on their arms and they don't live very long. They may look normal, but up here,' he tapped his skull, 'they're insects.'

'Pah!' Evie quite clearly found all this hard to believe.

'Well what do you think they are?'

'I dunno, just . . . nutters?'

'They're not just *nutters*, Evie. Surely you must have noticed that lots of them look the same?'

'That's because they're impersonators, look-alikes.'

'What?'

'They've all got some fantasy about being the same bloke, Don Whatsit—haven't they?' she replied, not to be swayed. 'He's the leader of some other country or something, and they all love him, and they want to look like him, and that's causing a lot of trouble. So someone's decided what's best is to lock them all up here on Dragonport Island, and keep them right out the way. *Insects,*' she snorted. '*Beetle people.* Who ever heard of that?'

Tom stared at her in frustration. He wondered just how much anyone in Dragonport really knew about this asylum.

'I'm sorry, Evie, but I promise you that is what they are. I know it sounds weird and strange, and believe me where I come from not very likely at all—but it's true. That is what they are: and I'm not. I'm normal, just like you. That's how you could tell I was different.'

Evie stopped her brushing and regarded Tom warily. He had a sense that she was at last beginning to believe him.

'Beetle people—eh?'

Tom nodded.

'Unwanted copies of Don Gervase Askary. They can't be killed because that would weaken him. So they are sent here to work until they die.'

'Evie! Where has that girl got to? Evie Spry!'

Nurse Manners's parrot-like voice squawked out from the corridor on the top floor. Evie swiftly stowed her dustpan and brush away in the bucket. She was obviously wanted.

'Which is why I have to get out of here,' Tom whispered as loudly as he dared.

'Oh you have, have you?'

'Yes.'

'An' how's that ever going to happen?'

'I don't know. I was wondering—' Tom paused: how to say this? 'You know this place really well, don't you?'

Evie shrugged.

'Well enough.'

'Maybe there's still . . . in the old days, long ago, there used to be places in this Museum that led from one place to another. Like portals. There was a wicker basket under the stairs that you couldn't feel the bottom of, and a hole in a wall on the ground floor, which transported . . . ' Tom stopped when he saw Evie's expression.

'No?'

Evie shook her head.

'Nope. I've cleaned all over this place, every corner, and I can fairly say there's nothing like that here. In fact they seem very particular about keeping you all in.'

Bad tempered footsteps marched to the top of the stairs.

'Evie Spry! Is that you?'

'Coming!' she called, gathering her bits together.

'But, if you did ever find anything like that, could you let me know? Because I'm serious.'

Evie Spry picked up her bucket. There was something very intense in Tom's face: he looked almost old and young at the same time.

'You don't have to tell anyone.'

'You're dead right I don't.'

And away she went. Tom stood for a moment in the darkness, wondering if Evie would confide in Nurse Manners, or Mr Grimal, or even Doctor Logan . . . something told him she wouldn't. Something told him that Evie disliked this place almost as much as he did. They were both, in different ways, trapped here. Slowly Tom began to trudge up the narrow winding staircase, and he had almost reached the top when his eye was caught by something bright lying in the centre of the dark step ahead of him. Stooping down, he picked it up. It was a small iridescent feather, glinting green and gold in the gloom. Obviously it had once belonged to some exotic bird: a parrot, or a hummingbird perhaps . . . Tom's first instinct was to hand it to Evie, thinking it must belong to her, but then another thought came into his mind . . . Carefully slipping the feather into his pocket, Tom ran up the rest of the stairs and out into the long corridor on the top floor.

'Don't talk to her, Mr Scatterhorn, she's busy!' called Nurse Manners from the desk at the far end without looking up. There was Evie, sweeping furiously in the corner with a scowl on her face.

'That's right, she's spent far too long yacking already and she's to have this corridor swept before I go home.'

'Oh.'

Tom put on his best vacant expression and innocently peered into Evie's dust bucket. There, in amongst the dirt, was another one, blue, fringed with gold, and at the bottom another—fire engine red.

'Where have the feathers come from?'

Evie dared not break her sweeping but nodded back to the narrow staircase.

'The middle landing,' she whispered, 'they's forever popping out from under the skirting board. Now you've got me in enough trouble already—'

'I said leave her alone, Mr Scatterhorn!' screeched Nurse Manners irritably. 'Evie Spry, you ignore him now!'

Evie lowered her head and began brushing faster, trying not to look at Tom rummaging about in the bucket.

'You don't half push it do you?' she muttered under her breath.

Tom slipped the red feather into his pocket and winked.

'I'm a nutter, remember?'

'Mister Scatterhorn if you please!'

With his best smile he looked up at Nurse Manners then bowed deeply.

'I'm so sorry,' he said. 'I really am.'

Nurse Manners rolled her eyes and went back to her notes.

Tom sauntered back down the stairs, and as soon as he reached the middle landing he dropped to his knees and immediately saw what Evie meant. In the corner, next to the wall, the skirting board had lifted away from the uneven floorboards leaving a narrow line of black air, just wide enough for Tom to poke his finger through. Strangely, he could feel no wall behind it. If only he had a torch he could peer inside . . . what was behind there? Quite clearly it was some kind of space, perhaps filled up with dirt swept off the stairs—or was it something else entirely? Tom didn't know, but his imagination began to race. Maybe . . . *maybe*—

For the next week the narrow black strip of air below the skirting board became Tom's obsession. He stuck a knife through the gap to find out how far it went back (inconclusive); he tried prising it away from the wall (impossible); he even put a glass to the wood and listened for any sounds inside (nothing whatsoever). Despite all this, Tom was convinced that there was some unaccounted space between the two new floors that divided the old West Wing. Again and again he clattered up and down the narrow staircase in his clogs, counting the number of steps, then comparing that with what he thought was the height of the ceiling in the floor below. Maths had never been his strong point, but Tom was almost certain that the ceiling was not high enough for the number of stairs, which meant that there must be some sort of middle space between the second and third floors . . . why this should be he did not know—maybe it was to do with the windows outside, but that didn't explain the feathers . . . The feathers . . . Tom's mind overflowed with possibilities; were there some relics of the Museum down there, left by accident, or perhaps even . . .

The real breakthrough came on Friday, just as Tom wearily stretched his last piece of shellac onto the board. Turning breathlessly towards the conveyor belt, he stood waiting in line behind the other exhausted children when he noticed something rolling around in the bottom of one of the empty wooden compartments coming up from below. It was a short, sturdy-looking chisel with a wide flat end. Obviously it had been dropped there by accident.

'Watch it, Tomsk!' shouted the girl in front as Tom shoved her out of the way and quick as a flash grabbed the tool and slipped it inside his sock. Shaking down his trouser leg he stood up to find Slim staring at him.

'What do you want that for, nutter-boy?'

Tom shrugged noncommittally and picked up his board.

'None of your business, Slim. And I'm not a nutter by the way.'

Slim scowled.

'I hear you's planning to escape.'

'Maybe I am.'

'What's the point in that? You'll be dead soon enough.'

'I don't think so.'

Slim looked at Tom and saw a fierce determination in his dark eyes that was most unusual for an inmate.

'You's serious, incha, Tomsk?'

Tom nodded.

'Maybe you can help me.'

'Help *you*?' Slim laughed brutally. 'Why should *I* help you?'

'Because you've got nothing better to do. Because you hate this place as much as anyone else. And why not?'

It was a question to which Slim could not immediately think of an answer. He scowled at Tom, then moved away.

Later that evening, when the stairwell was quiet, Tom set to work with his small steel chisel. After a few tentative prods he worked it along the top of the skirting and discovered that it made a perfect little lever. It only took a few minutes before there was a sudden loud squeak and one end of skirting board moved away from the wall—one more tug and . . . Tom's heart began to race. He felt behind it with his fingers: nothing there, nothing, it was empty, inviting; if he pulled it away now he could wriggle through the gap into . . . what? Supposing there was nothing down there? Supposing Mr Grimal or Nurse Manners found the skirting board lying on the landing? They would almost certainly have it screwed back so tight that Tom would never be able to get out again. No, he must stop. Be patient. Plan this out. That was the sensible thing to do. But at this moment Tom did not feel very sensible. He felt desperate. But desperation would get him nowhere. With a heavy heart Tom pushed the board back into place, shutting the door that had opened to him.

'So you won't be long, then?'

It was two thirty the following Sunday afternoon, and the whole asylum was snoring. Evie sat a couple of stairs above, watching anxiously as Tom began to carefully lever open each end of the skirting board. He had decided to take her into his confidence knowing she could replace the board at a moment's notice if anyone came past. And to make it easier he had removed the rusty old nails that held it in place and replaced them with some blobs of chocolate honey from the canteen to act like glue.

'It's hard to say,' whispered Tom. He couldn't admit to her that he hoped he would never be coming back. 'It might be five minutes, might be an hour. But if it's longer then don't worry. Just close it up and carry on.'

Evie sat on the step fretting, her narrow features knitted into a scowl.

'But what happens when they come to lock up the cells tonight and see you're not there? Cos it's me they'll be asking. Bound to. Cos they knows we bin talkin' an everythin'. '

'Tell them whatever you want, Evie. Except don't say I went down here.'

Tom lifted the skirting aside and peered into the darkness beyond. He could see nothing in the void, but the gap was just large enough for him to squeeze through.

'Won't look good though, will it? Supposing you get stuck?'

Tom turned to look up at her pale, worried face.

'I'm just doing a bit of exploring, Evie, that's all. I'll be back.'

'You'd better be,' she said, watching Tom wriggle through the narrow slot.

'Bye then.'

Slotting the skirting board back across the gap, Evie sat down on the stairs to take up reluctant lookout with brush and pan.

CHAPTER 7

SKIN, WOOD, WIRE, AND WIT

The space below was not as dark as Tom had imagined it might be, but it was certainly as strange. The gap between the ceiling above and the floor below was less than a metre high and, staying on his knees, Tom began crawling forward down what appeared to be a trench. Bricks, plaster, and rubbish had been piled up on either side, and here and there more brilliant feathers decorated the gloom. The whole place was absolutely filthy.

'Look, his feet is off the ground.'

Tom froze. A voice: somewhere to his left. Turning, he saw a diamond pattern of light. That must be the front of the building. But who—

'And he's stopped moving. Which equates to being dead. I win.'

'No he isn't! That was a twitch so it was!'

'Twitch, me arse! So hand it over.'

'Did you not see it?'

'I'm not falling for that old chestnut.'

The silence thickened. Tom inched forward and peered round the corner. Silhouetted in the dirt were two small black beetles, one with its spiky black mandibles clasped around the thorax of the other and lifting it off the ground.

'All right. I'll give it to you. *This* time. Again.'

Tom stifled a gasp as two very dusty and almost hairless creatures scampered out of the shadows and parted the duelling beetles to replace them with two more.

'Ready?'

'Achooo!'

Tom's sneeze surprised him almost as much as the two strange creatures. Startled, they stared in Tom's direction. Both had wizened, skull-like faces and each was missing an eye. Were they cats? Rats? In the dark it was so hard to tell, but they were *speaking*, weren't they?

'Hello?'

In the same second both creatures bolted.

'Hello?' he whispered again, louder this time. 'Anyone there?'

There was no one there. Tom wondered if he had imagined it. Then a hissing sound filled the gloom and built like a boiling kettle. Tom's instinct was to duck—but before he even had a chance something hard knocked into him from behind.

'Ow!'

Tom rolled over to find a bright light shining into his eyes, forcing him to shut them again.

'Please . . .'

'What do you think?'

'Escaper. Definitely. Look at this.'

Tom felt small sharp hands scratching at the numbers on his wrist—then something cold clambered up onto his face and bit at his fingers.

'Ow! Stop it!'

'Bury him?'

'What's the point?'

'Chuck him down the shaft?'

'It would be a kindness.'

'No,' began Tom, struggling to sit up. 'No you don't under-stand. I'm Tom, Tom—'

'Tom who? Tom Scatterhorn? Yes, yes, and I'm the pope.'

'No but I am. I am. Really.'

'Down the shaft—'

'Hang fire, my friends, hang fire.' Another voice sounded from somewhere further back and Tom opened his eyes a fraction. All he could see was a beak and an eye marching towards him, noth-ing more.

'Clear out of the way.'

The eye pressed closer, yellow and angry and bright as a but-ton. Tom knew the owner of that eye . . .

'Don't you recognize me?' said Tom quietly. There was silence. He could feel a prickly expectation in the gloom beyond.

'I do believe I do, boyo. I do indeed.'

There was a murmur of disbelief all around.

'He's good, then?'

'I think he might be. Tom Scatterhorn, eh? Well, well. How the mighty are fallen.'

There was a flick of a switch and at once the whole space was filled with small lights hanging from the ceiling in loops. Blinking hard, Tom found himself surrounded by a large and motley col-lection of papery, broken creatures: hairless, featherless, scaleless, with eyes hanging out and tails missing, but somehow, in some fashion, all still alive. For a long moment the strange creatures stared at the boy in his dusty brown uniform, and he stared back at them. There were so many questions it was hard to know quite where to begin.

'So what happened to you?' asked Tom.

'A question I would also like to ask, boyo,' replied the dodo, who despite being completely bald and with a large hole in one side had retained her Welsh accent. 'Because we certainly didn't expect you to be on the guest list of this place.'

'Neither did I,' admitted Tom. 'You first.'

'Well it's rather tedious. Do you want the long or the short of it?'

'Erm—'

'Our official capacity is insulation,' said what might have been the remains of a brush—or a porcupine—with feeling.

'Insulation?'

'That's it,' continued another familiar voice. 'Warm, bulky, light. Handy stuffing.'

Tom squinted into the darkness and saw the ghost of a small man squatting next to a post. He had an inordinately long and puffy nose and raised a shrivelled black hand.

'Hello, old bean.'

Tom smiled: even without any hair he could still recognize the proboscis monkey.

'This floor is obviously not quite a floor, but a void,' he continued. 'When those people destroyed our beautiful home, they wanted the window up there, and the windows down there, which left this awkward place in the middle, which was too small for anything much.'

'So they chucked us in,' continued the pangolin. 'Saved burning us, I suppose, but most unpleasant it has been.'

'Unpleasant? A living nightmare more like, for all and sundry,' continued the dodo. 'This place was filled from floor to ceiling with rubble, earth, dust, muck, you name it.'

'And we were just raw materials to be purloined by any passing rodent.'

'Rats took my eyes.'

'Moths ate my pelt—'

'Mice made nests in my belly,' nodded some unidentifiable mammal slowly. 'Oh lovely and snug it must have been—but what about me? I couldn't precisely move could I?'

'You're a sloth. You don't move.'

'I have moved. On occasion. At least I still look like what I'm supposed to be, not some leather sausage who—'

'So how did you get out of the rubble?' interrupted Tom, curious to see that all the old conflicts were still there, even now.

'Well someone had to take charge, didn't they?' snarled the dodo, puffing out her featherless chest. 'And it was unanimously agreed that, in my capacity as the senior survivor, I should actively address the issue, take the bull by the horns and really do something about our predicament.'

'My dear, that is not even remotely true,' demurred the proboscis monkey. 'I very much doubt whether we would have got anywhere at all had we not had a little assistance from . . . well, I think you may remember, Tom.'

'The eternal optimists,' hissed a flattened anaconda.

'Optimists of eternity, more like,' quipped a very misshapen meerkat. 'They just never know when they're beaten, do they?'

'Well said, brother!' came a high squeak from somewhere up above. Tom looked up to see lines of burnt chipolatas descending the wooden supports towards them.

'There's a song coming, I can smell it,' whispered the lemur, putting her hands over her ears. 'Here we go.'

The preacher shrew, now little more than a shrivelled pencil, opened his one remaining eye wide and pointed a needle-thin claw at the ceiling.

'Once we were the currants in the rock cake of time!'

His bald congregation squealed with delight and joined in.

'Our bodies were dus-ty, brok-en, em-pty—'

'Mummified for a millennium!'

'Cut off in our prime!'

'But were we *down*, sisters and brothers—did we panic?'

'Did we ever feel anything less than fan-tast-oceanic?'

'We rose up!'

'Like the bones.'

'And we dug—'

'So we did!'

'It took a century—'

'Maybe more—'

'To reveal this floor—'

'And then all our old friends were completely—'

'Utterly—'

'Definitely—'

'Dirtily—'

There was a squeal of delight as the preacher shrew raised his fist to the ceiling.

'Un-hid!'

There was a ripple of squeaky applause all around the rafters.

'Un-hid?' murmured the dodo.

'It's very, very slow to break you,' murmured the proboscis monkey. 'Imagine being hit over the head with a tiny hammer for the best part of two hundred years. You just have to give in, eventually.'

'So what happened to the rest,' asked Tom, 'all the larger ones?'

'Those with wits escaped, and those that didn't burned,' said the dodo.

'It was a terrible thing,' agreed the pangolin. 'To see them cart-ed off like that. Piled up on a bonfire and torched.'

There was silence for a moment as bad memories were stirred. Tom felt the atmosphere change.

'So the tiger—'

'Sold off,' said a hairless mandril. 'Boxed up, put on a train. Certainly never seen again.'

'But I'd put good money on her surviving somehow. Too clever by half, she was,' agreed the dodo.

'And The Deluge?'

'Gone. But there was never a noggin of nous between that lot.'

'The giraffe?'

The porcupine shook his head.

'Along with the entire African diorama and the South Ameri-can jungle. Up in smoke.'

'The mammoth?'

'Now he was particularly flammable as you will recall,' said the dodo knowingly. 'But somehow he earned himself a reprieve.'

'The privilege of the exotic,' muttered the sloth bitterly.

'So where is he, then?'

Tom secretly hoped that of all the exhibits the mammoth would have survived, despite the fact that he had the least chance.

'Last seen boarding a trolley, bound for the other side of the river. Together with all the other oddities. The luminous frogs, the two-headed cat—'

'Someone in Dragonport has bought them?' asked Tom.

'So we suppose,' replied the proboscis monkey. 'A collector of curiosities.'

'Seduced by flash and folderol—no eye for quality work,' sniffed the dodo. 'Whoever it is is guaranteed to be a man of rare vulgarity.'

Tom said nothing for a moment. It was quite clear that this had touched a raw nerve.

'And what about the eagle, have you seen him?'

'The king of the billabong—oh yes, he passes through from time to time on his walkabouts,' said the wombat. 'As rude as he ever was, I might add.'

Tom sat up, feeling a wave of hope rising within him.

'So, you mean, the eagle actually comes back *here*—to visit you?'

'Not here, exactly, and not us, exactly,' intoned the dodo loftily. 'But yes, to Dragonport. He has a struck up a friendship with that ludicrous pfeilstorch.'

'*Pfeilstorch?*'

'After your time, Tom. A white stork that just so happens to have a spear stuck through its neck. It flew all the way from central Africa to Germany with it lodged there and that makes it very special indeed—apparently.'

'The single-handed proof that birds migrate,' sighed the pangolin. 'And absolute confirmation that storks are birds of very little brains. Why didn't he pull it out, I ask you?'

'Someone found him in an attic. If only they could have left him there,' continued the dodo, 'but that's who the eagle comes to see. Every year without fail. Around Christmas.'

'Around Christmas?'

'It's a visit our once feathered friends find immensely exciting.'

There was a loud twitter of approval from the joists above, where rows and rows of what looked like small paper balls on legs were perched. A lucky few still had their plumage intact.

'Those that can go out after dark and he fills their heads with the most ludicrous stories about the battle at the end of the world. It's full of insects apparently,' tittered the porcupine.

'Highly entertaining,' nodded the one-eyed monkey, pulling out a tooth and polishing it. 'He's kissed the blarney, that one, make no mistake.'

Tom found his heart quickening a little.

'So, but, where is this pfeil—'

'Stork. Somewhere over there,' said the dodo, vaguely nodding out of the window. 'Down among the docks. It's kept in someone's office apparently. Some sort of mascot.'

'And do you think the eagle will be coming *this* Christmas?'

'Indubitably,' sniffed the anteater. 'That bird is a creature of habit if nothing else.'

'Always coincides with the big party here, doesn't it?' said the proboscis monkey. 'Why, I don't know. There must be a connection.' The creature squeezed his huge dusty nose thoughtfully. 'Do I sense a reason for all these questions?'

'Erm . . . maybe.'

'And what kind of maybe is that?'

It didn't take long for Tom to tell his story. Breathlessly he raced through everything as it had happened, but the imminent arrival of the eagle was so distracting that the words tumbled out any old how and he had to keep going back and repeating the unlikeliest parts until the animals finally understood. Or thought they did.

'Well you've got to hand it to the man—he must have a sense of humour,' sniffed the porcupine when Tom had finished.

'Why?'

'It's Don Gervase Askary's idea of a joke, isn't it? He doesn't like you, he can't trust you, so what does he do? He says you're an insect and bangs you up in the old Scatterhorn Museum to rub your nose in it.'

'Absolutely. It's a humiliation, the same as what he's done to us all,' agreed the civet, looking down at her dry papery body mournfully. 'To think of what I was. A dart of forest light. And now . . .'

'No no, it's more than that—a lot more,' said the proboscis monkey slowly. 'Do you know what I think, Tom? I think Don Gervase Askary's scared of you.'

Tom smiled bitterly.

'Why should Don Gervase Askary be scared of me? He could have killed me.'

'Could have—but didn't: remember that.' The ancient monkey cocked its head. 'You've upset him, no question—but squirrelling you away out here amongst all the unwanted echoes is the act of a desperate man. I bet he's never told anyone what he's done. You should take it as a compliment.'

'You really think so?'

'Absolutely so,' nodded the dodo in agreement. 'Old big nose is right. Whatever it is Askary is planning, he needs you right out of it. Which means you're special. Which is *precisely* why you are the best person to throw a right royal spanner in the works. I say you must *definitely* get out of this place. Then find out where the hell this vent-chimney-thing is, and when you know, you must do whatever you bloody well can to destroy Scara-whatever-the-hell-you-call-it. And if that changes everything around here—marvellous. So kiss my bum, Askary!'

'Well said, that lady,' said the proboscis monkey.

'We don't want to carry on living like this, Tom—scuttling about like moles in a box—but we can't do anything about it. But you, boyo, you *can* change things. And change things you must, by any means, fair or foul.' A muffled murmur of agreement rippled around the darkness and the dodo knew that she had spoken for all. She puffed out what remained of her papery chest with pride. 'And you can start by meeting up with Barry Billabong.'

Tom stared at the collection of broken, hairless, eyeless, half-squashed and dirty creatures nodding at him in the dark. They all looked quite crazy, but he felt the weight of their expectation.

'You think it's really possible to get out?'

'Certainly it's possible,' said the meerkat. 'All you need is a plan, and some luck. Now obviously from your sorry tale of woe you are the most luckless boy on the planet, but perhaps you might have a plan?'

Tom could barely admit the truth.

'Erm . . . well someone I know did, but unfortunately—'

'Right, we shall take control,' trilled the dodo, staring at Tom fiercely. 'Where's Plankton!'

'I think he's still asleep,' muttered the anteater.

'Well wake him up then.'

'Plankton isn't by any chance a white rat?' asked Tom, remembering the fat, pink-eyed, straw smelling rodent Jos and Melba once owned—and then lost.

'He is. Have you met him?'

'Erm, yes—'

'Must have discovered one of your routes, Tom, and for some reason August Catcher decided to stuff his head full of escape stories. Very appropriate it is too,' sniffed the bird, tapping her bald head with a knowing look. 'Oh yes, we've finally worked *that* one out. Clever man, August Catcher. Now will someone please find that rat . . .'

An hour later Tom crawled back to the stairs and gently tapped on the skirting board. There was a clattering of clogs on the steps above, and a moment later Tom saw Evie's worried face peering down at him.

'What took you so long?'

Tom wriggled out through the slot and sat up next to her, brushing the filth off his uniform. 'Was there nothing there?'

'Not exactly nothing, no,' he said, wondering how much he should take Evie into his confidence. 'Just lots of rubbish left over from the old museum days. No exits, unfortunately.'

'Oh.' Evie was a little disappointed. But strangely, Tom wasn't. Quite the opposite, in fact. 'So that's . . . bad, then?'

'No, it isn't,' he smiled. 'Because I am going to try and escape.'

'When?'

'On the night of the annual Christmas party. Whenever that is.'

Evie looked at Tom, puzzled.

'You mean Dr Logan's birthday? Next Saturday?'

'Next Saturday?'

'Oh yeah! It's a proper shindig. All the inmates, all the staff, plus his friends coming over from the town. Last year it was a right old hooley.'

Tom thought carefully for a moment. Next Saturday, was that enough time?

'But that ain't the night to get out of here, Tom. Definitely not. There'll be extra guards on the gate, floodlights . . . this place will be lit up like a castle. Won't that be a problem?'

Tom carefully replaced the loose skirting board, his mind whirring.

'Maybe. But not if you would consider giving me a hand.'

Evie stared at him hard.

'I knew you were going to ask that. I just knew it.'

'It won't be much more than you've done now. Just to look out, that sort of thing.'

Evie stared at the floor and blew hard through her teeth.

'But what happens if I get caught?'

'Who would catch you if they're all at the party?'

'But what if they did? Grimal will fire me, no question. And what would I do then? I'd have to join Slim in the factory. I did that once, what you do—every day for a year.' Evie nodded grimly. 'I'm never going to do it again. Never ever. I'd rather starve.'

Tom said nothing. Evie could not have made herself clearer and Tom knew that he would have probably felt exactly the same way.

'Slim and me don't have chocolate for breakfast every day.

There's no one helping us but us, so we've got to stick together—whatever. Otherwise . . . '

'What?'

'We could go the same way as Ma and Pa.' Evie turned over the brush in her hand sadly. 'There's these people about, see. Maybe they're the same kind as you've bin talking about. They all look the same and they're not quite . . . like us. You see them in vans roaming at night.'

'So they were taken?'

Evie nodded.

'They was working down in the wharves packing fish. Used to be loads of people working down there. Real busy. Not any more. They've all bin taken, no one knows where. That's why there are so many orphans in Dragonport. And the shellac works is the only place that'll have 'em.'

Tom said nothing for a moment. Slowly everything was starting to make sense. Perhaps this future Dragonport was not just a ruined town at the edge of the world . . . perhaps it was far more dangerous than he imagined . . .

'And these people you're talking about, where do they come from?'

Evie shrugged.

'I don't know.'

'Catcher Hall?'

'Mebbe. You can see the lights on across the water sometimes. Some big bloke owns it. Slim thinks it's a kind of research centre.'

'Slim? How does he know?'

'He's talked to people. And he's bin looking for Ma and Pa down in those old warehouses himself—many times. But he never found them. That part of Dragonport is very dangerous now: you wouldn't want to go down there alone. Definitely not at night.'

Tom said nothing. From the little those animals had told him he had a strong suspicion that was precisely where he would be going.

'You know, Evie, if I ever get out, I am going to do something to stop all this. Something that could close down this asylum, get rid of the people that took your parents—and everything else. Finish them off for good.'

Evie smiled at the very idea.

'It's true. That's what I'm going to try and do.'

The look in the boy's black eyes was almost frightening. He meant it.

'You really are a nutter, aren't you?' She smiled.

'Maybe,' Tom grinned. 'But I need to escape first. So would you at least think about it?'

Evie blew loudly through her teeth.

'All right then. Think about it. That's all.'

The next few days passed in a blur. Every evening, after his shift, Tom made a secret visit to the floor in between and discussed the plans with the animals down there. Apart from the escape itself, Tom's greatest concern was to somehow fool those thousands of tiny black beetles that descended into his cell every night to watch him. How was he ever going to dupe them? After a couple of days thinking it was Plankton the rat who came up with an ingenious solution to the problem, and on Thursday evening he demonstrated his idea—with a little help from the preacher shrew and his congregation.

'The Archimboldo technique,' he declared when it was over. 'What do you think?'

Tom was so amazed he could barely speak.

'I think you are the most remarkable rodents that ever walked the earth,' proclaimed the proboscis monkey. 'Bravo, brothers and sisters, bravo. But if I may suggest, with our good friend the lyre bird,' he nodded at a small brown shape on the rafters, 'we might be able to make this even more convincing . . . '

That evening was the first time that Tom really believed this whole crazy scheme might work. Even though the ragged hummingbirds could not tell him exactly where the famous pfeilstorch was, except that it was in an old office close to the water's edge, and he had no idea what might happen to him out in Dragonport once he had left the safety of the asylum, the excitement that he might actually escape was becoming harder and harder to contain. However Tom tried to keep calm on the outside, inside he was fizzing.

'You're looking very cheerful,' said Dr Logan, spotting Tom guzzling his breakfast as he made his rounds on Friday morning. 'Looking forward to a good day's work, are you?'

Luckily Tom could not reply immediately as his mouth was full of chocolate beans. He nodded violently.

'I hear you're very good at it, too. I must say I am surprised. Most of my patients hate it. Particularly the more intelligent ones.'

Tom realized that Dr Logan was expecting an answer, and pointed up at the line of bunting suspended above.

'Oh I *see*, that's the reason, is it? Well of course you're looking forward to my party—I know I am. It'll be the party of your life, I expect.'

Tom swallowed hard.

'Yes.'

'Nurse Manners has been very busy in the kitchens. I did hear something about a very special birthday cake. Triple chocolate sponge, white truffle fondant filling, chocolate on top and a small mountain of whipped cream on top of that.'

'Great,' said Tom, feeling his insides turn upside down at the thought.

'Yes, well at least you won't have to go and stretch shellac the next day. It's Sunday. You can sleep it off.'

Dr Logan smiled. Tom had the sense that he was attempting to be friendly, but he had no real idea how to do it.

'I suppose you've never seen the fruits of your labours, have you?'

Tom gulped down a slug of beetle juice and nodded politely. Dr Logan delved into his pocket and brought out a small brown packet.

'There,' he shook some small golden flakes out onto the table. 'Spong's handmade shellac, the finest handmade shellac in the world. Melt those down and you can use them for almost anything. Marvellous, isn't it?'

Tom could not have been less interested in what he spent almost every waking hour toiling over, but his eye was caught by the curious round stamp on the top of the packet.

'May I see?'

'Of course.'

Tom picked up the packet and examined the logo. 'Spongs', it read, in large letters around the rim. In the centre was the strange silhouette of a long-legged bird . . . it had an arrow through its neck.

Dr Logan observed his patient keenly. The boy suddenly seemed to be in shock.

'Does that seem odd to you?'

'Erm . . . no, I mean yes, very. Why, why—'

'Why does that stork have a spear through its neck? I have no idea. But it came from this museum. Old Ebenezer Spong is something of a collector. He bought that bird and liked it so much he decided to use it as his sign. You will find that stamp on every single packet of Spong's shellac. It's a famous symbol.'

'Wow,' spluttered Tom. 'That's . . . amazing.'

Dr Logan watched Tom curiously. These echoes really were intriguing. You could never guess what they were thinking.

'As a matter of fact I've invited Ebenezer to my party. He's very old now, but if you're interested I'm sure he'd be delighted to tell you more about it. I think he used to have it standing in his office.' Dr Logan smiled, then moved off to bother someone else.

Tom stared down at his heap of breakfast, his heart thundering. Maybe he wasn't the unluckiest boy on the planet after all. Suddenly something good had happened, something he could never have predicted. Ebenezer Spong's office, that was it: somewhere down in the old wharves . . . but how was he ever going to get there? After everything Evie had said, that part of Dragonport sounded very dangerous. But there was someone who might be able to help him . . . someone who had been there before . . . if he could ever be persuaded . . .

An hour later Tom was standing in a corner of room Nine A, waiting for the siren to signal the start of the shift. Slim leant casually against a steel post listening as Tom quietly explained what he intended to do. When he finished a small smirk spread across the boy's face.

'And if I tell Loagy about all this, what-cha gonna do then, Tomsk?'

Tom shrugged his shoulders as nonchalantly as he could manage. Slim took a small black lump of gum out from behind his ear and began chewing it thoughtfully.

'The way I see it, you need to be doing *me* a favour to keep my trap shut. Not the other way round.'

Tom was hardly surprised that Slim was trying to turn this to his advantage—and he was ready for it.

'If you did that, Slim, what would happen to me, I wonder? I'd probably be thrown into some jail, condemned to a life of hard labour, I'd never see my home or family again, in fact, I might as well not exist.'

Slim grinned toothily.

'You're right there, Tomsk. You'd be neck-deep in the doodoo river.'

'So what have I got to lose?'

Tom's eyes never once left Slim's sharp face as his grin turned into a snarl. Fair or foul, fair or foul . . .

'But of course, Evie would lose her job.'

'What?'

'And so would you, Slim. Maybe worse.'

'Oh yeah?' The boy turned to him angrily. 'And how does that tally then?'

'Obviously I would have to explain how she has been helping me.'

'She hasn't.'

'She has. And what's more, she has told you about it. So you're involved too. If you told Dr Logan you would be betraying her, and yourself.'

'He wouldn't believe a nutter.'

'Any more than he would believe you? There are plenty of hungry orphans round here, I'm told.'

Slim grimaced hard at the fires below. If Tom's veiled threat had any effect, he wasn't showing it.

'Please, Slim. Why don't you help me? You're the only person I know who's been down into the wharves. You know what it's like down there now. All I want to do is to find Ebenezer Spong's office. That's it. And apart from anything else, it would be fun, wouldn't it?'

Tom stared hard at the wiry, crop-headed boy who steadfastly refused to look him in the eye.

'On two conditions,' he murmured, his lips barely moving. 'First, you tell any of this crew what we's about and I'll kill you. Understand?'

Tom understood exactly. Slim could never continue to be the leader of this room if it was known he was helping a nutter. It was bad enough he was even talking to him.

'And the second?'

Slim pulled himself up to his not very impressive height.

'Whatever happens, I'm drivin'.'

Tom shrugged.
'All right. But *can* you drive?'
Slim turned towards him and flashed a toothy smile.
'No. This'll be the first time.'

CHAPTER 8

DOCTOR LOGAN'S BIG SURPRISE

And then suddenly it was Saturday. Tom slept very badly. First he dreamt that he had already escaped, and was running through the streets towards Ebenezer Spong's office, pursued by a gang of security guards on beetle-like motorbikes. Then he dreamt he had overslept, and he woke up convinced it was Sunday, only to see the great eagle flying away towards the pale sunrise.

'Come back!' he shouted, racing across the yard in front of the asylum, 'wait for me!'

He had scaled the heavy steel gates till he was standing at the very top, his hands gripping the coils of barbed wire.

'Get that boy down from there!' shouted Dr Logan. Rifles cocked, the guards took aim. 'Not that way! No!'

Suddenly Tom felt his balance waver and he tumbled back-wards—

Snap!

The spy hatch slammed open and an eye appeared in the cen-tre of the door.

'Everything all right in there, Mr Scatterhorn?'

Tom was sitting bolt upright in bed, sweating. It was still night, he hadn't overslept, and he hadn't been shot, either. He was still here. Locked up. In jail.

'Fine. Just . . . having trouble sleeping.'

There was a grunt from the corridor. Tom turned towards the window and through the jigsaw of reflections saw fat white snowflakes drifting down.

'It's snowing.'

'Don't you worry about that, son. You go back to sleep now.'

The voice was hard and in no mood for conversation. Feeling very conspicuous Tom lay down and meekly turned to face the wall. Would the snow make it harder? Almost certainly it would.

'Goodnight,' he said.

After what seemed like an eternity, the small metal spy hatch snapped shut again. Tom lay with his eyes open, staring at the grid of beetles motionless on the wall, their pink eyes glittering. How well can you see me? He stretched out a finger and held it above one's head. It didn't move. It would be so easy to crush it. Just one little squeeze and it would be gone. With great difficulty Tom resisted the temptation and closed his eyes. Wait until tomorrow . . .

Breakfast that Saturday morning was a tense affair—made tenser by Nurse Manners and her team of warders bustling about trying to rearrange the tables while the inmates were still eating.

'I'm sorry, but this is impossible!' protested a particularly befuddled Don Gervase, who was about to sit on a bench only to see it instantly removed.

'Just sit down and shut up,' blustered Nurse Manners, marching the bench across the room. She was in no mood for dissent—today of all days.

'Where should I sit down?'

'Anywhere.'

'But there isn't anywhere.'

'How about the floor?'

'The floor? You want me to eat my breakfast off the floor?'

'SIT ON YOUR BOTTOM! ON THE FLOOR!' she barked at the helpless man. Honestly, why Dr Logan persisted with these birthday parties was anyone's guess.

Tom kept his head down and found he had entirely lost his appetite. He felt as if he had swallowed a box of frogs and his head was spinning with all the things he had to try to remember. He ran the order over and over in his mind, convinced he was going to forget something. Maybe it *was* all too complicated, over ambitious . . . At last the siren sounded and all the inmates lined up for the long trudge down the tunnel to the factory.

'And here they are. Nutter number one and little boy blue.'

Tom blinked and found Slim Spry staring at him and Francis Catchpole. He had been so busy rehearsing his escape that he had barely noticed that he was already in room Nine A and the shift was about to begin.

'Gonna pull your weight today are we, Frankie?'

'I'll do my best, Slim,' said Francis, in that blank, innocent way of his that suggested he really meant it.

'You see he makes his quota, Tomsk,' Slim added, loud enough for the rest of the room to hear. 'Cos the way I sees it, one of you must be about to pop your clogs.'

There was a snigger at the back.

'What do you mean, Slim?' asked Francis innocently.

'I mean that you've been here three weeks, and Tomsk's had two, so my guess is that someone's charmed little life will shortly be coming to an end. Cos you don't live for long, do yew?'

'Don't we?'

Laughter rippled around the room and even Slim smiled. He was touched by Francis's innocence.

'Not to my knowledge, Frankie. Come Monday morning, I'm guessing one of you nutters will be gone to that big shellac factory in the sky.'

'Which of 'em will it be, Slim?' piped a boy at the back. 'Who's closest?'

Slim came forward, folded his arms and looked them up and down knowledgeably.

'Hmm, I'd say little boy blue's holding up pretty well. I'd plump for Tomsk.'

'Tomsk?' howled a girl. 'Not likely. He's almost as good as us. Frankie Catchpole is the goner for sure.'

Slim caught Tom's eye and gave him the merest flicker of a wink.

'I'll put money on it.'

'You're mad.'

'Wager me then.'

Tom and Francis stood watching as the children crowded around Slim and a flurry of small black coins changed hands.

'What are they doing?' asked Francis.

'Betting on which of us is going to die first.'

Francis seemed genuinely surprised.

'That's not very nice.'

'No it isn't.'

'You'd better be here Monday morning,' rasped a girl, jabbing Francis in the ribs as she went past.

'So it's really true then, what he said?'

'Maybe,' said Tom, trying hard to contain his excitement: he knew that the more Slim stood to win, the less likely he would be to back out now. Francis said nothing, but Tom noticed there was a peculiarly determined expression on his face.

The rest of the shift passed in a blur of noise and heat, and by the time Tom joined the procession trudging wearily back to the asylum he almost felt like that triple chocolate surprise.

'No touching the cakes if you please!' barked Nurse Manners as the inmates shambled back into the main hall, which they found entirely transformed. Lines of red and blue balloons hung from the ceiling, a small stage had been erected in one corner for a band, and the canteen was positively sagging under the weight of chocolate cakes of all shapes and sizes, stacked in pyramids like piles of elephant dung.

'Well, young Scatterhorn, what do you think?' Nurse Manners tottered across the empty hall with coils of streamers around her neck. 'I should think you probably remember lots of parties in here back in them "museum" days.' She smiled sarcastically.

'A few,' said Tom blearily. 'But nothing like this.'

'Oh I dare say,' she grinned. 'But you can't have much fun with a bunch of stuffed animals, can you?'

'No.'

'Well I expect you'll all want to go and tidy yourselves up,' she declared, addressing the entire procession. 'It's a mufti night tonight so you can wear whatever you please. That's right, gentlemen, no uniforms—just Your-Very-Best-Clothes!' Whatever they might be, she added to herself. Kilts and crowns and heaven knows what else.

'Let's be having you now!' she hollered, clapping her hands. 'CHOP CHOP! MUFTI NIGHT!'

The inmates wandered obediently away up the different staircases to do as they were told.

'Quite why she feels the need to shout all the time I do not know,' muttered a Don Gervase under his breath. 'Is she deaf?'

'Best obey, my friend,' replied another. 'If she treats us all like idiots then we have every right to behave accordingly.'

'I can't wait.'

Tom deliberately lingered until he was sure he was the very last to trudge up his staircase to the top floor. When he reached the dark landing he saw Evie's two steel buckets stacked neatly in the corner, as planned.

This is the beginning. From now on all he needed was luck.

Quite a lot of luck.

Carefully, very carefully, Tom approached the loose skirting and knelt beside it. He listened hard: no one coming up, no one going down. Good. Swiftly he removed the stumpy chisel from his sock and prised open one end just enough to see down into the dark space below.

'Arsenic,' he whispered as loud as he dared. Silence. There was a shuffling somewhere beyond, then a long black nose appeared out of the gloom followed by two beady eyes.

'Arsenic,' hissed the nose back at him. 'Tom? Is that you?'

'It is,' he replied, smiling at the anteater. 'Five minutes.'

'Very good. We're all set.'

Tom closed the board once more, carefully pressing in the corners so that the glue held. Then with as much nonchalance as he could manage he strolled on up the stairs to the top floor. To his relief he saw Mr Grimal at the far end besieged by anxious Don Gervases needing assistance with their hats and jackets and swords and other homemade finery.

'One at a time, gentlemen, please!' he bawled, trying to keep some kind of order in the chaos. Halfway towards his cell Tom passed Evie, who was on her knees scrubbing the floor.

'Hi there,' he said, his voice cracking weirdly with nerves.

Evie's elfin face peered up at him from beneath her orange beret. She was so nervous she could barely speak.

'You've—'

Tom was about to go on when a warder appeared out of the cell behind her and gave him a sharp look.

'Not changed yet?'

Evie returned to her scrubbing as if her life depended upon it. Tom cleared his throat.

'I think . . . you've left your buckets on the stairs.'

'Oh.'

'Well don't just stop there, girl, go and get them before one of these buffoons puts their foot in it,' scolded the warder. 'Go on.'

Evie scampered away down the corridor as the warder turned to Tom in a fluster.

'And you'd best get weaving an' all.'

'Yes, I must, mustn't I?' Tom replied. Avoiding the man's piggy eyes he returned to his cell, careful to leave the door half open.

He sat down on his bed, knowing he could do nothing more now than wait . . . Gradually the seconds turned into minutes . . . he could hear cell doors slam shut outside as inmates began to make their way down the corridor to the main hall . . . come on, Evie . . . At last the door opened and there she was with her brush and buckets.

'I'm to clean your room—sir,' she added loudly, and began brushing her way inside.

'Got them?' whispered Tom.

Evie nodded.

'Where?'

The girl glanced across at the two buckets behind her.

'Two bags, one in each, underneath. I'm not asking what's in 'em, but they's lumpy and jumpy, make no mistake.'

Tom leapt off the bed and plunged his hands into the two buckets, drawing out a long dusty canvas bag from each. They looked like two sausage-shaped cushions.

'Thanks, Evie,' said Tom, squirrelling them away under the blanket on his bed. 'Really thanks a lot.'

Evie smiled nervously.

'See you later then,' she said, and with a nod closed the door.

The moment she was gone Tom took off his uniform, stuffing his trousers inside his top and carefully placing it below the pillow, then he pulled his old clothes on. When he was ready he carefully reached under the blanket and undid the drawstrings on each bag.

'Everything all right?'

'It's rather reminiscent of the bad old days,' hissed a small voice. 'Could we have a little practice?'

139

Tom tiptoed back to the door and peered into the corridor. The Don Gervases had almost all gone down now, but Mr Grimal was still pacing about at the far end, attaching a straggler's epaulet.

'Go on then.'

'Ready, lads,' came a muffled whisper from under the blankets, 'remember your numbers and off we go.'

Ripples scurried up the bed and the next moment a motley collection of hummingbirds, rats, lizards, and shrews formed themselves in a pile on the pillow. The pile became larger and began to assume a shape . . . two pink shrews curled round each other to become an ear, a tail became an eyelid, a dark feather became a nostril, a white flank a cheek, a jumble of golden plumed hummingbirds a tangle of blond hair, and at the same time a collection of leathery shrews built themselves into two hands, palms, thumbs . . . fingers just above the blanket . . .

'Well, does it convince?'

Tom could barely contain his excitement. With the pillow and the blanket the illusion was complete. From the doorway, it was like looking at himself, lying asleep in bed, with his eyes closed.

'Amazing. It's . . . really incredible.'

'And do you want to hear the other bit?'

'I've been practising,' said a muffled voice under the covers, 'I think I've got it right now.' There was a pause. 'Amazing. It's . . . really incredible.'

The voice came from somewhere in the corner. Tom's voice, exactly.

'Wow.'

'Wow. Amazing. It's really incredible.'

'Once is enough, my dear,' squeaked the preacher shrew, who was now Tom's thumb. 'Convincing, eh?'

Tom was unable to stop smiling.

'But don't do anything until the door closes and locks for the night.'

'We know,' squeaked the thumb. 'And be back in the bags in the morning so that Evie can take us down. Everything's under control. Ready, brothers and sisters? Reverse numbers . . . go.'

As miraculously as they had appeared, the head and the hand dismantled themselves and scurried back under the covers.

'You trot along now,' said his own voice from under the blanket impatiently. 'Because it won't do to have two of us in here, will it?'

'Aha! I can see someone's made an extra effort.'

Tom whipped round to see Mr Grimal's large flaky face appear in the doorway.

'Erm . . . '

'You might at least have brushed your hair, lad. It looks like something you wash a bottle with,' he boomed, running his fat pink fingers through it.

'I don't have a hairbrush.'

'Don't have a hairbrush? Have you looked?'

'No really I don't,' said Tom, quickly but firmly positioning himself between the large pine-smelling man and his cell. 'I've never had one, honestly.'

Mr Grimal's moustache twitched. He was well aware of how useless these echoes were when it came to personal hygiene. Most of them had not the faintest idea.

'Perhaps I could borrow yours?' Tom smiled winningly, glancing at Mr Grimal's ferocious parting. 'It looks so . . . nice.'

Mr Grimal smiled awfully.

'Now that's more like it.'

And so it was that ten minutes later Tom walked out into the main hall, his face scrubbed, his hair flattened and combed into a regimental side parting with Mr Grimal at his side. It was worth putting up with all this, Tom told himself between his gritted teeth; if it meant he never had to see this place again it was worth it.

He cast his eye around the main hall, which was now filled with people. In the corner a small and noisy band were belting out a vaguely familiar tune, while on the dance floor groups of generals and Don Gervases in homemade costumes hopped and jigged about, enjoying themselves hugely. Tom noticed that several large warders prowled discreetly amongst them looking out for the first sign of trouble. Watching from the sidelines stood various guests that Dr Logan had invited up from the town. They were a strange bunch: hard faced men and dour, disapproving women, their cheeks flushed with the heat—watching the inmates in fascinated horror. It reminded Tom of another party, held hundreds of years ago in this very room for the opening of the museum. He could never have guessed that this is what the Scatterhorn Museum would become . . .

Tom knew he couldn't let his anger distract him. He glanced up at the clock—it was almost eight. Almost time . . . there was Evie, standing in one of the doorways beside the canteen, clapping her hands and laughing as the inmates began a conga. She caught his eye and nodded. Yes, she was ready . . .

'Come on, young Scatterhorn, let's see your dancing feet!'

Before Tom knew it a Don Gervase dressed as a pirate grabbed him and pulled him into the centre of the dance floor. Tom recognized him as the echo he had met on that very first morning.

'I've remembered it!' he cried.

'What?'

'What The Soap said!' he shouted. Tom's eyes widened and he struggled to hear above the thundering feet. 'I've remembered it!'

Kicking his legs wildly in the air they spun together, arms locked in a highland fling.

'Slow down!' pleaded Tom, but the Don Gervase just grinned madly and gripped his arm even tighter. Round and round they went, the shouting faces and clapping hands began to blur . . .

'Go on!' shrieked Nurse Manners, seeing that Tom was about to be sick. 'Spin him hard! Faster!'

'What did The Soap say?'

The Don Gervase laughed.

'The vent hole is not a hole!'

'What? What is it then?'

'It's hidden in a tree!'

'A tree? Which tree?'

'Next to the shack!'

'The shack?'

'The tumbledown shack! In the middle! There's a clearing. And you will need something bigger than a bomb to blow it!'

Tom racked his brains. Was it a riddle? Faster and faster they went.

'Bigger than a bomb, that's what he said. I knew I'd remember!'

Somewhere through the spinning kaleidoscope Tom glimpsed a line of cooks carrying a large square cake out of the kitchens. Two more followed on, bearing a vat of steaming white liquid slung between them on poles. A cheer went up as the sickly smell of melted white chocolate truffle filled the room.

'Aha, the grand finale!' shouted the echo, pointing at the second hand move up towards the hour. 'Do you see what I see?'

Tom felt his feet leave the ground. They were spinning so fast now it was impossible to stop.

'Eight o'clock, tick-tock! This is the end of my span, Tom Scatterhorn. That's me done. Life's run!'

Tom glanced up at the clock in panic. There was barely any time left.

'But you never said where it is!'

The clock struck eight, and that very moment there was a fizzing sound and the hall plunged into darkness. Instantly the Don Gervase let go and Tom found himself flying through the air . . .

Then everything seemed to happen at once.

'What the—'

Tom collided with three elderly men, crashing to the floor in a heap.

'Whoosh!'

Someone dropped something very large in the canteen. Suddenly the dancing inmates began skidding and slipping and tumbling into each other . . .

'Keep calm everybody! Keep calm!' shouted a warder from somewhere in the middle of the melee. 'Just a fuse, that's all. Just a—'

'Honey?' said a Don Gervase, bending down and licking his finger.

'With fresh cream,' said another.

'Pinch of cinnamon?'

'White truffle chocolate sauce?'

A thick gooey slick was spreading fast across the floor.

'White truffle chocolate sauce!'

There was a mad scramble as the inmates sank to their knees and began slurping at the sticky nectar like bees.

'Get up!' shouted Nurse Manners, tottering unsteadily into the white spreading lake. 'Up, you idiots! Someone call Mr Vee! Get the electri—oh!' And with a shriek she slipped backwards into the sauce. 'Dr Logan! Mr Grimal! Do something!'

But it was too late for Dr Logan or Mr Grimal to do anything. They could only watch as Nurse Manners writhed in the white slick like an oiled crocodile. Soon the entire room was a thrashing mess of inmates and guests sliding around in the dark.

'Foodfight!' shouted a pair of generals, grabbing some muffins from the tables. 'Get 'em!'

'Foodfight-foodfight-foodfight!' chanted the Don Gervases, ducking as the muffins flew, and returning them with interest.

'Stop!' shrieked Nurse Manners, as a bun hit her square in the face. 'Mr Grimal!'

Soon the air was thick with flying cake and Tom decided to make his exit. Dodging around the side of the chaos, he slipped away up the back staircase to the landing to find Evie waiting for him with a lantern and a broad smile on her face.

'I wish it was like this every day,' she said her eyes shining with excitement. 'It was so easy . . . I just tripped one cook and the others sort of followed like dominoes.'

'Well I suppose they deserve it,' said Tom as he levered open the loose skirting board.

'Too right they do. I'd never thought I'd dare do something like that.' Evie watched as Tom swiftly wriggled himself into the gap. 'So shall I leave it undone, in case you need to come back again?'

'I'm not coming back, Evie. Just put those two sacks back down here in the morning, then close this up for good.'

Evie looked down at Tom and saw the fierce determination in his eyes.

'Can I come with you?'

Tom shook his head.

'Sorry. It wouldn't work.'

Evie couldn't hide her disappointment.

'Honestly, Evie, it's better this way. I have to go alone. I wouldn't want you to get in trouble.'

'But I don't care if I do now. Now it's all started. I don't care about anything.'

Tom smiled.

'Bye, Evie.'

'Just one thing,' she said quickly, grabbing his arm as he was about to disappear. 'What you said about changing this place. Was you serious? I mean . . . could you really do it?'

Tom looked into her pale, worried face, so full of hope.

'I don't know. I'm going to try.'

'We're relying on you,' she said to herself, closing up the loose board behind him. 'And Slim, worse luck.'

Tom crawled slowly forward towards the dim diamond pattern of light ahead of him.

'Psst.'

'Hi,' said Tom to the darkness. 'Where are you?'

'Right up against the wall,' replied the voice. Tom quickened his pace and soon found himself face to face with a pair of very moth-eaten mandrills.

'Good job?' asked the larger of the two.

'The lights. He means the lights.'

'Oh perfect,' Tom smiled. 'It's chaos down there.'

One of the bald monkeys nudged the other and grinned, opening its mouth so wide Tom thought its jaw might pop out. He held out a large burnt fuse.

'They won't find this in a hurry.'

'But it won't take them long to get another,' muttered the anteater, his nose pressed against the gaps in the bricks. 'This looks like him now.'

Tom craned forward and saw a single headlight on the front of a small three-wheeled van rattle through the high steel gates and park in the corner of the snowbound yard. Out jumped a familiar figure with a scarf tied round his ears and, grabbing a tool bag, he hurried up the steps below.

'Right, Vee's in, number ones go,' hissed Plankton. Immediately the two mandrills started swiftly removing a small section of the diamond pattern of bricks. A keen wind began to whistle through the hole. The pink-eyed rat flipped a small hour glass hanging round his neck over and the sand began to run.

'You have five minutes to get to that van. We can't risk this with the floodlights back on.'

Tom stared down at the dark yard nervously. There were two sentries loitering by the gate.

'So you found a long enough rope?' he whispered, knowing that this was still not quite sorted out.

'Find, yes, rope—probably not what you are expecting,' replied the dodo, waddling up out of the darkness with something coiled around her neck. 'They are not being very cooperative.'

Unslinging the coil, Tom saw that it was made of leathery old snakes the colour of dust, whose heads and tails had been tied roughly together.

'That's it?'

'I'm afraid it is. Nothing else will go the distance down to the door.'

Doubtfully Tom picked up the tail of the end snake. It felt like old cloth in his hand.

'Yes—I feel about as brittle as I look,' hissed the ancient reptile.

'Come on,' muttered Plankton impatiently, staring at the hourglass hanging round his neck.

Tom took a deep breath: it was now or never, he knew it. Pulling his hat down low, he turned onto his belly and lay down on the smooth old plank the animals had placed opposite the hole with his toes just edging the bricks outside. Gripping the rope tightly, he took one last look back at the strange collection of hairless, dusty creatures bracing the rope in the darkness.

'Give 'em hell, boyo,' rasped the dodo, its beak full of snake.

'Send us a postcard,' chimed the porcupine.

'And see if you can't sort out this mess,' added the proboscis monkey, now acting as anchorman at the back. 'The vent hole thingy. Don't forget about us.'

Tom nodded nervously.

'I can't promise anything.'

'We know. Just—'

'Ready?' hissed the two mandrills, gripping his shoulders firmly.

Tom nodded, ignoring his galloping heart. They looked back at Plankton peering through the opening at the sentries below.

'Go!'

The next instant Tom was hurled feet first off the plank and out into the night. A second later the rope held and he slammed back towards the wall, his feet dancing across its surface like a fly. Down he slithered in a barely controlled plummet towards the gryphons above the front door, his fingers squeezing tighter and tighter as the old leather began to stretch and rip . . .

'That's my rattle I'll have you know,' hissed a snake angrily as the old hide ran through Tom's fingers, 'you can't just unrattle a—'

But the next second the bottom half came away and Tom thumped down onto the stone dragon's neck.

'Go up!' he whispered.

'What's left of me will,' said the snake curtly, passing the message up the chain. A moment later the tattered rope slithered back up the surface of the wall.

Kerchunk!

A bright blue light burned sparks into Tom's eyes almost knocking him off balance. Ducking down into the gryphon's shadow he saw all the lights had come back on—and there above was the snake rope, very slowly and deliberately being hauled in through the diamond shaped hole above. How could the guards in the yard not see it? But somehow, incredibly, they hadn't. There were no whistles, no alarms—just the howl of the wind. Huddling in the deep triangle of shadow Tom tried to collect his thoughts. Mr Vee had fixed the lights much faster than he had anticipated. That meant any moment now he would be coming back out to his van . . .

Boldly Tom crept behind the crumbling tablet that bore his name towards the darker side of the door. Suddenly everything had got a lot more complicated. The van was parked over in the far corner. How was he ever going to get over there, past the sentries on the gate, without being seen? He didn't know. But he couldn't stay here. No way. This was his one chance: he had to take it. Slithering off the side of the pediment Tom clung onto its rim with his fingers, then, bracing himself, he half-slithered half-dropped down the gap between the pillars to the ground. Ten breathless seconds later Tom crouched in the shadow of the doorway, his hands numb and scratched. Somehow that had worked. Now what? He stared at the expanse of floodlit snow between him and the van in the corner. Without the lights this might have just been possible, but those sentries at the gate were almost staring straight at him . . .

At that moment the door opened and a blast of the mayhem inside burst out into the night.

'Everything all right, Mr Vee?' shouted one of the guards.

'All fixed up very good,' said Mr Vee trotting down the steps and across the yard. 'Crazy party, you know. Crazy people. Fighting with cake.'

'Cake?' The sentries looked at each other.

'Cake fighting. Crazy people.'

Tom watched helplessly as Mr Vee slid open the door and threw his tool bag in the back. What could he do? In a moment he would get into the cab and everything would unravel . . . too complicated, he should have listened . . .

'Hey!'

One of the sentries suddenly unshouldered his rifle and ran into the centre of the yard. He stared up at the high wall topped with broken glass.

'Hey!'

Mr Vee turned round and looked. There was someone up there, a thin shadow, his arms outstretched, slowly placing one foot in front of another.

'Hey!'

Mr Vee's fingers left the door handle and he ran out to join the sentry. There was a boy up there with a look of intense concentration on his face. Tom could barely believe it—it was Francis Catchpole. He was escaping!

'Stop! Go back!' shouted Mr Vee. One of the guards took aim. 'No, gentlemen, gentlemen, please, he is in danger. Please! You no shoot him, he is crazy.'

An argument developed and Tom realized that this was his moment. Before he knew what he was doing he trotted out of the shadows and down the wide stone steps onto the snow. He kept his eyes down, hearing nothing but the thumping of his own heart. No shouts, no alarms. The vacuum of silence sucked him onwards. Left foot right foot, left again, hugging the shadows, every step closer to the van . . . he slipped around to the dark side and opened the door.

'I'm driving,' muttered Slim through gritted teeth, his fingers clamped to the steering wheel.

'Fine. But at least slide along and let me sit down.'

The thin boy with the shaved head ignored him.

'Slim?'

'I'm driving.'

The boy did not move.

'You're making this really difficult, you know.'

Stifling his anger Tom slid in behind him and closed the door as quietly as possible. Then he looked down at Slim's boots. Two large blocks of wood were strapped to the soles.

'You've really never done this, have you?'

'I watched old Vee. It ain't hard. Look.'

The next moment, he switched the large single headlight on, blinding the guards.

'Slim! What did you do that for?'

Mr Vee turned round in confusion and squinted towards the headlight.

'I'm warming the engine up.'

'But the gate's shut—don't you see! We can't go anywhere.'

Slim said nothing. Mr Vee began marching towards them. Tom realized that something had to happen very, very quickly indeed.

'If we get caught now, it's all your fault,' he hissed angrily.

Slim's grip on the wheel tightened. Even he looked nervous now. He slid down in his seat as Mr Vee levelled with the window and tried to peer at the shadow inside.

'When I turn this—go left, in a circle,' whispered Tom, his fingers gripping the key. 'And not too fast, got it?'

'All right.'

The starter coughed once, followed by a strange whizzing sound as the electric motor thrummed to life. Mr Vee leapt back as if stung by a wasp.

'What is it?' shouted a guard, spinning round to face the light.

'Someone is trying to steal my van,' he said.

The guards forgot about Francis balanced precariously on top of the wall and ran towards the vehicle.

'It's not working,' whispered Slim, pushing his foot hard to the floor.

Tom saw the guard's face through the window. His jaw dropped open.

'You! Get out!' he screamed and took aim. 'Get out now!'

'That's the brake.'

'The brake?'

At that moment there was a great creak and the two steel gates swung open. The guards looked at each other in disbelief as a large black limousine crunched into the yard and swept up to the steps.

'Go!' shouted Tom. Slim did not need any encouragement. He stamped on the accelerator and they rocketed forward across the yard.

'The gate!' gasped Tom. Wrenching the wheel hard over he slid the tiny van sideways, sending it bouncing off the barrier and out into the snowbound street.

'Now step on it!'

Slim jammed down his block of wood hard—and in an instant the two boys were thrown forward into the dashboard. The van spun in circles, then the engine spluttered—and died. For a moment time itself seemed to have frozen.

'What happened?'

Tom peered up at Slim groggily.

'That was the brake again.'

'Was it?'

'It was.'

Tom looked back in a daze towards the Scatterhorn Museum. A very old man was being helped out of the limousine: Ebenezer Spong himself. Dr Logan was rapidly trying to pull cake and truffle sauce from his hair as he trotted down the steps to welcome him. On the wall high above stood Francis Catchpole, arms outstretched and lit by searchlights. And a round silhouette was running towards them, waving his arms wildly.

'Stop! Thief!'

Everyone turned to watch Mr Vee lose his footing and tumble down into the street. He would be up again in seconds.

'Want to try again?' said Tom, leaning forward and pressing the starter motor.

CHAPTER 9

ODD WAY OUT

It was hard to know who was more terrified, Slim or Tom. Leaning forward over the wheel, Slim flung the tiny three-wheeled van down one alley after another, ignoring the blur of black buildings looming up like cliffs on either side.

'You can slow down if you like,' Tom gasped, bracing himself against the roof.

'No I can't!' shouted Slim above the whine of the engine. 'Not now they've seen us escaping. When that happens they lock this place down like a prison.'

Something large and black flashed across the street ahead.

'Is that a problem?'

At last Slim decided to use the brakes. Skidding the van to an untidy halt, they rolled out between two buildings.

'Not if you can swim, Tomsk. Ebenezer Spong's office is next to his wharf. Over there.'

Ahead was the stretch of dark swirling water that cut off old Dragonport from the mainland. To the left was the narrow causeway, but already a pair of large trucks were driving across it to form a blockade.

'Looks like they've beaten us to it. Like I said, it's a lock down.'

Slim was right—unfortunately. Shaking his head in frustration, Tom peered in the opposite direction to where a grey shadow loomed beyond a row of abandoned houses. In the mist it looked like the long rickety skeleton of a dinosaur, arching steeply across the water.

'What about that?'

'That's the old footbridge, built when the waters first came in. But it's rotten as anything now. I wouldn't even walk across it.'

'Have you?'

Slim spat nervously. He didn't answer the question.

'Listen, Tomsk—you don't want to be wandering about in them wharfs. Not if you've seen the things I've seen,' he hinted darkly.

'So how are we going to get there, then?'

Slim shrugged.

'Can we steal a boat?'

The boy laughed harshly.

'This is old Dragonport. There's nothing like that out here.'

Tom stared at the jumble of roofs swirling in the mist beyond the rickety bridge. He had a strong sense that Slim seemed to be giving up too easily.

'Looks like we'll have to drive across that, then.'

'Drive?' Slim's eyes widened. 'You're mad—this van's way too heavy.'

'Maybe it is. But I'm not going back, Slim. I mean it. So either you can do it or I will.' Slim's knuckles tightened on the wheel. He could tell that Tom was serious.

'Unless you're too scared.'

'Ha!' Slim bristled. 'I ain't scared, Tomsk. I ain't scared of nothing.'

Tom stared at him.

'Well?'

Slim glowered at the bridge.

'Can you drive?'

'Yes,' Tom lied. He'd driven a bumper car once, which was obviously more than Slim had done.

'Fine.' Slim shrugged as carelessly as he could manage. 'You can do it. I was getting bored anyway.'

'Right.'

Swiftly they swapped places, and Tom felt a quiet satisfaction as he turned on the engine. At least his destiny was in his own hands now.

'The accelerator's—'

'I know. Thanks.'

Carefully Tom pulled the little van out into the dark street and, hugging the shadows, drew level with the wooden bridge. Slim was right, it was very twisted and old and looked as if it had been casually lashed together with rope. There were no sides and several planks seemed to be missing. It really was very precarious.

'Like I said, that's got to be a hundred years old. So it will probably fall down. Everything else has,' shrugged Slim, pretending not to care.

Tom thrust the engine into reverse and backed up a small alley and stopped in the shadows. He stared at the long twisting ramp rising up into the mist. This was crazy, but he had to do it. For beyond that mist lay the rest of the world. He revved the little engine hard.

'Erm . . . y'know, Tomsk, maybe we *should* walk. In fact—'

Slim's words were jerked from him as the tiny van leapt forward. Tom kept his foot pressed hard to the floor and the little engine buzzed angrily as they flashed past buildings, bounced over the road and up onto the bridge. There was a violent trembling and wobbling beneath them.

'I told yer!' shouted Slim, his eyes wild with panic. 'And I can't swim neither!'

Tom urged the tiny van on and on, the wheels thudding on each plank like fingers on a piano . . . he was vaguely aware of splashing behind him as they raced up and up and up and, then— the front wheel left the bridge and it floated for a moment— there was the black water below . . .

Thump!

The van hit the other side of the bridge so hard that Tom and Slim bounced from the pit of their seats to the roof—and back, and on—down the other side, onto the shore and away—

'That was, that was . . . ' Slim could barely speak. His fingers were still pressed to the dash.

'Lucky,' breathed Tom, feeling the tingle of sweat break out on his back.

Lucky it was, certainly, but it couldn't have been more conspicuous. Every soldier on the causeway had watched in amazement as the tiny van shot out onto the rickety bridge and somehow managed to cross it as the whole structure collapsed behind. With a shout they leapt into their trucks and tore back over the causeway in pursuit.

'Which way now?'

Slim said nothing as they plunged into the labyrinth of ware-houses.

'Slim! Which way to Spong's wharf?'

'Go left,' he said, glancing back at a massive headlight turning into the alley behind them. Tom obeyed and almost immediately found a shed straight ahead of him.

'Now?'

'Right.'

'Right?'

'It's further along the shore. Just keep going round and you can't miss it.'

Tom did as he was told. The birds had told him that the stork was kept in an office next to the water . . . it made sense. Out of the corner of his eye he glimpsed more lights flashing through the gaps between buildings, hunting them down . . .

'Left here.'

Tom banked hard. Every wooden alley looked just the same.

'You're sure about this?'

'Definitely,' said Slim. 'Straight on. Through that arch. That's it.'

Shooting under the wide wooden arch at the end of the alley they suddenly found themselves in a large circular yard, hemmed in on all sides by old wooden sheds. Exits ran off on all sides like the spokes of a wheel.

'Which way now?' said Tom, sliding the van at speed round the edge.

Slim stared down each dark hole grimly. He said nothing.

'Slim?' Tom shot him a harsh look. 'Slim!'

'Easy, Tomsk, I'm trying to remember—give me a chance.'

Tom slammed on the brakes and the van skidded to a halt in the snow. They sat in silence for a moment, listening to the throbbing engines thundering in the distance.

'Well?'

The boy stared out of the window, avoiding Tom's angry glare.

'Are we lost?'

Slim seemed almost paralysed with fear.

'Slim!'

'They're coming. They're going to come.'

'I know that. Which is why—'

'There's no way out.'

'What?'

Slim shook his head.

'You're a fool, Tomsk.'

'What are you talking about?' Slim refused to look at him. 'Slim? What's going on? Evie said—'

'Forget what Evie said,' he replied savagely. 'Evie knows nothing. Nothing about anything.'

Tom stared at the shaven-headed boy. And then suddenly he realized.

'You've never been here before, have you? That was a lie you told her—about coming down to look for your parents after they disappeared. You made it up.' Slim shrugged and bit his nails hard. He did not deny it.

'Didn't you?'

'Kind of.'

'Kind of! What are we going to do now?'

'Wait.'

'Wait? Wait for what?'

A ghost of a smile crossed Slim's lips. Tom's mouth fell open.

'No . . . you . . . you didn't, you wouldn't have . . . '

'What did you expect, nutter?'

Slim . . . he had lied—and now he had betrayed him too.

'Why?'

'Needed the money. Mr Grimal says old Loagy will pay top whack to get you back. Turns out you're very special indeed.'

Tom jumped out of the cab, slamming the door so hard it almost fell off. He felt a surge of white hot anger pulse through him: he was so stupid, he should never have trusted Slim, why did he ever believe him? So foolish . . . but he was never going back to that asylum, not now . . . he would rather die . . . Tom looked around wildly. Headlights began appearing down the alleyways, surging towards them from all directions . . . It was a trap . . . He glanced at the blanket of white cloud above. If only it would come down and swallow him up. *If only* . . .

And then he saw it. Like a black cross high above, moving with a lazy grace in and out of the white mist . . .

'HEY!' he screamed. 'HEY!' Tom began frantically leaping around in the snow screaming his head off. 'HEY! DOWN HERE!'

'What you doing, Tomsk?'

'THE EAGLE! THERE IT IS!'

Slim looked up to see the great bird flying directly above.

'The eagle?' He'd never seen such a thing before.

But Tom was already back in the van and reversing at top speed.

'You ain't escaping now, nutter. You can't.'

Tom ignored him and accelerated hard across the yard, skidding round a couple of bends then retracing the pattern, before looping a circle in the middle. The great bird watched the van careering drunkenly around in the snow. The wheels were forming a pattern . . . S . . . O—and then in a flash it understood.

'Ahh!'

There was a thump on the roof and the head of an enormous shaggy raptor suddenly appeared upside down through the windscreen. It blinked. Slim screamed again.

'I don't bloody believe it! Tom Scatterhorn, is that you?'

'Hi!' Tom swerved dangerously to avoid the first truck that skidded into the yard and began to chase them round.

'What are you doing out here, kiddo? Or is that a daft question . . . whoops!'

The great bird ducked as another truck swung in front of them and joined the pursuit.

'I've been trying to find you.'

'Me? But—'

'Don Gervase put me in the asylum and—'

'Bloody Hell Fire! Not *that* place?'

Tom nodded, spinning the wheel wildly as more and more men and vehicles began to appear from the alleyways.

'I knew you were coming tonight so I escaped and—'

'You escaped! With your mate?'

Tom glanced at Slim, whose expression was fixed in absolute terror.

'He's not my mate. He's no one.'

The bird glared at the boy cowering in his seat.

'Can you help?'

The bird glanced around. Every exit was blocked now and soldiers were leaping from their trucks . . .

'Dang it, Tom Scatterhorn. Just hold out as long as you can.'

There was a scratching on the roof and the bird had gone.

'You ain't getting out of this, nutter,' hissed Slim, rapidly recovering himself.

'Aren't I?' Tom accelerated hard. There was Mr Grimal descending from one of the trucks.

'No you bloody ain't. This is business.'

In that same second Slim stretched across the dashboard and ripped out the key, flinging it out of the window. Instantly the engine died and they scrunched to a halt in the middle of the yard.

'You're going back where you belong, Tomsk. Now.'

Tom's first instinct was to punch the smile off Slim's bony face—but he knew that wouldn't solve anything. Ripping open the door he tumbled out into the snow and saw the soldiers all around, their rifles levelled at him.

'Hands up!'

Tom did as he was told and squinted into the lights.

'What a shame. And you was doing so very well.'

The heavy form of Mr Grimal came forward from the shadows and Slim stepped out of the van. He looked across at Tom with a sneer.

'Here's your echo, boss. Delivered just like you said.'

'Nice work, Spry. Well done.' There was a pause. 'Now, Master Scatterhorn, that was quite an adventure, wasn't it?'

Tom glimpsed the men closing in from all sides. He had a vague sense that he shouldn't move, shouldn't look up, or even glance behind him . . .

'Don't make it difficult, lad. We don't mean any harm.'

Grimal gave a grunt and the soldiers lowered their weapons. He took a step closer and Tom instinctively took a step back.

'All we want to do is to get you home. Where you belong.'

Tom kept his hands up. Whatever might happen, must happen right now. *Come on*, he whispered to himself. Please.

Mr Grimal stared at the boy. Why was he standing like that? He seemed to be waiting for something . . .

'Get him.'

The ring of men moved forward. And in the same instant a dark shape cannoned out between two buildings. Grimal turned to find something big flying straight at him.

'Shoot it!' he screamed. But even as he said it the soldiers instinctively flattened themselves against the snow as the bird swept through their ranks. The next second Grimal dived out of the way and Tom felt two great talons grasp under his arms . . . up he swung, just glimpsing Mr Grimal's horrified face before they were over the roofs and out of sight.

'Cutting a little fine,' rasped the eagle. 'You OK?'

Tom nodded. He opened his mouth but no words would come.

'Just hang on a little longer, kiddo.'

Tom felt the shudder of the bird's vast wings as they swept out across the river towards the silhouette of the church bell tower, rising from the swirling black water. A moment later the raptor dropped Tom gently onto the roof and then swooped in to make a clumsy landing himself.

'What a bunch of nongs,' it muttered, glaring back at the lights flashing through the wharves. 'Like blue-arsed flies the lot of them.'

Tom stared at the great bird: it seemed to be more of a

mishmash of odd feathers and colours than he remembered, and most of its grey ruff was missing. Eventually it turned and fixed Tom with its angry yellow eye.

'Now my old mucker, before we go any further, how's about you tell me precisely what is going on?'

Five minutes later the eagle had listened to Tom's tale in grouchy silence. He had kept it brief and simple, sticking to the essential details.

'Sounds like you've made one helluv'an enemy there, kiddo,' it sniffed. 'And something tells me Askary ain't going to take kindly to this little escapade.'

Tom nodded—that much was obvious.

'Maybe Dr Logan won't want to admit that I've got out,' he said, trying to sound positive. 'Especially if I'm some kind of prize prisoner.'

The bird snorted disdainfully. 'That's a maybe and a half.'

It looked back towards the museum in the distance. The engines were quieter now, and Tom thought he could almost hear the noise of the party once more.

'But even if he wants to, I'll betcha Logan won't be able to keep a lid on this for long. Boy mysteriously rescued by tatty old bird: it's bound to get back somehow. Not to mention all them brave little critters in your cell. What the hell's going to happen to them?'

Tom shrugged guiltily: he had almost forgotten those animals piled up on his pillow.

'Strikes me that you're in a chutney of extraordinary proportions, kiddo. Perhaps we both are.'

Tom said nothing. Somehow the bald facts didn't scare him any more.

'Which is why I have to find that vent hole.'

'*You* have to?'

'Well someone does. Someone's got to try and destroy it. Why shouldn't it be me?'

The raptor stared at the scrawny thirteen-year-old boy, his black eyes blazing. He could think of a whole heap of reasons . . .

'Are you sure there isn't something you aren't telling me?'

'What?' said Tom, the colour rushing to his cheeks. 'What do you mean?'

'That there isn't some other reason behind all this?'

Tom shook his head angrily.

'Of course there isn't.'

But of course he hadn't mentioned what had happened inside his head. That his mind had been beetleized, that any moment Don Gervase could just invade it, screaming commands . . .

'You could just go home, you know. Go home, go to bed: forget it ever happened. Like a bad dr—'

'I don't want to go home,' spluttered Tom angrily. 'What would be the point? He'd still find me. He'd find me anywhere I hid. Which is why I have to destroy Scarazand. And anyway, this is not just about me any more. It's bigger than that.' Tom paused awkwardly. 'It's about all this. What's happened here. To this place. To everything. I'm serious.'

'I don't doubt that you are, me little bushranger, I don't doubt that you are. It's just—'

The bird didn't want to hurt the boy's feelings, but it was

like listening to an ant proposing a fight with a bull elephant—a whole herd of bull elephants, in fact.

'I'd give you a hand, if only I had the durndest idea where that chimney was. But you can guarantee it's going to be extraordinarily well-hidden. And as for the protection . . . ' The eagle shook its great shaggy head. It was hard to imagine that whatever forest the vent hole was hidden in wouldn't be stuffed with all manner of hideous beasts . . .

'Perhaps we're in need of some assistance here: advice from a couple of blokes who spent a fair amount of time looking for that chimney themselves. Though of course, they never had the tip off that you have.'

Tom felt his heart quicken.

'Yes, me old gulabong. August Catcher and Sir Henry Scatterhorn.'

'So . . . they are still alive—even now?'

'In their own fashion, never livelier.'

Tom's heart leapt.

'And you could really take me to them . . . from *here*?'

'Could? Interesting word, could. I'd say yes, only there are two large snags. The first being they have absolutely forbidden me to let anyone know where they are, on account of being hunted themselves.'

'Oh.'

'Ever since our little excursion to Scarazand last year Askary's been on to them, searching every hidey-hole on the face of the planet. Guess he didn't take kindly to us finding out what he's up to down there. Hence they's holed up in the thickest of thickets. If I took you to 'em I'd be breaking my word, and that's bad, mate. Specially with them.'

Tom could not hide his disappointment.

'That's a no then?'

The great raptor paused, clearly thinking hard.

'Secondly, you ever seen what's living in those windmills up there?'

Tom shook his head blankly. The quilt of grey mist had remained unbroken ever since he had arrived.

'Hmm. Maybe that's a good thing.'

'What is it?'

'They's black and spiky and roosting on the columns. Look like vultures, only a lot less lovely. When I arrived the air was thick with them. Seem to be guarding the place. I got through, but that's because I was unannounced. The question is, are they wise to your escape? Because if they are . . . ' the bird shook its head. 'No dice, kiddo.'

Tom looked up at the mist scudding overhead. 'Couldn't we fly low over the forest, stay under the cloud?'

'That's not desirable. You ain't seen much of this world, have ya?'

Tom couldn't pretend that he had.

'Believe me, you don't want to. It's not pretty. No mate, the only ways in and out of this godforsaken world are up there, where the moon is. Moon equals moonbeams, shadows, reflections, the edges of things. There ain't no other way round it.'

Tom looked up at the grey blanket glumly. It looked so soft and harmless.

'Maybe we'll be lucky.'

'That's rich. From what I've heard you don't have a single lucky bone in your body, Tom Scatterhorn.'

'Except that I'm here, right now, talking to you, when I could be dead, or back in that asylum. That's something—isn't it?'

The eagle looked at the boy. He didn't look as if he was going to take no for an answer.

'A very small something.'

'Well then?'

Two minutes later a dark shape ascended over the rooftops of old Dragonport. Tom crouched in the deep fold between the bird's wide wings, staring down at the remains of the town rising up out of the water like a pile of boulders. At the far end, set slightly on its own, stood Catcher Hall, now shuttered and dark.

'Do you know who lives there?'

'No idea, mate,' rasped the bird, glancing down at the great house. There were no lights on in the windows. 'No one you'd want to be friends with, I'd guess.'

Tom nodded grimly. He could just make out neatly manicured lawns and closely clipped box hedges rising up out of the woods below: whoever it was obviously looked after the place.

'Euch! Hold your nose!'

Tom sniffed and instantly recoiled. The air was filled with the stench of rotten eggs, stinging his eyes. Whatever it was felt very poisonous.

'Horrible ain't it?' The bird slipped sideways towards the dark sea and the next second they were out of it. 'I always know I've arrived when I get a whiff of that. Must be that factory of yours. That's the Dragonport smell.'

Tom closed his eyes: the taste in his mouth was making him feel very sick, and somewhere far away he thought he could hear a low distant thud, like a hammer in a cellar . . .

A moment later the wall of white cloud enveloped them. On they flew, ascending through the milky darkness. Tom felt nothing but the wet air soaking his face.

Whoosh!

Something sliced through the cloud just in front of them, so fast it was barely visible. Tom's fingers gripped tighter to the bird's back.

'What was that?'

Whoosh!

Another shape carved the mist in two . . . There was a deep throbbing, a humming somewhere above.

'Turbine blades—remember? Windmills. It's a forest of them!'

Up and up they went, the eagle steepening its climb as the humming grew steadily louder. At last they burst through the wisps of cloud and Tom felt as if he had just risen out of some primeval swamp. There in the pale moonlight were hundreds of spinning windmills, stretching away in lines above the clouds.

'Look to the mast tops,' shouted the eagle, 'you see 'em?'

Tom strained his eyes to look: the white steel columns were black and mottled—as if some sort of mould was growing on them. Only it wasn't mould, or anything like it . . .

'Here we go . . .'

Out of nowhere the first outriders appeared, circling around them inquisitively. Moonlight glinted off their shiny carapaces and flat eyes . . . they reminded Tom of a giant horsefly he had once seen, except these creatures were considerably bigger.

Suddenly one of the insects dived in and attached itself to the eagle's head.

'Now there's no need for any of that nonsense. I ain't gonna—OW!' With a vicious lunge the insect skewered him hard in the eye. In a flash the raptor ripped it away with a talon and crumpled it to bits.

'Dang it but that was unnecessary. Keep your head down low, Tom. Give 'em half a chance and they'll make a hole in your head. The last thing we want is to antagonize 'em.'

Tom pressed himself deeper into the eagle's back. On they flew, deeper into the forest of spinning blades, followed by the curious buzzing cloud.

'Can you see an opening anywhere?'

The eagle shook its head.

'Not a sausage. Just a daggy grey mess. Let's head over to the power station, all that electricity might give us a bounce.'

The bird adjusted its course and made for the chimneys in the distance. By now some of the insects seemed to have lost interest and were returning to their nests.

'That wasn't so bad,' whispered Tom. 'Maybe they were just inquisitive.'

'Save the champagne, me old fruit,' rasped the bird. 'We've one helluva way to go yet.'

The eagle had barely finished speaking when something seemed to pass through the air all around, an invisible ripple that lifted the cloud of insects like a gust . . . the next moment Tom felt a heavy thud deep inside his skull. It was a signal . . . an order . . . but for what? Looking back, Tom felt the hairs on his neck stand on end. There, silhouetted against the violet sky was a small dark shape cannoning in their direction. Already part of the black swarm had broken away and began chasing it down hard.

'But that can't be *him*, can it? He wouldn't bother, not in person,' reasoned the eagle. The hissing grew louder. 'That's gonna be an assassin or something like that.'

'EXACTLY!' shouted Tom. 'COME ON!'

'Right you are,' exhaled the great bird, 'I knew this was a bad idea.'

Angling its wings into the shape of an arrow, the raptor plummeted towards the clouds beneath. In an instant they plunged back into the grey darkness.

'Whoops!'

The eagle twisted violently, narrowly lifting over a blade that scythed left—then weaved under another cutting right. On they went, slaloming through the steel forest of masts and spinning blades.

'This is really most ill-advised,' complained the bird. 'Haven't we lost them yet?'

Tom glanced back. He couldn't see a thing, but there was a hissing somewhere close by . . .

'Maybe . . . possibly.'

'All right. Let's have a gander. Up periscope!'

Bending into a steep climb they skimmed back out above the cloud.

'That's better. At least I can see which is blinkin' up and d—'

The eagle stopped. The cloud of insects was tracking them directly overhead like a black cloud, so thick they blotted out the moon.

'Time to get drastic!' it roared. 'Hold on, Tom Scatterhorn.'

Turning suddenly, the bird dived straight towards the nearest windmill.

'What you doing?'

'Ever played Russian Roulette?'

Whatever Tom said was lost in the rush of air as they accelerated hard towards the centre of the propeller. It was a kaleidoscope of spinning steel and clouds . . . Unable to keep his eyes open Tom glanced back: he lost count of the number of dark shapes racing behind like a pack of hounds, trying to barge each other off their quarry . . .

'Hold on!'

The blades came up so fast that Tom barely had time to screw his eyes shut before the eagle twisted, riding an invisible kink in the air. The first ten insects smashed into the windmill, exploding like bombs, but the rest slipped past effortlessly and closed ranks for the kill. With a sudden burst of speed they darted forward in unison, clinging to the eagle's tail feathers and feet.

'Get off!' shouted Tom, kicking and flailing at the black creatures—but it was no use—in seconds the others had joined and now a cloud of insects billowed below them like a great sack, dragging them down.

'What are we going to do?' shouted Tom.

The eagle did not reply—it was struggling to stay airborne.

'I think I should be jettisoned!'

'Not yet, mate!' rasped the bird as two insects clamped themselves over its eyes and beak. 'We've got one last option. Can you swim?'

'Yes—but—'

'Hang on to your hat!'

Suddenly the eagle stopped flapping and they spiralled down through the clouds in a barely controlled plummet, emerging just above a dark landscape of forests and hills.

'Dang it! I thought this was the sea!'

'There!' shouted Tom, spotting a small lake with a cottage beside it, nestling between the trees.

'That'll do!'

With all its strength the great raptor surged forward, dragging the seething cargo below.

'You's gonna have to let go, mate.'

Tom fought and kicked at the biting insects all around and glanced at the rapidly approaching black water. It looked cold and hard and horrible.

'OK.'

'I'll pick you up after—just get as far away from them as you possibly can.'

Tom's eyes widened as the lake rushed up towards him.

'Are you sure—'

'Yes! Here we go!'

The next few seconds were a blur. Tom was vaguely aware of a colossal splash, and then he was tumbling down through the darkness. The water was so cold it felt like an electric shock. Closing his eyes he began to swim, and he swam and swam and swam until his lungs began to burst and he could go no further. He headed up. One stroke more, two, three, one for luck—and with a gasp he burst up into the clear night air . . .

'Hey!'

Tom gasped, and gasped again. Beyond was a mass of insects, kicking helplessly in the lake. There above was the vast shaggy eagle, bedraggled but flying once more.

'Grab me undercarriage, mate!' it roared, arcing down over the water's glassy surface. In one movement it caught Tom up in its talons and hurled him up into the air.

'WHUMP!'

The next moment Tom landed in the thick wet feathers of the eagle's back.

'This is becoming a bit of a habit, ain't it! I thought you's a gonner then. Why did you swim so far?'

Tom was so breathless he could barely speak.

'You said get away, so I just . . . got away.'

'So you did, mate. We both did.' Tom looked down at the black stain wriggling on the surface of the lake. 'Water's the one thing they can't cope with. Remember that.'

'You've done that before?'

'Once—in extremis. I didn't think I'd make it—but was pleased to find out one of me relations was a shag. So swimming was on the agenda.'

Tom smiled, amazed that this brave, strange creature was so resourceful.

'Now, Mr Scatterhorn, let's get ourselves somewhere more friendly. Without having another battle with Johnny horsefly and all his mates.' The bird scouted ahead towards the end of the lake. There the smallest gap in the clouds was just beginning to open up, and a small patch of moonlight began dancing across the water's edge.

'That's my beauty. One of you little moonbeams should do us just fine.'

CHAPTER 10

I RECOGNIZE THAT FACE

Tom had no idea how long they had been travelling, it might have been seconds or hours. Half-waking, half-dreaming he saw cities hove into view and dip past: at one point he thought he recognized London: there was St Paul's Cathedral, and the Thames snaking through Tower Bridge far below, then when he looked out again there was the Eiffel tower . . . but mostly it was a black and endless expanse of sea. Gradually Tom was lulled to sleep by the constant whoop-whoop of the bird's lazy rhythm, but had he stayed awake, and had he been alert, he might have noticed a dark speck on the horizon, ever present, following their course like a shadow . . .

When he awoke dawn was breaking over the horizon. Tom looked up groggily to see cliffs plunging down into the sea ahead.

'Where are we?'

'Dead close now, kiddo,' rasped the eagle, lifting over the grey rocks and swooping down into a narrow ravine carpeted with pines and boulders. 'Glad you've had some kip.'

Five minutes further and Tom was beginning to feel ravenously hungry—he could barely remember the last time he had anything to eat—or drink. He looked down longingly at the crystal streams tumbling over the rocks below.

'Is there no chance of—'

'In a moment, yes,' announced the bird, nodding ahead. At the end of the ravine stood a pale mountain pointing up at the sky accusingly. At its summit, glowing pink in the dawn, Tom could just make out a pitched roof and small, square windows. The walls seemed to come directly out of the rock itself.

'Is that their house?'

'Not theirs, exactly; and not a house, precisely.'

The great bird swung down into the shadows and bounced to an awkward halt amongst the pine trees. 'It's a monastery.'

'A monastery?' repeated Tom in surprise. August and Sir Henry were many things, but religious was not one of them.

'On the outside. In fact it is the refuge of an ancient order. They've been here about a thousand years, but they's a secretive bunch. They don't exactly invite visitors, or even advertise their existence. It's all very hush hush. Hence that.'

The eagle nodded over to a rough wooden platform close to the bottom of the rock. Tied back in the branches of a tree was a large basket, about the size of a coracle, with three high wicker sides.

'That basket's the only way up. Or down. But I don't think those boys ever come down. Once they're up—they're up, for life. And what a lot of fun that must be.'

'And what are they called?'

'The Legion of the White Ant. Odd, ain't it? I doubt you've ever heard of them.'

The name was vaguely familiar, but Tom could not remember

why. Beside the basket was a small stone basin catching water from a stream and a chipped china cup. Tom helped himself to a long, deep draught.

The deliciously cold, icy water sharpened his senses. Glancing up again he followed the line of the rope dangling against the rockface to a distant platform hanging against the pale dawn sky. It seemed a very long way.

'So they pull you up?'

The eagle nodded.

'Hand over fist, right to the top. I could have taken you there myself, course, but erm . . . ' The eagle seemed a little embarrassed. 'It ain't a hotel, see. The brothers don't like my comings and goings—it's a bit of a sore point, in fact. So I usually slip in at night when no one's looking.'

Tom saw that there was no choice in the matter. But if it was this hard to get in, how was he ever going to get out again?

'And you're sure they'll be there?'

The eagle shrugged.

'August was a month ago. But he may not be quite what you expect. Remember, kiddo, he's been alive one heck of a long time. Just so's you're not too disappointed.'

'And Sir Henry?'

'I'm not sure. He's less predictable.'

Tom steeled himself and climbed into the basket, sitting on the rough seat.

'Give that a yank, it usually works.'

Tom tugged at the rope and waited. A moment or two later it tightened up and the basket swung off the platform with a jerk.

'There you go. Good luck.'

'Thanks.' Tom sat still, moving in rapid jolts up through the trees. 'Will I see you again?'

The eagle frowned at him as if that was the most stupid question he had ever heard.

'Does a frog have a waterproof bum?'

Tom grinned, and soon he was heading up into the sunlight, which despite the early hour was surprisingly hot. Shielding his eyes, he tried to catch a glimpse of who it was hauling him up, but he couldn't. Up the side of the rock they went, till the long twisting ravine unravelled like a green snake, at the end of which Tom could just glimpse a small dot of blue—the sea, glinting in the dawn light. The Legion of the White Ant . . . Tom remembered the name now—they had held a meeting in Dragonport once, down by the docks . . . Lotus Askary and her gang of thugs had burnt it down . . . so *they* were sheltering August and Sir Henry . . . what was he going to say to them when they finally met?

Tom found himself trying to rehearse the scene in his mind, imagining all those awkward questions and realizing he had very few answers. No, he didn't know why he had been sent to an asylum in the future. Neither did he understand the pictures of Betilda Marchmont. He didn't even know why or how he was supposedly going to betray his parents . . . so what did he know? Only that he wanted to destroy Scarazand for ever. That was all. Why? Tom stared at the trees diminishing below. Why you, Tom?

If you really want them to help you will have to tell them everything. Which means the truth.

'But I can resist him. Honestly I can, if I think hard enough.

179

I've done it before, for a short while . . . if I concentrate he can't control me completely . . . '

Tom shook his head angrily. That was the truth. And he hated it. It sounded so feeble. Suddenly all those secrets he had managed to keep were swimming up to the surface as surely as he was rising up the side of this mountain . . .

A moment later Tom found himself emerging through a hole in a wide wooden platform. To one side, working the block and tackle, were two young men wearing pale grey robes. Their heads were shaved and the sweat was glistening on their temples. With a grunt one braced the rope while the other hauled the basket onto the platform and paused a moment, breathlessly.

'Ya soo? Boro na sas voeetheeso?'

Tom turned round to see a wiry man with closely cropped hair and bright shining eyes staring at him. He was angular and athletic looking, like a dancer: not at all what Tom imagined a monk should look like.

'Hi. Thanks for pulling me up.'

The man said nothing. He kept smiling, probing. Tom noticed he was slightly cross-eyed. Behind him stood a high wall and a narrow wooden door. It was closed.

'I'm looking for someone. A friend. August Catcher. I used to be his assistant, many years ago.'

The silence continued. Actually this monk was very cross-eyed, and Tom had trouble choosing which brilliant blue eye to focus on.

'I wondered . . . that is, I was hoping I might see him.'

There was no response.

'Or Sir Henry Scatterhorn? Is that possible?'

'Brothers are not permitted to take visitors,' the monk replied in English—quietly but firmly. 'Our order does not permit that.'

'But it's urgent. I've come a very long way. I'm in trouble, and I have to see him,' said Tom, his voice rising slightly. 'I need his help.'

The monk's smile remained fixed. He was wondering, calculating whether this was yet another ruse. The boy had come up with the right name, but anyone could do that. And there were reports that they were becoming better informed . . .

'How did you come here, young friend?'

Tom swallowed nervously: what was he supposed to say to that? The monk's eyes had narrowed a fraction. This was a test . . .

'I . . . I erm . . . I had heard about the monastery, and I was just walking up the ravine . . . erm . . . hiking, when—' Tom looked down at his shoes and swore silently.

Don't embarrass yourself. You are not a tourist. Remember—the truth!

'OK, OK. My name is Tom Scatterhorn. I am from Dragonport, England. I came here on the back of a bird, a kind of eagle made by August Catcher many years ago when he was a taxidermist. The eagle knew that this is where August and Sir Henry were hiding and that is why he brought me here.'

There, he had said it. The speech was met with silence, but the monk did not seem surprised. He glanced at his two companions, then back at Tom.

'Scatterhorn?'

'Yes,' said Tom, wiping his brow. Suddenly his heart was thumping loudly in his throat. 'Tom Scatterhorn.' He could barely say his own name.

The monk's smile turned into a cold glare, and he turned and stepped through the narrow door behind him. Tom stood waiting in the harsh sunlight. Neither of the other monks would look at him, but they didn't leave, either. Either they were about to push him off, or let him down again. Whichever it was, Tom found himself wondering if the eagle knew all this was going to happen. He stared angrily at the valley far below, the harsh lines of smoky sunlight burning through the mist.

'Scatterhorn?'

The monk had reappeared in the doorway. He stepped aside, and in the dark square beyond a figure emerged in a monk's cowl. A ghostly face, crisscrossed with lines, and pale, sparkling eyes . . .

'August?'

Tom unconsciously took a step forward and the two young monks instantly did the same. Tom sensed that they were ready for anything he might do next.

'Is that you, Tom?'

The voice was rattling—but it was his: wasn't it?

'Yes, it's me.' Tom smiled. 'The eagle brought me.'

'Very good.' The white face in the doorway nodded vacantly. 'Still jabbering away in that strange Russian accent of his, is he?'

Tom was flummoxed. Maybe August had forgotten.

'Russian? Erm . . . No, he speaks English, with an Australian accent.'

'Oh yes, so he does, quite right,' said the voice distantly. 'And why does he do that I wonder?'

Suddenly the words of the bird came dancing back. *He may not be quite what you expect* . . . Why was August asking him these questions, to which he obviously knew the answers, and why was he not coming out to greet him?

'It's the aboriginal dictionary you put inside his head. That's how he learned to communicate with birds.'

'Oh . . . oh yes.'

Something was wrong, Tom could feel it. The monks regarded him belligerently.

'So you've come from Dragonport?'

'That's right. Just now. It took all night.'

'How is the old place?'

'It's very . . . different. You wouldn't recognize it. It's all changed.'

'Oh dear. That's a shame. But the cathedral's still there, isn't it? I used to love going in to listen to the organ.'

'Erm—'

'And Dragonport Athletic—don't tell me they aren't still at the bottom of the fourth division?'

'Well . . . '

Tom squinted into that pale white face he had known so well. There was no cathedral in Dragonport, and as for football, August Catcher wouldn't be seen dead inside a football ground. Not the August he knew, anyway. Maybe that's why these monks were protecting him. August Catcher was alive, but a shell of his former self. Maybe Sir Henry was, too. Suddenly Tom felt a wave of regret wash over him. He should never have come to this place.

'I'm really sorry. I've made a mistake. Sorry.' Tom turned back to the two monks who had pulled him up. 'Please, I think . . . could you let me down again?'

There was silence. All eyes were on Tom. A bird screeched far below.

'You want to go down again?'

It was the cross-eyed monk that had spoken.

'Yes. I do.'

August Catcher still stood in the dark doorway: just a frail twig . . . a ghost of that vital, brilliant man he had first met all those years ago.

'Bye, August. I'm sorry to have troubled you.'

With a heavy heart Tom turned towards the basket. He was aware that still no one had moved.

'Are you *quite* sure you want to go down again?'

That frail voice, but the tone was different.

'Yes. I'm certain.'

'Excellent! What did I tell you, gentlemen?'

Tom turned round and his mouth fell open in astonishment. The frail figure in the doorway disintegrated before his eyes, his skin a mass of pale moths that fluttered away in all directions. The cowl dropped to the floor and from the darkness beyond stepped a sprightly bearded figure, whose shock of white hair stood upright on his head.

'Well, well, Tom Scatterhorn! This is a surprise indeed.'

Tom could barely gasp before the bespectacled man was wringing his hand furiously.

'August?'

'Yes, yes. Apologies. New idea that needed testing. We have to be extraordinarily careful, my fellow monks and I, against unwanted guests.' He turned back and the younger monks smiled, all the tension seemingly evaporated.

'This young man is very remarkable indeed,' he said, clapping his hand on Tom's shoulder. 'Not only has he been to Scarazand, but he has come back to tell the tale.' The monks nodded approvingly. 'Though not to *too* many people, I hope,' added August, his quick eyes glinting somewhere inside the piles of wrinkled skin.

Tom smiled with relief.

'No.'

'Good good. Come come, I expect you are ravenously hungry, as boys always are,' and with that he turned on his heel and trotted away into the darkness. Tom moved awkwardly between the curious monks and into a dark, cool corridor of vaulted stone. The ceiling glinted with gold mosaics and a heavy smell of incense hung in the air.

'They've been very good to me, these chaps,' said August, ducking through a small arched doorway and down a spiral staircase. 'Got my own suite, dare I say it, which is mightily useful, given all the clobber I carry around. You probably remember that, don't you, Tom?'

Tom did indeed remember August's remarkable workshop in a cave on that island in the Himalayas, and he also remembered that August had seemed much more frail the last time they had met. He seemed not only to have shrunk, but somehow become much more energetic.

'Here we are,' he said, opening a wooden door and descending a few steps into a large irregular shaped room. Three small windows cut into the massive walls provided the only light, and the room was crammed full of August's paraphernalia that spilled across every surface.

'Still got the airborne encyclopaedia,' said August, raising a hand over the table piled high with books and specimen glasses towards the far wall where lines of shoebills stood on racks, staring ahead impassively. 'Which of course have to be kept updated,' he said, sweeping along a line of albatross. 'And then of course there are the errors,' patting a pair of mournful-looking geese on the head. 'And even errors have errors,' he winked at a rather bewildered storm petrel. 'But that's the march of progress, isn't it, gentlemen? Knowledge waits for no one.'

There was a muffled shuffling of feet.

'And the moths?'

'Rhodi moths. Take a little cajoling, but they can turn them-selves into most things. And the nicest thing about them is that they are desperate to please—rather like puppies,' he said. 'And they know what you are thinking.'

Tom laughed.

'They do?'

'Absolutely they do.' Picking up a small box from the table he shook a collection of speckled creatures into Tom's palm. 'Think of something. An object. Something small.'

'Anything?'

'Why not? Something you really want.'

Tom looked at the fluffy insects walking around his palm in circles, their wings buzzing. What could he think of? He closed his eyes and found all he could think about was food—he was so hungry. An apple, red, crisp, juicy—

'There you are.'

He opened his eyes and an apple—or rather, something like the ghost of an apple, stood on his palm. It was made of moths.

'Colour's no good, I know, but the intention's there, all the same. That *was* what you were thinking of, was it not?'

Tom looked at the white and brown speckled apple quivering there and nodded.

'How do they do it? They read it, from your hand. From the electricity humming in the nerve ends, they knew precisely what you wanted. You are expressing yourself through the air. We can't see these thoughts, but they can. They can feel them, and feel compelled to illustrate them. Uncanny isn't it?'

Tom set the grey apple carefully down on the table. Actually, even looking at it was making him feel extremely hungry.

'You see the air around us is not the empty, clear space our eyes would lead us to believe,' continued August, rummaging through some drawers enthusiastically. 'It's a kind of soup, filled with infinitesimally small things through which we can communicate without speaking—or even seeing. In fact, it is probably jam-packed with a blizzard of thoughts, dreams, unspoken wishes . . . '

'I don't suppose you have an apple?'

'What?'

August was so carried away with his own enthusiasm that he had quite forgotten what Tom had wanted.

'Do you have anything to eat?'

'Eat? You mean food? Food! Why yes, dear boy, of course. There I was wittering on like some mad old fish while you're dying of starvation . . . of course. Gosh I must be getting old!' he winked. 'Sit down. Relax. Give me half a second.'

Later, as Tom sat in contented silence eating his way through a loaf of flat bread, a hunk of cheese, olives, a whole jar of honey, followed by the best part of a bowl of fruit, August patiently explained the history of the Order of the White Ant.

'Formed originally by a group of medieval knights who had heard of a lost kingdom beneath the earth, a place made of gold and silver and jewels and peopled by insects. They went in search of it, some died, some went mad, and many years later, quite by accident, three knights found an entrance to Scarazand in a marsh . . . down they went into that astonishing world . . . two came back, but one never did. Unsurprisingly, no one believed their incredible tale but they wanted to keep their secret alive, so they built this monastery, as far away from anywhere as possible. Some of their descendants are still here, though nowadays the monks are mainly fugitives from Don Gervase Askary—and a fair few criminals, I dare say . . . '

Tom ate and smiled and nodded politely when required until at last he began to feel normal again.

'So you really *were* hungry, then?' said August, looking in some amazement at the empty table. That was more than he would have eaten in a week, and despite it all, the boy still managed to look thin and rangy.

'I was. Very.'

'In which case I know the perfect way to round it off.'

August disappeared, returning a minute later with a large white porcelain cup.

'A special gift from the kitchen,' he said, setting it down before Tom. 'Anyone who has escaped from Scarazand cuts the mustard around here.'

Tom took one look at the swirling, steaming brown liquid and closed his eyes. That smell, so sweet, so sickly . . . August was a little mystified at Tom's reaction.

'Don't tell me you're the only boy in the world who doesn't like hot chocolate?'

Tom's head began to swim. Actually he really did think he was about to be sick.

'I do like it. Normally. It just . . . it just reminds me of something.'

'What does it remind you of?'

And then the whole story tumbled out, words rushing over themselves like confused waves. This time Tom kept his promise: he left nothing out. August sat patiently listening, his expression gradually shifting from mild intrigue to acute concern. When it was all over, he sat for a long time staring out of the window at the mountains beyond. Strangely, he had not seemed surprised when Tom told him about the cark beetle that had burrowed into his brain: in fact, it seemed as if he already suspected this might have happened.

'And you have told no one else about this?'

Tom shook his head.

'And you've never told your parents about that prediction, either?'

'No.'

August's fingers twisted around themselves restlessly.

'Then you're braver than I thought. To tell me, that is. '

'That's why I just . . . I just have to destroy it. Even if Don Gervase forgets about me—which he won't—but supposing he did: how can I ever forget about him? It's like he owns me, somehow, and there's this grenade inside my head that I'm waiting to go off at any moment.' Tom sighed deeply. 'That's what it feels like. Maybe I'm crazy.'

August glanced at Tom, his quick, grey eyes twinkling.

'You're not crazy, Tom. Far from it. Headstrong, perhaps, but that is hardly a fault. Who knows, a little reckless bravery may end up saving your life . . . '

Tom waited for August to elaborate, but he didn't. Instead he chose to change the subject.

'So it all boils down to finding that little vent hole, doesn't it? Take away the Queen and Don Gervase is nothing. That chimney is Scarazand's single weakest point, its Achilles heel. And according to your echo friend it's hidden in a tree, close to a tumble-down shack, in the middle of, possibly a wood, or more likely a forest, somewhere on the face of the earth.'

Tom looked glum: he couldn't pretend this was much of a clue.

'But don't you think it sounds familiar?'

'Not to me it isn't—but perhaps you're right. Perhaps that's the reason why Sir Henry and I never managed to find it. We spent years trudging across various deserts, jungles, and mountain ranges, following one educated guess after another—right into the back of the back of beyond. Not a sausage. Never mind,' he chuckled. 'Collected some lovely butterflies.'

Tom smiled weakly.

'But even though it may *sound* familiar, Tom, you can be certain that these woods, forests—wherever they may be, are extremely well-protected. They must be, to have kept the secret for a thousand years.'

'I know.'

Tom sat in silence, fidgeting. It annoyed him that this little chimney was the one thing in the world he wanted to find, and yet he had already been so close to it last year, in Scarazand . . . It had happened by accident, when they were escaping down through the honeycomb of tunnels in the black rock and he had suddenly spotted an entrance to the Queen's chamber. Ignoring the danger and the swirling gasses he had crept down it and peered out over the precipice . . . there she was, far below, the Queen of Scarazand, its heartbeat, white and glistening and throbbing like some vast maggoty submarine . . . and a hundred metres above, through the swirling mists of gas, shone a tiny speck of light . . . that was it, the vent hole, the only place the Queen made direct contact with the ground . . .

'But supposing by some miracle you did find it, Tom, and imagine that you did manage to hurl down some handy bomb concealed about your person, you would not necessarily kill her.'

'Why not?'

'She's much too big. The explosion would hurt the Queen, certainly, but not kill her outright. To do that you would need something much, much—'

'Bigger than a bomb.'

'What?'

'That's just what the echo said. The Don Gervase, I mean. Something bigger than a bomb.'

August paused for a moment, lost in thought.

'But the likelihood of that is minimal. Unless . . . *unless*—' August rubbed his ancient brow thoughtfully. He was miles away. Then he smiled, oddly.

'What?'

'Just daydreaming, old chap. But however it is done, the object remains the same. To cause the Queen so much distress that she utters a sila scream.'

'A sila scream?'

'Yes. It's a fanciful name, but that's what I call it. I've seen it happen in termite mounds, ants' nests . . . when the queen is fatally wounded she booms out a distress signal to every single creature loyal to the colony. It's a great bolt of magnetic energy that says, help me, protect me, save me. And that is exactly what they try to do—every single one of them. They have no choice.'

'And can they save her?'

August shook his head.

'Never. And what's more, the effort required to produce the scream is so great that the queen cannot survive. She is like a bee that loses its sting. She becomes weaker, more erratic, and her subjects run around like misfiring mechanical toys until eventually they just give up.'

'And you really think this is what would happen in Scarazand, too?'

'Of course. They are insects. But remember, Tom, Scarazand is the greatest and most extraordinary colony of beetles that there has ever been. The death scream of the Queen would be beyond anything we could imagine. That bolt of energy would be felt on the edges of Space.'

'Wow.'

'Wow indeed.'

'What about Don Gervase—couldn't he save her?'

'He could try, but he might as well try directing a tidal wave. The sheer power of it would be colossal. I suspect that if it ever happened, Scarazand would implode in a spectacular fashion. Everything connected with it would be utterly destroyed.'

'Everything?'

August did not seem to notice the hint of concern in Tom's voice.

'Well not quite everything,' he mused. 'Somewhere in that great edifice a small group of beetles will surround a young female and escape, flying away to start a new colony afresh. She will become their new queen, and they will be loyal to her alone. So out of death there will be a rebirth of sorts. A silver lining.'

Tom said nothing for a moment.

'And . . . if this scream happens, what would it do to me?'

Tom's voice was timorous, almost a whisper. Even in the deep shadows of the room, August could see that beneath his thicket of blond hair Tom's black eyes were blazing. It had only just dawned on him what the boy was really asking. Should he tell him the truth? Many long, arduous years of studying insect behaviour could not be ignored . . . August wiped a hand across his brow uneasily.

'There is always an exception to every rule,' he blustered. 'Perhaps you will manage to disregard her, just as you have done before. Is that not possible?'

Tom grinned savagely. What Don Gervase had done to him using the mesmerion was mere childs' play compared to this.

'And don't forget you have escaped from Scarazand alive. Many people would consider that in itself an impossible feat. It would be foolish, Tom, to mistake the probable for the inevitable.'

Tom sat very still, feeling his insides twisting around like snakes. He found it hard to share August's optimism. He could see the future now, for the first time: *really* see it, and in a way, it was almost a relief to know. If he ever did manage to destroy the Queen, then he would die too. Their fate was bound together. He was part of the colony, part of Scarazand, whether he liked it or not . . .

'Tom?' August was staring at him, his ancient brow deeply furrowed. 'Are you all right, old boy?'

'Sorry. I was just . . . thinking, that's all.'

August nodded kindly, and cursed himself for being so honest. 'But none of this is ever going to happen,' he said, breezily changing the subject. 'Scarazand will carry on in its own sweet way, and we can do the same. And knowing what I know now, that is absolutely for the best. Don Gervase Askary has got the elixir, the mesmerion, you have escaped, and whatever he wants to do now is entirely his business. We can stay well out of it.'

'But what *am* I supposed to do now? Just hide up here from the world—for ever?'

'That's one possibility,' August replied. 'The monastery is safe, surprisingly pleasant, and off the radar, so to speak. Many of the brothers of the Legion have chosen to do just that. It's not such a bad life.'

Tom frowned. He hadn't even considered that this might be an option, but now he could see that it was all he had. Could he really stay up here, among the monks? Maybe, just for the moment . . . just for a bit . . . until he worked out more of a plan . . .

'I know it's not a very exciting prospect, old bean, and I am sure at your age I would have felt much the same way. But until one of us can think of something better.'

August smiled kindly as Tom Scatterhorn continued to stare into the racks of birds with a distant, almost lost expression on his face.

'And of course Sir Henry's back tomorrow, and he can see the lie of the land out there far better than I can. In fact I am rather hoping he has some news that will be of great interest to both of us. Tom?'

The boy looked up at him. He didn't seem to have heard a word he'd said.

'Yes?'

'Why don't I show you something?'

CHAPTER 11

A TALE OF THE UNEXPECTED

The rest of the day was spent in a blizzard of experiments. August Catcher had decided that what Tom needed was entertaining and educating and he set about both with gusto, teaching him first how to communicate with the rhodi moths and then giving them a series of ever more complex tasks, culminating in making Don Gervase Askary's face from nothing more than Tom's own memory.

'So you see, it's not unlike taxidermy,' he smiled as the great yellow head dissolved in Tom's hands and fluttered down onto the table. 'Creating something that is alive out of nothing. Had enough?'

Tom nodded: his mind was spinning.

'And it's extraordinary what one can achieve with practice. If there is a memory hanging in the air somewhere these little chaps will find it. It's really very surprising what they reveal.'

Tom did not doubt it. He looked down at the pile of grey moths on the table feeling utterly exhausted.

'I see I have been a little over eager,' smiled August as Tom yawned loudly. 'But I wouldn't want you thinking that I'm some funny old chap who sits about all day doing nothing.'

'I don't,' said Tom, watching him brushing all his moths back into a jar. If anything August Catcher seemed more dynamic than ever.

'Excellent,' he smiled, glancing at the first stars appearing in the sky. 'Now let me see if I can persuade the brothers to let you have Sir Henry's cell for the night. Because you are staying, aren't you?'

He closed the door and bustled away. It was obvious that August was doing his best to make Tom feel at home, and Tom really appreciated it, nevertheless . . . could he really spend the rest of his life in this monastery? Others had. It was safe. It was warm. He stared at the lines of birds lurking in the shadows. And there was so much he could learn. Maybe he really could become August Catcher's assistant this time . . . the problem was—

'All arranged,' said August merrily, reappearing at the door with a lantern. Beside him stood the cross-eyed monk Tom had met earlier on the platform. 'Visiting rules are extremely strict, but for you they will make an exception.'

The monk smiled and bowed a little.

'I rather think you've become something of a mascot,' August added quietly. 'The boy who escaped from Scarazand. They're all talking about it. So I'll see you in the morning, old bean. And when Sir Henry returns I'm sure we'll get you out of this tangle.'

'I hope so.'

'You *hope* so? Don't be ridiculous, of course we will!' laughed August. With his wild white hair and long grey robes, he looked more like an Old Testament prophet than ever. 'Goodnight.'

'Please,' said the monk, and he led the way up the steps and around the edge of a narrow cloister. In the centre was a small fountain glittering in the dusk.

'Sir Henry has the room directly above. It's not far.'

They climbed a stone staircase in the corner and threaded along a balcony until they reached the last wooden door. Setting down his lantern, the monk fiddled with the heavy lock, then stepped through into the small dark cell. As Tom's eyes adjusted to the gloom he could just make out a chaise longue, an antique rifle hanging on the wall, an orderly shelf full of books, and a small black desk. Unlike the muddle and tempest of August's cell this was the room of a neat man who was never there, and somehow that made Tom feel uneasy, as if he was trespassing. Which of course, he was.

'The bed is through there,' said the monk, indicating a small adjacent room where a starched sheet was just visible. 'You can use it if you like.'

'But he's not . . . you're not expecting him back tonight, are you?'

The monk smiled like a cat.

'He is not expected. That doesn't mean he is not coming.'

'Oh.'

'But you are his relation. He will be pleased to see you, yes?'

'Erm, I hope so,' said Tom, sounding a lot more certain than he felt.

The monk cocked his head.

'My name is Gregor.' He held out his hand and Tom took it. 'Welcome.'

'Thank you.'

Gregor bowed and left, silently closing the door behind him.

For a moment Tom stood awkwardly in the half-light, wondering quite what to do. Walking over to the desk, he picked up a framed photograph of Sir Henry dressed in a linen suit, sitting on a Greek column. He looked friendly and relaxed, his quick, piercing eyes almost curling into his large white whiskers. That was his great-great-great-uncle. This was his room. Tom couldn't just sleep in his bed. It was impossible. He felt like Goldilocks.

Pushing the shutters aside, Tom Scatterhorn walked out onto the narrow balcony and leant over the stone railing. It was still warm to the touch. The smell of rosemary and cistus wafted up from August's windows directly below, then the cliff wall fell away in a sheer drop down to the dark carpet of pine trees. How far was that? A hundred metres, two, maybe, a long, long way . . . Tom looked up at the moon and knew that he had just swapped one kind of prison for another. But maybe he would get used to it. After a while, maybe it wouldn't be so bad. If only he could forget about Don Gervase Askary and that low pulse inside his head. That was the problem.

Wandering back inside, Tom found a dark woollen blanket thrown across the chair and curled himself up on the chaise longue. A minute later he was asleep.

It was hard to know how long he had lain there, but it was the soft scraping of shoes on stone that woke him. Tom opened his eyes and glanced at the photograph hanging on the wall reflecting the dark room beyond. He stared into the patch of light that was the window. After a moment a shutter eased open a fraction and a figure appeared from the balcony. His face was obscured by a monk's cowl. Was that Sir Henry? Tom remembered the monk's words; almost certainly it was, maybe he came and went all the time surreptitiously. But how did he get there? Surely he hadn't climbed up the cliff face . . .

Tom watched the shadow hovering on the edge of the room. He seemed very cautious. Perhaps he sensed that someone else was here, perhaps Tom should reveal himself . . . but then—then Tom saw something else that made his heart freeze. That starched white sheet at the end of the bed in the room opposite—it was no longer flat. There was someone in it . . . someone was very definitely sleeping *in* Sir Henry's bed. Tom's heart began to pound in his temples. If that . . . so who was this?

'Hello?'

The figure swivelled towards Tom with blinding speed. In his hand was a long, narrow dagger. Moonlight glinted off its polished surface. He seemed stunned to see a blond boy suddenly appear from behind the chair.

'Who are you?'

Tom saw the white fingers on the blade tighten. Its end was so keen it melted into the darkness. This could be a very big mistake . . . He tried again, louder this time.

'It's me, Tom Scatterhorn.'

'I can see that. Stay where you are.'

The man's voice was muffled, dangerous. He looked around slowly. Tom's heart pummelled in his throat. He thought he was going to be sick.

'Sir Henry!'

'Sir Henry is not here,' hissed the figure, glancing back at the rumpled bed.

Tom did not understand.

'I think . . . I think you should tell me what's happening,' stammered Tom. 'Is there . . . why—'

'Put the knife down. Now.'

Another voice suddenly appeared out of thin air. It was high and commanding. Tom was stunned. He glanced over the monk's shoulder to see a shadow standing in the doorway beside the bed. Another monk?

'That's right. Put it down. Gently—before I make you.'

The monk bristled; in the darkness Tom thought he saw a ghost of a smile from somewhere inside his hood.

'Very well,' he muttered, carefully setting the blade at his feet.

'Good. Now step back. Slowly.'

The monk bowed his head. He did not move. Tom sensed that he was quivering all over, trembling almost, raising his shoulders . . .

'BACK!'

In the next instant the monk rolled backwards and hurled himself at the figure in the doorway. But whoever that was was ready for him. There was a flurry of kicks and punches and before Tom could even blink the monk had smashed down onto the desk and slipped to the floor out cold. His cowl had fallen away to reveal his face: it was one of the shaven-headed monks who had hauled him up in the basket that morning. There was a dark line of blood running from his nose.

'He'll live,' whispered the other monk, feeling his neck. 'Give him another half an hour and he'll probably be trying to attack me again. He must have seen me coming.'

Returning to the bed the monk pulled out a rucksack from

under the sheet, then with a flourish shook off the heavy robes. At first Tom was so surprised at the transformation that he could say nothing at all.

'So, Tom Scatterhorn. You remember me?'

Tom stared at the girl, her cat-like face: her milky eyes, that arrogant smile—

'Lotus?'

There was a pause as Lotus Askary picked up the table, then set the upturned chair down next to it. She sat down casually and began to tighten her laces.

'He probably thought I was an assassin. He was protecting you, Tom. You should be flattered.'

Tom stayed close to the wall. He was trying to remind himself that this was Lotus Askary, *the* Lotus Askary: Don Gervase's daughter, the scourge of Scarazand, who had already tried to kill him several times and failed. It was like being in the same room as a leopard.

'What are you doing here?' he said, as belligerently as he could.

'I followed you. From Dragonport.'

'Dragonport?'

'That's right. I had a feeling he'd put you in that asylum. It was so predictable.'

'You were with your father I suppose?'

Lotus snorted dismissively.

'No. I was alone. But he probably knew I was there. That's why those insects in the windmills attacked me—and you too.'

Tom didn't move. None of this made any sense . . . it was surely a trick . . .

'Why were you looking for me?'

'Because I wanted to find this place. This monastery is a very well kept secret and I needed a guide. I suspected that this is where the eagle would take you. Because you couldn't very well go anywhere else.'

Tom stared at the girl with deep mistrust.

'You don't believe me, do you?'

'Why should I? I know what you are, Lotus.'

'Oh that's good, very good.' Lotus grinned sarcastically. 'You have no idea who I am, Tom Scatterhorn. Not one single clue.'

'Why would those insects try to kill you, Lotus—*you*: Don Gervase's own daughter?'

Lotus shrugged haughtily.

'I . . . it was inevitable. Now that my position has changed.'

'Changed? How?'

Angrily she kicked the monk's hand with her toe. It was clear she really would rather not have to explain any of this.

'I am . . . no longer considered *reliable* enough, or *capable* enough, to be the heir of Scarazand. So, I'm not. I'm a fugitive. An enemy of the colony. Like you, Tom.'

'What had you done?'

'Nothing!' she hissed, her eyes blazing. 'Nothing at all! All I did was follow a particular lead, which apparently . . . apparently I should not have followed. It was treason. So on the flimsiest evidence I was thrown in jail. It was all just a tissue of lies to get me out of the way. A pathetic excuse.'

Either Lotus had become a very good actor, or she seemed to be telling the truth.

'What was this lead?'

'I was looking for Nicholas Zumsteen, as it happens. Who, as you may remember, is Don Gervase Askary's brother. And you may also remember that several years ago he rashly decided to climb out of the vent hole, uncovering Scarazand's greatest secret, and jeopardizing its whole existence. It is a crime for which Zumsteen is being pursued to the ends of the earth.'

Tom nodded: he knew as much.

'And I suppose you found him?'

Lotus shook her head.

'No. I didn't. That's why I followed you here. I need to talk to August Catcher and Sir Henry Scatterhorn face to face.' Tom stared at Lotus hard. Her milky green eyes gave nothing away. 'I need to find out the truth behind a rumour.'

'What rumour?'

'They know something about Nicholas Zumsteen. That is all I am prepared to say. I need to talk to them.'

'You mean you want them to tell you where he is so that you can kill him?' Lotus smiled and shook her head. 'Or maybe you're hoping that if you capture him and bring him back to Scarazand Don Gervase will reinstate you as his heir?'

'Tom, please: I'm not that stupid. I just want to ask them a few questions, nothing more. That is the truth.'

Tom could hardly believe he was having this conversation. Even if it were true, and Lotus really was a fugitive, how much could he trust her? Supposing this was a bluff?

'They are not here,' he said boldly.

Lotus grinned like a cat.

'Come on, Tom, you've just spent the whole day with August Catcher, and as for Sir Henry, I happen to know he has just arrived. This evening.'

'He hasn't.'

'Oh but he has. We shared the same basket up to the monastery. He didn't recognize me. And if you are wondering where he is now, I can tell you he is with August downstairs. I saw them talking through the window as I climbed up.'

Tom was finding it very hard to conceal his irritation. How many more answers did Lotus have up her sleeve? He looked at his watch. It was three o'clock in the morning.

'Well maybe you should go and ask whatever question you have right now. I'm sure they'll be thrilled to see you again.'

Lotus smiled at Tom's sarcasm.

'That is why I was hoping you might come with me.'

Tom snorted.

'To what, confirm your story? Give me one reason why I should do that?'

'Because it's true.'

'Is it, Lotus?'

She did not like the last remark, but Tom did not care.

'Remember those insects in the windmills, Tom. I had to fight them off just as you did. That wasn't easy. And to put it bluntly, if I had wanted to kill you, or Sir Henry, or even August Catcher—I would have done so already, wouldn't I?'

Tom glanced at the monk lying on the floor and frowned. Unfortunately, that was probably true: and despite everything, there was a change in Lotus—she did seem different somehow. That arrogance that she used to wear so lightly was starting to crack.

'Please, Tom? As a favour?'

Tom shook his head and glanced out at the inky sky beyond.

He could never have believed that he would be doing this.

'OK,' he said, between gritted teeth. 'But you owe me.'

A minute later they were standing in the dark stone corridor be-fore August's cell door. Tom knocked four times, bright and clear, and waited. Moths danced drunkenly around a lantern at the far end.

I must be as mad as she is. This is Lotus Askary. How can I ever vouch for her?

Lotus hung back in the deep shadows, fidgeting. Tom sensed that she was almost as apprehensive as he was. There was a loud creak and the door finally opened, revealing a tall shadow wear-ing a long white shirt.

'Trouble sleeping?'

The voice was the same, and so was the face, that high brow, aquiline nose, and eagle-like eyes, ancient and watchful.

'Good to see you, old chap.'

Tom smiled and clasped Sir Henry's large sinewy hand, feeling its familiar lock-like grip. But still he hovered on the threshold.

'Is there something wrong?'

Tom shifted uncomfortably, trying to separate himself from the girl behind him.

'Erm . . . there is someone here to meet you.'

Sir Henry Scatterhorn opened the door wider, throwing a shaft of light out into the dark corridor. There, hovering beside a pil-lar, stood the slim shape of a girl he almost recognized . . . . in a flash Sir Henry grabbed Tom and flung him into the room and slammed the door, knocking the hasp home.

'What on earth is going on?' asked August, standing bewildered at his table.

Sir Henry glared back at Tom angrily.

'I might very well ask the same thing,' he growled. 'Is that who I think it is?'

Tom nodded. 'I don't know how she got up here, honestly, but she's followed me from Dragonport. I had no idea—'

'You had no idea?' interrupted Sir Henry. 'Do you know what this means?'

'Who is it?' asked August.

'It's Lotus Askary.'

'What?' August turned to Tom in disbelief.

'She says she's changed.'

Awkwardly Tom fumbled through the events upstairs, making it quite clear he had no sympathy for Lotus whatsoever. Sir Henry and August listened in surly silence, and Lotus was listening too, as when he had finished her feeble defence there was a tentative knock at the door.

'And you don't think this is some elaborate trick to kill August?'

It was Sir Henry who asked the question, and Tom felt the searchlight of his anger burning into him.

'They have been trying to find him for years, you know. Scouring the four corners of the earth like devils. They're everywhere. Only extreme caution has kept us alive so long. And don't forget she personally set fire to our last place. Burnt it to the ground.'

Tom shifted uncomfortably. Somehow he felt that this was all his fault.

'But she's come alone. Maybe judge for yourself.'

Sir Henry glanced at August. He seemed deeply sceptical.

'It's a risk, old chum. A serious risk.'

August shrugged.

'People do change. Maybe she has.'

Sir Henry shook his head. He clearly did not approve.

'Very well.' Calmly he went over to a drawer and took out a revolver, spinning the chamber to check it was loaded. Then he tucked it into his waistband behind his back. 'Open the door, Tom.'

Obediently Tom did as he was told. There in the doorway stood Lotus. She did not look like a killer. She looked like what she was: a slim, fifteen-year-old girl, dressed in sombre, strangely old-fashioned clothes, wearing something like a penitent expression on her pale, porcelain face.

'I should warn you I am armed,' growled Sir Henry, standing to face her. 'I won't hesitate, young lady.'

'I understand. But you won't need to.'

'I'll be the judge of that.'

He motioned her to come forward. Quietly Lotus closed the door behind her and stepped down the stone steps into the room. Sir Henry stood arms folded before the table, with August a little to one side behind him. It was clear whom he was protecting. Lotus ventured as far as the corner of the carpet then stopped before Sir Henry told her to. Tom had never seen her so nervous. An awkward, intensely hostile silence descended upon the room. Had anyone else been standing there Sir Henry and August would have been models of courtesy and decorum, but now they were behaving as if they were in the presence of a highly poisonous and unpredictable snake . . . Lotus stood alone, unwanted, loathed . . .

'Thank you for agreeing to see me,' she began with an awkward smile. 'I'm very grateful.'

The words hung in the empty air. Not one single sign of encouragement.

'Obviously this is something of a surprise. For myself as well. Believe me, I never imagined I would be doing this given . . . what has happened between us in the past.'

Silence. They waited for her to go on.

'I . . . as Tom explained, I have come because I have a question to ask you. Well, more than one as it happens. That concern Nicholas Zumsteen.'

'Who you are intent on capturing and giving to Don Gervase Askary, to try to win back his favour?' snapped Sir Henry.

'No, not at all—'

'So it's us you're after then?'

Lotus searched their faces for any shred of sympathy. She was shocked to find none.

'You knew Nicholas Zumsteen, didn't you?'

'You know we did,' growled Sir Henry. 'What sort of a question is that?'

'But before. I mean, before he joined you on the island of Tithona. When he was younger.'

'Of course,' said August, watching her carefully. 'Nicholas grew up at Hellkiss Hall in Dragonport.'

'What was he like?'

'Nicholas? He was a crazy sort of a fellow, as perhaps the youngest sons of all great families are entitled to be. The Zumsteens were diamond traders, rich as Croesus and very serious minded, but Nicholas couldn't have been more different. He was

like a butterfly; charming, mad about aeroplanes, animals, anything that took his fancy. And his family spoiled him rotten. I
mean, take all those extraordinary tableaux—'

'Why do you want to know this?' demanded Sir Henry, plainly
not approving of August's rambling history lesson.

'It's important,' she replied, politely but firmly. 'Of course you
have every reason to feel angry, and I am sorry for what has happened . . . but I just want to find out the truth.'

'And what "truth" might that be, young lady?'

'The truth about me!'

The words echoed around the room. Lotus seemed beside herself. August stared at her curiously.

'As I was trying to say, I heard a rumour when I was looking for
Nicholas Zumsteen—'

'A rumour—from whom?'

Sir Henry's glare burned into her. What was the point in concealing any of this?

'From Jos Scatterhorn as it happens—'

'Uncle Jos!' Tom started forwards, his fists clenched. 'What did
you do to him?'

'Nothing! I just asked him some questions. Which if you must
know, was how I discovered that the police were looking for
you, Tom. Then I discovered that you had last been seen up near
those garages. So I went up there and realized what Ern Rainbird
had done. That he had somehow abducted you and carried you
through an opening in the forest to the future. So I followed, because I wanted to find out what had happened to you—*that's all.*'

Tom glared at her murderously. If she had killed Jos, or
Melba . . . if—

'And what else did Jos Scatterhorn tell you, young lady?'

Lotus shook her head defiantly, sensing the atmosphere turn even more hostile.

'All I asked him was why Nicholas Zumsteen never lived at Hellkiss Hall. He told me that something had happened there a long time ago. Something terrible. A secret.'

'What kind of secret?' asked August.

'That long before Nicholas was married, he had a girlfriend called Amy Dix.'

There was silence.

'And that when Amy was sixteen, she had a child that no one knew about.'

'Go on.'

'And that . . . ' Lotus turned crossly towards August who was standing behind the table. 'Why are you making me tell you what you already know? You were there, weren't you?'

August held her gaze, but didn't flinch.

'This has nothing to do with anything,' said Sir Henry firmly. 'Frankly—'

'I can make my own decisions, old friend,' said August, raising his hand. 'Of course this is why you have come. And though you do not deserve to be told the truth, you shall have it.'

'Thank you.' Lotus stared humbly at the floor.

'Yes I was there, at Hellkiss Hall, that evening in September. I was visiting Nicholas's father as it happens. We had some business together, and I was designing him a coat of arms. Just before sunset I looked out of the window of the library and saw Amy pushing the pram out across the lawn. A large white pram, I remember it well. It was a charming scene, the evening sky was clear and the forest below was a blaze of gold. Amy Dix looked very picturesque in a cornflower dress and wide straw hat. She was a pretty thing, dark hair, pale skin, but so young . . . anyway, Amy took out a newspaper from the pram and felt in her pocket for her sunglasses. She didn't have them. I knew what she was thinking. She looked down at the sleeping baby and, seeing that all was well, she ran swiftly back across the grass into the house. She can't have been gone for more than a couple of minutes at the most.'

'And then?'

'Old man Zumsteen called me through into the hall to discuss his crest.'

Lotus stared at August blindly. The silence was so intense even the air seemed to be humming.

'But . . . but you do know what happened next—don't you?'

'Yes, as it happens, I do. In those few brief minutes while Amy Dix was gone, the baby died. The family kept it all very quiet. It was a terrible shame, but it was probably for the best. The Zumsteens never really approved of Amy. Her family were not rich or well-connected, and those things mattered to the Zumsteens. They had much higher ambitions in mind for young Nicholas.' August watched a small moth crawl up his finger. 'Was that the rumour you heard?'

Lotus nodded.

'But you didn't believe it.'

'No.'

August fixed her with his quick grey eyes.

'Well, you're right.'

Sir Henry turned to his old friend in surprise.

'The child didn't die. It was stolen.'

Tom's mouth fell open.

'Stolen? Stolen by whom?'

'A tall man, very tall, and narrow shouldered. He appeared out of the trees dressed in a long khaki coat and cap, looking for all the world like some kind of gardener. In his hand was a bucket. He scooped the precious bundle out of the pram, placed it in the bucket and slipped away into the forest. Never to be seen again.'

That was enough for Lotus. Her mask-like face flashed with anger.

'Are you saying—are you saying that Don Gervase Askary stole his own brother's child?' said Sir Henry, making sure he understood correctly.

'Yes. But more than that,' said August, looking at Lotus steadily. 'Does that answer your question?'

Tom looked from August, to Lotus, and back again.

'Yes it does. Thank you.' She paused. 'That child is me. I am Nicholas Zumsteen's daughter. Don Gervase Askary is . . . '

She never finished her sentence.

'A deeply, *deeply* unpleasant individual,' said Sir Henry, wiping a hand across his brow.

'But if you said you never saw it,' Tom began, 'how—'

'Thanks to these little fellows everything has been revealed,' said August, setting down the jar of rhodi moths on the table. 'It's about a hundred years too late, but there we are. Some acts linger in the air for a long time.'

A strange, uneasy silence descended upon the room.

'But I can't understand why Don Gervase would do that,' said Tom at last.

'I've got a pretty good idea,' August replied, looking steadily at Lotus. 'The rivalry between those two brothers runs very deep indeed. May I?'

CHAPTER 12

THE MISSING CHAPTER

August moved round the table towards his avian library, aware that all the attention had now shifted onto him.

'But before I begin I'm curious to know how you pieced this jigsaw together. What made you suspicious?'

Lotus looked at her audience uneasily. August had been honest with her . . . to gain his trust she should be the same.

'After I met Jos Scatterhorn I found out more about Amy. She had died long ago in a car accident. But her sister was still alive in Dragonport. I went to find her. She didn't really want to talk about it much, but it was clear that Nicholas Zumsteen had abandoned Amy. He obviously blamed her for what happened—he never forgave her. Sounded like he treated her very badly indeed. Perhaps . . . he even suspected who the thief was.'

'That wouldn't surprise me,' murmured August. 'So where did Don Gervase Askary take you?'

'To Bolivia. At first he had a nurse look after me, or rather several, because I was very demanding. And then, when I was about four I think, I was sent to a convent. It was very strict and there were plenty of punishments, but that is where I grew up, with the nuns.'

'And did Don Gervase ever tell you about your mother?'

'Only that she had died when she had me,' Lotus replied, matter of factly. 'He was always away, "on business"—that is what he said. I thought he was a cocoa trader. And on the rare occasions he did visit I never felt that he liked me much. Then one day, when I was eleven, he came up to the convent and we sat in the garden and he revealed to me the great secret. Of what we really were, what *I* really was, and what we must do, which was find the elixir—your elixir, as it turned out.'

'Were you surprised?'

Lotus smiled.

'No, strangely, I wasn't. I had always felt so different. I was excited. And I had had more than enough of the nuns by then, and they had certainly had more than enough of me. So that's when our travels began. I was desperate to impress: prove to him what I could do. Which perhaps made me a little more . . . ruthless than necessary.'

Lotus paused, allowing her words to sink in.

'And did he ever tell you about changing form?'

Lotus took a deep breath. She had never spoken to anyone about this.

'To begin with, I mean the first time—it just happens. But then, after a while, you can learn to control it. Make yourself angry enough, then . . . it's as if invisible steel bars are squeezing you in and the only way out is to explode . . . and I have, many times.'

August watched Lotus incredulously. He had never expected such frankness. What an extraordinary creature she was: a perfectly ordinary-looking girl who could metamorphose into a full-sized beetle at will. And the more he looked at her, the more he could see the rebellious spirit of her real father.

'But why did he do it?' asked Tom. 'Why would you steal your own brother's child?'

'Desperation, probably,' suggested Sir Henry. 'Perhaps he was looking for the elixir and he wasn't getting anywhere. Having a daughter provides a useful cover story, doesn't it? But he couldn't take just any old baby. It had to be someone like him. Someone special. Playing the grieving widower must have opened a few doors.'

Tom said nothing. He remembered this was precisely what had happened the very first morning he had met Lotus and Don Gervase on the steps of the Scatterhorn museum. The story of the widower and his daughter had worked . . .

'And now that you know all this, does it make you feel any different?'

Lotus was aware that they were all watching her across the table. Her smooth, doll-like face was as impassive as a mask.

'Actually, no. I don't feel anything at all. It just confirms everything I had always suspected. But then I'm not like you, am I? I'm different.' She paused. 'Though there is something I can't understand. How did he know about me? I was an accident. A secret.'

August smiled and rubbed his hand across his forehead.

'I'm not sure there can ever be any secrets between identical twins. No matter where they are they always seem to know each other's business.'

Lotus glanced at August awkwardly.

'But Don Gervase Askary and Nicholas Zumsteen aren't identical twins. How can they be, when they look so completely different?'

The words drifted out into the dark corners of the room and were left unanswered. Lotus found August and Sir Henry watching her and the colour began to rise in her cheeks.

'What?'

'So he never told you?'

'Told me what?'

'About where he came from originally? His family—your family?'

'We never talked about those sorts of things,' Lotus replied defensively. 'I assumed they were all dead. And if it was a long story I probably wouldn't have listened because I'm not interested.'

Sir Henry raised his eyebrows.

'In fact it is a surprisingly short story, young lady, given the time that has elapsed.'

'And it explains a good deal of what has happened between those brothers ever since,' added August, seeing that Tom was now looking at him in anticipation. Of course, he knew none of this either. August picked up a jar of rhodi moths fondly. 'Thanks to these little fellows I have been able to make a study of those boys. Some events leave their shadow burning in the air for a very long time. Particularly if they are violent.'

Lotus wasn't sure she wanted to hear any of this. But curiosity got the better of her.

'All right,' she said shortly. 'I'm listening.'

'Your father and his brother were born Dorian and Caleb Rust,' August began.

'Rust?'

August nodded.

'In Dundee, on the east coast of Scotland many years ago. And unlike yours, their mother really did die in childbirth. The twins' father was away at the time, working as a deck-hand on a tea-clipper, plying its way back and forth from Bombay to Liverpool. Unfortunately Mr Rust never met his two sons, as rounding Cape Horn his ship hit a storm. While taking in the sail from the topmost spars a wave as high as a house hit the ship broadside, knocking it flat and carrying Mr Rust away into the foam. He was never seen again. So the twins were placed in the care of the House of Mercy, an orphanage that took in the children of lost sailors. And there they grew up, surviving on whatever charity the good-hearted Taysiders could afford.

'Now the Rust boys' life in the House of Mercy was tough, but it was about to become a good deal tougher when a certain Martin Dander appeared. Dander was a missionary, and by all accounts a man as keen on the strap as scripture. He punished himself as much as he punished everyone else, and would often leave church with a bloodstained shirt, having pummelled his breast so vigorously. Dander already had two children of his own. Hope, a spiteful, ringletted little thing, and Isaac, who was much older. But when Dander saw those two dark, spindly boys dressed in rags, their watery grey eyes melted his iron heart. The missionary was overcome with an urge to save them from the hell fires of damnation into which they would inevitably fall if left to fend for themselves in the back streets of Dundee. I'm sorry, but as you may have noticed, the more I know about Martin Dander the less I find there is to like.

'So the missionary had his way, the House of Mercy was paid, and like it or not the young Rust twins found themselves promptly embarking for New Zealand, making for the South Island and a new mission that Dander had been promised there. But Martin Dander quickly discovered that these two waifs were not all they seemed. Caleb was weak and constantly ill, and there was something very peculiar about Dorian. He was a blank shell almost, with a coldness that was amplified by his refusal to speak. He preferred to communicate through scribbled bits of paper passed to his brother. Compared to golden-haired Hope and tall, strong Isaac, chorister, captain of football, these two sickly boys were unwanted cuckoos, whose arrival Isaac and Hope deeply resented. But Martin Dander ignored this, just as he ignored everything else: the greater the challenge the more determined he was to succeed, and turn these ungrateful paupers into model citizens. So off they went, across the vast Pacific, until they reached the tiny island of Tithona.'

'Tithona?' repeated Lotus, wondering if this was just a coincidence.

'But no further,' added Sir Henry quietly.

Lotus looked up, an expression of intense concentration on her face.

'What do you mean?'

'At that time Tithona was a remote tropical paradise,' continued August, 'formed from a large and dormant volcano that rose out of the centre of the island. It was a popular spot for ships to reprovision, and on arrival Dander found they had a week on their hands before their journey could continue. With nothing much to do in the rickety little town, Dander looked up to the mountain rising out of the jungle, and was told about the mysterious secretive tribe who lived there. The prospect of saving some souls excited him. So borrowing a sailor's pistol for protection, and shoving a stack of Bibles in his bag, Martin Dander dragged his family up the hot, steep road into the jungle, and made camp in the crater. Back in those days the crater was like the garden of Eden. The locals considered it sacred—they didn't hunt in it—and consequently it was filled with rare birds, mammals, insects: all remarkably tame. At the centre stood a maze of iron boulders containing many narrow passageways leading down into the mountain. It was while exploring these one afternoon that, so the story goes, the Rust twins got lost, and never returned. But I'm afraid there is more to it than that: much more.'

'How do you know?'

August glanced across at Lotus.

'As I said, the air is a soup of memories, which was how I could piece the story together. Those twins didn't just get lost by accident. They were fleeing in fear of their lives.'

'Fleeing? Why?'

'Because they stood accused of murder.'

Lotus's jaw fell open in amazement.

'Whose murder?'

'The murder of Hope Dander.'

They waited silently for August to go on. Tom noticed that the first grey streaks of dawn were forming in the sky, but August seemed to show no signs of flagging; quite the opposite.

'After lunch the children descended among the rocks and began to explore. Isaac, being older, braver, and more reckless than the rest, led the way deeper and deeper into the maze until eventually he lost them. When Dorian and Caleb finally caught up, they found Isaac standing on the far side of a narrow chasm that plunged down to the crater floor. Isaac began to taunt the twins, daring them to jump across, then hurling abuse at them when they didn't. They recognized very well the spite in the older boy's eyes. But they would not jump. And then little Hope appeared. She saw her big brother on the far side and he began encouraging her to jump instead. "I'll catch you, show those cowards how to do it, go on, show those cowards, Hope . . ."—you can imagine the rest.

'Hope was smiling now, pleased at the chance to better the two waifs. But Dorian could see she would never make it. "Don't!" he scribbled on a piece of paper, "too far!" And Caleb warned her too. But little Hope would not listen. She trusted her big brother to catch her—why shouldn't she? And she loathed with a passion those thin, pale boys who had spoiled her life. So she leapt . . . but not far enough.

'The scream echoed around the crater, bringing Martin Dander rushing up to the scene. In the blink of an eye Isaac accused Dorian of pushing his sister off the boulder. He knew Dorian would not answer back. Martin Dander stared at the little pink dress at the base of the rock in terror, then lashed out at Dorian, knocking him to the ground. Frantically he descended the rock to where Hope lay, but it was futile. His daughter was dead, her neck broken. The missionary was consumed with grief, rage, and his eyes burned with zealous determination to teach that unlikeable, silent boy a lesson he would never forget.

'Dander marched Dorian back to the camp by his ear. He tied him to a tree, like a goat set out for a tiger. The jungle fell silent. Slowly Dander took off his coat and rolled up his sleeves. Then he cut himself a length of cane.

'"Please," Dorian whispered. "It wasn't me."

'"Deciding to speak when it suits you, boy?"

'"It wasn't me. I didn't do it. I didn't."

'Dorian watched Dander take off his pistol and holster and lay it carefully on his coat. He looked at Caleb imploringly, but his brother was paralysed by fear. He daren't come between the monster and his meat. Neither did Isaac. They stood in silence and watched as the blows began to rain down, and continued on and on and on, until the sun dipped behind the trees. At last Martin Dander threw his stick down into the dust, split and bloody.

'"You will never, ever, lie to me again, boy," he foamed, his face and shirt all spattered red. Picking up his gun, he staggered into the jungle. Isaac followed. Caleb could barely look at his brother. His back and legs and arms and neck were nothing but a grisly pattern of bloody red stripes and torn flesh. But somehow Dorian Rust was still alive, just, and burning with a silent and all consuming hatred: and an iron determination to escape. Caleb must have felt it too. The next morning, the Rust twins' tent was empty.'

A thick silence filled the room. The grey dawn light was creeping in between the shutters.

'Well, you can imagine what happened next. Martin Dander was now faced with a double tragedy. He may have believed Dorian had killed his precious daughter, but he did not want two more deaths on his conscience. From dawn to dusk he searched the iron boulders, calling the boys' names. Not surprisingly, they didn't answer. After a couple of days he went down to the town and returned with a dozen policemen. They searched too. But the locals took umbrage at all these strangers trampling over their precious crater. To them the white man had awoken bad spirits which had taken the twins. So the policemen left and refused to come back. And after ten days Martin Dander was forced to abandon his search. His boat was leaving. He buried little Hope in a lead casket, packed up with Isaac and left, never to be seen again.'

There was silence for a moment. Tom glanced across at Lotus to see that she was genuinely shocked.

'So Don Gervase really never told you any of this?'

Lotus shook her head.

'I didn't know anything about it. I'd be surprised if anyone does, apart from his brother. It's rather shameful, isn't it?'

'Shameful?'

'To be beaten like that. Shows weakness.'

'I'm not sure there's much the boy could have done about it, young lady,' murmured Sir Henry, somewhat surprised at her re-action. 'Martin Dander was a monster.'

'And is that why he hates people so much?' asked Tom.

'Who knows?' shrugged August. 'He may have changed his identity but he certainly still bears the physical scars. That strange line bisecting his forehead, that curious way of stand-ing, as if on tiptoes . . . Dander probably whipped the skin off his feet. He's carried it all with him. And he's probably nev-er forgiven his brother for standing by and letting it happen, either.'

'I can't see how you could ever forget,' mused Sir Henry. 'If you're looking for the speck of grit that has started this whole thing off I suspect that's it.'

Lotus sat in sullen silence. So many things were at last starting to make sense.

Tom said:

'And what happened next?'

'Well, the twins took refuge inside the mountain, where they were infected by that extraordinary Kafka beetle, and from there they found their way down into Scarazand, just as you did,' continued August. 'And once there, one presumes they grew up, bound together by their difference in that strange, alien world.' He looked up at Lotus. 'Perhaps you know the rest?'

She shrugged.

'Only what he told me, which is not very much. They began as lowly workers, doing mundane, boring things . . . Don Gervase always said that his life only really began when he heard that there was an elixir of life out there somewhere. As soon as he realized that, he could think of nothing else. It became his obsession.'

'Why?'

'It's obvious, isn't it? He didn't want to stay as some lowly worker all his life. He wanted power. He wanted to control Scarazand and make it the greatest insect colony there has ever been. And he realized that the only way he could ever do that was to give the insects what they craved more than anything else: more life—because they had so little of it. So finding your elixir was the key.

'And did he ever talk about his brother?'

Lotus shook her head.

'Not really. I assumed that he didn't care much about the great project, and that he was a bit of a waster. But I suppose that's not true, is it?'

'I suspect it is, partly,' smiled August. 'Caleb probably didn't care very much. I suspect Dorian's single-mindedness was pretty suffocating. And maybe as they grew up Caleb did feel that weight of guilt hanging over him, that perhaps he should have done more to try to save his brother. Maybe Dorian wouldn't let him forget—those scars must have been a constant reminder. And perhaps Caleb was uncomfortable that Dorian, who had always been the weaker of the two, the twin who had refused to speak, had suddenly found a purpose in his life that he hadn't. Whatever the reasons, once he'd grown up he needed to find a new identity far away from Scarazand. Which was how he chanced upon a young diamond prospector camping beside his aeroplane in the Namibian desert.'

'Nicholas Zumsteen?'

'Exactly. Nicholas Zumsteen. Adventurous, handsome, rich, carefree Nicholas Zumsteen. He was everything Caleb wanted to become. So, he did.'

'He did?'

'Remember the beetle that infected those brothers was very special indeed. It was a Kafka beetle, the rarest beetle in the world. Probably only half a dozen of them ever existed, and they are now almost certainly extinct. The Kafka beetle is a parasite with a unique ability: not only can it change form to get inside its host and become that person, it can also metamorphose back into a beetle again in an instant: as we have just heard.'

August glanced at Lotus and she nodded. Tom knew this, of course, but he still found it almost unbelievable.

'And did Dorian ever find out about his brother's new identity?'

'Almost certainly. And by then he had one, too. The thin, disfigured, limping boy had become a cocoa planter from Peru,

Don Gervase Askary. With a daughter, and my elixir, which presumably had the desired effect?'

Lotus nodded.

'We returned to Scarazand for the great gathering, the Contagion, and Don Gervase presented what he had found. A single blue bottle from your workshop—empty, but with the stopper still on it, trapping that precious gas inside.' She smiled briefly at the memory. 'And yes, the Chamber were completely astonished. They were the council of old men who had controlled human matters in Scarazand for centuries. They never really expected us to find it. They dismissed the whole search as a joke. But that was their downfall. A few days later there was a bloody revolution and Scarazand was ours.'

'And did you ever see Nicholas Zumsteen?'

Lotus shook her head.

'Apparently he was there at the Contagion. And I heard he met Don Gervase later that night in secret. Whatever was said between them who knows, but at the end of it Zumsteen escaped out of the vent hole. Which was not very clever, as that was absolutely forbidden and punishable by death. He knew that. So in a way he signed his own death warrant.'

'Perhaps, my dear, he had no choice,' murmured Sir Henry, stroking his moustache. 'Maybe it was the only exit left open to him. Nicholas must have sniffed what was coming. There's only ever room on the throne for one, isn't there?'

'So why then hasn't he destroyed Scarazand?' asked Lotus. 'That is what I can't understand. If he knows where the single weakest point is, why hasn't he done something about it?'

There was silence as a bell rang somewhere above. August

turned back to Lotus. Beams of low dawn sunlight were slicing through the room now, lighting up his shock of white hair like a halo.

'That is a very good question. Until this evening I would have been unable to answer it. As I said, Nicholas always seemed to me a happy-go-lucky sort of chap, blown by whatever fancy took him. Certainly without that single-minded craziness of his brother. But now it seems that appearances can be deceptive.'

They waited in silence for August to go on.

'Well?' prompted Lotus.

'Nick Zumsteen does not want to destroy Scarazand, because he intends to take it over,' said Sir Henry. 'He's busy planning a little revolution of his own.'

'What?' spluttered Lotus. 'I mean, how do you know?'

'He told me. We had lunch at my club in London. The Travellers Club. He was rather keen that August and I should get involved.'

'But how is he going to do it?'

August turned to Tom.

'Do you remember the last time you met him?'

Tom thought back to that moonlit platform high above the crater on Tithona. That tall, dark-haired, nervous man, sitting there in the branches, watching him curiously.

'Yes.'

'And you will remember then, those two long bags he carefully stowed away in his rucksack?'

'What are you talking about?' demanded Lotus.

'Those white, pearly things?'

'Exactly. All the time Nicholas Zumsteen was my assistant on Tithona he was secretly collecting them. It must have taken him the best part of two years. After tropical storms he would go down to the beach and find them washed up in the flotsam—they'd probably floated up from deep trenches around there. Had I known I would have warned him off and he probably guessed as much, which is why he was so cagey. Hid them in a hole in a tree, I believe.'

'But what were they?' asked Tom. 'Some sort of egg?'

'Yes. The egg of a particular creature. A gorogona.'

'Gorogona?' repeated Lotus, who had never heard the word.

'Gorogon-arh,' corrected one of the dusty shoebills, stepping forward off the shelf. 'The a is long.'

'Right,' she said, somewhat surprised by the croaking bird. 'You know, I suppose?'

'Of course. Gorogona.' It cleared its throat. 'Gorogona is the name given to the last of the great snake-like insects to roam the earth several million years ago. Presumed extinct, they are now worshipped as gods on certain Pacific islands, where they have been attributed certain magical powers such as swallowing mountains, breathing fire, creating whirlpools—'

'Ha!' Lotus snorted dismissively. 'Well that sounds highly likely. You are obviously an expert.'

The shoebill did not seem very pleased.

'Actually gorogonas *are* rather unique,' said August. 'Not only can they spit poison, which ignites, but slice one in half and two spring up in its place, quickly growing to the size of the original. Imagine a giant fire-breathing worm that can multiply ad infinitum and you get the picture.'

Tom thought back to those bags of pearls, and then he remembered this was precisely what Don Gervase had interrogated him about before he had left him for dead in the museum. Maybe he also knew exactly what these gorogonas were . . . but obviously he had never told Lotus. She sat in the corner sulkily, unable to pretend she wasn't irritated by any of this.

'And I suppose Nicholas Zumsteen is incubating those eggs somewhere?'

Sir Henry nodded.

'Indeed he is. Actually August and I have been trying to catch up with Nicholas for some time now, and so has his brother. Last year Askary almost managed it, trapping him in a ship in Siberia. The vessel had been attacked by some sort of giant centipede and there was not a soul left alive on board. Amazingly Nicholas escaped, and we followed his trail up into the forest. After several days tracking we arrived at a hut on the edge of a wide valley. There was no one there, but we had a good nose about anyway. That's when we realized he was breeding something . . . there were these strange balls of ice all over the place. But we didn't know exactly what was inside them until Nicholas told me himself.'

'And I suppose he also told you when they are going to hatch?'

Sir Henry smiled.

'He's a very odd fish, your father. Plays his cards extremely close to his chest. But my guess is that it will be soon. Very soon. He's planning "an insect Waterloo", so he called it. "A battle to decide the future of all things."'

'Up in that valley?'

'Possibly. August recalled seeing an old volcano on the far side. Perhaps he's going to use that to forge some entrance down into Scarazand.'

Tom thought back to Betilda Marchmont's painting. Was this what she had seen? He was finding it increasingly hard to remain calm about any of this.

'Now whether Nicholas Zumsteen wants to return Scarazand to that peaceful, harmless place it once was, or use for his own ends, I don't know. But he was very keen to tell me how perfectly odious his brother was, and how we should all come and help overthrow him. He is quite convinced his gorgonas are going to win, and frankly I'm inclined to believe him. If each and every snake can divide ad infinitum . . . well—it doesn't bear thinking about. The only snag is, once the gorgonas hatch Nicholas hasn't a cat in hell's chance of controlling them. But he didn't seem too bothered about that. He laughed out loud in fact. Found the idea hilarious.'

There was silence for a moment. Tom began to wonder if Nicholas Zumsteen *was* actually quite as crazy as his twin, despite appearances to the contrary. Sir Henry yawned loudly and looked at his watch. It was now almost six o'clock in the morning. He leaned back in his chair and threw his arms behind his head.

'So as you can see, this is all shaping up into a family spat of colossal proportions, and you know what I say? Leave them to it. Sooner or later the gorgonas will hatch, and then presumably Nicholas will attempt to invade Scarazand. Don Gervase will probably lead his armies out to meet them, and there will be an almighty punch up. A will destroy B, or vice versa—either way someone will end up in control of the Queen, and that will be that. Does it really matter who wins?'

'It matters to me,' muttered Lotus. 'Don't think I'm going to just stand by and let Don Gervase succeed. Not now.'

'And it matters to me too,' added Tom quietly. 'A lot.'

Sir Henry glanced at the boy who was looking a little sheepish.

'Ah. Well yes, of course, I had clean forgotten about that.' Sir Henry stole a glance at August. 'That is a problem, isn't it?'

Lotus peered through the shafts of light, trying to read Tom's face, half-hidden in shadow.

'Perhaps even more reason not to get involved. How about we leave it till the morning then?'

'It is the morning,' August replied.

'You know what I mean. It's been a very, very long day.'

CHAPTER 13

ECHOES AND EGGS

It was late afternoon when Tom woke again. He had curled up under a blanket on the chaise longue in Sir Henry's room, and despite everything that had passed the night before he had slept deeply and well. Pulling himself groggily to his feet, he stretched.

'Finally you're awake.'

Tom squinted past the dazzling beam of white light pouring in through the window. There was Lotus sitting curled up in the deepest patch of shadow like a spider.

'I'm amazed how you can sleep when all this is going on.'

Tom yawned.

'I'm very tired. I've been working as a slave in a shellac factory, remember?'

Lotus continued watching him closely. 'I didn't know you were a convert. Don Gervase kept that very quiet.'

Tom pushed the tangled mess of hair out of his eyes. So she had guessed. He could hardly deny it, and there was no point pretending.

'Can he control you with the mesmerion?'

Tom stared out of the window and sighed.

'August gave me a grub to eat so my conversion was not complete. It stopped before . . . you know. So he probably can't kill me. And I am getting better at ignoring him. But yes, in answer to your question, Don Gervase can control me—a bit.'

A ghost of a smile crossed Lotus's lips. This obviously made a great deal of sense to her.

'And that's why you want to destroy Scarazand: to get rid of it—that part of you that belongs to him, or Zumsteen, or whoever has the mesmerion. Remove the itch you cannot scratch. I understand now.'

Tom sighed. It occurred to him that Lotus had been giving this a great deal of thought.

'Isn't it the same with you?'

Lotus shook her head.

'Like August said, Kafka beetles are unique—they answer to no one. I can't even hear the Queen. Isn't that odd? Neither can Don Gervase—nor Nicholas Zumsteen I imagine.'

'Oh.'

Lotus's relentless unblinking gaze was becoming uncomfortable.

'So, Tom, I have decided that I want to help you. I want to help you find that vent hole and I want to help you destroy Scarazand, because I can't see the point of it either. Not any more.'

Tom was somewhat thrown by this sudden change of heart.

'But what about your father?'

'I don't need another father. Especially if he's anything like my old one—which it sounds like he might be. Supposing I did join Zumsteen in this great battle, and we won—what then? Sir Henry's right, there's only ever room on the throne for one.

Eventually I'd just get in his way. So the best thing to do is get rid of the lot of them, and do the world a favour.' Lotus's pale face glowed like a moon in the shadows. She seemed to be serious. 'Are you hungry?' she said, suddenly changing the subject.

Tom had to admit he was, a little.

'I'm famished. I have been waiting ages for you to get up. Sir Henry told me the monks wouldn't take kindly to a girl wandering around their monastery—particularly one who had just beaten up one of their brothers—so I thought for the first time in my life I might try to do as I am told. It's been very difficult.' With a grin she uncurled herself from the chair and strode over to the door. 'Shall we?'

With an unmistakable spring in her step Lotus led the way down the stone steps to the small cloister below. Several monks stopped and stared at them as they passed. Lotus ignored them all and boldly knocked on August's door. As they waited more monks gathered to watch the slim girl and lanky boy. They did not look particularly pleased to see them. At last the hasp rammed open and the door creaked and there stood Sir Henry on the threshold.

'Good morning. Or should I say, good afternoon.'

Tom smiled awkwardly.

'Breakfast, lunch or tea?'

'Anything, please.'

They went in to find August lolling on the balcony under a canvas awning. He was wearing a battered straw hat and on the table before him spread a large meal waiting to be eaten.

'Aha, the kraken has awakened,' he twinkled. 'How are you feeling?'

'Fine.'

'Please—tuck in.'

'Thank you.'

Lotus flashed her sweetest smile, and sat down opposite Tom. In silence they began to devour the plates of bread and honey and figs and yogurt set out before them. Tom noticed several shoebills standing patiently in the doorway.

'We've been wrestling with your problems and not getting very far I'm afraid,' said Sir Henry, pulling up a chair to join them. He stared out at the carpet of trees far below. 'I've been half-wondering whether we shouldn't just try flying into Scarazand like we did before. Find an entrance, then construct some sort of Trojan horse in the shape of an insect. August could knock one up. Then fill it full of dynamite, fly it inside, and . . . '

Lotus stifled a discreet smile.

'No?'

She shook her head.

'Ever since you flew your aeroplane into the cave everything has changed. Scarazand is a fortress now. There are no visitors, no tourists—only workers going in and out. Tens of thousands of holes have been stopped up—and those that haven't are now all heavily guarded. No stranger will ever be able to find their way in again: by accident—or otherwise.'

'You seem very certain about that.'

'I am,' she said, picking up a fig between her long white fingers and peeling it methodically. 'It was my job to see that it happened. And it did. I was quite ruthless. Getting inside Scarazand is now impossible.'

Sir Henry rolled a ball of bread between his fingers and flicked it over the balcony restlessly.

'Hmm. Well I did have a suspicion you might say something like that. That was my contribution. I'm stumped. Anyone got any bright ideas? Tom?'

'Only that the Don Gervase in the asylum was right. The best way has got to be to find that vent hole. Hidden in a tree, close to a tumbledown shack—'

'Somewhere on the face of the earth,' snarled Sir Henry, spotting a fly on the table. Lining up another ball of dough he flicked it straight at it, knocking it backwards. 'Trouble is, we've already spent ten years looking for that blasted hole.'

'And even if we find it, it will take something bigger than a bomb to blow it up,' August sighed. 'With all the consequences of that. Yes those words have begun to haunt me too.'

Lotus had sliced the fig into small regular sections. She popped one segment into her mouth and chewed it carefully, like a mouse.

'Actually I too have been giving this a great deal of thought.'

She swallowed, took a small sip of water, then began chewing the next segment. It occurred to Tom that he had never seen Lotus Askary eat before. It was clearly not something she did very often.

'As I have just been telling Tom, I have no interest in helping Nicholas Zumsteen, or Don Gervase Askary for that matter. Not any more. So I will help you find the vent hole.'

'That's very good of you, young lady,' smiled August, acidly. 'And how might you do that?'

Lotus took another sip of water.

'I have an idea. It's a very good idea. But it needs . . . something. Something to tempt Don Gervase Askary out of his lair.' They sat waiting, watching her eat very precisely. 'When you met Nicholas Zumsteen did he happen to tell you where he was going afterwards?'

'Possibly.'

'In other words, yes. May I ask where?'

Sir Henry hesitated. Even now there was something about the girl that did not inspire trust.

'Well I don't suppose it matters. He's going to be at a party in Mexico tomorrow night.'

'Whose party?'

'His name is Golding Golding. An American. He has made his fortune as an arms dealer, and he is always looking to create new and peculiar weapons from the insect world. Nicholas discovered his interest a while ago and he has become quite pally with him. A natural ally perhaps—though I wouldn't trust Golding Golding further than I can throw him. Which is not very far, as he is built like a Buddha.'

Lotus frowned.

'Golding Golding?'

'That's right. You've heard of him, then?'

'Of course. And you're right, he is entirely untrustworthy. He pretends to collect art, but in fact he has been stealing whatever he can from Scarazand for a long time. We know all about Golding Golding and his little schemes.'

Sir Henry and August eyed her carefully.

'I mean, not that I care. Why should I?' Lotus blustered, a little embarrassed. 'Did he tell you who else was going?'

'Quite a lot of strange and colourful people apparently,' Sir Henry replied, standing up and rummaging about in his jacket that was hanging over the chair. 'Socialites, scientists, villains . . . Nicholas told me Golding Golding had invited "anyone with an interest in plundering the spoils of Scarazand". His words, not mine. Nicholas was as cagey as ever, but I had a definite sense he was going to tell them all about those gorogonas he's breeding and the great battle to come. Why, I don't know. But he was very keen for August and me to show our faces.'

Sir Henry slipped a heavy cream card into Tom's hands. The writing was large and gold and embellished with many confusing squirls. It was addressed to August and Sir Henry.

Mr Golding Golding is having an important birthday.
He would very much like you to come and celebrate it with him.
It will be extraordinary. Dress accordingly.
RSVP etc etc.
Hacienda Favorita, Xilitla, San Luis, Potosi, Mexico.

'August and I were just debating whether one of us should go. Invitations from Golding Golding are rarer than hen's teeth, and I wouldn't mind seeing what he's got squirrelled away out there. It's a very strange set up by all accounts. Artistic, you know.'

'May I?'

Tom passed the card to Lotus and she examined it hungrily. Then a strange smile crossed her lips.

'But this is it.'

'This is what?' asked August.

Lotus flipped over the invitation. Her smile was broadening by the moment.

'Don Gervase Askary will be at this party.'

'He will?'

'He has spies watching Golding Golding very closely. He will know the kind of people who have been invited. He might even know about Zumsteen and his lecture. He will be there, I guarantee it: and he will try to capture and kill as many undesirables as possible. Including you.'

Sir Henry raised his eyebrows quizzically.

'You seem very certain about this.'

'I used to watch Golding Golding myself,' she said simply. 'It was one of my many chores. I knew quite a lot about him as a matter of fact. But I never saw an invitation like this. You're right, this is a rare opportunity. I guarantee Don Gervase will not let it pass.'

There was an uncomfortable silence for a moment. Lotus's complete confidence in her own ideas was a little disconcerting. August said:

'But, my dear, even if you're correct, and Askary does plan to turn up with his henchmen in tow, what could he possibly hope to do? Everyone would see him coming a mile away. We certainly would.'

'Not necessarily.'

'What do you mean?'

Lotus smiled oddly. She put the card back down on the table and placed her knife neatly in the centre of her plate. She had spent most of the night thinking about how this little secret fitted into the scheme of things, and now she was convinced she knew. It was time to reveal it.

'It's not necessarily him that you would see. You would see Tom Scatterhorn. Obviously not this Tom Scatterhorn. I mean, his echo.'

'Tom's echo?'

'Yes. Tom's echo.' Her large green eyes slid across to him. 'Because you do have an echo, Tom—a real one.'

No one spoke. Only the cicadas, far below.

'You were bitten by an insect when you first arrived at the asylum, weren't you?'

Tom nodded.

'I knew it.' A cruel, clever smile spread across Lotus's face. 'Let me tell you what has happened, and correct me if I'm wrong— but I won't be, because I spent long enough with Don Gervase Askary to know how he thinks. It's like this. Don Gervase is a powerful, lonely leader: he trusts no one. He is convinced that one day Nicholas Zumsteen is going to try to take Scarazand away from him, and he knows that he has been collecting gorogonas to do just that. He is terrified of these creatures—but what can he do? Two things. He sends legions of spies out into the future, hoping they will come back and warn him what is going to happen. And in the meantime he makes a few investigations himself. He is embarrassed about these, as they show him up as paranoid and weak—so he tries to keep them secret: I know this because he tried to keep them secret from me. But somewhere along the way he discovers that you, Tom, have a crucial part to play in his future. Am I right?'

Tom nodded: he noted that for all Lotus's breezy confidence, she did not know what this role was.

'Don Gervase finds this immensely irritating. Because he knows that as a half convert, you cannot be completely controlled, or even relied upon. Perhaps you even dared to tell him so. So what should he do? He could ignore the warning, but that would be reckless. He could kill you, but then you will never play any part in his future—so that's no good either. So instead, he decides to make a secret copy, a forgotten echo, that he can completely control then hide away, ready to be useful. It's very cautious, a little peculiar, but this is how Don Gervase Askary operates. He never leaves anything to chance.'

August and Sir Henry sat in silence for a moment, allowing Lotus's words to sink in.

'But why didn't he kill Tom once he had made the copy?' asked August.

'He couldn't. Killing an original destroys the echo: they are linked together. No one understands why, but it's a fact.'

Sir Henry ran a hand across his brow, wondering whether to believe a word of this.

'So what you are saying, young lady, is that hidden away somewhere deep inside Scarazand is Tom's echo. And Don Gervase is going to bring him along to Golding Golding's party as some sort of bait?'

Lotus nodded.

'I'm sure of it. That's exactly what he'd do.'

'But if you and Tom go, instead of us, then you can somehow make a swap with the echo,' said August, seeing at once where this was leading.

'Exactly.'

'A swap?' Sir Henry looked mystified. 'Why?'

Lotus continued.

'Because by playing the part of his echo, Tom would be taken down into the very heart of Scarazand unopposed, and then . . . ' she paused for effect.

'I could climb up that chimney . . . and out of the vent hole.'

There was silence. Somehow Tom had said the words before he really understood them.

'That was precisely my idea,' nodded Lotus, a trifle annoyed that she had been beaten to the punch line of her brilliant plan.

'You could climb *up* the chimney, and *out* of the vent hole.' August repeated the phrase slowly. 'And obviously then discover exactly where it is. But that is a small stroke of genius.'

'Unless you get found out. Or lose your footing. And even if you manage it what happens when you find yourself alone in the middle of some forest surrounded by lord knows what. Excellent!' Sir Henry snorted. This was quite plainly one of the maddest ideas he had ever heard. 'How on earth is Tom going to climb up that chimney?'

'I don't know, but Zumsteen managed it,' shrugged Lotus defensively. 'He got in from one of the attics up in the palace. It can't have been that far to climb.'

'Which attic, precisely?'

'I was told it was right above Don Gervase's bedroom.'

Sir Henry pressed his fingers to the bridge of his long aquiline nose and shook his head.

'This sounds like a wild, wild fantasy. I'm amazed that you are even considering it, August.'

'But it *is* a plan, that much can be said for it,' answered his friend. 'By impersonating the echo Tom gains immediate access to Scarazand, which as Miss Askary says is now otherwise impossible. And by climbing up the chimney, at one stroke he eliminates the hardest part—namely, having to find the blinking vent hole—which you and I didn't manage in ten years. And we don't have another ten years. I'm not sure we even have another ten days. But yes, I agree, this scheme is not without its hazards.'

Sir Henry laughed bitterly.

'Not without its hazards. I like that. Very good.'

There was an awkward silence. Tom thought back to that high chimney and that tiny speck of light hovering like a star. Was it really possible to climb up there? Maybe it was . . .

August cut himself a thin slice of bread and cheese and chewed it thoughtfully.

'Well, Tom, no one can ask you to do any of this, and no one can do it but you. This is your call.'

Tom was sitting quite still, trying to ignore his galloping heart. Beyond the balcony the shadows in the valley were lengthening, the pine forest burning brown and gold.

'I think I have to do it.'

'You're quite certain about that?'

Tom turned to August's ancient, craggy face. His eyes were blacker than ever.

'How else can it end?'

'It can end by Nicholas Zumsteen and those gorogonas winning the battle,' growled Sir Henry.

'But that might not happen,' murmured Tom. 'You said yourself he can't control them . . . and even if he does—what then? I will always be a slave to whoever controls the Queen. They will always own me. And I can't help thinking that whoever that is will always want to do bad things. Not to me, exactly, but, just because they can. It's so powerful . . . if you can do anything . . . ' Tom sighed in frustration. He couldn't find the words to express what he felt. 'And this is not just about me any more. I've seen what he's doing to the world out there, I've seen what it's like. I have to do this. I want to do it.'

Sir Henry's eyes narrowed.

'Those are quite different things, you know. Think, Tom: *think*— even if you do succeed in getting down into Scarazand, sooner or later Askary's bound to find out that you are not an echo. Maybe he even knows already. There won't be a way back if—'

'I don't care!'

Sir Henry was stunned by the boy's anger.

'I don't care any more! It's fine, all right? Just fine. I know the risk. I'll take it. Just leave me alone.'

Tom's outburst rang out across the valley. They sat in awkward silence as a bell tolled somewhere up above. Tom stared out at the small slither of sea in the distance, biting his lip. His eyes were full of tears.

It was almost evening when they met up again. Tom found the atmosphere in August's room too suffocating to stay sitting down, and making his excuses he wandered off into the monastery. He paced down dark cloisters, stared into bubbling fountains and watched the brothers going about their quiet, ordered lives, tending vegetables, pressing olives, praying in the chapel . . . August was right: this was a good place. Tom could see why fugitives from Scarazand would seek sanctuary up here: they joined the Legion, and suddenly that weird insect world and all its dangers seemed to melt away, they would never have to confront them again . . . could he ever do that? Even now, despite his outburst, Tom wasn't completely sure. He couldn't pretend that he wasn't nervous about this plan, and everything that went with it . . . the chances of being found out, the sila scream . . . he didn't know if he was doing the right thing at all. But even up here Don Gervase Askary could control him: that voice in his head would always be there, always. And then there was everyone else who was depending on him. Wasn't he the only one who could finish this?

'Thought we'd lost you.'

Tom looked up from his daydreams to find Sir Henry sitting next to him in the cloister.

'How are you feeling, old chap?'

His hawk-like eyes watched him keenly.

'Fine. The same, in case you're wondering. I still want to do it.'

'Thought you'd say that. Stubbornness is a Scatterhorn trait.' Sir Henry grinned, then patted him on the back. 'I won't make any more attempts to persuade you otherwise. But I would like you to take this.'

Tom looked down at the small grey stone shaped like a cone in his palm.

'What is it?'

'Think of it as a little beacon. When you crawl out of that chimney and find yourself in some forest in the middle of nowhere, this will help us find you.' Tom ran his finger over the stone's rough surface. It didn't look like much. 'Don't ask me how it works. August found it in a junkshop somewhere—he thinks it used to belong to a shaman. I always take it with me wherever I go. Curiously accurate little instrument. But your need is far greater than mine.'

Tom smiled awkwardly.

'Thanks.'

'No problem.'

They sat side by side, watching the fountain for a moment.

'Well, everything's set. Miss Askary has persuaded August to summon the transport, and she has come up with rather a novel plan of how to slip into Golding Golding's party incognito.'

'Oh?'

'You will go via somewhere called Marchmont Castle. It's some draughty old place in Scotland. Bit of a wreck apparently. Once the home of an artist—'

'Marchmont Castle?'

Sir Henry saw Tom's expression and grinned knowingly.

'Yes, that's precisely what I thought. Highly unlikely. You've heard of it, then?'

'Erm . . . vaguely.'

'The girl is convinced there is a direct connection between it and Golding Golding's hideaway. She is absolutely insistent in fact—but refuses to say more. I suspect there is some business there we don't know about. But if Askary is going to be at the party, he will undoubtedly be watching every arrival very closely.

And as the Villa Favorita is ten miles out into the jungle with only one road up to it, I suppose it makes sense to use this most unlikely sounding back door.'

Tom sat in silence, watching the bubbling water. Actually, he was not as surprised by this as he might have been. He knew that Lotus and Don Gervase had used such secret connections before. After everything he had heard about some great final battle, and those gorogonas, it sounded very much as if Betilda Marchmont had travelled herself . . .

'What does August think?'

'You know August—he hasn't the first idea of the danger. What interests him is the idea that the earth contains webs of secret connections that he knows nothing about. According to his encyclopaedia that castle is riddled with hidden passages and hidey holes.'

Sir Henry paused.

'But—and I know you do not want reminding—it will be very dangerous, Tom, and I don't mean just climbing up the vent hole: I mean travelling with Lotus Askary. She may look quite respectable but she's about as subtle as a sledgehammer. I suspect you will have to pour a lot of oil on troubled waters, old chum—smooth the way, if you know what I mean.'

Tom nodded: unfortunately he did know exactly what Sir Henry meant.

'And you will have to start by convincing your taxi man. He's not exactly enthusiastic about his new passenger.'

'The eagle?'

'Precisely,' Sir Henry smiled. 'He won't listen to reason, and you seem to have far more influence over him than anyone else.'

'Don't come the raw prawn with me, mate!'

It was evening, and the sun was just beginning to touch the edge of the sea in the distance. At one end of August's balcony perched the motley raptor, its wings hanging down the rock face.

'I know what you are thinking,' whispered Tom. 'And I agree with you—a bit. Well, more than a bit. But she's going to help me. I can't think of another way.'

'*But she's the freaky beetle bloke's daughter,*' it hissed, peering at Lotus hovering in the background. 'And not just any old beetle— she almost tore me blasted beak off.'

'I know. You don't have to say yes. It might just be useful, that's all.'

The eagle stared at Lotus in utter bewilderment.

'You're putting me in a position here, make no mistake. Can't you go on your own?'

Tom shrugged helplessly.

'Sorry.'

'GF, GF,' it muttered to itself. 'There is only one reason I'm even considerin' doing this, just one, and I'm lookin' at him.' The bird bent its great shaggy head forward conspiratorially. 'You and me have got to stick together, chum. I mean it. Specially now,' it hissed. 'Things are dangerous enough for us out there without—' The eagle glanced round at Lotus who was waiting expectantly.

'So that's a yes, then?'

The raptor muttered strange curses to itself.

'Note I'm narked—with a capital N.'

Tom looked back at Lotus and nodded briefly. She broke out

into a wide grin and came forward, smiling as charmingly as she could.

'Thank you very much. It's very good of you to—'

'This has nothing to do with you, missy. If I had my way, why you'd—'

'Please.' Tom held up his hand. 'Please.'

'All right,' snarled the bird. 'But any metamorphizing or other fancy malarkey and I'll have you off quicker than a . . . than a . . . don't even contemplate it.'

'I won't.'

The eagle grunted and, with an ungainly turn, swung its back round to face them.

'Well, what you waitin' for?'

Tom clambered up between the bird's great wings, and Lotus followed. Awkwardly they sat, one behind the other.

'Nah nah nah. If you want to stay on, missy, you's going to have to put your arms around his waist—nice and cosy. Understand?'

Tom felt very uneasy as Lotus grabbed him, and he in turn threw his arms around the bird's neck.

'That's the ticket,' it rasped, 'pretend we're like one big happy family.'

Sir Henry and August stepped through the doors to watch them depart.

'Good luck!' shouted Sir Henry.

Lotus smiled and waved back.

'Bye, Tom. Pecker up and all that.'

Tom tried to smile but found it impossible. Was this a very bad idea? It was the only idea . . .

'Hold on,' grunted the great bird, and with one ungainly hop it dropped off the balcony and out of sight.

Sir Henry and August moved forward and watched the great brown shape swoop down over the canopy and accelerate towards the hills beyond.

'Poor old Tom,' murmured August. 'You know what he's thinking, don't you?'

Sir Henry nodded.

'That he has to sacrifice himself. That he doesn't have a choice. And that somehow it's the noble thing to do. He does seem very determined to die.'

'Very.'

They watched the bird as it swept up over the crest of the ridge, its wide wings burning in the low sun.

'You don't think they stand much chance, do you?'

Sir Henry grimaced.

'Frankly, no. But there's no persuading them. Two more pig-headed young people you could never hope to meet.'

August sighed.

'Well, perhaps you're right. But such blind determination might buy us a little time, if nothing else.'

Sir Henry turned to his old friend and saw a mischievous glimmer in his eye.

'A little time? For what, exactly?'

August's eyes sparkled.

'Something the boy said earlier. It's given me a bit of an idea.'

CHAPTER 14

WING AND PRAYER

Tom took one last look at the monastery then felt a great rush of air as the eagle lifted over the ridge and swept down into the next valley. Keeping low, it dipped down over the shadowed green flanks and accelerated towards the sunlit trees ahead.

'This is one of my favourite places, kiddo. There are always loads of openings up here—laid out like junctions in a road.'

Swooping down they began weaving through the great oak trees shining gold in the last rays of sunlight.

'I've got a lot better at this,' it continued. 'Them little swallows taught me pretty much everything they know. There's one.' The eagle nodded towards a ray of light glinting off a rock. 'Did you see that?'

Tom glanced sideways, but already it had gone.

'How do you know where they lead to?'

'You can usually get a glimpse: but sometimes not. Scotland, back in your own time, you say?'

'If possible.'

'Okey-dokey.' The eagle flew on towards a mighty cedar standing slightly on its own. 'That's strange,' it murmured, peering at the sunbeams bursting through the crown.

'What's he saying?' asked Lotus.

The raptor eyed the tree mistrustfully.

'Do you get a sense something's watching us?'

Tom squinted into the zigzag patterns of light and shadow bouncing all around.

'I can't see anything.'

'Hmm.' The bird dipped even lower, its wings barely beating above the ground. 'Well neither can I, but I tell you, kiddo, we're not alone.'

'Is there a problem?' asked Lotus, sensing the eagle's unease.

The bird did not reply. It swooped around the clearing and began to retrace its path through the sunlit wood, muttering to itself.

'Could be a trap. I've seen them before. Never mind. We'll put in a swift shimmy and then dink it.'

'Dink it?' repeated Tom, feeling Lotus clinging to his waist tightly.

'Hang on to your hats!'

Rocks and earth flashed past as the great raptor began to ac-celerate straight towards the mighty cedar, flying straight up the edge of a thick shaft of light nudging between the uppermost branches. Tom screwed his eyes tight shut and held on . . .

WHOOSH!

The eagle darted left as nimbly as a swallow, twisting through skins of time so fast that Tom and Lotus lifted off its back—blue, green, white—

BLACK. Silence.

They were through. It was night. Streets of terraced houses

drifted peacefully below. They were on the outskirts of a large, dark town. The eagle seemed rather surprised.

'Must have been wrong then.'

'About what?'

'I'd swear I saw—'

BANG!

'Gadzooksarama!'

'B-B-B-BANG!'

The eagle dived sideways, almost throwing them off.

'Apologies!' rasped the bird wheeling left—

'B-B-B-BANG!'

The explosions were so close they pulsed right through Tom's head and out the other side. Even the air seemed to be on fire.

'What's going on?' shouted Lotus, clearly terrified.

'You tell me, missy!'

There was a shuddering whine somewhere behind. Tom looked back. In the darkness he could just make out the outline of what looked like a Spitfire . . . except it wasn't a Spitfire . . . it was a black, shining insect with whirring wings, a blunt snout and dead eyes . . . cannons were strapped to its sides and mounted behind its head was a narrow glass cockpit where a pilot sat, grinning crazily. A second followed close behind.

'Satanflies,' breathed Lotus. 'They're fast. This is not good.'

'I'm a bird, mate!' shouted the bird. A burst of yellow fireballs whizzed past, so close Tom could have almost put his hand out and caught one.

'Careful! Those things'll kill ya!' roared the raptor. Another burst and the eagle dived straight towards the grid of moonlit streets below. Suddenly they were at street level and flying dangerously fast . . . walls, shop fronts, traffic lights zipped past . . .

'Have we lost them?' rasped the raptor, swerving around a bus.

Tom glanced back down the street.

'I think so!'

'No we haven't!' shouted Lotus, pointing at a dark shape flying in the next street parallel. Then the first dipped round a corner and joined the chase. Instantly the eagle swung into an alley and over a line of gardens, its wings barely lifting above the fences.

'What the hell are those things?' it muttered.

The question was left hanging in the air as a burst of fire ripped through the wood—sending splinters flying.

'Well?' Tom glanced back at Lotus's pale porcelain face, which was a picture of terror.

'Satanflies hunt in threes. We can't outrun them,' was all she could say. It seemed that the sudden appearance of these armoured creatures had stung her to the core. At the end of the row of gardens the bird dived right through a blackened railway arch and twisted up onto the tracks.

'Now let's see what you're made of!'

With a surge the eagle's great wings began to beat faster and they accelerated like an arrow down the line. The speed was so great it made Tom's eyes water, yet through the darkness he could just make out the square shape of a goods wagon ahead . . . then another, then a long line of wagons and an engine straining towards . . .

'A tunnel!' gasped Lotus, seeing the black hole gaping in the hillside beyond. 'If we can—'

'Get in there before they do!' shouted the bird. 'That's right, missy—that's the only way we'll lose these maniacs!'

Already the two dark shapes were hurtling low along the track behind them, gaining at ferocious speed. Another ball of fire flashed past.

'Strewth, leave that out, won'tcha!'

The eagle closed rapidly on the wagons, and soon they were over the top of them. Tom could see they were filled with white rocks.

'Down flew the mad bird, carrying Tommy Scatterhorn—

'Up came the insects one two and three—'

The raptor sang to the tune of Waltzing Matilda, oblivious to the fireballs splashing in all directions. Tom glimpsed the straining engine closing fast on the tunnel's mouth, in seconds it would be there . . . if they could just slide in ahead—

'Come on . . . ' urged Tom, '*come on!*'

'And his ghost may be heard as you pass by that billabong . . . '

There was the driver leaning out of his engine in horror—there was the first Satanfly almost directly behind them—Tom could see the pilot's face grinning weirdly . . . tentacles seemed to be opening out from the mouth of the insect . . . time seemed to be slowing down—

'Oh my lord,' breathed Lotus, grabbing Tom tighter, but somehow he couldn't tear his eyes away. There was the tunnel entrance, right there—

'You'll come a-Waltzing Matil—'

And then the third Satanfly emerged from the tunnel's black mouth.

'ABORT!'

In an instant Tom felt the weight of Lotus slam into him, knocking the air from his lungs. It was so quick but somehow they had turned ninety degrees and were flying vertically.

BANG!

At the very same moment a colossal explosion erupted below. Out of the corner of his eye Tom saw the Satanfly crumpled to bits by the racing engine. Then the second smashed into the hillside above and dropped onto the hurtling wagons, colliding with the third.

'Go get yourselves some flying lessons, boys!' shouted the great bird triumphantly as they swept up and away. 'What the hell were they all about?'

Tom looked back at Lotus and saw her grim expression. She had been telling the truth when she said she was hunted the world over . . . but did that mean him too? Had his escape already been discovered? He didn't even want to think about it . . .

By dawn they had left the town far behind and arrived at the corner of a great wood straddling a hillside. With an ungainly hop and a bounce the eagle landed on a deeply rutted track amongst the trees and set them down. Tom felt so stiff from being cramped in one position he could hardly stand up.

'Not dead already are you, kiddo?' asked the bird.

Tom could barely muster a smile.

'Pins and needles,' he groaned, trying to shake some life into his fizzing legs. 'Is this the right place?'

'It is,' said Lotus, stretching like a cat. 'Marchmont Castle is just down there, isn't it?'

She pointed at the grey turrets surfacing from the sea of mist in the valley below.

'That's right, missy, but you'll have to do the last bit on foot as I ain't goin' no closer. Not after meeting that reception committee.'

Lotus smiled at the motley raptor. Now that she was out of danger her old confidence was returning.

'Well thanks for getting us this far—and through all that. You saved my life.'

'Excuse me, it was *my* life I was savin'. You two just happened to be on board. What the hell were those hooligans doing? And how did they know we were coming?'

Lotus shrugged, returning the eagle's suspicious glare with her best blank expression.

'I suppose it must have been a coincidence.'

'Coincidence? Hmm. Well isn't that a thing?' The eagle muttered angrily to itself. 'An ambush I'd call it.' The raptor glanced over at Tom hobbling through the leaves. At last his legs seemed to have come back to life. 'You all right, me old mucker?'

Tom winced painfully. 'Just about.'

'I don't mean yer legs,' it hissed, stalking over to where he stood. 'I mean, are you all right about, y'know, going on down there with spit-and-catch-it.' The bird shot a glance at Lotus, now standing at the edge of the wood staring down into the valley. 'Cos this is the last chance saloon.'

'I know,' said Tom quietly. 'It's OK.'

'You don't sound very certain. And I don't blame ya. Never trust an insect, mate. Specially not one that can—'

Lotus turned round and looked back at them. There was an uneasy silence as the girl, the boy, and the eagle faced each other.

'I'll take that chance,' whispered Tom, knowing he had no choice. Going with Lotus was the only way he could finish this.

'All right, kiddo. It's your funeral.'

'Thanks.'

The great raptor shook out its feathers grumpily, then turned to go. But before it did it couldn't resist a parting shot. Marching forward, it bore down on Lotus and fixed her with an angry yellow stare.

'Now hear this, Miss Fancypants, if I ever find out you've played us all for fools, and this is all one big wheeze to get yourself back in there with Mr Askary, I guarantee I will rip that pretty head right off your shoulders and feed yer brains to the crows. D'you understand me?'

The bird thrust its long grey beak right into her face and Lotus took an involuntary step backwards.

'Well do ya?' The raptor looked so ferocious that Lotus nodded. She could hardly do anything else.

'Right then.'

The bird turned and in a couple of bounds it took off and soared away above the trees. It never once looked back.

'Charming creature,' said Lotus, smoothing back her hair to regain her composure.

'He means it,' said Tom, secretly pleased that Lotus seemed to be so ruffled by his threat.

'Listen, Tom, you may still find this hard to believe—but I have no secret plan to get back in with Don Gervase Askary. He's trying to kill me, isn't he? I would have thought after what we have just been through that much was obvious.'

'So they *were* expecting you, then?'

Lotus kicked the mud off her boots and said nothing.

'Lotus?'

'Something triggers when I go through a hole. I don't know how. Ever since I have escaped from jail it's been like that.' She glanced at him. 'But obviously I couldn't tell you, or him, otherwise he would never have agreed to take us.'

Tom shook his head in amazement.

'Great. So now he must know we're here.'

'I doubt it. They were all killed, weren't they? And anyway, news travels very slowly.'

'But supposing—'

'What!' Lotus's eyes flashed angrily. 'Supposing Don Gervase Askary thinks I'm in Scotland, so what?'

'But it's not just *you*, it's me and the eagle. If he knows we're—'

'What difference does it make? If he knows or he doesn't know—it's not going to stop us now, is it?'

'No. But—'

But Lotus had already flounced down the hill, her willowy form fading into the mist. Tom took a deep breath. Lotus Askary was a tricky customer, there was no doubt about that. Perhaps this was all going to be much harder than he had imagined.

'Wait!' he called, and ran down after her.

Five minutes later they had slithered down the steep path and reached the narrow road that ran along the bottom of the valley. In the distance was the outline of Marchmont Castle, rising up like a black cliff beyond the trees, with turrets on each corner and battlements fading into the mist.

'I suppose you have a plan?' puffed Tom, as they hurried up the empty road.

'Of course I have a plan, I always have a plan.'

'Are you going to tell me, or do I have to guess?'

Lotus exhaled deeply, her breath steaming in the chilly air. She was clearly still furious and could barely be bothered to explain.

'All right. It's simple. Betilda Marchmont was a traveller, like you.'

'I gathered that much.'

'And she used to visit Golding Golding.'

'I guessed that too. But how?'

'Golding Golding built his hacienda right out in the middle of the jungle. Why? Because it is the site of an ancient insect colony, with many old tunnels connecting it to different times and places, including one that leads to Scarazand. Golding Golding is obsessed with Scarazand. He collects things from it. That is how I know about him—that is why we have been watching his house, seeing who comes and goes . . . and one of those people was Betilda Marchmont. How did she get there? Not by road. Not by trekking up through the jungle. She must have used one of the other old tunnels. Probably discovered it by accident.'

Tom nodded. He could just about believe this was possible, after all August and Sir Henry had found the remains of another miniature Scarazand high up in the Himalayas where he had visited them last year . . .

'And you're certain Betilda Marchmont travelled there from *here*?'

They had rounded the corner to find the castle looming up before them. In front stood a small gothic gatehouse.

'Definitely. She must have done, as she was a recluse. Betilda never left this place—barely even left her own room. She spent all day painting weird pictures up in the attics.' Lotus waved vaguely in the direction of the shuttered windows on the top floor. 'It was only when August told me that this castle was riddled with secret passages that I realized she must have found some secret connection. Obviously there is a hidden staircase, a tunnel, a cupboard, somewhere up on the top floor that took her straight there. No one ever realized she had gone. All we have to do is find it.'

They had almost reached the drive when an engine revved and a milk van emerged from the fir trees further up the valley. They watched as the headlights swung round the low wall and the van stopped beside the little gatehouse. The door opened and out jumped the milkman, swiftly going about his business. He hadn't seen them.

'Lotus wait. Don't you think we are a bit suspicious-looking?'

Lotus marched on purposefully, pretending not to have heard him.

'We need a story. How did we get here?'

'Does it matter?'

'Yes it does,' said Tom holding her back. 'People don't just turn up. Not on foot, in the middle of nowhere, first thing in the morning. What are we doing here?'

Lotus shrugged.

'I don't know. Maybe we've been in a car crash.'

'What?'

'Maybe we're lost. Maybe you're ill. Maybe we took the bus.' She pointed at what might have been a stop sign, barely visible in the gloom.

'Lotus, just—'

'Tom, I have done this sort of thing many times before, all right?' Carefully and deliberately she removed his arm from her own. 'I know exactly what I am doing. Kindly leave this to me.'

And off she marched towards the van. Tom trailed in her wake with deep misgivings. He wasn't sure what Lotus knew about anything beyond her own strange world, and Sir Henry was right: she could be about as subtle as a sledgehammer. The milkman emerged from the gatehouse blowing on his purple fingers. He stiffened a little when he saw the two odd-looking children appear out of the mist.

'Hello there,' said Lotus, smiling cheerily. 'How are you?'

'Chilled to the bone,' spat the milkman, who was wearing a balaclava under his hat. 'How are you?'

'Oh very well. We've come to see Marchmont Castle.'

'Oh aye. Well there it is, lassie. Grim and gruesome.'

'Is it open?'

'Not at six o'clock in the morning it isn't,' he said, putting down his empty bottles in a crate. 'And whether it ever will be again I don't know. What you want to go in there for?'

'Oh actually it's a social call. Betilda Marchmont is our mother you see. It's been such a long time since we've seen her. Is she at home?'

What sounded most natural to Lotus sounded very bizarre to the milkman. He was about to climb back into his van when he stopped.

'Betilda Marchmont is your *mother*, you say?'

'That's right. She's invited us to breakfast. Is the house locked?'

The milkman stared at the strange children. The girl was very pale, with a face as smooth as soap, and dressed in some kind of grey cape. The boy was thin with dark eyes and a shock of blond hair that looked as if he had just been pulled through a hedge backwards. He knew he should be getting on with his round, but there was something very suspicious about these two . . . could it be . . .

'So you don't know, then?'

Lotus smiled painfully and flexed her fingers like a gymnast. She was already tiring of these questions.

'Know what? What precisely is there to know?'

'About the murders.'

'Murders?' Lotus laughed out loud. 'What murders?'

The milkman's expression hardened. Maybe it was them: the papers said there might have been two, and killers always returned to the scene of their crime, didn't they? They did—it was a fact. Carefully the milkman pulled out his mobile phone. He smiled falsely, then knocked a large blob of snot bobbling on the end of his nose.

'You want to go inside, you say?'

'That's it.'

'Aye. Well I tell you what. Why don't you stay there and I'll see if I can rustle up the key.'

'Thanks,' beamed Lotus. 'You're very kind.'

The milkman turned and with his thumb punched in three quick digits. Then he walked furtively round the back of his van.

'This is not good,' whispered Tom, quickly remembering what had happened to the people who lived here.

'Why do you say that?' hissed Lotus. 'He's being helpful.'

'Police,' growled the milkman. 'Marchmont Castle.'

'No he isn't,' murmured Tom between his teeth. 'Don Gervase killed the people who lived here. I read it in the paper.'

Lotus saw that Tom was serious. The milkman was edging away as he spoke hurriedly into the phone.

'That's right. Two. No, no, they're standing at the gate. Up the road. Odd looking kids. I have no idea.' The milkman glanced at them and smiled again. 'He's gone for the key. He'll be up in a jiffy.'

'That is a shame,' sighed Lotus watching the man turn back to his conversation. Coolly she walked around the side of the van and picked out a bottle of milk from the rack. With one swift throw she cracked it over the back of the milkman's head, knocking him out cold. The phone tumbled from his hand. Tom stood there in shock, then without thinking ran forward to pick it up.

'Hello? Hello? Sorry, my dad didn't mean any of that,' he said hastily into the receiver. 'He's . . . not very well; it's part of his condition—to make prank calls, he keeps doing this, I'm sorry. Please don't take any notice. Sorry.' Tom switched the phone off and put it back on the ground. He stared at it for a moment, breathlessly, barely able to believe what he had just done.

'That was the police,' he mumbled.

'You're more ingenious than you look, Tom Scatterhorn,' smiled Lotus, 'I would never have thought of that.'

'Thanks,' said Tom, noticing the hint of condescension in Lotus's smile. He might have added that Lotus was far less charming than she looked, but he didn't.

'I don't know whether they believed me.'

'No. We haven't got long. And he'll come round in ten minutes.'

Leaving the milkman sprawled on the grass they ran on up the gravel drive, passing lines of close-trimmed yew bushes and up the wide stone steps. The front door was locked, but a small window round the back was open, and soon they were hurrying across the dark oak hall and up the winding staircase, past lines of grim-faced Marchmonts and faded tapestries until they reached the top floor.

'Now where?' whispered Tom, noticing his breath steaming. It was almost as cold inside this old house as it was outside.

'Any ideas?'

Lotus was already halfway down a twisting landing that seemed to lead towards the back of the house, and by the time Tom caught up with her she was standing at the end of a small corridor before a black door. There was a smile of satisfaction on her face.

'This must be it.'

'How do you know?'

Lotus pointed at the words painted on the wooden lintel above.

'Nunquam minus sola—quam cum sola,' she read. 'It's Latin.'

'Thanks. I'd guessed.'

'Never less a lonely lady—than when a lady alone.' She translated for his benefit. 'That sounds like Betilda, doesn't it?'

Lotus tried the door. It was locked. In fact a large, brand-new padlock had been fixed across it.

'Maybe this is the crime scene. The room where those—'

But Lotus had already unceremoniously kicked the door off its hinges.

'We have to get in somehow, don't we?'

Tom swallowed hard.

'Fine, just . . . it doesn't matter.'

The room was small and bare, like a monk's cell, with nothing but a bed, a small chest of drawers, and a fireplace. Around the walls hung a few unframed paintings of odd-shaped people, half human, half . . .

'Half-breeds, how interesting,' said Lotus, examining one peculiarly misshapen man with an old tam-o'-shanter perched on the back of his head. Tom stared at him. He looked vaguely familiar . . . next to him was another portrait: it was of a small woman, wearing a velvet dress and a blue turban, with wide, bulging blue eyes.

'Betilda?' wondered Tom out loud.

'Wow! Come and look at this!'

Tom followed Lotus through into a long, low room and felt as if he had entered a dark forest. Covering every wall and stretching up to the ceiling were long slender tree-trunks weaving an endless pattern, and in amongst them Tom began to see strange, nightmarish scenes from a fantastical realm that he half-recognized, half-wished to forget. This was the world of Scarazand . . .

'I don't believe it.'

Lotus had wandered to the far end where there was a large painting of a battle taking place in an icy valley. It was a huge swirling mass of creatures and men, violent and intricately paint-ed. In the foreground, a knight in a black spiked suit of armour galloped on beetleback towards a vast rearing cobra, driving his spear deep into its thick white neck. Below him lay a man, raising his hands in terror. The whole image had been splattered with white bleach. Tom recognized it immediately—he had seen it in the newspaper what felt like a lifetime ago.

'Just remember that's not you, Tom. That's your echo. Betilda Marchmont never even met you.'

Tom stared at the boy's scratched out face: the determined jaw, the black eyes . . . it might not have been him, but it was still deeply unnerving. And so was that huge, cobra-like serpent rear-ing above Don Gervase. That was a gorogona, wasn't it? It must be . . .

Spotting a dusty box on the windowsill Lotus hefted it onto the floor and threw open the lid.

'Ha!' Kneeling down, she picked up the pile of waxy green papers inside.

'These are from Scarazand.'

'Are you sure?'

Lotus nodded.

'Someone must have given them to her. I can't believe she had the guts to go there herself.'

Tom peered over her shoulder to read the headline.

'Wolfskidder's cannons no match for boy,' it read. Beneath was a shimmering portrait of Tom's echo dressed in the same distinc-tive suit of armour. He looked very heroic and determined. An ugly black beetle lay dead at his feet. Lotus tossed it away then read the next, 'Boy sets new course record', and the next—'All in a day's work for Tom'. Each waxy cutting carried its own tale of derring-do—another creature vanquished, another enemy despatched. Tom felt his stomach start to crawl.

'But I thought you said my echo was being kept hidden, like a guilty secret?'

'Well I was wrong, wasn't I?' snarled Lotus angrily. 'Don Gervase is obviously creating a new hero for the people. A puppet he can control, who they can idolize . . . and he's even dressed him up in the Scaramoor.'

'The what?'

Lotus slapped her hand down hard on the newspaper.

'That armour. It's famous. It belonged to the first man to discover Scarazand, a thousand years ago. A knight named Inigo Marcellus. You won't have heard of him. He became the first king of Scarazand. He's the halfbreeds' hero. He liberated them, gave them status, and they made him the Scaramoor in return. It has over ten thousand pieces, each cut from the strongest, lightest chitin in the world. I was never even allowed to touch it.' Lotus leafed through the papers faster and faster, barely able to control her fury. 'The finest suit of armour ever made, now worn by a mere echo. Dumb enough to save his master in battle, who will be conveniently killed afterwards. Betilda Marchmont was completely obsessed.'

Tom turned away, his mind throbbing. He really didn't want to see any more . . . but Lotus was right: that knight was everywhere . . . rampaging through forests, scaling walls, diving through pools and slicing up insects great and small . . . and then it dawned on Tom why Lotus was so angry. This echo had taken her place. He was the reason why she had been thrown in jail. He was the new heir to Scarazand. And his name was Tom Scatterhorn.

'I think if I stay here a moment longer I'm going to be sick,' hissed Lotus, flinging the rest of the papers to the floor. For the first time in a long while Tom was in complete agreement. 'Let's just find out how she got down to Golding Golding's house.'

'Before the police get here.'

'Exactly.'

Lotus strode around the room, flexing her fingers. 'If it's some old hidden passage it's probably behind these paintings. I bet if we rip them all away we'll find it.'

'You can't just rip all the paintings off the wall, Lotus.'

'Why not?'

'I don't know, it's a work of art, isn't it?'

Tom walked back into the small bedroom and stared at the portrait of the eccentric little woman. If that was Betilda March- mont then she didn't look very athletic.

'It's bound to be somewhere really obvious—'

CRASH!

Tom turned to see Lotus kicking a hole right through the mid- dle of a wooden panel then tearing it off the wall.

'LOTUS!'

She glared at him angrily.

'What? We've got to find it.'

'You've got to control your temper.'

'Says who?'

'I do. Stop smashing everything. Let's just think for a moment.'

Tom shook his head. It was like travelling with a wild animal.

Lotus scowled, but she decided not to rip the next panel from the wall. Instead she sauntered back and joined him in the bare bedroom.

'Well?' she demanded sulkily. 'I'm thinking. Are you?'

Tom scratched his head. There were no cupboards, wardrobe, chest of drawers, nothing. He glared at the portrait in frustration.

'Betilda wasn't a gymnast, was she? It's got to be staring us in the face. Somewhere.'

'Where exactly?'

'I don't know.'

Lotus shot him a withering look.

'Are you actually stupid or do you just enjoy pretending to be?'

Tom decided not to rise to the bait. Instead he crossed the room and crouched before a strange little picture painted directly onto the panelling. It was of a waiter riding a penny-farthing, bearing a tray of drinks. For some reason Betilda had forgotten to paint his mouth. Lotus saw what he was looking at and strode across to read the Latin inscription painted along its rim.

'"Parva sed apta mihi: nec tamen hic requies." Hmm.' She frowned, then folded her arms across her chest.

'Which means?'

'This little house is perfect, but I'm restless. Could be an allegory. Or some strange private joke. Ha ha. Betilda wants to travel, on a bicycle, with a waiter—'

'Stop.'

Tom stared at the waiter: why had Betilda not painted his mouth?

'Because he's dumb,' he whispered. 'Because he's dumb.' Tom gasped suddenly. 'That's it! He's dumb . . . a dumb waiter!'

'A dumb waiter?' repeated Lotus, as if this was some kind of code.

A moment later Tom was running his fingers around the painting. Feeling the panels, he slid one open and found a small wooden compartment.

'There it is. That's a dumb waiter. It's a lift—for food. From the kitchen.'

'Isn't it a little small?' said Lotus, deliberately pointing out the obvious. 'Unless you're suggesting Betilda Marchmont was a midget.'

'Supposing she just used the mechanism.' Lotus seemed nonplussed. 'It's a lift. So it's on a pulley, isn't it?'

Tom began pushing the adjacent wooden panel in each direction. With a squeak it shunted a little, and then suddenly slid sideways, and very easily, too.

'There,' he said triumphantly. Behind the panel was a narrow stone shaft with a rope dangling down the centre. At last Lotus understood. She peered down into the darkness.

'So what you're saying is that this shaft might go down *beyond* the kitchen, into a cellar, or a dungeon, or—'

'A tunnel. So Betilda can go up or down in secret. It's got to be, hasn't it?'

'But if we hang onto that rope, what's to stop us just crashing into the ground at the bottom?'

Lotus was right. Betilda must have used something to balance her weight. Tom looked again at the wooden box. In the rough stone wall behind it there was a large loose block.

'Supposing she slides the block onto the top of the box to counterbalance her weight?'

To demonstrate, he reached in and pulled the block on top of the wooden box. Slowly it disappeared down into the shaft and the rope began running up. There was a rumbling of wheels somewhere above. After what seemed like an age the rope came to a halt. At its end was a lead counterweight wide enough to stand on, and a couple of loops Betilda had tied to the rope to hold on to.

'See? It's so easy.'

Lotus was forced to agree. She smiled.

'All right. You win. Very clever, Tom. I stand corrected.'

She peered down into the black shaft then back at Tom. There was no fear in her eyes, only excitement for what she knew lay ahead.

'Do you want to go first, or shall I?'

CHAPTER 15

SURREALISSIMO

The first sound Tom heard, strangely, was a dinner gong. Then came laughter and applause, followed by a trumpet. Cautiously he stepped through the wooden door in front of him and found himself in a small hollow. It was night, and the air was hot and wet and humming with all the sounds of the jungle. Climbing up through the ferns he found himself in a garden, filled with twist-ed concrete shapes sprouting out of the ground and bridges lit by lamplight. The high laughter was coming from further down the hillside, where Tom could just make out the silhouette of a house. It sounded like a party was going on.

'Lucky Betilda to have found this entrance,' whispered Lotus, emerging through the small door and climbing up through the bushes towards him. 'You have no idea how remote this place is. We are right out in the middle of nowhere.'

'So Golding Golding is some secretive evil villain, then?'

Lotus smiled.

'Secretive? Definitely. As for evil, in the scheme of things, he's a very small fish indeed. Unlike something else.'

'Something else?'

'I know what he's been collecting,' she said, with a half-smile. 'He deals in arms, but he adores the weapons of Scarazand. Airborne poisons, unbreakable armour, pheromone guided missiles, that sort of thing. He has a few of them, but is always trying to get his hands on more.'

'And he keeps them all here?'

'So we believe. Come on.'

Lotus led the way down the steep gravel path between fountains and stone pyramids towards the party. Tom did not know much about plants but even he could tell this garden was very peculiar: carefully tended lines of pitcher plants clung to coiling black branches, vast red ferns towered overhead like parasols, and concrete spiral staircases rose up into the night sky without reaching their destination.

'It's all pretty strange, isn't it?' whispered Tom as they carefully skirted around a giant red hand emerging from the undergrowth, the fist closing around a tree trunk.

'It's art, Tom, can't you tell? And very expensive, too. After insects, this is Mr Golding Golding's obsession.'

Dropping to her haunches Lotus slid across a large plastic ant and peered over the parapet wall.

'Ah. That's . . . interesting.'

Tom took his place beside her. For a moment he too was amazed.

'But the invitation said nothing about fancy dress.'

'It will be extraordinary. Dress accordingly. I had forgotten.'

The courtyard before the house was thronging with guests who certainly had read the invitation. There were women in long green dresses made entirely of iridescent beetles, men in sailor suits with dorsal fins on their heads, medieval knights with wings, red centaurs, women whose naked bodies were painted blue and decorated with white clouds . . .

'So these are the people plotting the downfall of Scarazand?'

'I very much doubt it,' growled Lotus. 'They must be Golding Golding's artistic friends. Any genuine travellers will be either well-disguised or waiting elsewhere. These people are just a front. They're very rich, very curious, or very bored: high society, Tom, hiding away in the jungle with nothing better to do.'

The venom in Lotus's voice was unmistakable.

'So you don't approve of them, then?'

'Approve?' Lotus snorted dismissively. 'I was locked up in a convent with their daughters, remember? Actually, no I don't— not that it matters any more. There he is.'

Lotus pointed into the melee at a large, heavy man, as bald as a Buddha, whose skin was glistening with oil. All across the folds in his neck and shoulders hundreds of brilliant blue butterflies were feeding. Tom stared at Golding Golding and found it hard to imagine this ridiculous oily lump was an arms dealer. Only his small reptilian eyes suggested any kind of menace.

'We're not exactly going to fit in down there, are we?' said Tom, staring down at the exotic throng. 'And supposing Don Gervase is wearing some crazy costume?'

'What, he's come dressed as a fish? I don't think so,' muttered Lotus. 'Let's go closer.'

Quickly they descended through the trees and stepped out onto the steep dirt drive that led up to the house. All along its edge lurked a procession of Rolls Royces, Mercedes, Ferraris, parked end-to-end and gleaming magnificently in the moonlight.

Chauffeurs hovered in the shadows, the ends of their cigarettes glowing like fireflies.

'Quick, someone's coming,' said Lotus, hauling Tom back behind a tree. A group of girls in long red dresses and matching fox hats trotted up the track towards them, talking excitedly. Hanging in their shadow was a tall, wiry man wearing evening dress. His face was hidden behind a white mask and his dome of black hair glistened in the moonlight. Up the steps they swept, and the man prowled after them, taking in two steps at a time.

'I don't believe it.'

'What?' Lotus was already watching as another Rolls Royce arrived, and two elderly green lizards climbed out.

'I think that was him,' whispered Tom. 'Nicholas Zumsteen.'

'Really?'

Lotus turned to see the quick, nervous man melt into the throng.

'Are you sure?'

'No, not exactly, but . . . the way he walked . . . at least he looked a bit like that.'

Already Lotus was running up through the shadows towards the steps.

'Lotus!' Tom chased after her breathlessly. 'What are you going to do?'

'I don't know—find him.'

'And then?'

Lotus's face was whiter than ever as she forced her way through the crowd, pushing past centaurs and angels.

'Careful!'

'Look where you're going can't you!'

Lotus ignored the irritated looks as she pursued the masked man, now with a glass in his hand. He strode out to the edge of the crowd and, standing beside a large urn, took out a cigarette from a silver case and lit it.

'Like I said, I'm not completely certain,' whispered Tom. They watched as he turned away and stared towards the jungle. Lotus took a deep breath and strode forward.

'Nicholas Zumsteen?'

The man spun round. His eyes were just black holes beneath the mask and he seemed rather surprised.

'It is you, isn't it?'

Zumsteen smiled a moment.

'Is it that obvious? I suppose I do feel a little underdressed.' He looked the scruffy girl and boy up and down. 'But then you're not precisely dressed for the ball either, are you, my dear? Are you a friend of Golding's?'

Lotus shuffled uneasily. This was her real father. A total stranger. He had no idea who she was. Suddenly whatever she had intended to say had just evaporated from her head.

'My name is Lotus. And this is Tom. Tom Scatterhorn.'

Zumsteen blew a cloud of blue smoke out between his teeth. He looked at them again.

'Tom Scatterhorn. Of course you are. And Lotus Askary. *Quelle surprise*. I would never have put you two together.' There was an awkward silence. 'So what are you doing here?'

'Erm . . .'

'Because you certainly weren't invited. I could have you thrown out right now. In fact I rather think I should. Is this some pathetic attempt at spying for your father?'

'I have nothing to do with him any more. Or Scarazand. I've been banished.'

'My heart bleeds.'

'And you know Tom isn't,' she continued. 'We're not spying for him. Honestly.'

Zumsteen stared at them both in silence. Behind his mask it was almost impossible to tell what he was thinking.

'So you recognized me?' she asked suddenly.

'Obviously.'

'But do you know who I really am?'

'Should I?'

Lotus shrugged.

'Maybe not. But as it happens I'm your daughter. Your real daughter.'

Nicholas Zumsteen snorted. Then he uttered a loud, high laugh.

'I never had a daughter.'

'Actually you did. You know you did. Before you were married. Her mother was called Amy Dix.'

Nicholas Zumsteen took a long pull on his cigarette, then stared at the dark haired girl, her pale white skin, her milky green eyes.

'It was a long time ago,' persisted Lotus, 'and everyone thought she had died in her pram one afternoon. But she didn't die. She was stolen.'

'Stolen?' repeated Zumsteen. Again he laughed his strange, braying laugh. 'What a ridiculous story. Stolen by whom—my wicked brother, I suppose?'

'*Yes*, as it happens,' said Lotus, growing steadily angrier by the second. Though she didn't care, it needled her that Zumsteen seemed to be taking all this so lightly. 'He was not getting any-where in his search for the elixir, so he decided that having a daughter would be a useful prop. But it couldn't be just anyone. It had to be someone like him—like you. So he stole me.'

'Ha!'

Zumsteen tossed his cigarette over the balcony and stared out into the jungle beyond. Tom sensed that he must be finding the truth very uncomfortable.

'So you never knew?'

Zumsteen's silence was deafening. He fidgeted with his glass, then drained it.

'Didn't you even suspect?'

Zumsteen turned to her, his eyes just dark holes.

'What do you want me to do, play happy families? My dear Lotus, it's a little too late for that.'

Lotus stared at her father in surprise. August was right: Nicho-las Zumsteen was a very peculiar man.

'I don't want to play happy families. I hate families. And I don't want you to pretend to be my father, either. I just wanted to let you know, that's all. Because it's the truth.'

'That's very good of you. I'm much obliged.' Zumsteen's thin lips had tightened into a grimace. 'Incidentally, who told you I would be here?'

'Sir Henry Scatterhorn,' said Tom.

'Did he indeed. Is he coming?'

'No.'

Nicholas Zumsteen seemed surprised.

'That's a shame. Well I suppose they will find out sooner rather than later. There are some rather big changes afoot.'

Tom nodded.

'We heard. The gorogonas.'

Zumsteen smiled wryly.

'Yes, of course. He has told you everything. Well if you want my advice, stay as far away from Scarazand as possible. It's going to be no place for meddlesome children.'

'Is that a threat?' demanded Lotus.

Again Zumsteen laughed his high, strange laugh.

'You have no idea.'

'Nicholas? Is that you? Because I can't be sure . . . oh but I think it is. Nicholas!'

A large gold shape rolled towards them.

'So do you want to be thrown out?' asked Zumsteen, watching Golding Golding approach. 'It wouldn't be pretty.'

Lotus crossed her arms and shrugged nonchalantly.

'Let me guess, you don't care?'

'Not really.'

Zumsteen grinned despite himself. He rather liked this girl's attitude.

'All right. Stay. But be very careful, Lotus Askary. Or would you prefer Zumsteen? You too, Tom Scatterhorn. *Au revoir.*' With the briefest of nods he stepped forward into the throng.

'Nicholas!'

'Golding!'

'Nicholas, I need a quick word before you make your speech . . .'

They watched in silence as the large gold man threw one glistening arm around Zumsteen's shoulder and they disappeared into the crowd. For a moment they said nothing. There was nothing to say.

'Was he that strange when you met him before?'

'Erm . . . not quite that strange. But almost. What did you expect?'

'I don't know.' Lotus seemed bewildered. 'I don't know. I thought he might be a little more . . . friendly, perhaps?'

Tom watched the two men walk up the steps to the balcony above. They were still locked deep in conversation.

'Maybe we should stay and hear what he has to say. If he is going to make an announcement about the battle, maybe say when—'

'I'm not sure that would be a good idea,' whispered Lotus, touching Tom's arm. He followed her gaze down onto the path below. There, striding purposefully up through the trees was a group of men whose silhouettes all looked the same. At their centre was a very tall, narrow man, with a green mask across his eyes. There was a boy at his side, slim and identically dressed, his thick blond hair slicked back . . . Tom felt the hairs on the back of his neck stand up. Was that his echo?

'What shall we do?'

Lotus glowered at the tall man and the boy moving up through the shadows . . . this was the first time she had seen Don Gervase since leaving Scarazand.

'We need to separate them somehow . . .'

There was a peal of laughter high above.

'But Geegee, you promised! Please!'

Above them a line of faces spread out along a balcony of the hacienda. The crowd turned and looked up to see Golding Golding reluctantly emerge at the centre, the butterflies still floating around his head.

'Oh go on, Geegee!' shouted the woman again. She was dressed as a cockatoo, and carried before her a long silver tray. Golding Golding smiled awkwardly.

'My dear, do you have any idea how much these cost?'

'Don't tell me, they are priceless!' wailed the woman with glee.

'Everything has a price, Solange. Even you.'

'Oh you miserable old pudding!'

'But these are by Fabergé, my dear. Fabergé.'

'Geegee darling, if anyone can afford it you can.'

Golding Golding looked down and hesitated.

'Please,' simpered Solange. 'You did promise us a glimpse of her. Just one little sneaky peeky?'

There was an excited murmur amongst the guests as they began pressing forward towards a railing at the side of the courtyard.

'I have no idea,' whispered Lotus, anticipating Tom's question. Sliding quietly through the throng they reached the front, and found themselves looking down upon a large dark pool carved out of the side of the jungle directly below. Beside it was a small shrine that held a single spluttering candle.

'So that's where he's keeping it.'

'What? Keeping what, Lotus?'

'But must it be these?' protested Golding Golding, looking down at a glittering array on the tray. 'Any old trinket would do.'

'But I don't want it to be any old trinket!' screeched Solange. 'I want it to be special. Super special. Birthday special!'

'Zink of it, Geegee,' intoned a deep French voice behind Golding Golding. 'Zer greater zer sacrifice zer more beautiful zey are.'

'But they already are very beautiful, Herve.'

'Maybe so, double G,' replied Herve, a tall man with a lobster on his hat. He peered over Golding's shoulder. 'But zey are so precious zat you are afraid of zem. Zey own you. Do you want people to know zat zer great Golding Golding is owned by some piffly little eggs?'

'Piffly little eggs!' shrieked Solange.

There was a murmur of laughter and Golding Golding smiled weakly. He had the look of a man who had been hijacked.

'What are they talking about?' whispered Tom. Lotus was about to reply when a slow handclap began.

'Free yourself, Geegee! To freedom! Art!'

'Freedom! Art!' screamed the guests with glee.

Golding Golding stared at the delicate jewels on the tray, then down into the black water below, trying to convince himself.

'Very well. To art!'

With one motion he tipped the tray. A dozen golden eggs, each encrusted with diamonds and jewels, tumbled down and broke the surface of the pool like drops of rain. And then there was silence. The faces lined along the parapet watched and waited. And Lotus and Tom watched too. Something swirled in the water, moving just below the surface. There was a gasp from above.

'Oh, see the little ones, too. How adorable!' shouted Solange. 'I want one.'

'This is true surrealissimo, no?' intoned Herve gravely. 'But what is she, Geegee?'

'A caddiscapula. Like a water scorpion, only larger. She lives under that rock with her brood. It's an old Spanish shrine. She collects anything that glitters.'

'And did you breed her?'

'No, Herve, I stole her. She is from an extraordinary colony of insects in the future.'

Herve smiled, wondering whether this was a joke at his expense.

'But my dear, how perfectly marvellous,' said a short man dressed as a pirate. Ripping off his large hooped earrings he tossed them into the water. A tail, then something like an armoured body, sliced through the dark surface.

'Bravo!' he shouted.

'Did you make a wish, Archie?'

'Of course! I wished I could steal everything that she has squirrelled away down there and I would be a very rich man.'

'I don't think there's much chance of that,' smiled Golding Golding weakly.

'Why not?'

'She'll defend that little cave of hers to the death. I'm afraid that's the last I'll see of my eggs.'

'And these.' Solange pulled a small glass bottle from her pocket and held it up for all to see. Inside there were three small white pearls. 'I knew they must be precious because you kept them locked up in the same cabinet as the eggs.' Suddenly Golding Golding's whole attitude seemed to change. His eyes narrowed dangerously.

'Put those down, Solange.'

'Not unless you tell me what they are, Geegee,' she said mischievously rattling them under his nose.

'They are a gift from a friend and they are no concern of yours. Solange, please. Give them back.'

'Are those what I think they are?' whispered Lotus.

'They must be,' breathed Tom.

The other guests had gone quiet now, sensing trouble.

'So you won't tell Solange what they are?' she said, in mock sadness.

'Certainly not.'

Solange smiled crazily.

'Solange?'

'Don't let's have a scene, darling. It's your birthday!'

With a shriek she tossed the small glass bottle down into the dark water. A small silver splash . . . then something large and black and scaly sliced across it and the bottle was gone. The applause was deafening. Golding Golding wiped the sweat off his forehead. He could barely believe it. He turned to his tormentor with a murderous expression only for Solange to plant a kiss on his nose.

'Oh come come, Geegee! Now you are free! You must be strong. Like a lion!'

'Yes I am a lion, Solange. But that was cruel. So now Geegee is rather a sad lion.'

'A sad lion!' shrieked Solange. 'Geegee is a sad lion!'

Peals of laughter echoed across the jungle, followed by a blizzard of earrings and bracelets and watches splashing down into the pool.

'What tremendous fun all this is,' said Mr Golding Golding with a grimace as he was propelled away from the parapet and back into the house.

Tom and Lotus watched the feeding frenzy down in the pool below.

'These people are crazy,' whispered Tom. 'If those had been mine I'd—'

He stopped as Lotus pressed her fingers to her lips and glanced back towards the steps. Tom just glimpsed the group of masked men and their leader trotting swiftly down the drive.

'He's going to retrieve them,' she whispered.

'Retrieve them? From there? He can't—'

'He can . . . ' Suddenly Lotus's eyes widened. 'It's perfect. This is your chance. Our chance.'

Tom looked at her doubtfully.

'What are you talking about . . . Lotus?'

But Lotus was already hurrying back down the steps and out onto the moonlit drive.

'Come on,' she hissed, sliding over a wall and dropping down into the undergrowth. She began making her way swiftly towards the pool. Tom had to run to catch up.

'Obviously Don Gervase wants those gorogona eggs almost as much as he wants Sir Henry, or August, or anyone else here,' she whispered breathlessly. 'Wouldn't you want to know what the secret weapon is that your greatest enemy is planning to use against you? Here they are—on a plate. It's the perfect opportunity.'

'But what about the caddiscapulas?'

'He's not going to do it himself. The Glorious Leader doesn't go jumping into pools full of dangerous beasts—he's not that stupid. He's going to get that puppet to do it for him. Your echo.'

Tom stumbled on through the darkness, not wanting to believe what Lotus had in mind.

'That's insane.'

'Maybe it is—but I know him, I know how he thinks. I used

to have to do this sort of thing all the time. Get this, find that—believe me, I know,' she whispered. 'And now that boy has taken my place he will be doing the dirty work.'

Dipping through the umbrella ferns they crawled forward till they reached the edge of the pool, and hid in the dark overhang of a rock. High above was the hacienda, lit up like a glittering castle. There was no one left on the balcony. Tom stared at the inky, silvered surface, trying to ignore the hammering in his chest.

'OK. Supposing all that is true. What am I supposed to do?'

'Just wait. Sooner or later they will come down here, and when the boy jumps into the water, we'll slip in too. I'll deal with him and you can swim up in his place. Simple—no?'

'Deal with him?'

'There's a cave at the back. That's what Golding Golding said. I'll hide in there with the echo till you've gone.'

'And then?'

'Then I'll take him back to Betilda's house. Meanwhile you—'

'Take his place—I know.' Tom swallowed nervously. 'But—'

'No buts, Tom. This is the perfect moment, don't you see? It's dark, it's under water, he's alone. The echo goes down—you come up—no one will know the difference. We won't get a better opportunity.'

Tom tried to ignore his spinning head. There were large black shadows moving through the marbled depths.

'What about them?'

'I can help you with them,' she whispered, looking down intently. 'I know about caddiscapulas. Yes, they have lots of teeth and a snapping tail—but they trap air in a long bubble beneath their abdomen, which allows them to stay under water longer. We can use it if we have to.' Lotus plucked a reed and handed it to Tom. 'Just slip this under the shell, hold your nose—exhale, then breathe in. Simple.'

Tom looked at the reed pipe doubtfully. Lotus's confidence was breathtaking.

'And the bottle with the gorogona eggs?'

'Just say you couldn't find it. Make an excuse. Say a caddiscapula ate them or something like that.'

'He might make me tell the truth.'

'Well, resist him. You said you could. You can, can't you?'

Tom stared at the reed.

'Lotus, I'm not doing this.'

'What?'

'I'm not like you. Sorry. It's impossible.'

Lotus smiled in disbelief. It had never occurred to her that Tom might actually say no.

'Why not?'

'I'm not jumping into a pool full of giant piranhas. I'll die. There must be another way.'

A loud whistle split the darkness—silencing the hiss of the jungle. Heavy footsteps crunched up the gravel track towards the pool.

'Well you'd better think of it very, very quickly,' she growled. 'Because here they are.'

Pressing themselves deeper into the shadows they watched as four men marched out into the moonlight. They were the squad of identical bodyguards flanking Don Gervase earlier, only now two of them had machine guns casually slung over their shoulders, while the other pair held a knife and a pistol in each hand. They stood at the water's edge, staring down.

'Anything?'

A short, ginger-haired man with round spectacles marched up the path to join them. He was wearing a white suit.

'Can't see it, sir,' grunted one of the men, the moonlight chiselling into his deeply pock-marked face.

The white suit peered into the depths, his glasses glinting in the moonlight. He looked dainty and clever, and a little irritated.

'Who's that?' whispered Tom.

Lotus stared at the short man keenly. He seemed to be in some position of power, and that annoyed her. But she was sure she had seen him before somewhere . . .

'Make quite sure we're alone,' he snapped, staring directly across the pool to the rock where Lotus and Tom crouched.

'Yessir.'

The three men began to fan out through the undergrowth. Slowly they moved round towards the rock. Tom stiffened.

'I haven't thought of anything.'

Still Lotus continued to stare at the white suit.

'Lotus?'

'Take off your clothes,' she hissed.

'Why?'

'Do it. Quickly.'

Tom didn't argue. As the armed men moved towards them a familiar figure appeared in the shadows on the far side.

Don Gervase Askary, and with him a boy, his white skin glowing in the moonlight. He was wearing dark shorts and nothing else. Don Gervase bent down and began speaking furtively in his ear, then patted him on the back. Lotus and Tom were so intent on watching them that they hadn't noticed the bodyguard with the machine gun barely ten metres away. He seemed to be looking directly into the shadow in which they crouched . . .

A high whistle echoed from the far side of the pool and the man turned. The pock-faced leader made a signal, and immediately his three companions broke off their search and returned to the other side. Putting down their weapons they slipped off their jackets and shoes. Long knives glinted in their waistbands.

'What now?' whispered Tom.

'They're all going in. They're going to help him.'

Lotus was right. A minute later the boy and the four men slipped into the moonlit pool and disappeared. Only Don Gervase and the man in the white suit stood in the broken shadows, watching.

OK. I'll go first—you follow. Keep to the edge, away from the cave.'

Tom's heart was thundering in his temples.

'You really think we can do this?'

'Of course. Believe in yourself, Tom Scatterhorn. Your echo does. It might help you stay alive.' She smiled cruelly. 'For a little longer, anyway. Let's go.'

Silently Lotus slipped into the water beneath the rock. In a second she had gone.

I must be mad, thought Tom. He felt the water. It was warm and black.

I don't know why I am doing this.

He filled his lungs.

I'm as crazy as she is.

CHAPTER 16

THE NEST OF TEETH

Tom followed Lotus down, keeping close to the edge of the pool. Lotus's hair fanned out behind her as she swam with long, powerful strokes. Beyond, two men were swimming towards the great caddiscapula that hovered like a black shark just under the lip of rock. Its offspring darted through the shadows in and out of the cave. Tom could not see his echo anywhere . . . The two men swam closer, their knives glinting and ready—they seemed to be trying to goad the great creature out . . . perhaps so that the echo could swim inside.

Closer they went . . . closer still, waving their glinting knives like matadors before the stumpy black nose . . . Suddenly the caddiscapula shot forward, and with a terrifying jerk its whole head seemed to unzip and slide up. Its huge jaws bit savagely into the nearest man's leg, ripping a chunk away, then a second later it darted back beneath the safety of the rock. Black blood started drifting up from the gaping wound but the man didn't turn back. He carried on. Again the creature darted out and snapped, the inner working of its head hideous to behold. This time the second man's knife made contact and the great creature twisted away angrily. The small caddiscapulas, sensing danger, began racing too and fro in blind panic. Tom glanced around . . . where was Lotus? He couldn't see . . . but then the great creature saw him. In a flash its head shot out—the armour plates sliding back to reveal the nest of teeth within . . . Tom dodged sideways, forcing himself round . . . what had been water was now a swirling storm of silver bubbles . . . it had missed, just, he was alive, just, but in the turn of that second Tom realized that unless he found air instantly he was going to drown. A primeval urge took over and, forgetting everything else, he kicked upwards, instantly colliding with the body of a small caddiscapula twisting in the water above. Its head had been ripped clean off . . . Tom's eyes widened, obviously the mother's furious attack had killed her offspring instead of him, but its shell was still intact . . . its shell . . . the next moment he jammed the short reed tube under its hard carapace and, letting the precious air bubble escape from his lungs, clamped his mouth around the reed and gulped in . . . air. Air! He exhaled gratefully, sending a cascade of bubbles skywards, then breathed in again . . . how much was trapped there didn't matter, it was enough: but Lotus . . . where was she?

Suddenly Tom felt a tap on the shoulder. There was the pock-faced man from earlier. With a frantic expression he urged Tom down towards the lip of rock. Tom pretended not to understand, then out of the corner of his eye he saw Lotus dart out of the shadows above the great mother. Ignoring the man, Tom swam away just in time to see Lotus pounce on the creature from behind, thrusting a knife into the back of its head . . . The caddis-capula squirmed and bucked as she held on, plunging the knife deeper . . . with a savage twist it threw her off and smashed into its two attackers, before tearing off around the pool, kicking like a broken toy. Seconds later it stopped and, rolling over, hung in the water motionless, its hideous head stretching open to reveal the jagged city of teeth . . . and there, lodged in a crevice, was the small glass bottle, somehow intact . . .

In an instant Tom swam towards it, and so did Lotus, but neither was fast enough. Out of nowhere a small caddiscapula swung past, its rider snatching the precious bottle and tearing off into the shadows. Lotus grabbed hold of another that seemed to be going in the same direction and set off in hot pursuit. Tom waited for them to come back but he couldn't be sure who was who as shadows burst past in all directions. It seemed that everyone was chasing everyone else in a game of underwater dodgems . . . suddenly there was Lotus again—then the pock-faced man, then someone else hurtling straight at him. Instinctively Tom grabbed at a passing caddiscapula and it jerked him down into the shadows . . . thump! Tom's head banged against something sharp . . . instantly he let go and through the swirl of moonlit bubbles he saw something silver spinning down through the water . . . there it was! The bottle . . . the rider must have dropped it . . . Tom reached out and the moment his fist closed around its neck a hand shot forward and grabbed his wrist. Tom tried to prise it away but the grip held, and as the curtain of silver bubbles began to clear he stared into what might have been a moonlit mirror. A rangy boy, with blond hair and deep-set black eyes was floating there—staring at him. His echo. For a second the two boys hung motionless, caught in the watery reflection . . . Tom felt a strange fizzing electricity in their contact that united and repelled at the same time. He could see anger in the echo's eyes, and a fear too:

he looked dangerous, but alone . . . Did he even know who he was—could he feel what he felt? Somehow Tom sensed that he did . . .

And then, in an instant, the mirror shattered. Lotus Askary had chosen well, but aimed badly. Shooting past on the back of a caddiscapula, she ripped the echo's hand away dragging him down towards the cave. But the force of her attack had sent the precious bottle spinning . . . Tom barely had time to see them disappear into the darkness before he realized what had happened. In blind panic, he lunged at the small silver shape, its top falling open as it tumbled down. Somehow his fingers closed on a single egg . . . what about the rest? No time left . . . the pressure in his lungs urged him upwards and he kicked and kicked and burst the oily surface, gasping and spluttering.

So this was it . . . he had got what he wanted. And somehow it had all happened far sooner than he had expected. Now all he needed was some luck . . .

In a couple of strokes Tom reached the water's edge, and clung on to a stone to catch his breath. Then slowly, purposefully, he climbed out.

'Well? Find anything?'

The man in the white suit walked out of the shadows, the moonlight reflecting off his glasses. At close range Tom saw he had a thin ginger moustache, pale freckled skin, and held his hands clasped neatly before him like a priest.

'What's happened to your shorts?' he demanded.

Tom looked down and was somewhat relieved to see his underwear hanging in tatters. Strangely, his feet and hands were covered in scratches.

'It was a bit of a battle down there,' he mumbled, looking at the man's black and white brogues. They were polished so bright he could see the moon in them.

'But did you find anything, yes or no?' persisted the man impatiently.

Tom wasn't sure who this was, but decided he'd better present his find. Opening his palm, he revealed the single, solitary egg.

'Here.'

The man did not look very impressed. Tom smiled apologetically.

'The bottle had broken. There was only one left. Sorry.'

'Did you search the cave as instructed?'

Tom shook his head.

'I didn't have to. It was caught in the creature's mouth.'

'Well obviously you must go back down and search the cave. Go on.'

'Wait, Dr Culexis.'

A tall silhouette came forward from the shadows, the moonlight carving a deep line down the centre of his forehead. Despite the warm night air Tom felt a shiver run down his spine. Surely *he* would know, *he* could see . . .

'You're cold, boy?'

Tom looked up into those large yellow eyes, burning into him, inquisitive. He smiled nervously.

'Yes. A bit.'

'Then of course you mustn't go down there again.'

Dr Culexis shot an angry glance at Tom.

'Supposing he's not telling the truth?'

'He is, Culexis, I am quite sure of that.'

'But my lord—'

Don Gervase silenced him with a mere flick of his head. It was the smallest gesture, like a tiger irritated by a fly, but it was enough for Tom to realize that Don Gervase Askary not only believed him, but he was protecting him, too. Why? It couldn't be out of compassion. And this other man, Dr Culexis, obviously considered that a threat.

'And did you see Lotus Askary down there?'

'Erm . . . '

Why was Dr Culexis asking him that? Tom glanced down to Don Gervase's side and saw his long fingers twisting idly around a clear rubber ball decorated with patterns . . . the mesmerion, of course. Don Gervase was using it to control him, only it wasn't controlling *him*, exactly, it was controlling his echo . . . but he was expecting the truth.

'No. I didn't see her. Just those creatures.'

Don Gervase's fingers twitched and hovered above the mesmerion's clear surface.

'You're quite certain?' pressed Culexis.

'Yes. But it was very dark,' he added quickly. 'There was a lot going on.'

What about those other men—if he lied would that expose him? Don Gervase smiled.

'In that case those clothes you found on the far side must belong to someone else.' Tom followed Dr Culexis's impatient glare over to his pile of filthy clothes and shoes, lying accusingly in the dust. He could barely look at them.

'My lord, we *know* the girl is here. She has been seen. There is good—'

'I am aware what you are suggesting, doctor. But even if there is some mysterious cave down there, do you really think Lotus would be so foolish as to hide in it? With all those caddiscapulas? I think I know my own daughter.'

Don Gervase had no idea quite how close to the truth he had come. Tom glanced up to find Dr Culexis still staring at him with a vexed expression on his face.

'And you seem to be forgetting that this boy is entirely in my control. He is not capable of deception.'

'Wouldn't it be prudent to at least—'

'Oh will you shut up!' barked Don Gervase. 'She's not here and I am not having this ludicrous debate a moment longer. There is far too much to do. I want what happened here tonight recorded in your usual style.'

Dr Culexis's moustache twitched violently. He was beaten.

'Your grace.'

'And those other men are dead, so you'd better find me some more.'

'Your grace.'

'Now go away.'

Culexis bowed again and withdrew with a painful smile on his lips.

'At last.' Don Gervase turned to Tom, still dripping in the dust. 'May I see it?' He held out his hand and Tom placed the egg into his long fingers.

'Thank you.' Don Gervase lifted the small pearl up into the moonlight and examined it carefully. 'So small. So perfect. You've no idea how precious this is.'

'Is it the egg of an insect?' asked Tom innocently.

'Something rather more than that, I hope,' he said, curling his fingers around it and slipping it into his pocket. 'Now I expect after that little diversion you want to put your clothes back on and get on with the task in hand. There is much to do.'

Tom smiled with grim enthusiasm as Don Gervase led him down the moonlit track to where a large brown Bentley lurked under the trees.

'Be quick,' he growled, ushering Tom inside and closing the heavy door. Tom sat down in the rich dark interior and his lungs filled with a cocktail of cedar wood and chocolate. On the seat opposite he saw a pile of neatly folded clothes. A dark red silk shirt, a blue, almost black velvet suit, heavily embroidered and buttoned up to the neck, grey socks, and a pair of black patent leather shoes. An identical uniform to Don Gervase. The charade had begun . . . Play the role and you can end all this, Tom told himself. Climb the vent hole and you can destroy Scarazand . . . But doubts tumbled through his mind as he hurriedly changed into the clothes that fitted him exactly. That boy in the water: his expression, so serious, so determined . . . yet vulnerable too, like a hunted animal—what did he know that Tom didn't?

'Very good,' said Don Gervase as Tom stepped out into the moonlight, trying to look as relaxed as possible. 'Hair.'

He produced a brush from his pocket and Tom obediently brushed down his unruly mop into a parting.

'Thank you,' said Don Gervase when he had finished. 'Now let's return to the house and see if we can find Sir Henry Scatterhorn and August Catcher.'

'Who are they?'

Don Gervase shot an impatient glance at Tom.

'Must I really explain it all again?'

Tom did his best to look apologetic.

'Very well, but this is the last time. Now concentrate, boy. As I already explained, August Catcher and Sir Henry Scatterhorn may be elderly, but they are extremely dangerous. They know more about our world than anyone else, and they have been using that knowledge to help Nicholas Zumsteen plot my downfall. Which is why they, and anyone else who recognizes you tonight, must be dealt with severely. Understand?' Tom nodded obediently as Don Gervase produced a pair of green masks from his pocket and thrust one at him. 'Now put this on and do what you are told.'

And so disguised they climbed the steps. Don Gervase nodded briefly at the liveried servants either side of the door and followed the voices down the hall and through into the ballroom. At the far end was a small stage on which a table and two chairs had been placed. To one side stood a lectern and a screen. Several rows of seats and armchairs had been arranged below.

'A lecture. How curious.' Don Gervase seemed genuinely surprised. 'That is not what it said on the invitation.' He cast a glance around the room, scrutinizing the guests in their exotic costumes.

'Do you know any of these people?' whispered Tom, nervously.

'Unexpectedly I do.' Don Gervase pointed to an old man in a red frock coat and a Napoleon hat. 'That is Dr Briniville, the world's foremost inventor of airborne poisons. His work is very interesting—but so obvious. He is talking to Mikael Ropov, a weapons designer currently developing a chitin tank based on the wolfskidder beetle.' Tom looked at the dark-suited young Russian hovering on the balcony. 'Golding Golding stole one for him, you see. And that purple concoction behind them is Professor Mary Senior, the parasite expert. She's just bred a spider that will suffocate you silently while you sleep. No doubt she is explaining all its boring detail to the Ginzberg sisters, who do their own little line in cyanide maggots.' Tom looked from the large purple goddess to the two hollow-faced women she was lecturing. 'Meddlesome amateurs—pathetic, isn't it?' muttered Don Gervase irritably. 'Now if anyone recognizes you be sure to let me know.'

'But what am I—'

'Go,' he hissed impatiently. 'To work, boy.'

With a small but deliberate shove Tom was propelled into the room. He glanced at Don Gervase shrinking back behind a pillar. Tom took a deep breath. He had no choice: he was his echo now. But at least he had his mask. Keeping his eyes to the floor he slipped in amongst the crowd, willing himself to be invisible. Who could be here? No one he knew . . . please make it no one.

'Well, look who it is.'

Tom's heart began thumping wildly. An American voice, right behind him. Don't look back.

'Hey, honey, is that you?'

Ignore it. Walk on. Tom ducked behind a large pyramid of glasses.

'Tom Scatterhorn?'

A slim hand touched his shoulder.

'Why it is you!'

'It's not,' mumbled Tom.

'But it is. Tom? Say Tom, what's the matter?'

A tall, flame-haired woman stood before him, her pale skin glinting with diamonds. She was wearing a long green dress made entirely of iridescent beetles, and held a feathered mask in front of her face.

'Don't you remember me? It's Trixie. Trixie Dukakis.'

Trixie dipped her mask aside and Tom looked into the wide, smiling, happy face as if he had seen a ghost.

'Are you OK?'

'Erm . . .'

'Denholm! Over here, chuck, come and say hello.'

A broad, cheery-looking man sidled through the crowd, wearing a white tuxedo and a scarf, also made of green beetles.

'Tom, this is my little brother, Denholm Dukakis.'

'It's a pleasure,' he said, in a deep melodious voice, wringing Tom's hand.

'You remember a couple of years back, I told you about that place I went with Sir Henry?'

'Sure. Your awfully big adventure.'

'Well . . . here's that Tom Scatterhorn.'

Denholm Dukakis looked impressed.

'All right! *That* Tom Scatterhorn. Well well. Pleased to meet you,' he grinned. 'So I guess you're not really supposed to be here either?'

Out of the corner of his eye Tom spied Don Gervase through the crowd, watching them intently.

'I'm sorry, what did you say?'

'You *know*,' teased Trixie.

'Do I?'

'The lecture. Guess you must be really excited to hear what he has to say.'

'Erm. Whose lecture?'

'My, how mysterious you are.' Trixie laughed at his confusion. She bent down and whispered quickly. 'Nicholas Zumsteen. Why else would we want to mix with these folks? Oh please no. It'll be starting anytime around now I suppose. See, everyone's gathering. So where's August and Sir Henry?'

Tom glanced back at Don Gervase and tried to move out of sight. He was finding it hard to control his rising panic.

'Erm . . . they're not coming. They didn't think it was safe to come.'

'Well I guess they're probably right. But hey, once you've been to *that* place it becomes a bit of an obsession, doesn't it?' she winked. 'Denholm has a theory Zumsteen's got a secret plan to start a revolution and overthrow you-know-who. Tonight he's going to tell these folks all about it. Can you imagine if he succeeds? Maybe he'll open up Scarazand into some sort of crazy theme park.'

Denholm smiled, but Tom was not smiling at all. He glanced back to see the mesmerion revolving rapidly through Don Gervase's fingers. What was he doing?

Trixie frowned.

'Tom honey, you seem very distracted. I'm worried about you.'

Tom turned his back on Don Gervase and leant forward.

'You should leave. Quickly. Please.'

'Why?'

'And if you see anyone else—tell them to too. Leave now—before it's too late.'

Trixie and Denholm stared at him without understanding. Tom lowered his voice even further.

'Please. You've got to get out of here. It's a trap.'

Tom turned abruptly and walked away. A moment later he was back at Don Gervase's side, anxiously watching the mesmerion still spinning in his palm.

'Well done, boy. Good start.'

'But I don't know those people. I've never met them before in my life.'

Don Gervase never took his eyes off Trixie.

'Of course you haven't. But they thought they knew you, didn't they? That is the point.'

'But—'

'The man I have no idea about, but that woman in the green dress I have been seeking for a long time. Not because she is important, but because she had the audacity to fly an aeroplane right into the heart of Scarazand. Can you imagine that?'

Tom watched as Trixie and Denholm moved out onto the balcony, locked deep in conversation. They seemed worried.

'You must be mistaking her for someone else,' said Tom quickly. 'She told me she was a . . . a spy—a secret agent. She's working for us.'

'I think not,' smirked Don Gervase. 'And anyone who tells you they are a secret agent is a barefaced liar. Ahh.' His fingers twitched, then steadied, holding the mesmerion quite still. 'There it is. Right there. Excellent.'

Don Gervase's eyes never left Trixie and Denholm as they began heading for the door.

'What are you doing?' asked Tom, his eyes widening.

A lizard-like grin spread across Don Gervase's mouth.

'Don't tell me you didn't recognize the beetles? No? That dress, his scarf, very decorative but unfortunately for them, they are meloids.'

'Meloids?'

'Blister beetles. Boiling with poison.'

Tom watched in horror as Trixie's and Denholm's expressions began to change. They seemed to be heating up, their skin changing colour, reddening . . . starting to swell . . .

CHAPTER 17

BEFORE THE COCK CROWS

It was unbearable to watch. No sooner had Denholm and Trixie Dukakis strode through into the hall than they began to scratch . . . they looked at each other in confusion, then panic . . . Trixie began dancing in a circle, ripping at her dress, Denholm pulled at the green scarf that had clamped tightly about his neck, trying to get away from the seething mass of beetles each delivering their deadly drops of yellow poison. Trixie screamed and fell to the floor.

'Water! Get a doctor!'

'A knife, a knife to cut it off!'

'Oh that's a shame,' muttered Don Gervase, as the cries brought guests running out into the hall. 'I had rather hoped that these people in particular would enjoy a little dance of death.'

'Let me through!' shouted a woman in a wide-brimmed hat brandishing a pair of scissors.

Tom stared grimly at the concerned crowd now gathered around Denholm and Trixie who had collapsed to the floor.

'Will they survive?' he growled, failing to disguise his anger.

'Unfortunately they might. But the pain will be excruciating and last for months. Which is something. Right. Onwards and onwards. Let's see if anyone else recognizes you. Now remember, if August Cat—'

'He's not here.'

'You seem very certain.'

'I don't recognize anyone. Let's go.'

Don Gervase smiled in surprise.

'I hardly think you are the one to decide—'

'You'll never win, you know. Not like this. Never.'

Somehow the angry words came out before Tom had a chance to stop them. The Glorious Leader stared at his young protégé in surprise. Strange, but there was real venom flashing in those eyes now . . . as if something suddenly had woken up inside him.

'Oh but I think we will. Who is going to stop us—this rabble? The ludicrous Mr Golding Golding and his little zoo?'

Tom said nothing, his knuckles clenching white with rage. How could he be a part of this?

'I can see that you're angry, boy. You may not like my methods. But sometimes one cannot choose one's weapons. One must strike first with whatever one has to hand. That's a useful lesson for you to learn.' Tom flinched as Don Gervase's cold finger grazed his neck. It was like being touched by an eel. 'Now, if you don't mind, we will continue our search.'

Tom looked down to Don Gervase's fingers spinning across the mesmerion. He could see he had no choice. They moved out into the hallway where a stream of guests were already taking their coats and trotting down the steps.

'You see? Anyone with any sense has decided it is not safe here. They're not stupid.'

Don Gervase growled behind his mask.

'Hmm. Perhaps it was a little dramatic. But Catcher and his mob may be lurking upstairs. You will lead the way.'

'Fine, but I think you should let me go on alone.'

'Alone?'

'If August Catcher is here he might approach me. But he won't if he sees you hanging around.'

Don Gervase appreciated the logic of this; the boy's tone irked him nevertheless.

'Very well. But I will be following.'

Tom nodded: of course he would be, but if there was any way he could prevent another disaster . . . up the wide staircase they went, and on into a series of dimly-lit rooms that Tom was relieved to find empty. There was nothing here but more curious artworks: a pair of giant boots made as feet, horses emerging from eggs, a rubber mouth full of spiders . . . it was all vaguely reminiscent of Betilda's paintings—strange and somehow pointless at the same time.

'Definitely. Who else could do something like that?'

'And the boy, did you see him?'

'No. But he's here with that girl. Nicholas has spoken to them.'

'He's *spoken* to them?'

Tom dipped into an alcove just as two men in capes and bird masks swept down the corridor.

'It's a disaster. Golding Golding should never have been trusted.'

'But surely we must hear what he has to say?'

'Must we? The whole thing's a sham.'

A door clicked shut, and when Tom emerged from his hiding

place the corridor was empty once more. There was no sign of Don Gervase. Had he given him the slip? That would have been too much to hope for—but he couldn't see him. He hurried on to the end where there was a giant pair of red lips that was a sofa. It was a dead end. On one side there was a window, on the other, a velvet curtain concealing a wooden cupboard door. Tom opened it. It was full of mops and buckets. Those two men must have gone some other way, but . . . wait. A mark on the back wall caught his eye. It was a fleck of white paint, only it wasn't exactly a fleck . . . it was an ant, carefully painted. A white ant. The legion of the white ant . . . Tom's heart quickened . . . beneath it was a small black handle. It was warm to touch. Could he find whoever it was that had just passed through this door, warn them what was happening, and then get back before Don Gervase noticed he'd gone? Maybe he could . . .

With a last backward glance Tom opened the cupboard door and found himself on the top landing of a narrow staircase. It was dark here, and much, much colder. Though Tom longed for this to be another part of Golding Golding's hacienda—the servants' quarters perhaps—somehow he instinctively knew it wasn't. There was a damp mustiness hanging in the air, mixed with the smell of turpentine. Large cracks streaked the walls and the skylight above was black. This was another place entirely—it had to be—another connection, just as Lotus had said. But to where?

Tom looked over the rickety banisters into the narrow hall below. At the far end a door stood ajar, and Tom could just make out shadows flickering against the walls. He listened. There was a low hum of voices . . .

'I tell you he's there now, with that boy—'

'But that's impossible. If you are suggesting—'

'I am not suggesting, I am telling you. It's a fact. Did you not see the picture in the paper? He's wearing the Scaramoor and he's saving Askary's life! It's him!'

'It's not.'

'He's even admitted he's under Askary's control.'

'Rubbish! When?'

'In the monastery. I overheard him tell August Catcher. But the silly old fool did nothing about it. He should have handed him over to us there and then.'

There was an uneasy muttering all around. By now Tom's heart was thumping in his temples. He had a terrible feeling he knew who these people were. Closer he crept along the threadbare carpet towards the door . . .

'So it's a trap, then?'

'Of course it is. The boy is the lure. Bait.'

'Then we must protect the connection. It's taken us years to find anything like this. Barricade up the door and get out of here right now—'

'Exactly.'

'Let's go.'

There was a scraping of chairs and Tom froze, crouching in the centre of the corridor. Where could he hide? Nowhere . . .

'Wait, my friends, wait. Please—a moment.'

The noise stopped. There was silence.

'Forget about the boy. Think about this in a different way. This is the first time in months we know Askary's left the safety of Scarazand. And he's come without his hordes of insects. And he doesn't even know we're here. He's *vulnerable*. We've got people, weapons—we could finish him off right now—'

'I think not.'

The voice was as low as a distant train, and it was right inside Tom's ear. He spun round to find Don Gervase looming over him like a giant bat.

'Well done. White ant. How observant.'

'But—'

'Hush.'

Don Gervase pressed a soft black glove to Tom's mouth and marched him forcefully backwards down the hall towards a broken window.

'Well well,' whispered Don Gervase, quickly taking in the scene beyond. 'Right under my very nose. Very clever—'

Tom sank his teeth deep into the thin leather, biting for all he was worth.

'STOP THAT!'

Tom was thrown back against the wall so hard that stars danced before his eyes. Don Gervase thrust his bitten hand between his legs and rubbed it hard. With his other hand he took out the mesmerion, his fingers squirming across its surface.

'You are playing with fire, boy. I have half a mind, half a mind . . .' He glowered at Tom murderously, then thought better of it. There was only one reason why this boy was still alive . . . his life hung by a thread.

'Where is this place?' panted Tom.

'London, of course. Dukes Square. Can't you recognize the headquarters?'

Tom looked out on a square of dark, narrow houses. Through

the trees on the far side he could just make out a grey building from which a stream of shadows were running towards them . . . For the first time in a long while Tom felt a distant thumping in his head. A hammering, knocking, blinding wave was starting to build . . .

'What are you doing?' he gasped.

'I have sounded a general alert in this area. I am glad to say you will have to suffer it,' he smirked, his fingers spinning the mesmerion.

Tom closed his eyes, trying to shut out the noise, but the dark horizon opened up before him and he saw a thin red line rumble forward, gathering speed, a raging red wave of static and shouting voices . . . detain them detain them detain them detain them DETAIN THEM!

Tom sank to his knees as the pulse surged through him, tingling every nerve in his body.

'Now, as this is your discovery, I would like *you* to announce our arrival,' sneered Don Gervase, pleased to see the discomfort Tom was in. 'I'm sure they will be most intrigued. Up.'

Tom staggered to his feet, sweating. He glanced out of the window. A large group of men in black overcoats had gathered on the pavement outside and were looking up expectantly for the signal. Tom wiped a hand across his face. The spring was coiled—the trap was set. All that remained was to present the bait. Which was him.

'Yes, we are all waiting for you, boy. Now go.'

With a rough shove he thrust Tom down the corridor. Tom glanced at the mesmerion spinning through the tall man's fingers . . . he was being controlled again—if only he could think of something . . . anything, to get out of this . . . Tom had always had a blind faith in his ability to get out of situations on the spur of the moment: he had always managed to do it, somehow. But right now his mind didn't seem to be working. The harder he thought, the blanker it became. He was sleep-walking. All he could feel was Don Gervase's eyes burning into the back of his neck. Raising his hand, he could hardly bring himself to knock.

'Come in?'

The voice was gruff, a little surprised, even. Tom opened the door in a daze and saw twenty or thirty weather-beaten, well-travelled people gathered around a long table on which maps and photographs were strewn about. At the head of the table stood Gregor, the cross-eyed monk from the monastery. He stared at Tom in open-mouthed astonishment. Suddenly there was a crash from below as the door was stove in.

'Oh my . . . good god . . . what's that?' cried a woman at the back. Footsteps began pounding up the stairs. Gregor's hand reached for a knife on the table.

'Who are you?' he murmured.

'What do you want from us?' demanded another.

Tom felt their accusing eyes burning into him . . . how could he ever explain what was happening? Don Gervase sniggered in the corridor.

'You really . . . don't know who I am, do you?'

'No,' growled Gregor.

Suddenly the door creaked open and Don Gervase Askary stepped into the room. The assembled company were so aston-ished that they could barely move. He put his hand on Tom's shoulder and instantly a tall, shaggy-haired man moved forward out of the shadows . . . beside him stood a small, raven-haired woman, her dark eyes burning with anger. At first Don Gervase seemed confused, and then he began to realize who they were . . .

'Are you the parents of this boy?'

Silence. Tom did not understand the question. In a blind daze he hunted through the weather-beaten faces, and then . . . no . . . no . . . *no*, they were supposed to be in South America. Don Gervase could barely contain his glee. They *were*—more Scatterhorns—this *was* a surprise . . .

'I'll take that as a yes.'

'He's got nothing to do with this! Nothing at all!' shouted Sam Scatterhorn.

Don Gervase's smirk widened.

'You really never guessed, did you?'

'What,' said Poppy, nervously staring at Tom. 'Guessed what?'

Suddenly Tom felt as if a bomb had exploded inside his head. He knew this scene—every word—he had read it a hundred times, scribbled on that scrap of paper. He knew how it would end. He looked at the frightened, shouting faces in a daze . . .

'Young Tom is the reason why you are here. And he is the reason why we are here, too. He has set you up. He has betrayed you.'

Tom caught his mother's eye and shook his head fiercely. It's not true . . . not true . . .

'What?' demanded Sam, seeing his son's anguish. 'What are you talking about?'

'Oh I know, it's hard to take. Why would *he* do a thing like that? So trusting. So foolish. It's tragic.'

Gregor made a sudden lunge at Don Gervase but the tall man was too quick. Stepping sideways he caught his outstretched arm, twisted it behind his back and sent the monk's head crashing into the wall. Before anyone else could move he had stalked out of the door pushing Tom ahead of him. The squad of overcoated men crouched waiting at the top of the stairs. At their head was Ern Rainbird, with a crowbar in his hand.

'Remove them,' ordered Don Gervase. 'Destroy the evidence. See that they are taken down to join the rest of the riff-raff.' Rainbird nodded once and grinned cheerily at Tom. The next second they burst in, moving as a single black fighting swarm . . .

Tom Scatterhorn could not bear to listen to the screams and vicious thumps a moment longer. In a daze he covered his ears and dragged himself away up the stairs, trying to find somewhere, anywhere where the pull of this nightmarish whirlpool would not reach him . . .

'Traitor!' screamed one man as he was thrown down the stairs. 'Bloody traitor!'

Tom slumped down on the top landing and leant against the wall. The inevitable had happened. He couldn't stop it. What did he feel? Nothing. Just numb. Disconnected. Almost as if this was a dream and it was all happening to someone else.

Some time later, when it was all over, Don Gervase Askary clattered up the stairs with Ern Rainbird trailing in his wake.

'A very good haul, my lord,' gushed Ern Rainbird, 'and didn't they half have a nerve? Plotting right here, with headquarters just across the square.'

Don Gervase stopped on the landing and examined the small door in the back of the cupboard.

'The legion of the white ant—why didn't I think of that?'

'Oh I'm sure you did, your grace,' Rainbird flashed a greasy smile. 'It's just them echoes do have a habit of getting lucky.'

'A commodity that cannot be underestimated, Rainbird.'

'Indeed, your grace.'

'Now stop up this particular hole then follow us back to head-quarters. And you, boy, will come with me.'

Don Gervase turned to where Tom Scatterhorn sat on the floor, his head leaning against the wall.

'Did you hear me, boy?'

Tom hadn't heard him. He was completely and utterly asleep. Rainbird moved forward, intent on giving him a hearty slap in the face.

'Wait.'

Rainbird looked up at his master expectantly.

'No?'

Don Gervase Askary stared down at the boy, more than a little mystified.

'Send him along later,' he said. 'I suppose it has been a very trying evening.'

'Very good, your grace.'

Don Gervase smiled benevolently. Then away he swept, down the stairs.

CHAPTER 18

A DUCK REMEMBERS

'I think you might be right, old bean.'

'I rather hoped you'd say that. Seems odd, doesn't it?'

'Very. Very odd indeed.'

Sir Henry yawned and flung himself down on the sofa. He had to admit he was feeling rather exhausted. Picking up a handful of pistachio nuts he shelled one and tossed it into his mouth. He glanced at August poring over his large map of the world once more. He had spent the entire night pursuing his theory—turning it upside down, back to front, inside out . . . it was exhausting to watch. He was a man possessed. Sir Henry couldn't understand it.

'And you're sure Arlo Smoot picked up the same thing on his radio?'

'Oh undoubtedly,' said August. 'Though at the time he didn't know what it meant. Which is probably the reason he never thought it was significant.'

Reaching across the table Sir Henry picked up the dog-eared red notebook labelled 'For Smoots Eyes Only'. Arlo Smoot was a radio spy who could listen to any conversation from the past, present, or future . . . this little book contained all his greatest secrets . . . How August came by it is another story. Sir Henry read the closely scribbled words in silence.

'You don't think this could be a mistake?'

August shook his head.

'To my mind Arlo Smoot never made mistakes. That was his great skill. He always copied down what he heard exactly. And I'm sure I recall something similar, but what was the blasted date?'

Sir Henry frowned. He flung the book back across the table and watched the dust mites dance up through the pools of sunlight.

'What I can't fathom is why the hell Askary's got a shellac factory out in Dragonport. What's the point in carrying mashed up beetles all the way from Asia out there?'

'Precisely. Why indeed—unless he wants to maintain a presence. Keep an eye. Protect something.' August squinted at his calculations then checked them against the red notebook.

'What about this one. December fifteenth, 1899.' He turned to the corner cupboard labelled 'Assorted Diaries—Woefully Incomplete', where lines of stuffed birds stood waiting in the gloom. 'Any takers, gents?'

Somewhere on the top shelf a gloomy brown duck shuffled forward and cleared its throat.

'Aha! Is it you?'

'It is I indeed,' droned the bird. 'I am that year, and that year is me. The last volume of your diary in that long and eventful century.'

'Well?'

The duck cleared its throat elaborately, sensing the occasion.

'1899. The sunset of an age. When the late, great, going down—'

'Oh do get on with it,' said Sir Henry, flicking a nut in the duck's direction.

The duck was not pleased. As 1899, being asked anything at all was a rare occurrence.

'I suppose you want me to skip straight to that date?'

'If you wouldn't mind.'

'But there are many other, finer—'

'If you wouldn't mind,' repeated August. 'December fifteenth if you please.'

The duck sighed.

'Very well. December fifteenth. Friday. Grey. Windy. Bitterly cold. But mercury somehow rising. Began work on kingfishers. Chops for lunch, plum tart to follow. New telescope delivered. Ten by thirty. Not bad. Can even see into Mrs Cattermole's—'

'Yes, we'll skip that bit, thank you,' interrupted August.

Sir Henry grinned.

'Must we? I was rather enjoying that.'

'Please—' said August. 'Continue.'

The duck began again:

'All afternoon stuffing kingfisher. Fiddly. Tea: fruitcake. Inedible. Had to throw on fire not to disappoint. Agnes Cuddy is a fine housekeeper but appalling cook. Around 10.45 p.m. boy came about job. Extraordinarily late. Tom is his na—'

'You see I knew it,' interrupted August excitedly. 'That's the connection. Go on go on.'

'Very scruffy he is too. Took fright when showed him telescope. Seemed confused and appalled by prospect of a life in taxidermy.

Not sure why he bothered. Not sure *he* knew either—'

'And I was right, he would have made an appalling taxidermist,' smiled August. 'Continue.'

'12.44 a.m. Woken by tremendous noise. Storm raging outside. Snow, thunder! Then—lightning? Most peculiar meteorological phenomenon.' The duck paused. 'That's it.'

'So there we have it. 12.44 a.m. I was meticulous to a fault.'

'But you never actually saw the lightning strike?'

'No. This only confirms what Arlo heard. To be quite certain, we would have to go back and see it for ourselves. Back to that time where—'

'We already are, old bean—which breaks our cardinal rule: never interfere with your own life.'

'But we wouldn't be interfering. We don't want to meet ourselves, we don't want to talk to anyone: in fact we don't want to change anything at all. All we want to do is to observe.'

Sir Henry exhaled loudly. He chucked another nut into his mouth.

'That will not be easy, August. Not talk to anyone? We're bound to foul something up. Every action has a consequence, even the smallest, as you well know.'

'But supposing it provides the answer to everything? This is more than just a coincidence, Henry. We can't just ignore it. Think about the boy. Lord knows what's happened to him by now.'

Sir Henry looked up at his old friend. Somewhere within the deep folds of skin his clear eyes were sparkling.

'Well? What do you say?'

Sir Henry harrumphed loudly. He glanced at the duck, then stared out of the window. At last he said:

'I seem to remember it was very, very cold that winter. Can you manage that?'

'I managed it then, I don't see why I can't manage it again.'

'All right. Let's go then. Tonight.'

'Tonight?'

'Isn't time of the essence?'

August grinned.

'Bravo, Scatterhorn.'

CHAPTER 19

THE DEVIL YOU KNOW

SPLASH! The cold water smacked across his face and brought Tom spluttering to his senses. Opening his eyes, he stared up at the bare branches of trees against a dark sky.

'That's done it. Clever thinking, Gordon.'

'But look at the state of him. He's all wet now.'

Tom sat up and found himself sitting in the centre of a dark square. He could see the lights of buildings through the trees, and heard the sounds of traffic in the distance.

'Where am I?' he shivered. 'Who are you?'

A burly man in a thick overcoat leant forward, his squashed face seemingly too small for his considerable frame.

'I'll give him another.'

'Wait.'

A second man stayed the bucket of icy water in his hand.

'Don't go storing up trouble for yourself, Seamus. We was only told to wake him—not drown him. Have a care, man.'

Seamus grunted. The boy certainly would not appreciate being soaked again. In fact, his dark eyes were starting to look very angry indeed.

'You was out for the count, my lord. And Mr Rainbird's instructions were to bring you round by any means necessary. No offence, you understand, but we's been having the very devil of a job. So *he* thought—'

'*You* thought—'

'I didn't—'

'We both thought this was the last resort.'

Tom stared at the two square-shaped men, their caps pulled well down over their ears.

'Seamus and Gordon Garnish, my lord, at your service.'

'Mr Rainbird was most partic'lar. We was to get you up 'fore you went inside, so's not to cause The Leader any embarrassments,' continued Seamus carefully.

'He is waiting for you,' added Gordon Garnish, flicking his eyes up towards the top floor of the large concrete block lit up on the street opposite.

Tom was rapidly coming to his senses and remembering what had just happened. This was London. Dukes Square. He was back in his own time. And that was Don Gervase's headquarters.

'IMPAI?' said Tom, reading the large gold letters above the door.

'That's it, HQ,' said Seamus cheerily. 'You've got to be ever so clever to work in there. Or born to it. One or the other.'

Tom shivered a little. IMPAI . . . International Movement for the Protection and Advancement of Insects . . . He remembered what the letters stood for now. Streams of men and women walked through the revolving doors. It was just the sort of faceless, joyless place he had always imagined it would be. Then turning round he saw the shabby house in the far corner of the square. The front door had been kicked in and a couple of burly shadows loitered on the street outside, standing guard. That was how he had got here from Golding Golding's party . . . that was where the connection was. It was all coming back now . . . But his parents, why were they there? They knew nothing about any of this . . . and where had they all been taken? There were so many unanswered questions . . .

'Best not keep him waiting too long, my lord,' smiled Seamus, pulling his cap down lower. 'Cos you know how he's the very devil for punctuality.'

'Very devil,' echoed Gordon.

'Yes,' said Tom, standing up with grim determination. 'Of course. Let's go.'

'Erm, maybe,' Seamus hesitated, then produced a slim black comb from his pocket. 'Just to save you the bother—eh?'

Tom took it warily.

'You know how he is. That hair of yours always seems to stick in his craw, don't it?'

Seamus and Gordon watched approvingly as Tom scraped the blond tangle away from his face.

'Will that do?'

'Perfect, my lord, quite perfect,' nodded Gordon Garnish. 'Every inch the prince.'

Tom tried to ignore whatever that might mean and thrust the comb into his breast pocket, his fingers brushing against a scrap of paper. A neatly folded scrap of paper . . .

'This way, my lord.'

Up the steps they went, and in through the revolving doors

into the brightly lit foyer. What was that scrap of paper? . . . A security guard stepped forward to prevent the Garnish brothers going any further, but the moment he saw Tom he fell back in respectful silence. Seamus smiled nervously and pressed the button for the lift, which instantly appeared.

'And may I say once again how particularly sorry we is about the dousing,' he murmured. 'We meant no offence, only—'

'It's all right, Seamus,' said Tom, stepping quickly into the dark panelled lift. The Garnish brothers stood slightly bowed, waiting. And so did everyone else in the foyer.

'Erm . . . which floor?'

'The usual, my lord,' nodded Gordon.

'Twenty-three,' whispered Seamus helpfully. 'There are so many we all get a little confused sometimes.'

'Thanks.'

Tom pressed the button, then waited for the doors to close. The grey-faced men and women in the foyer waited too, watching him as if he were on stage. Why were they staring at him so? At last the doors closed and Tom hurriedly extracted the folded slip of paper and smoothed it out with trembling fingers. It was a rough scribble in pencil—and barely legible at that. But the handwriting might have been his own.

> *'I must be more polite.*
> *I must not ask any more questions.*
> *I must be very careful of Dr Culexis.'*

Tom's mouth felt dry as he read the scribble again. Were these the thoughts of his echo? It seemed so. But why were they here? Perhaps he had been instructed to write them down by Don Gervase, perhaps he had decided to write them down himself . . . either way it was a glimpse of what was expected of him.

The lift slid to a halt and the doors revealed a dimly lit corridor at the end of which stood an imposing mahogany door. A small green light above it winked, beckoning him forward. Tom knocked, tentatively.

'Enter.'

Be more polite, don't ask questions . . .

Taking a deep breath Tom found himself in a large grey office. The room was filled with curious machines, half-mechanical, half-insect, buzzing in orderly rows along lines of tables. In the centre stood a large leather desk loaded down with stacks of yellow reports.

'Good evening.'

Tom glanced towards the wide marble fireplace, decorated with golden beetles. Don Gervase stood with his back to him, greedily sucking the warmth out of the blazing fire in the grate.

'You're looking very pleased with yourself.'

Though his back was turned, Tom realized Don Gervase was watching him intently in the large fisheye mirror hanging above the mantelpiece. His considerable forehead and huge yellow eyes were magnified to seem more insect-like than ever.

'Feeling better now, I presume?'

'Much better thanks.'

'I'm glad. Sit down.' Don Gervase swivelled round to face him, grinning widely. 'Have you seen the evening paper?'

Assuming not, he flung one in Tom's direction. Tom picked up the *Scarazand Star* and saw an image of himself with one foot on the caddiscapula. 'Terror in the Jungle!' shouted the headline. 'Boy's secret mission revealed!' Tom read on with mounting amazement. According to Dr Culexis—'the young hero's trusted friend'—Tom had just returned from the most dangerous adventure of his life. He had heard that Golding Golding, 'a cunning and devious enemy', was hard at work in his secret jungle laboratory, 'breeding a particularly dangerous creature with which to attack Scarazand. The caddiscapula.' The boy had asked the Glorious Leader's permission to destroy them. Permission was refused. So the young hothead decided to go it alone. Armed with 'nothing more than his sword and a mountain of cunning', the boy killed each and every one of them, single handed—then despatched Mr Golding Golding himself. On pages two, three, four and five there were more pictures: Tom scaling a cliff; diving into the jungle pool; duelling caddiscapulas in their underwater lair; chasing Golding Golding across a roof . . .

'But it's not true,' Tom gasped, reaching the end.

'Not entirely. But that is what facts are for. Dr Culexis has excelled himself. Every day the legend of the hero is growing.'

Tom stared at the pictures feeling very intimidated. He couldn't help wondering what the point of all this was.

'Don't you enjoy playing the role I have given you?'

Tom cleared his throat awkwardly.

'Erm. Of course—'

'You don't seem very enthusiastic. Or grateful.'

Don Gervase Askary wandered over to the window and peered out into the dark square.

'You are the people's hero, boy, the defender of Scarazand. Thousands would kill to be in your position. Plucked from obscurity, trained up, chosen to wear the Scaramoor—even Lotus Askary was not worthy of that.'

Tom smiled weakly.

'Maybe she didn't want it.'

'Oh I think she did. More than anything. But Lotus, dear Lotus, she was too headstrong, too moody, too unpredictable—she never cared if anyone liked her or not—and they didn't. She made too many enemies, so she had to go—it was as simple as that. And between ourselves, Lotus would *never* have defended the Glorious Leader to the death. Unlike you.' Don Gervase turned back, his eyes darkening. 'And it won't be long now.'

'I'm sorry?'

'No, you haven't heard. But while you have been napping Nicholas Zumsteen has been traced. He was even at that party— can you believe it? Apparently about to announce his imminent assault on us. Possibly even as soon as tomorrow.'

'Tomorrow?' Tom tried to cover his confusion with a smile. 'Are you certain?'

'His gorogonas are about to hatch in a forest in Siberia. A spy has confirmed it. And it is a very good place to attack us from. There is a hollow mountain there, an old volcano, that leads straight down to Scarazand. I had it blocked up, but Nicholas has realized it is very easy to reopen. So as soon as we receive the word we will have to get up there first and pick them off as they hatch. One by one.'

Tom stared into the fire blindly. But this was all so soon, too soon . . . what about climbing up the vent hole and everything else?

'We are in for the fight of our lives, boy. Soon you will lead the troops out into battle, and it will be the greatest battle there has ever been. Doesn't that excite you?'

'What? Oh very much so. I . . . I can't wait.'

Don Gervase looked at Tom quizzically.

'You are *ready* to defend your Glorious Leader to the death?'

Tom could do nothing more than grin helplessly. So Lotus was right, he *was* some sort of mascot to be sacrificed . . .

'I will do . . . everything I have to do.'

Don Gervase smiled generously. 'I understand. You're nervous, aren't you, boy? You didn't expect it to happen so soon. Neither did I. And so much is expected of you. You want to acquit yourself well.' He paused. 'Sometimes I too feel the burden of responsibility. What would happen if I suddenly vanished into thin air, swapped all this for the life of a simple dung beetle. Toiling away through the dirt. Rolling balls of dung about.' Don Gervase chuckled. 'I could do it—like that,' he clicked his fingers sharply.

Tom tried to read Don Gervase's expression. Was he joking? He didn't seem to be.

'But would you?'

'Of course not. It would be absurd. But escape is always an attractive option, is it not?'

Tom felt his cheeks begin to burn and there was nothing he could do to stop it.

'No—not now, when I have come so close to achieving everything.' Don Gervase stared out of the window, across the square, and into the past. 'You know, when I was your age I could see my goals lined up like trees marching towards the horizon. First, find the elixir. That I did. Then take over Scarazand by bloody revolution—that I did. Then control the Queen and make Scarazand the most powerful colony that ever existed. That I have done too. And when I had achieved all that, I promised myself that one day I would use this great power to steal from the world what the world stole from me.'

Tom could guess what he meant. Don Gervase wanted revenge, for that vicious beating, for all the life that was denied him, revenge for being Dorian Rust, the hated, lonely orphan.

'And how were you going to do that?'

'Oh . . . I had a few ideas. Still do,' he smiled. Lights flashed across his strange features. 'He doesn't know it, but in collecting those gorogonas Nicholas might have done me a great favour. He is about to unleash a storm he cannot possibly control. The world will change—for ever, I suspect. I shall have to be ready to adapt.'

Tom did not understand this cryptic talk and Don Gervase was not about to explain. He turned away from the window. With a friendly grin he walked towards the chair where Tom sat perching on its edge.

'Tell me something. In amongst that meddlesome riff-raff we captured this evening were a man and woman who seemed to recognize you. Who did you think they were?'

'Erm . . . ' Tom coughed nervously. This was an extremely dangerous subject. 'I . . . I don't know, exactly. But I felt . . . ' Don Gervase loomed over him, waiting for the answer. 'I felt . . . like I was connected to them somehow.'

'Connected? In what way?'

Tom's heart began to gallop.

'Just a feeling I had. Like they might have been . . . that I was maybe . . . related to them, or something. That's all.'

It was a performance of sorts. Don Gervase considered this answer carefully.

'Would you mind if I killed them?'

Those yellow eyes seemed to be burning holes right into Tom's skull. He could not lie.

'Yes, I would mind. I don't want you to.'

This answer seemed to satisfy Don Gervase. He had heard of this phenomenon in echoes before, a kind of ancient memory that somehow survived inside them, despite their duplication.

'So you're not going to, then?'

'Kill them?' Don Gervase smiled. 'Anyone caught plotting to assassinate me can expect little mercy. They have been interrogated, and admitted to working for Golding Golding. They have been for years, apparently, collecting rare and poisonous insects for him to play with.'

Tom clenched his fists so tight it hurt. Was this really the truth? If it was, why hadn't they told him?

'Had it not been for the coming battle they would have been liquidated. But as it is they will now find themselves defending Scarazand alongside everyone else. We will need every footsoldier we can get.' Don Gervase smirked. He noticed the boy still seemed extremely agitated. 'Parents are not something I'm familiar with. But I suppose I am your parent now—in all but name. I have chosen you—encouraged you, instructed you. So from now on I shall expect you to behave as any son should. Is that understood?'

Tom was still so confused he could barely think.

'Is it?'

'Yes . . . of course. Your grace,' he added.

'Your grace.' Don Gervase smiled. 'That is good but I think . . . *father* would be better. It may not be entirely true, but it will help you to understand your role.'

Tom felt Don Gervase's cold fingers climb up onto his shoulder like a crab, and did everything possible not to flinch.

'Very well.' He just couldn't say it. 'If you like.'

'Excellent. Now,' Don Gervase leapt up and strode across the room to the door. 'I think it is high time you and I returned to Scarazand to prepare for tomorrow. There is an army to organize.'

Silently Tom followed the tall man down the narrow corridor and into the lift. Down they went at speed.

'Forgotten your comb, boy?' tutted Don Gervase, staring at Tom's hair, which despite his earlier efforts was rapidly becoming unstuck.

'I've only just brushed it.'

'Well I'll have to do it again. Give.' Snatching away the small comb he set about Tom's untidy curls with manic intent, oiling them down with spit into something like his own. Tom stood in sullen silence, concentrating as hard as possible on the small row of numbers in front of him. He would put up with anything now—just so long as it took him down into the heart of Scarazand. He must climb that vent hole immediately, tonight— before the battle, before he was discovered, before this maniac destroyed everything . . .

'That's better,' growled Don Gervase as the lift shuddered to a halt. 'I can tolerate many things but unruly hair is not among them. You will have to make more of an effort.'

Thrusting the comb back into Tom's hand he stepped directly out of the lift onto the platform of a tube station. It was crowded with workers, their overcoats streaked with rain. No one had noticed the Glorious Leader's arrival.

'A-hem.'

The crowd reacted to the low growl as if stung by an electric current. Instantly they backed away, allowing a pair of scurrying half-breeds to roll out a battered red carpet that snapped over the platform's edge. Tom suddenly felt very conspicuous as hundreds of pale, yellowed eyes turned towards him. Could they tell who he really was?

'Three cheers for the Glorious Leader!' shouted a young man at the front. 'Hip-hip!'

'Hooray!'

'Hip-hip!'

'Hooray!'

'And Tom Scatterhorn too! Hip-hip!'

'Hooray!' The entire platform raised their fists in salute. Don Gervase bowed his head graciously in acknowledgement.

'You see? Your fame precedes you, Tom,' he murmured, his lips barely moving. 'People need to dream of heroes, do they not?'

Tom smiled awkwardly, and followed Don Gervase down the red carpet. He stared back at the men and women, their young faces strangely old and cracked like earth in a drought. Here and there a tie slithered straight, a jacket buttoned itself, a skin umbrella furled. Tom may have been back in his own time, but he had no doubt who these people were . . . His eyes met those of a woman who was holding a copy of the *Scarazand Star*. She was goggling at him in amazement.

'My lord, may I be the first to shake your hand,' she whispered adoringly. 'The Revolution needs chaps like you.'

'Thanks,' Tom replied, a little embarrassed.

There was a loud blast on a whistle, and instantly a single-carriaged train thundered out of the tunnel, squealing to a halt beside the red carpet. The carriage resembled a gleaming, golden maggot, with thousands of black and gold beetles swirling across its pressed aluminium flanks. There was a loud hiss, followed by a collective gasp from the crowd as the double doors swung open to reveal the interior. It was unlike any train they had ever seen: velvet walls, deep black leather armchairs, a rich Persian carpet, a tiger's head mounted on the wall—there was even a fireplace containing a small electric fire. It was like the inside of a jewelled box, and radiated a rich and overwhelming smell of chocolate.

'After you,' smiled Don Gervase, ushering Tom inside. He was about to step in when a shy voice whispered something behind him.

'Sir? Please, sir?'

Tom turned and saw three identical schoolgirls standing on the edge of the carpet bearing copies of Tom's photograph and pens in their hands. Don Gervase raised an eyebrow: that was a nice touch—clever Dr Culexis had thought of everything.

'Well go on,' he instructed.

Awkwardly Tom went forward and scribbled his name across the picture of himself. The girls could barely contain their excitement.

'There,' he said, finishing the last one. He raised his hand to the crowd. 'Goodbye.'

The entire platform grinned back at him.

'GOODBYE!' they shouted as one.

'My lord!'

Suddenly a familiar squat figure appeared breathlessly at the doorway, brandishing a brown packet in his hand. It was Ern Rainbird.

'My lord,' he rasped, 'my lord, I—'

'What is it, Rainbird?' demanded Don Gervase, somewhat irritated to find his henchman spoiling the moment.

'This . . . has just arrived. For you.' Marching down the red carpet, he bowed low, then thrust the packet forward towards his master. 'Dr Culexis insisted you should see it. As soon as . . . ' Ern Rainbird dissolved into a violent coughing fit. 'Ahem—Excuse me. I wouldn't have presumed, only the matter did seem most particularly pressing.'

'Very well,' snapped Don Gervase, somewhat perplexed but not wanting to make a scene. He took the package. 'Thank you, Rainbird.'

'Your grace.'

Ern Rainbird bowed again and watched them step aboard. The doors clanged shut, and Tom felt Rainbird's lizard-like eyes burning into him as they sped away. Something was wrong, he could sense it. Lowering himself uneasily into a black leather armchair he glanced at the brown package that Don Gervase had casually placed on the small wooden table.

'You don't like alcohol, do you?'

'Not really,' Tom replied, seeing Don Gervase return from the sideboard with two slim crystal glasses each filled with clear golden liquid.

'This might change your mind. Honeyed firewater. Straight from the distillery.' He set down a glass beside Tom and folded himself into the chair opposite. 'Chin-chin.'

Tom watched him take a sip and pick up the package, ripping open the end.

'What is that?'

Don Gervase pulled out the yellow report and seemed somewhat mystified by the hologram on the front cover.

'Security Failings at Dragonport. An enquiry conducted by Dr K. Logan, acting Head of Facility.'

A knot of fear began to tighten in Tom's stomach.

'So . . . so is there . . . a problem?'

Don Gervase turned the page in mild irritation.

'Some misdemeanour or other I expect.'

Taking another sip of his firewater Don Gervase Askary began to read. His expression gave nothing away. The carriage thundered on in silence. Tom stared at his shoes. What could he do? Surely this was what he thought it was? He tried to take his mind off it by looking around the carriage, and his eye was drawn to the tiger's head mounted on the opposite wall. It was ancient and faded and it seemed to be staring straight at him. Had he not known better Tom might have assumed this was the faded, dusty man-eater from the Scatterhorn Museum. Unless that's precisely what it was, and Don Gervase had cut its head off to keep as a memento . . .

'Odd, isn't it, how the desire to save one's own skin surpasses all others,' rumbled Don Gervase at last. 'Sometimes I wonder if I will end up running every single part of this empire myself. Even this lowly prison at the edge of the world.'

'Why is that?' asked Tom innocently.

'Three days ago this place was in chaos. Though, of course, it has been concealed from me until now. There was a power cut, followed by a chocolate flood, followed by a cake fight, and then a full-scale riot.'

'Oh. Really?'

Don Gervase read on in mounting disbelief.

'Someone called Nurse Manners broke her leg. An echo named Francis Catchpole fell off the perimeter wall, landing on Ebenezer Spong, who was killed stone dead. Then a certain Mr Vee's van was hijacked inside the yard by two inmates. It was driven at speed around the town, until one thief was eventually apprehended. But the other . . . ' Don Gervase turned the page. For a moment he said nothing. A spark of red fury danced in his eyes. 'The other managed to escape. He has not been seen since.'

With a supreme act of will Tom bit his lip and said nothing. How could he not suspect? Or maybe he was just beginning to . . . At last Don Gervase flung the report down onto the carpet and pushed it across to Tom with his toe.

'Dr Culexis is very concerned. Clever Dr Culexis. Always full of clever theories. And now he's got old Rainbird hopping mad. Read it,' he commanded.

Tom obediently did as he was told and opened the file in the centre. All the blood seemed to freeze in his face. There was the photograph of himself taken by Dr Logan when he first entered the asylum.

'So . . . erm . . . do you know where . . . where he is?'

'That is a very good question.'

Don Gervase shook the mesmerion out of his sleeve and held it thoughtfully in his fingers. Tom glanced at the ball—how long had he got? No time. No time at all. Already everything had moved too fast . . .

'Do you recognize him?'

Tom grinned inanely, what else could he do?

'Obviously he looks like me.'

'Go on.'

'So that means . . . '

Don Gervase's milky green eyes bored into him like lasers. Tom was not sure how long he could keep this up.

'There are two of us. Him and me. He's out there . . . somewhere. Is that a problem?'

Don Gervase was already revolving the many possibilities of this deceit through his mind. If this was the real Tom Scatterhorn, how could he have swapped with his echo, right under his nose? It must have been at that party. Underwater? Probably. But then what was he doing here, right now, with him? He must want something . . . something he is risking his life to find, and he is either being very foolish, or very brave, or perhaps both . . . Don Gervase watched the boy looking innocently back at him. It was impossible to tell the difference. They were identical.

'You're smiling,' he said.

'Am I?'

'Why are you smiling? Did you think you'd get away with it?'

Tom watched Don Gervase's fingers spin the mesmerion. He felt a burning wave building inside his head.

'YOU WILL TELL ME THE TRUTH!' barked a voice. 'THE TRUTH!' It shouted louder. 'STAND UP!'

Tom stayed sitting down. He breathed away the thunder inside his skull. Don Gervase stared at him coldly, not moving a muscle.

'I don't know what you mean,' he whispered.

'STAND UP WHEN I TELL YOU!'

The voice screamed higher this time. Tom felt beads of sweat break out on the back of his neck, his cheeks. With iron concentration he kept staring blankly at Don Gervase.

'If I knew what you meant—'

'GET UP!'

Tom closed his eyes. The thunder was overwhelming. His hands were shaking and he could resist no longer. Despite every effort it was too much. With eyes clenched shut he staggered to his feet and stood there, waiting. Don Gervase's thin mouth stretched into a sickle grin.

'Tom Scatterhorn. What are you playing at?'

Tom looked down at the glass of firewater on the table.

'What is this, some desperate attempt to kill me? Do you have any idea who I am?'

The thunder was beginning to roll away. Tom's breathing quickened.

'What are you doing here?'

Tom clenched his fist. One chance . . . this was it.

'LOOK AT ME WHEN I AM TALKING TO YOU!' screamed Don Gervase, in wild fury.

In the next instant Tom reached down and flung the glass into the tall man's face.

'AHH!'

Don Gervase barely had time to wipe the stinging liquid out of his eyes before Tom reached the cabinet and flung the decanter at him. Don Gervase dodged and it smashed into the fire, bursting into flame.

'You . . .'

Tom flung another bottle, this time hitting Don Gervase square on the forehead, then glasses, books, anything else he could find . . . but the tall man was on his feet, walking towards him with a wild look in his eye.

'Very foolish . . . ' he muttered, the mesmerion spinning in his fingers. 'Provoke me any more and you know what will happen . . . '

Tom ran round to the far side of the carriage, trying to ignore the thunder rushing in his head. He knew what this threat meant . . . in an instant Don Gervase could turn into a giant black beetle and kill him.

'What about the battle?' he gasped, edging along the wall. 'Don't you want me to save your life—'

'To hell with that. You'd never do it.'

Desperately Tom wrenched a clock off the wall. With every sinew of strength he hurled it hard, knocking Don Gervase off balance, then kicked over a small table, causing him to trip. Almost by accident Don Gervase found himself slammed back against the opposite wall.

'Right. That's it.'

With a smirk Don Gervase moved forward and in that moment something hard and cold grabbed him by the scruff of the neck. Before he could resist he was shaken violently from side to side like a rat. The tiger's iron jaws clamped across his neck and it would not let go . . . Don Gervase smiled at Tom weirdly, his face changing colour, blotching red and orange as if he was starting to boil inside . . . Tom knew what was about to happen . . . he was about to metamorphose . . . transform . . .

'No,' he gasped. 'No!'

Without a thought he ran forward and grabbing a standing lamp in both hands brought it crashing down on Don Gervase's head. Instantly the lights went out. The tiger let go, and the Glorious Leader sank to a crumpled heap on the floor. For a moment there was silence. The carriage thundered on into the darkness.

'Just in the nick of time.'

Tom looked up. In the flickering light of the fire he saw the tigress staring down at him.

'Thank you, Tom Scatterhorn. You have no idea how much pleasure that gave me. That'll teach him to slice me to bits. Pity I couldn't kill him too and do us all a great favour.'

Tom looked down and saw the mesmerion still gripped between Don Gervase's white fingers. A thin steel tentacle had slithered out of his cuff and was curled protectively around it. Dare he try to rip it away? He must try . . .

'Not a good idea,' advised the tiger, seeing Tom reach for the ball. 'That's his security. You cannot break it, and if you try you will wake him up.'

'Are you sure?'

'Most certainly. And surely you have something better to do?'

Tom looked down at the mesmerion desperately. Did he really need it? Not if he could climb up the vent hole in time . . . Could he? He didn't know. But if he got caught now, there would be no escape. Don Gervase would never forgive this, never . . .

'Almost there,' growled the tiger as the carriage began to slow. 'I'd get cracking if I were you.'

CHAPTER 20

KING OF THE MOON

All too soon the golden carriage screeched to a halt. With a loud hiss the doors opened and Tom stepped out to find himself at the tunnel's end. Beyond, there was a piece of corrugated iron leaning casually against the wall and a large pink-eyed insect crouching above. He took one last glance back into the carriage. There lay Don Gervase Askary, surrounded by a mess of broken glass and upturned furniture, his feet and hands bound as tightly as Tom had dared. And there was the mesmerion, still locked beneath that thin steel feeler inside his fingers . . . if only there was a way—

'No you mustn't,' growled the tiger. 'Don't even think about it. Go. Now.'

Tom grimly wondered if he wasn't making a colossal mistake.

'All right. What about you?'

The tiger fixed him with her flame coloured eyes.

'Don't be so sentimental, boy. What can he do to me? I died years ago.'

'Bye then.'

'Good luck, Tom Scatterhorn.' You're going to need it down there.

Ignoring the stony gaze of the insect, Tom Scatterhorn slipped behind the corrugated iron and found himself on a narrow rock ledge. Beyond was a slender stone bridge that spiralled steeply down into the darkness. Tom knew this place—he had been here before. This was one tentacle of the great hidden labyrinth built by the beetles of Scarazand, protecting them and connecting them to every place and time . . . Tom had a distinct feeling this was Don Gervase's private entrance. Well at least it might get him there a little quicker . . .

The next five minutes were a blur as Tom hurried down into the darkness, keeping his eyes fixed on the path as it cut an elegant sweep through the tangle of white bridges that snaked away in every direction. He was dimly aware of insects and men moving above and below him but he didn't stop to look or catch their eye: his mind was set on one thing only, to slip into the great city of Scarazand unnoticed and climb up through the attics of the palace into the vent hole . . . at last the path began to rise and, passing through a rock face, he entered a short tunnel that ended in a circle of white light. This was it . . . instinctively Tom slowed, listening to the chaotic din in the chasm beyond, the thunder of millions of spiky feet on stone, the hiss and throb of the insects, and the deep, relentless heartbeat of the Queen that began to pulse loudly in his brain.

And then suddenly there it all was, laid out before him exactly as he remembered. A vast cave, in the centre of which stood Scarazand, a thick black spike of rock that over thousands of years the beetles had hollowed out and infested. All around its flanks hundreds of skeleton-thin bridges stretched out towards the cave walls, and every single one of them teemed with every kind of life—insects, beetles, half-breeds, men, and plenty else besides . . . it should be easy to hide amongst that lot, Tom reasoned, no one would notice him down there, and then . . . Tom squinted across at the rickety town, clinging precariously to the upper reaches of the rock. Above it, almost at the point where the black column narrowed to a spike and touched the ceiling of the cave, was a tumble of roofs fanning out like bats' wings . . . that must be the palace, right up there, at the very top. And at its apex Tom could just make out a small round window nestling under the eaves like the eye of a snake . . . that was where he must aim for—

'Ohh!'

Tom started back as a black gondola slid up before him. It was a little like a cable car. There were two velvet seats inside. Should he get in? Obviously he should. Did that mean he had been seen? Perhaps . . . but it's still all right, he told himself, it might be some sort of automatic machine, and it might save him time . . . Hesitantly Tom took his place and watched as two long levers hinged down from above, stretching out cords of jelly-like elastic either side of the gondola. The elastic creaked and hummed . . . suddenly the gondola fired out into the air like a stone from a slingshot, skimming over the chasm towards the town. Far below faces turned up in amazement to see the black shape whizzing over their heads and Tom could just imagine Don Gervase's delight at seeing his subjects from this angle; in fact, he probably invented it for precisely this purpose . . . In a moment the gondola had glided down towards a long balcony. Four cloaked figures slunk forward to catch the contraption, setting it gently on the ground.

Remember who they think you are. Remember what is expected of you.

'Thank you,' said Tom, jumping out with purpose. The dark figures backed away deferentially. Each was tall and gaunt and entirely hidden inside their thick black cloaks that bore the same red insignia. They might have been men, they might have been insects, it was impossible to tell. Skrolls—Tom suddenly remembered their name: Don Gervase's hated secret police—he glanced up at the palace high above. Dare he ask them to take him up there? He could try . . .

'Your Grace, if I had only known I could have been more ready.' A man in a neat black and gold uniform appeared in the doorway, his small round glasses glinting. 'Time is not on our side. The scouts you sent out have just returned and—' Dr Culexis stopped mid-sentence when he realized Tom was alone. He glowered at the empty gondola, then back at the boy.

'What is this?' he demanded. 'Where is Don Gervase Askary?'

'He's tied up. H-h-held up. I mean he's got held up.'

'Held up?' The doctor's thin ginger moustache twitched. He peered at Tom accusingly. 'Held up by what?'

'He saw your report about an escape somewhere, and he said he wanted to check some facts,' blustered Tom. 'He said I should go on ahead and prepare the colony for . . . for everything we must prepare for . . . He will be here shortly.'

Dr Culexis did not seem remotely convinced.

'But did he read my report?'

'Of course. I saw Rainbird give it to him myself.'

'Then what other facts could he possibly want to check? Everything was in there.'

Tom shrugged. It was all he could do to return his suspicious gaze.

'Is this some sort of joke?'

There was a muffled shout and Tom turned to see a cloud of insects spread themselves against the cave wall like a vast curtain. The shimmering surface flickered a moment, then formed the head of Don Gervase Askary, smiling like a waxwork. 'One leader!' boomed a voice. An automatic cheer rose up from below. The face dissolved, and to Tom's horror it was replaced with his own, dressed in that elaborate black spiked armour. 'One champion!' the voice boomed again. There was an even louder cheer. 'To lead us in one battle! A battle to end all battles! To decide the future of all things!' Wild cheers. 'Tomorrow!' A hushed silence fell upon the millions watching below. 'We will be attacked at dawn. From the valley beyond the northern gate.'

'Def-definitely tomorrow then?' stammered Tom, trying and failing to sound unconcerned.

'Yes,' snapped Dr Culexis irritably. 'The scouts have just returned and confirmed it. Which is why it was imperative that I broadcast this announcement, despite . . . '

'Prepare to defend your colony!' boomed the voice, echoing around the cave. 'Prepare to defend Scarazand! Arm yourselves!'

A roar erupted and the hissing and clattering began again, rising to an almost deafening pitch.

'We must be there at daybreak, at the very latest. Frankly there is so much for the leader to organize. Quite apart from the small matter of . . . ' Dr Culexis glared at Tom poisonously. 'I suppose even *you* understand what this means?'

Tom smiled painfully.

'Of course.'

'Good. Well you'd better get ready then.' Dr Culexis snapped his fingers and a Skroll approached. 'Escort him to his room,' he barked. 'Unless his lordship would prefer to try and find it on his own?'

Tom ignored the barbed remark, and with a determined smile made straight for the doorway. What world had he just plunged himself into? Culexis knew, perhaps they all knew . . .

In they went, Tom blindly weaving through the dark labyrinth of passages that all looked the same. Soon Tom became hopelessly disorientated—had they gone up, down, walked in a circle? The Skroll wasn't about to tell him. The creature slunk behind like a constant shadow, Tom sensed it would follow him off the edge of a cliff should he so choose . . . Turning a corner he was relieved to find himself at the end of a high vaulted hall teeming with activity. There were officials bearing piles of instructions, soldiers pushing trolleys laden down with crossbows, insects hauling catapults and other strange contraptions . . . the colony was preparing for battle all right, and Tom dived purposefully into the crowd, searching the signs above each archway: Ministry of Duplication . . . Ministry of Poison . . . Ministry of Repair . . . Ministry of Pulp . . . where was the palace?

'Aha, the famous warrior returns—with yet more scalps, I hear?' A familiar figure strode through the chaos sporting a wide-brimmed hat festooned with thin red worms. It was Gord, the ringmaster from the stadium. Tom recognized him from his last visit.

'Excellent hunting, excellent,' he grinned, squeezing Tom's hand. Tom did his best to smile at the group of young cavalrymen trailing in his wake. All wore long leather boots and thick padded costumes. Their faces were a patchwork of cuts and stitches.

'Nice work, your grace,' said the girl in the middle. She had a shaved head, and seemed to know him well. 'So there was really fifty of 'em caddiscapulas then?'

Tom nodded awkwardly: they had obviously read the evening paper.

'Erm . . . it was dark, I couldn't see much. Maybe.'

'Maybe?' She glanced at the others and giggled. Obviously they did not expect such diffidence. 'What, you've lost count, then?'

'I mean maybe there were more.'

'More?'

'Yes. A lot more.'

'OK,' she laughed, clapping him on the back. Tom laughed too, but inside he was seething. *Be more confident . . . arrogant. Otherwise this will never work.*

'So are you looking forward to tomorrow, sir?' asked one of the boys.

'Definitely.'

'We're buzzing, aren't we, folks?' tittered Gord. 'And so's 'em bladgers. Hootin' and blowin' in their stalls, gone right off their food. They got the nose up for a proper show, see. But that's cavalry for you—smell blood before they see it!'

Tom nodded, having only the vaguest idea what the old man was talking about.

'People say they's like snakes we'll be fighting. Snakes as long as this room,' continued the girl excitedly. 'Fire breathing snakes.'

'Gorogonas, Viola,' corrected Gord. 'That's what Culexis said.'

'You ever seen a gorogona before?'

Tom nodded casually.

'A few times. We've nothing to worry about.'

'No?'

'They're not nearly as bad as they look.'

'Hear this!' wheezed Gord, clearly approving of Tom's breezy confidence. 'So will you be sayin' a few words at the address tonight?'

The smile began to freeze on Tom's face.

'Erm . . .'

'You did promise,' added Viola.

Gord pressed forward till the red worms around his hat were touching Tom's shoulder.

'A word or two from you will do wonders for morale, my lord. You know how them half-breeds love a whinge—especially the night before a battle. And a proper battle at that.'

Tom found them all looking at him expectantly.

'I'll think about it. I'm very busy. You know . . . how he is.'

'We do, sir. That we do,' winked old Gord. With a toothy smile he led his troops away. 'Now don't forget to grease that visor. And sharpen that sword!'

'Bye,' waved Viola.

Tom turned on his heel, his heart quickening. Everything was happening so fast—if he wasn't very careful he was going to be sucked into the heart of this battle without realizing it—and it wasn't only him . . .

'I need to go up to the palace this instant,' he demanded of the large Skroll still hovering behind him. 'You will lead me through this rabble.'

'My lord.'

The Skroll bowed obediently and set off towards the wide staircase at the end. Tom kept his eyes fixed dead ahead, trying to avoid the admiring glances on all sides, but he couldn't help feeling he was being watched . . . at last they reached the stairs, and barely had they climbed a couple of steps before Tom noticed some sort of commotion at the top. He looked up. There was Dr Culexis, surrounded by a gang of Skrolls. He was barking instructions and pointing frantically down towards Tom: and at his side stood Ern Rainbird . . .

A knot of fear tightened in Tom's stomach. Rainbird! He must have returned to Scarazand by some other way . . . had they found the carriage? It surely wouldn't be long now . . . Rainbird and three Skrolls were forcing their way down through the crowds towards him.

'Actually . . . actually this is going to take too long. Can we take another way up?'

'Does my lord require the private lift?'

'Yes. Quick.'

The Skroll bowed, and to Tom's relief it turned back down the stairs and moved with stealthy speed towards an archway on the far side of the hall.

'My lord,' it hissed, holding open a small door.

Tom instantly sat down on the single wooden seat and waited.

'I do not want to be disturbed, you understand? Not by anyone.'

The Skroll bowed again.

Tom glimpsed Ern Rainbird's grim face advancing through the crowds.

'Why isn't it moving?'

'Tap once for chartroom, two for library, and three for private apart—'

Tom's thumping heel interrupted the shadowy creature and the next instant there was a great scrabbling below. Something unseen shoved him vertically up the dark stone shaft at speed, and barely seconds later Tom was brought to a giddy halt before an ornate door. Feeling a little dizzy, he stood up and stepped off the platform.

'Don't go anywhere,' he commanded whatever was lurking beneath the chair. 'That is an or—'

Too late. The lift dropped back into the gloom. What did that mean? Tom preferred not to think about it. Stepping through the door he found himself in a grand mirrored hallway. It was dark, silent: there was no one here. Was this the right place? It certainly looked like a palace. The attic above Don Gervase's bedroom . . . Tom sincerely hoped that Lotus was right about that. Carefully he walked through one empty gilded room after another, their walls covered with mirrors and tapestries. It was all as lifeless as a doll's house. Perhaps Don Gervase never even came up here . . . Finally Tom reached a pair of high doors and, opening one, found himself in yet another ornate room, as neat and symmetrical as the rest . . . but in the centre stood a carved black bed. And in the corner was a small circular window. Glancing out, Tom saw the rooftops tumbling far below. This must be that window he had spotted at the very pinnacle of Scarazand, the eye of the snake . . . this *must* be it. But how to get up?

Directly above the bed hung a large glass chandelier. He could try . . . but that would mean—Tom kicked his scruples to the back of his mind. There was no time for niceties now. Only one thing mattered. Swiftly Tom closed the door and wedged a chair under the handle. Then he grabbed another and, placing it on the bed, stood up and grasped the chandelier. Kicking his legs away he pulled hard, twisted, spun it round and round and round . . .

'Come on,' he muttered, rocking it to and fro. Something cracked above, a snap, a rip, then—

Suddenly Tom fell back down onto the bed and the chandelier smashed all around him. Glass balls bounced across the floor and the air was full of dust . . . but when he looked up, he saw a small round hole in the ceiling . . . he'd done it! In a moment Tom was back on the chair and hauling himself into the beams above . . . Where now? The rafters fanned out in a circle from a column of black rock . . . that must be the outer wall of the chimney, so how had Zumsteen got into it? He must have made himself a hole . . . Stepping through the thick wooden joists Tom reached the circular wall. He could barely see anything, but when he ran his hands across the surface he felt a patch that seemed rough and brittle, and warm, like paper . . . a repair? Without thinking Tom banged his elbow against it and it tore straight through. Instantly a thick swirl of sulphur swept into the attic . . .

Tom's heart leapt . . . this was it! Right above Don Gervase's own bed! Lotus was right. No one would dare do this . . . no one except Nicholas Zumsteen. Barely able to believe he'd found it, Tom covered his nose and peered out into the deep well. Hundreds of metres below lay the great white Queen, the size of a submarine, pulsing, glistening, swirling in gasses . . . The heartbeat in Tom's head was deafening but he forced himself to look up . . . Yes! A small circle of light, only not so small and not so far now . . . how high was that? Thirty metres, maybe less . . . the rock was pitted with holes and ledges . . . he could do it, just as Zumsteen had done, ignore the heavy pulsing air and climb up to the vent hole and then find some way to stop all this before—

Suddenly a door banged open somewhere below. The noise was so loud that Tom jumped. He looked back at the hole in the ceiling. There were footsteps approaching, and muffled voices, too.

'He's in here,' growled a low voice, rattling the bedroom door angrily. 'He's locked himself in.'

That was Ern Rainbird, who else? Blooms of sickly yellow gas drifted past . . . don't think about him, just go, Tom. Now! With both hands Tom stretched out and grasped the nearest ledge. It felt secure . . . don't look down . . . whatever you do, don't look down—

'Shall we smash it, sir?' hissed a voice.

There was silence. Tom edged out into the chasm on tiptoes. Don't look down . . . Forcing himself to stare at that chink of light he began to climb . . .

'Sir?'

'All right.'

The crash tore both doors from their hinges. Tom closed his eyes. The booming inside his head was tremendous. Right hand. Left hand. Keep going up—

'Rainbird!' The shout echoed through the apartments. 'Rainbird! Ernest Rainbird!'

Suddenly Tom's foot slipped. Desperately he regained his footing. No, it couldn't be . . . He glanced down in terror at the opening below. His head began to swim . . . so high—so high up . . . his fingers wouldn't move. His arms had suddenly locked. Fear was paralysing him, gluing him to the wall—

In the bedroom below it was chaos. The gang of Skrolls nervously backed away from the broken doors, hurriedly concealing their axes within their cloaks. Ern Rainbird hastily kicked as many glass balls as he could under the bed.

'I'll do the talking,' he whispered, 'we're in the right here, lads, don't wor—'

'What is the meaning of this?' demanded Don Gervase Askary, striding into the room. There was a long cut across his forehead and his face was white with anger.

'My lord, I must explain—'

'Indeed you must. Why have you broken down the door of my bedroom?'

'We—there's been a—'

'Why have you ripped down that chandelier?'

Ern Rainbird smiled desperately, squirming before his master.

'My lord, it's not what you think—'

'Are you about to tell me what I think?'

'No, no no I—'

'Then what are you doing destroying my private apartment?'

'Because . . . because, that is Dr Culexis said—'

'Spit it out, Rainbird.'

'The Scatterhorn boy, your Grace—the real one, he's escaped and—'

'Nonsense. Drivel. Claptrap.'

Ern Rainbird's eyes bulged in confusion.

'My lord, I beg you, please believe—'

'That will be all, Rainbird. '

Ern Rainbird stared at his master open-mouthed. Had he not read Dr Culexis's report?

'But Dr Culexis. Doctor . . . '

Don Gervase cocked his head and waited. Ern Rainbird flailed one finger towards the door, then up towards the hole in the ceiling.

'The boy. He's hiding. Up there.'

'Get out, Rainbird, and consider yourself very fortunate you are not in jail for this wanton vandalism.'

Ern Rainbird blinked.

'But I was only—'

'I'm not going to ask you again.' Don Gervase's voice was so poisonous the words seemed to drip from his lips. The stocky henchman stood motionless. He saw the mesmerion spinning through his leader's fingers.

'GET OUT OF MY SIGHT!'

A second later Rainbird and his crew dived for the safety of the hall and thundered down the stairs. Don Gervase turned his milky green eyes towards the hole in the ceiling.

'That was not very intelligent, boy.'

There was silence from above.

'And now you will obey.'

A second later Tom Scatterhorn tumbled headfirst through the hole and bounced down onto the bed. He looked up, dazed, to find Don Gervase Askary standing beside the window with a cruel smile on his face.

'So that's what you were looking for. A way *up* into the vent hole, finding out where it touches the surface from the inside out: very resourceful. Very clever. But you haven't the brains to work that out yourself, boy. Who gave you the idea?'

'Lotus,' mumbled Tom, somehow unable to stop himself.

'Lotus Askary, of course. And I suppose she told you that this is how my brother did it, too. I see. And you swapped at Golding Golding's little soiree. In that pool, was it?'

Tom nodded in response.

'And once you had climbed up the vent hole, what were you planning then?'

'I don't know.'

'You don't know? You don't *know*?'

'LITTLE FOOL!' screamed the voice in his head 'HOW DARE YOU!'

Tom tried to cover his ears. The noise was overwhelming, like a hot knife slicing right through his skull . . .

'What about Catcher and Scatterhorn? Are they helping you in this?'

Tom shook his head.

'No? Nicholas Zumsteen, then?'

'He knows nothing about it.'

Don Gervase knew that the boy had no choice but to tell the truth—for what it was worth.

'Escaping before the battle. I never took you for a coward, Tom Scatterhorn. Arrogant and disobedient, but not that.' Don Gervase paused to stare out at the teeming chaos below. 'Dr Culexis was right of course, and Rainbird too, they know very well who you are. They are only trying to protect me. On any other night we would not be having this little scene. I would have killed you already. But now, unfortunately, it is too late.' He turned back to find the boy curled up on the bed, his hands over his ears.

'The battle you were trying to escape is only a matter of hours away, and even I am not so foolish as to deprive Scarazand of its precious mascot.' He spat out the word as if it stung. 'They may hate me, but they love you. So you, boy, will have to do. Now get up. GET UP!'

Tom staggered woozily to his feet to find the Glorious Leader's slippery, bloodless face centimetres from his own.

'Now listen very carefully, Scatterhorn. From now on you are not the scrawny, miserable scarecrow you appear to be. You are something better. You are the people's champion. You have risen from their ranks, proven yourself to be a great fighter. Tomorrow morning, at dawn, you will set them an example. Which means doing everything possible to protect me. Do you understand?'

Tom stared dizzily at Don Gervase, breathing away the pain in his head.

'Do you?'

'Why have you done this? What's the point in turning me into some sort of hero?'

The question irked Don Gervase more than he could say. To think his fate, *his fate*, was bound up with this loathsome thirteen-year-old boy . . .

'It's those pictures, isn't it?'

'Pictures?'

'Betilda Marchmont's pictures. You're scared she might have really seen the future. You think I'm going to save your life.'

Don Gervase laughed mockingly.

'I've no idea who you are talking about. Betilda Marchmont?'

'Don't pretend you've forgotten. Why else did you scratch out my face—and yours, too. You had to know.'

Don Gervase sneered.

'Oh that. You think I set any store by the doodlings of some madwoman?'

'But that's why I have an echo, isn't it? That's the reason. Just in case it's true. Lotus was right. You're pathetic. But I'm not your puppet. You can't make me die for you.'

'Can't I?'

Tom glared at Don Gervase belligerently.

'No you can't, Dorian Rust. You're on your own.'

The smile hardened on Don Gervase's face. Despite everything, Tom sensed the power was shifting . . .

'Do not presume to play games with me, Tom Scatterhorn.' The tall man's eyes narrowed. 'Perhaps you're right. Perhaps I cannot control you as much as I would like. And if you choose not to fight tomorrow—so be it. Stay in bed. There is nothing I can do.' Don Gervase paused, dangerously. 'But, if you refuse to lead them on the battlefield, the millions of your supporters down there will be left very disappointed. They've been expecting great things. If they realize their hero is nothing but a coward, afraid of war, afraid of death, well—' Don Gervase turned away from the window, his thin lips breaking into a cruel smile. 'I won't be able to stop them. Scarazand can be a brutal, savage place. They will rip you apart.'

Don Gervase walked over to the door and opened it.

'Think about what choices you really have, Tom Scatterhorn. Think about them very carefully indeed.'

The Glorious Leader marched Tom down the stairs into a dark passageway. Flinging open a rough wooden door he pushed him inside.

'You,' he growled at the Skroll standing at the end. 'No one is to disturb Mr Scatterhorn until tomorrow morning. Double the guard.'

'My lord.'

Don Gervase took one last look at Tom.

'And there is something else you should bear in mind. Goro-gonas are vicious, clever, almost perfect creatures. They are unlike anything you have ever seen. Whatever happens tomorrow, I guarantee it will take every ounce of your wit and cunning just to stay alive.' Don Gervase smiled darkly. 'But of course, if by some accident you do—consider yourself free. I release you. You shall never hear from me again.'

The door slammed. Tom listened to the footsteps clattering away up the stairs. Did he believe him? It hardly mattered any more. He doubted Don Gervase would ever make a promise he knew he wouldn't have to keep. Sitting down on the bed, Tom's eyes began to fill up with hot tears and he blinked them away angrily. If *only* he had had the courage to climb up the chimney, he could have escaped by now and maybe everything would be different . . . but would it? Really? Right from the start he had been borne along by Lotus's crazy confidence, by the sheer audacity of the idea, but when it actually came to climbing up the inside of that chimney, trying to ignore the choking yellow gas, the hammering in his head, the Queen pulsing far below . . . it had been like hanging off the edge of a skyscraper . . . He couldn't do it. He'd frozen. He'd failed. Tom Scatterhorn wiped his eyes, and for the first time in a long, long while began to wish he was just an ordinary thirteen-year-old boy, and that none of these remarkable adventures had ever happened to him.

But Tom Scatterhorn was not very good at feeling sorry for himself for long. Already he was becoming distracted by the contents of this room. That it was his echo's he had no doubt. But it was as ordered and tidy as his own was messy and chaotic. A line of shoes stood neatly under the bed. Coloured pencils were arranged in order on the empty desk. There were two more charcoal grey velvet suits hanging on the wall, identical to that which he was wearing, immaculate and neat. Who was his echo? Was he really like him?

In the corner, on its own, stood an ancient wardrobe, encased in thick, steel bands. Tom opened the heavy door, and for a moment he could do nothing but stare. There, framed against the dark space, was the most extraordinary suit of armour Tom had ever seen. It was the Scaramoor—he recognized it instantly. Reaching in, he touched its gleaming black and gold surface. It felt warm. He peered at the hundreds of spiky shapes that made up the breastplate, the intricate sliding layers around the collar, and the helmet—which was even more elaborate than Betilda had painted. The visor was a snarling, wolf-like snout, inlaid with silver teeth. Tom lifted it a fraction and it squeaked shut. There were two long slits for eyes, a sharply ridged head, bristling with jagged spikes, and on each side two black and red antlers, twisting and polished. The Scaramoor was intricate, beautiful, terrifying—but it was not for show. The surface was covered in tiny scratches and dents. It had been worn in battle before—perhaps many battles . . .

Suddenly Tom felt very intimidated. Supposing his echo was not just some hollow puppet: supposing he had really worn this, and fought in it, too? Tom reached into the darkness and gingerly drew the sword from its scabbard. The grip felt worn, well-used. The blade was perfectly balanced. Tom swished and cut at the air angrily, then, feeling a little self-conscious, slid the sword back into its scabbard. Tomorrow, whatever happened, it would be Tom's turn. With a heavy heart he carefully replaced the sword and closed the door. And it was only then that he noticed the small folded square of paper that had been wedged beneath it . . .

CHAPTER 21

STONE COLD TRUTH

'Well, what do you think?'

'Very good. Perfect. If I didn't know, I would never know, if you see what I mean.'

'Excellent, August. Now if you wouldn't mind.'

Taking a door each, Sir Henry Scatterhorn and August Catcher pulled them shut on the long low boatshed. Beyond was a grey expanse of frozen river. Only the most discerning eye would have spotted the outline of a biplane hidden behind the piles of sacks and crates.

'Burdo will have not the foggiest that it is even there,' said Sir Henry, clamping the padlock shut and pocketing the key. Wrapping themselves up against the wind, the two ancient men turned towards the small cottage through the trees.

'Feels a little rude not to at least say hello,' said August, noticing an oil lamp burning in the downstairs window.

'Like you said, can't talk to anyone, old chap,' murmured Sir Henry, pulling a dog-eared book of tables from his pocket. 'You're going to have to keep unnaturally quiet.'

Sir Henry looked up at the new moon and flipped open

a compass. Taking a bearing he ran a finger down the list of numbers.

'Dammit.' He checked his watch, then squinted at the tables once more. 'Rattlesnakes. I can't believe it. I've done it again.'

'What is it?'

'We're late.'

August pulled out his fob watch and stared at it: it was almost six o'clock.

'How late is late, old bean?'

Sir Henry wrinkled his eyebrows into a knot.

'A whole week late. It's the *twenty-third* of December, 1899. Drat it.'

With a grimace he shoved the tables back into his coat pocket.

'That really is very, very annoying. I apologize. I'm afraid without that little lodestone of yours my skills are not what they should be.'

'Have you lost it?'

Sir Henry shook his head.

'I gave it to the boy. His need seemed greater. I didn't antici-pate doing much precise travelling.'

'No.'

'But if we tried again we might not get any closer. Indeed it's highly likely we might end up even further away.'

'Quite.' August drew up his scarf against the buffeting wind. 'Well, it's not a disaster. We're here now. There seems no point in trying again. Even if we cannot witness the event itself—the evidence will surely still be there.'

'Meaning?'

'The woods. The tree. The lightning must have left some trace.'

'Right. Right.' Sir Henry looked up at the thin moon galloping through the clouds. 'Well I suppose there's no point wasting the trip. Better get our skates on.'

August grinned.

'Indeed. I've been rather looking forward to that.'

A minute later two stooped figures emerged from the edge of the woods and slid quietly along the frozen river. They were wrapped up in tweed and wool with balaclavas pulled so deeply over their brows they might have been mistaken for a pair of trees, were it not for the long elegant swishing of their skates and a certain quickness of their movements. Ahead of them burned the lights of the ice fair, the stalls sparkling pink and orange against the night sky.

'Strange to think we are actually here already,' murmured August. 'Can there be any rules about seeing oneself?'

'Probably not advisable, old boy. But I have no memory of bumping into an ancient old tramp claiming to be me—do you?'

'If I did, it didn't make much of an impression.'

A minute later they were in amongst the noisy stalls, skating quietly through the marzipan sellers with lanterns on their hats, barrel organs with monkeys leaping about, children laughing and racing each other, dogs pulling toboggans, and in the centre of it all the pale green ice castle, complete with battlements and turrets.

'I'd forgotten what fun all of this is,' murmured August as they reached the shore. Stamping up onto the frozen ground they took off their skates and put their shoes back on.

'Yes, but have you noticed?'

Sir Henry nodded past the lines of chestnut braziers that ringed the waterfront to a chandlery shop window. Outside stood two identical, pinch-faced men dressed in black swallowtail coats, staring into the crowds.

'I remember those two . . . why that's those doctors, Shadrack and Skink,' said August.

'Are they who I think they are?'

'Most definitely. Don Gervase's spies. They even came and gave me some medical advice on your condition.'

'Then even more reason to keep a low profile, old chap. A very low profile.'

'Right.'

Silently August and Sir Henry watched the two hunched doctors slip away down an alley, then stowing their skates in a bag, struck out into the tide of people moving down towards the ice fair. They kept their heads down so low they barely noticed other identical doctors moving stealthily amongst the sailors and orange sellers and girls with hoops—

'Mind yer backs, mister!'

There was loud jingling and a horse and trap thundered up the street behind.

'I say!' roared Sir Henry, jumping up onto the pavement. August attempted to follow but he was not so nimble, and before he knew it he had tumbled to a heap in the gutter. The two dogs running behind pricked up their ears and sniffed at him curiously. In the next instant their hackles rose and they set upon August, barking and biting at his arms and legs.

'Get off! Shoo!' shouted Sir Henry, kicking at the hounds in vain.

'That's it! Have a go, old man!' laughed a crowd of young lads, enjoying the sight of one tramp trying to help his fallen friend. 'Stick it to 'em! That's it!'

The driver glanced back and hauled on his reins.

'Footloose! Fancy! Come away from there! Come away!'

But the hounds sensed something strange about these two old vagrants, and they were persistent.

'What you's all standin' about for?'

A round form elbowed through the crowd to see the two old men and dogs fighting in the snow.

'Get along with yer, you nasty mutts!'

With a tremendous crack the woman brought her cane down on Fancy's side, making the dog howl in pain. The boys cheered.

'And that!'

Footloose yelped as the cane whipped across his back.

'Have a care, missus! Them's my bloody dogs!'

'Well yew larn 'em some bloody manners then! Git along there!'

Footloose and Fancy needed no further encouragement and scampered away to their master.

'Come here!' the man swore, and with an angry backwards glance cracked his whip and the trap lurched on up the street.

'Are you hurt?' asked the woman, helping Sir Henry pull August to his feet.

'Quite all right, thank you. Remarkably well-padded as it happens, which was fortunate because . . . good lord.'

August wiped the snow away from his face and saw that his saviour wore a dark shawl and a small black bonnet perched on the back of her head. She looked more than a little like a dodo.

'Don't I know you, sir?' she said, in a high, singsong voice.

She cocked her head to one side and August smiled helplessly. It was Mrs Spong, and there were her five daughters lined up behind her like a row of ducks.

'I . . . I'm not sure you do, madam. We've just arrived—'

'From the ferry—just now,' intervened Sir Henry pointing in the direction of the docks. 'We're tourists.'

Mrs Spong looked from one wrinkled face to the other. Come to think of it, *he* looked familiar too. Very familiar—aristocratic, somehow. Both of these tramps were quite obviously not what they appeared to be.

'You've been extremely kind,' smiled Sir Henry politely. 'Thank you so much.' He bowed formally, and Mrs Spong could not help dropping a small curtsey. Taking August's arm Sir Henry motioned him away into the crowd.

'What did you do that for, mother?' asked one of the girls, watching the two old men slither up the hill.

'I don't know. Really I don't. Most peculiar.'

Sir Henry and August continued up through the town in silence. Gradually the houses and people began to thin out as they climbed up the lane, past cottages and fields until they reached the iron gates of Catcher Hall. It was darker now, and the wind seemed to be blowing even harder. There was no sign of anyone about.

'I suppose walking straight in won't do any harm,' suggested Sir Henry. 'What do you think?'

'It's my house, I can do what I like,' huffed August, and they set off down the drive. After a couple of bends Catcher Hall loomed up before them, its lights throwing shadows across the snow. August looked up at the narrow oval window in the attic directly above the great front door.

'You know I can barely believe I am doing this. That's my workshop up there. That's probably me,' he said, pointing at the vaguest silhouette behind it.

'Armed with your brand new telescope,' whispered Sir Henry, drawing August back into the shadows. They skirted around the terrace towards the rear of the house and stopped on the edge of the croquet lawn. To the left there was a greenhouse and a walled kitchen garden, and beyond that ground fell away into a jumbled mass of trees.

'Well there they are. The woods. I must say I find this rather extraordinary. As you say, this is your house, August.'

'I know. It is unsettling, to say the least. But why else did Askary buy the place? And why else has he been so obviously protecting it ever since? I am ashamed to say I know nothing about it.'

Sir Henry moved out onto the moonlit grass and stared at the black shapes below. The wood was encircled by a high wall.

'How do we get in?'

'There's a door from the kitchen garden, but I seem to remember it's always locked. The gamekeeper has a key, and there's another hanging behind the scullery door.'

'Behind the scullery door? You mean, in the house?'

'Of course.'

'August, that really is not very helpful.'

'No. Quite.'

'Why did you keep your woods under lock and key?'

August seemed mystified.

'I seem to remember it was something to do with gypsies making themselves at home . . . boys making dens . . . I don't know, the gamekeeper was very insistent.'

'Who is this gamekeeper of yours?'

'He's not really a gamekeeper. More of a gardener cum

watchman. Has a little cottage at the bottom of the hill. Ralph Rainbird is his name. The family's been here generations.'

'Ralph *Rainbird*?' Sir Henry raised his eyebrows. August looked at the ground sheepishly.

'Oh dear. I haven't been very observant, have I?'

Sir Henry said nothing.

'But there is another way in . . . I think. My sister and I used to do a bit of exploring when we were younger. Might be able to find it. Come on.'

Ignoring Sir Henry's despairing glance August led the way across the croquet lawn, slipped through the gap in the yew hedge and followed the track along the edge of the high wall. It was dark down here, very dark, so that when they reached the small silver birch August was searching for it seemed to be almost glowing.

'There,' whispered August, pointing at the slender white branches that just reached over the crest. 'We used to shimmy up over that.'

'And how old were you when you last did this?'

'Eight or nine maybe.'

Sir Henry smiled and shook his head.

'If it wasn't so important I would say not on your ninny.'

'I know. I'm sorry.'

'Do stop apologizing.'

'Sorry.'

A minute later, and after much cursing and wheezing, the two ancient men found themselves standing in an overgrown thicket.

'Well if you ever thought it might be a jungle, August, you were not mistaken,' gasped Sir Henry, glancing around. 'This place looks as if it hasn't been entered for centuries.'

'I don't think it has. My sister and I never got very far. We heard there was some old gardener's shack in the middle some-where—completely fallen down. We never found it.'

Sir Henry looked up at the trees and listened. Above the sound of the wind there was something else. Barking and branches breaking . . . it was coming closer.

'Is Ralph Rainbird a vigilant man?'

'Erm . . . I assume so.'

'Did he have three dogs?'

'Why?'

'Well, someone's coming up the hill. With three dogs.'

'Really?'

'Yes. Really,' said Sir Henry, listening hard. The barking seemed to be behind them, then to the front, circling around. 'I suspect it's him. He's heard us crashing about and he's coming up to investigate.'

They pushed on blindly, ignoring the jumble of brambles that tore at their hats and ripped their trousers, driving a path through the confusion of rotting stumps and dead branches.

'Look!' said August suddenly. There was something rushing through the trees ahead. A shadow racing . . .

'That's one of them. Stay behind me,' whispered Sir Henry firmly. Without a thought he pushed forward towards the sounds, and a minute later they reached the edge of a small, oval-shaped clearing. The dogs were barking somewhere to the left.

'It's all right, we're downwind of them,' panted Sir Henry, hanging back in the shadows. 'Do you think that could be what you and your sister heard about?'

August peered into the jumble of blue and black shadows to

see the vaguest outline of a roof and the remains of what might have been a chimney. The whole structure was entirely covered in ivy and a tree had collapsed on top of it.

'It could be. I don't know.' He shrugged vaguely. 'I'm ashamed to say I have never seen it before in my life.'

Sir Henry pulled out his small notebook and thumbed through to the back.

'The vent hole is not a hole . . . ' he whispered. 'It's hidden in a tree next to the tumbledown shack. That's what the echo told Tom. Doesn't say which side but those are his words exactly.'

They stood in silence a moment, absorbing the strange, ancient atmosphere of this unexpected place. And then they noticed that just beyond the clearing, half-hidden behind a row of narrow pines, stood a vast stag-headed oak, its dead branches reaching up towards the sky like a hand.

'That's odd, isn't it?' whispered August, indicating the tree. The oak was so dilapidated that iron bands had been used to hold its trunk together, and it seemed out of keeping with everything else in the wood. It was much, much older, as if it was the last remnant of some secret, pagan place.

'What do you think?'

'Unfortunately it doesn't appear to have been recently struck by lightning,' murmured Sir Henry. The dogs were closer now, crashing through the undergrowth and converging. 'But if there's something odd they'll sense it. Come.'

Withdrawing into the thicket Sir Henry and August dropped behind a rotting trunk and watched as the three hounds burst into the clearing, yelping excitedly. They were large, liver-coloured, slathering things, all teeth and gums, and they bounded straight over to the hut, barking excitedly. Then one peeled away and, following its nose, quartered the ground towards the ancient oak. Barely had it reached the base of the tree before it danced back, as if the ground was burning its feet. Its excited yelps turned to confusion, then alarm . . . A sharp whistle pierced the gloom and a burly man dressed in a thick green coat stalked into the clearing. His features were hidden in the shadow of a stovepipe hat and a shotgun was crooked over his arm.

'Rainbird?'

August glanced at his old friend and nodded.

'Come away from there!' shouted the gamekeeper fiercely. The dogs obediently ran to their master, and then back to the tree, barking excitedly. 'Leave it!' Ralph Rainbird approached the tree cautiously and then glowered into the woods all around. He could see no one.

'Heel!' he bellowed, and whistled his dogs away into the thicket, his hat merging into the trees.

'I wonder what his real job is,' whispered Sir Henry as the silence returned.

August stared after the shadow.

'We weren't precisely well-acquainted.'

'I can see that. Come on.'

Carefully they stepped out into the clearing once more and walked across to the ancient tree that rose menacingly against the sky.

'You're right, August, there's something very odd about this,' said Sir Henry, examining the iron bands almost submerged beneath the gnarled bark. There was no gash or broken branches to be seen. But there was no grass growing round it, either. Just bare earth.

'Maybe it's been scorched up there,' suggested August.

'All right.'

Fearlessly Sir Henry grasped a low branch between his thick gloves and began hauling himself up. August barely noticed that his friend had gone. He was peering into a small black hole near the base. Picking up a twig he slid it inside. There was a hiss, and when he tried to withdraw it he couldn't. The twig had been caught. Locked in.

'Most peculiar,' he murmured.

'What are you doing?' called Sir Henry from above.

'I'm wondering if this is even a tree at all,' August replied, noticing some white liquid oozing round the hole. Carefully he wiped a bead onto his finger and sniffed it—there was a vague smell of burning hair. 'Do your gloves feel hot?'

Sir Henry stopped breathlessly and looked at his hands.

'Yes they do rather,' he said examining his fingers. The leather of his gloves seemed to be melting. 'Why, what is it?'

'Must be some defence mechanism,' muttered August, 'and probably not the only one. I don't think it likes you climbing all over it!' he called out.

'Well I've almost made it,' Sir Henry replied, glancing at the branches above. Just above his head was a great cleft from which the five dead limbs sprang out towards the sky. 'Come on, old boy.'

August did not need any prompting. Grabbing the same low branch he began hauling himself up to where Sir Henry sat.

'It really doesn't like us,' puffed August, watching the acid eating away at his mittens as he climbed higher and higher.

'Here.'

Grabbing his hand, August scrambled up until they stood side by side in the centre of the tree. The cleft formed a wide platform, flat like the palm of a hand. There was no sign of a lightning strike.

'Wrong tree?' muttered Sir Henry sitting down on the large circular bole in the centre. Years ago it might have once formed the massive main trunk, but obviously it had either been cut or fallen down, and now the bark had formed a shallow dome over the top of the scar. August scratched his head.

'I can't understand it.'

'Neither can I,' said Sir Henry, drumming his fingers on the bole. 'Nothing here.'

'Wait.' August stared at Sir Henry's fingers. 'Do that again.'

'What?'

'That. What you just did with your fingers.'

Sir Henry obliged and they listened. The bark rang hollow. He slid off the dome and stared at it in amazement.

'You don't think?'

August nodded, his eyes shining.

'I do. It's a lid. Look.' He pointed to the six thin ridges that ran up the sides of the bole and met in the centre. 'It opens up like the petals of a flower.'

'How ingenious,' murmured Sir Henry, suddenly recognizing the object for what it was. 'But it's closed.'

'My guess is this tree has sensed us climbing up. Maybe the moment we touched it triggered the defence mechanism. It's entirely plausible that the vent hole should have such a device to keep it hidden.'

Sir Henry stood up and scratched his head.

'But if this lid closes the main chimney, the gas must still be escaping from somewhere—'

'Oh it is—can't you smell it?' They stood still, sniffing the sulphurous reek in the air. 'I suspect it's coming out of the branches: they're probably all hollow. The beetles must have drilled minuscule holes in them.'

Sir Henry marvelled at the cleverness of it all.

'So actually it's not a tree at all, it's a large lung. And I suppose it's waiting for us to go down before it opens this again,' he said, kicking the dome with his toe.

'Which won't be long, because of the acid.'

Sir Henry looked at his gloves. The leather was almost burnt through.

'Do you think this is all Askary's idea?'

'Must be long before him, old boy. This chimney is fundamental to the existence of Scarazand. It's evolved over the centuries—growing like any other tree, getting larger as the Queen did. It's a perfect disguise.'

Sir Henry was finding it hard to contain his frustration.

'If only there was some way of breaking the damn thing open. If I had an axe or a sledgehammer I'm sure I could knock this lid clean off. Then we could go and get some fireworks or gunpowder or—'

'No point. She's too vast. It would be like attacking an elephant with a peashooter.' August stood up and looked at the dome thoughtfully. 'A lovely bolt of lightning really would have been quite perfect. In one second it would have shot through this vent hole, pierced the Queen's fat pulpy body, and ignited the gas. She would have released that colossal scream and Scarazand would have collapsed, just like that.'

'Something bigger than a bomb.'

'Exactly.'

'But lightning never strikes twice, does it?' growled Sir Henry, his voice rising with exasperation. 'And frankly, how do we even know it hit this tree? This lid looks perfectly intact. I think Arlo Smoot can't have heard it correctly.'

August had to admit Sir Henry was right. It didn't make sense. Crouching down, he examined the bark around the dome once more. In the darkness it was almost impossible to tell, but he thought he could just make out a jagged ridge running away from it down the trunk. Was that a scorch mark? A burn? It might have been . . . traces of white liquid still oozed out of the wound.

'Unless something *else* took the full force of the strike,' he murmured. 'Which, of course, would have triggered the mechanism and closed the dome.'

Sir Henry watched his old friend running his finger down the line in the poison bark.

'You've lost me, August.'

'Perhaps you're right. Perhaps the lightning didn't strike this tree directly.'

'It didn't?'

'Not directly. Perhaps it struck someone *hiding* in this tree that night. And perhaps this tree has already repaired itself.'

Sir Henry was even more mystified.

'But who on earth would be hiding in this tree?'

'Remember which night we are talking about. December fifteenth 1899.'

August stood up and smiled at his oldest friend's confusion.

'You can't mean Tom Scatterhorn.'

'Obviously not. But what if there was another boy up in Catcher Hall that night, someone answering my advert for an assistant taxidermist. And supposing he was also called Tom.'

Sir Henry snorted.

'Tom? Why Tom?'

'Because as he was sitting in the kitchen, warming his toes, waiting to see me, Tom Scatterhorn suddenly appeared upstairs, having travelled back from his time to this, and we all thought they were the same person.'

Sir Henry scratched his head.

'But is that what happened?'

'I don't know, but Agnes Cuddy my housekeeper and little Noah certainly met Tom Scatterhorn on the landing upstairs that evening. They sent him up to my workshop where I was expecting him. It never occurred to them he was someone else. Tom Scatterhorn just walked into the past as if it was the most natural thing in the world.'

Sir Henry was flummoxed.

'So who was this "Tom", then, and how did he come to be hiding in this tree?' August paused to think for a moment.

'If he had seen my advertisement in the paper, he could have been anyone. Some boy from the town, a gypsy here for the ice fair: Dragonport is full of strangers, isn't it? And as for finding himself up this tree . . . ' August shrugged. 'Maybe he didn't actually want the job at all, he just wanted an excuse to come into the house to steal something. And supposing he *did* steal something. He waited till he was alone in the kitchen then pocketed something small and valuable, easily missed, some silver cutlery maybe, then he ran down into the garden, shimmied over the wall like we did, but instead of finding his way to the bottom he got lost in this thicket. Ralph Rainbird got wind of him, so he decided to hide in the biggest—'

'But this sounds like the most extraordinary coincidence,' interrupted Sir Henry, exasperated. 'And what about the acid? His skin would have melted.'

'He didn't have to linger. All he had to do was climb up, which triggered the lid to close—and then the lightning struck.'

'Killing him outright and unwittingly saving Scarazand.' Sir Henry watched his gloves steaming with a vexed expression on his face. 'Well it's one hell of a story. And if it's true I'd say the lightning bolt put him out of his misery.'

August stood in silence. He imagined those dogs barking below, the boy's burning fingers and feet, unable to go up or go down.

'But you were told nothing of this at the time?'

August shook his head.

'Obviously not. But then I don't seem to have been told very much about anything at all.'

'I suspect there might have been a reason for that, old bean.' Sir Henry smiled wryly. 'Back in those days your head was filled with higher concerns. Dioramas, displays, elixirs of life . . . you spent so much time up in that workshop of yours stuffing stuff I doubt you even knew what day it was.'

'That's not true. I wrote a diary. Meticulously.'

'But you were rather obsessed, old chap. Slightly odd, and quite unworldly.'

August seemed rather surprised and a little hurt.

'Was I?'

'Yes I'm afraid you were. And if, as you say, there was a boy hiding in this tree, then I wouldn't be at all surprised if Rainbird didn't quietly dispose of the body without telling a soul. He didn't want policemen poking around, not down here, of all places. It's probably his job to guard this damn thing. One does wonder though, why the boy's family never came round asking questions. You'd have thought he would have been missed.'

August said nothing. He was still smarting at the idea that he might have been able to prevent this tragedy, if indeed this is what had happened.

'Perhaps we should pay a visit to the graveyard before this blasted thing melts us alive,' said Sir Henry, clapping his old friend on the shoulder. 'If he's anywhere he'll be in there. And a freshly dug grave is a good place to start, isn't it?'

Five minutes later two elderly gentlemen slithered into the churchyard at the bottom of Catcher Hill. It was dark now, and a thick blanket of snow covered all but the tallest gravestones.

'Where do you think they'd put him?' muttered August, stamping his feet against the cold.

'Against the far wall, methinks. Isn't that where most unwanted paupers end up?'

August nodded grimly.

'All right.'

Quietly they picked their way through the drifts towards the low flint wall in the furthest corner. Here, as Sir Henry had predicted, there stood a line of thin wooden crosses poking out above the snow.

'Four hundred Fletcher, gentleman of no fixed abode . . . Hannah Drew, trampled by a bullock . . . Martin Round, fell through the ice, never found . . . '

August rubbed away the snow and peered at a cross larger than the rest.

'Alice Simkins, Merry Simkins, Patience Simkins, George Simkins, *Samuel* Simkins, taken by typhus the same night! Aged nine, seven, five, three and one . . . little wretches,' he muttered. The names scratched into the bare wood were already beginning to fade. 'I suppose they can't afford any better.'

Sir Henry did not reply. He had moved towards another small wooden cross set directly against the flint wall. Wiping away the snow with his glove he noticed it had not been long in the ground.

'Have a look at this.'

August knelt down beside him and peered at the rough ink scrawl.

'Killed by lightning. December fifteenth, 1899. Known only . . . to God?'

'The date is correct. But was it a man, woman, boy, girl . . . ' Sir Henry paused, scratching his chin. 'I would say that is a deliberate omission. Even a cat has the dignity of being called a cat.'

The two old men stared at the small wooden cross in silence. A bitter wind was blowing in off the estuary, sweeping little drifts across the ground.

'We could dig it up.'

'Don't be ridiculous,' snorted August, appalled. 'I think it has to be him, doesn't it? Rainbird probably dumped the body at the church door then wrote that scribble himself. It's too anonymous to be anything else.'

Sir Henry shook his head mistrustfully.

'I must say I still find it all the most extraordinary coincidence. The fact that the boy should choose to shelter in that tree, of all trees, and stand up at the precise moment the lightning struck, taking the blow that would have destroyed the Queen lurking below. Isn't it all a little too . . . neat?'

'Listen, I'm as suspicious of coincidences as you are,' muttered August. 'But here is the evidence: how else do you explain it? That boy, whoever he was—some unwanted, unmissed waif—is the single reason why Scarazand still exists.'

They stared at the grave in silence for a while.

'Shame, isn't it?' muttered Sir Henry at last. 'One almost wonders, would it not be sensible, given everything that happens from this point onwards . . . '

'I know,' murmured August. 'If there was only some way of preventing him ever climbing up that blasted tree.'

'Or better still, persuading someone who is already here to knock that lid off with an axe, just to make quite sure.'

'Indeed.'

The two old friends glanced at each other a moment: each knew precisely what the other meant.

'But that really would be breaking the cardinal rule. You cannot play fast and loose with the past, August, it's utterly forbidden. It would change everything.'

August frowned.

'Would it? I can't see how anything on the surface would be disturbed at all. A boy would still come up to the house, find a way down into the woods, and obviously a bolt of lightning would still strike that tree. But instead of hitting him, the vast colony of Scarazand that has been hidden below for thousands of years would be wiped out. Nothing else would change.'

'But what about this?' said Sir Henry, indicating the grave. 'Someone is still going to die, aren't they? Or are you saying we ignore that?'

August shook his head slowly.

'We won't have to Because I'm afraid a boy will still die.'

'But Tom needn't be struck by lightning?'

'No—but he will do anything to destroy Scarazand, regardless of the consequences to himself. He knows what they might be.'

Sir Henry understood. But he had never imagined August could be so ruthless.

'It's a high price to pay.'

August nodded grimly.

'But it's the only way Scarazand can ever be destroyed. And that is what he wants, isn't it?'

Sir Henry stared up at the rind of moon racing through the clouds.

'So we must find him. Get him back here on that very night to answer your advert in the newspaper.'

'Which, assuming he hasn't lost that little lodestone, he should be able to find very precisely—unlike us.'

Sir Henry grinned, already he was relishing the thought of the challenge ahead.

'All right. But there is one other problem. A rather large problem. Assuming Tom has not climbed out of that vent hole already, he's about to take part in the greatest battle there has ever been.'

'Oh. Yes. I'd quite forgotten about that.' August raised a quiz-zical eyebrow. 'But that's good, isn't it?'

'Is it?'

'We know exactly where to find him. Because there's only one place that can be.'

CHAPTER 22

LOTUS AND THE ECHO

'This is very, very, *very* annoying.'

Lotus Askary threw away the empty box of matches and stared at the meagre pile of wood in the fireplace. This was not going to work. It was too damp, there was no paper, and she dare not go in search of something drier. Standing up, she drew her coat around her and walked over to where the boy lay stretched out on the sofa. There was a large bruise on his forehead, but he was still fast asleep. That was something. She glanced down the drive to the gatehouse where the police car was parked, a grey silhouette against the snow. Various officers had come and gone during the course of the afternoon but no one had yet searched the attics of Marchmont Castle. Lotus sincerely hoped it would stay that way. She had chosen this old storeroom because there was a key in the lock that worked and there was a small window out onto the roof at the back—and if anyone came searching there was plenty to hide behind: the room was crammed with tea chests, trunks, old toys, doll's houses— sprawling across the floor and the four poster bed.

Moving aside a moth-eaten fox's head, Lotus flung herself into an armchair and scowled at the snow-covered hills beyond. She had to admit that she hadn't really thought about this. She had thrown all her energy into making the swap between Tom and his echo happen, and now that it had, she wasn't sure what to do. She couldn't kill him, because killing echoes weakens the original: that's what everybody always said. But she had to keep him out of the way so there was no chance of him ruining everything. So reluctantly Lotus had waited in the cave until the kerfuffle at the pool had died down, then she had carried the boy back up the garden and through into Marchmont Castle. It had been exhausting work, but she knew she couldn't stay here for long. Somehow she had to find out if Tom had made it or not . . . but how? Lotus bit her nails angrily, oblivious to the two rooks sitting on the battlements watching her. This was ridiculous. She really hadn't thought this through at all . . .

'Where am I?'

Lotus Askary swivelled around to see the boy sitting upright on the sofa, blinking groggily.

'Marchmont Castle. It's in Scotland.'

The boy seemed shocked to hear another voice. He turned to see a slim, dark-haired girl swinging her feet impatiently in an armchair by the window. In the gloom he could just make out her pale, wide face and her large green eyes. She looked like a doll. A very irritated doll.

'Who are you?'

'Don't you recognize me?'

The echo stared at her a moment, then felt the large bruise on his head. He had a vague memory that she had given it to him.

'You were in that pool—'

'Correct.'

The girl stood up and walked towards him like a ballerina. The cold was sharpening his senses by the second.

'You're the one who kidnapped me.'

'Gosh, aren't we clever?'

'Why? Who are you?'

'My name is Lotus Askary.'

The boy seemed momentarily shocked. Lotus was rather pleased with that reaction.

'That's it. Lo-tus As-kary. So you have heard of me?'

The boy knew exactly who she was. Lotus Askary was being hunted the world over, for good reason—

'You are a traitor.'

'Am I?'

'You are helping Nicholas Zumsteen. You escaped from the jail and are plotting against us. You are a traitor.'

The boy's dark eyes held hers. She recognized that stubborn anger only too well.

'And who told you that?'

'Your father. Don Gervase Askary.'

Lotus stood before him with a mocking curl on her lip. The echo sensed that there was something dangerously unpredictable about this girl.

'You won't get away with this, you know.'

'Won't I?'

'Not if I can help it.'

'Not if *you* can help it?'

'My name is Tom Scatterhorn. I have been chosen to protect and defend Scarazand.'

'Defend Scarazand? You sound very important. But you're not doing much defending now, are you?' Lotus sensed the echo's anger was building, and she was rather enjoying it. 'I'll tell you exactly what you are. You are a pale imitation of an average boy, who just so happened to be in the right place at the wrong time.'

The echo glared at her furiously.

'I'm not.'

'Oh but you are. I know the real Tom Scatterhorn, you see. And you have met him too—in that pool. You came face to face with him, in fact. Or maybe your tiny echo mind has already forgotten.' Lotus's eyes blazed, unable to contain the venom she felt. 'To think that you, *you*, a mere echo, could take my place.'

It was hard to know who moved first, such was the speed. In the next second the boy flew at Lotus like a wild animal. Tumbling across the room she only just escaped his grasp, but the echo sprinted after her and, grabbing a broom handle, hurled it at her like a javelin. Lotus ducked and it smashed into a picture directly behind her head, shattering the glass. With an angry hiss she sprinted forward and launched a kick into his chest, but the echo was too quick—rolling underneath he snatched an old golf club lying under the bed. The moment she landed he swung it at her chest and she was only just able to sway back in time. Unnerved by the boy's skill, Lotus grabbed another golf club and began to duel him back across the room, round boxes, over the bed until she had him trapped in the corner—but just as she was about to move in he hauled up a line of flex, whipping away her feet and sending her thumping to the ground. Irritated to the point of metamorphosis Lotus roared and leapt at the light, swinging off it and slamming down hard into the boy's chest. In a second she had him pinned to the floor with her knees.

'You're not bad—for an echo,' she panted. 'Had enough?'

'Almost,' he growled between gritted teeth.

The next moment Lotus found herself flying backwards—thumping into the upturned armchair. The fox's head fell into her lap. For a second she lay still, breathing hard. Already the boy was back on his feet and ready for more. Neither moved. Lotus's eyes were bright with excitement.

'Who taught you to do that?'

'None of your business,' he said, rubbing his wrist. 'I've been trained to deal with people like you.'

Lotus wiped a trickle of blood from her lip.

'So I can see. Except you haven't dealt with me. You've been kidnapped.'

'But you can't stop me escaping.'

'You sound very certain about that.'

'I am. You won't.' The boy glanced out of the window at the darkening landscape. The police car had gone. 'As soon as it gets dark I am going back to Scarazand. Perhaps I'll take you with me as a prisoner.'

Lotus said nothing. Pulling herself to her feet, she straightened her clothes, realizing that unfortunately the echo was right: it was going to be very hard to stop him leaving. He may look like Tom Scatterhorn, but the Tom she knew would never have been able to fight like that. She was going to have to think of something else to keep him here—and fast.

'So why did you kidnap me? What was the point of the swap?'

Lotus did not reply immediately. She wondered just where his loyalties lay.

'The real Tom Scatterhorn has something very important to do which you, as his echo, could never have done.'

'Which is?'

Lotus paused. Perhaps she should trust him . . .

'He's going to destroy Scarazand.'

The echo grinned.

'So that's it. I understand now.'

'You understand nothing.'

'When I grabbed his arm in that pool I sensed he was trying to do something impossible. It was obvious. I felt it.'

Lotus watched the boy very carefully, trying to decide if he was telling the truth. She had heard of such phenomena before . . . unconscious electrical connections between echoes and their originals.

'All right, maybe to you it was obvious. But that is why he has taken your place. Tom is going to climb up into the vent hole using the same route as Nicholas Zumsteen.'

'Which is completely forbidden. And then?'

'We are going to destroy the Queen. Blow her up. The plan is all worked out. But don't expect me to tell you.'

The echo smiled a little.

'You're lying. But it doesn't matter, because Tom will never make it up the chimney.'

Lotus laughed hoarsely.

'Won't he?'

'No, he won't. Because he hates heights.'

'And you sensed that too, I suppose?'

'Once I was made to climb up the lift shaft of Scarazand. I couldn't move.'

Lotus fumed silently. She knew that getting angry with this boy would not solve anything. And it was possible he was telling the truth . . . an uneasy silence descended between them. Lotus decided upon a different approach.

'So you're a professional fighter. You're not bad. In fact I might even admit you're very good. Were you a gladiator down at the stadium?'

'I never became one, but that's where I began,' the echo replied tersely. 'I was an apprentice, sharpening swords, cleaning equipment, taking small parts in the shows. I wasn't special and I wasn't the best either . . . I was just another fighter with all the others. I wasn't born lucky like you.'

'But you did get lucky,' smirked Lotus, ignoring the jibe. 'Very lucky indeed. Why do you suppose that was?'

The boy shrugged. To his credit, he seemed genuinely confused.

'I don't know. One day Don Gervase came down to watch us training, and when it was over he took me aside and told me that he wanted to promote me. And not only that, he wanted me to learn how to behave . . . learn how to become a leader. He said he would organize a few battles in the stadium for the people to watch—which of course I won. But with the mesmerion on my side, I could hardly lose, could I?'

The boy smiled sheepishly, and for the first time Lotus smiled too. She could just imagine the real Tom saying that—in his strangely diffident way. But this echo obviously had no inkling of the dark scheme behind it all. He had no idea that the only purpose of his short life was to defend Don Gervase to the death in that great battle with the gorogonas, whenever it might come, after which he would almost certainly be put to death. It seemed a shame to tell him.

'So you became the new hero of the revolution,' she smiled. 'Defender of Scarazand. What an honour.'

The boy shrugged.

'It is what he wanted. I went to live in the palace. I trained and trained and trained . . . that was that.'

It was almost dark outside now, too dark to see the shadows of the rooks gathering in the trees.

'And did anyone mind that you had been elevated in this way? Apart from me, of course.'

The boy nodded.

'Definitely. Dr Culexis minded.'

'Dr Culexis?' Lotus paused, thinking back to that man beside the pool. 'Small, neat, with a thin moustache and shiny shoes?'

'That's him.'

'Didn't he used to work in the Ministry of Poisons?'

'He did—before. Somehow Culexis wormed himself out of that and into writing stories for the paper, then all the other propaganda too. I would have to play along with whatever he wrote. He's very creepy. He never liked me at all.'

'Why not?'

The boy took a deep breath. He wasn't quite sure why he was saying any of this, and to Lotus Askary, of all people. He had never spoken about it to anyone before.

'I think he was jealous that I had been taken up by the Glorious Leader. He never understood it. Him and Ern Rainbird, they were the inner circle. They had special jobs no one else knew about. Rainbird was a thug, but harmless enough. He didn't care too much about me. But Culexis . . . '

'What about him?'

'I was given a suit of armour. It was from the old time, worn by a great warrior hundreds of years ago, who became the first king of—'

'I know it, The Scaramoor.'

'Culexis was obsessed with it. He was forever telling me how famous it was, how precious it was, what a great honour it was for me to wear it. It was obvious he didn't think I was worthy of it. As an echo, I mean.'

'He's right,' said Lotus shortly. 'Whoever wears the Scaramoor guarantees the allegiance of every half-breed in Scarazand. It's a famous symbol. I was never even allowed to touch it.'

The boy paused, wondering if he should continue. It was clear this had touched a raw nerve.

'I just had a feeling that one day he would take it back. See that it was given to someone more deserving.'

'And how might he do that?'

'I don't know. He was so particular about it.'

Lotus stared out of the window and frowned at her own reflection. What chance was there of Tom knowing any of this? None . . .

'It would be much better for Tom if you didn't try to get back to Scarazand tonight,' said Lotus quietly. 'I realize that might be hard, given your loyalties, but as soon as Don Gervase realizes you've been swapped Tom won't stand a chance. Not down there. He will be punished—severely.'

'Killed you mean?'

'No, not killed. Because when an original dies, the echo dies too—and Don Gervase wants you alive. Which is why Tom was kept alive in a prison so that you could go and live in the palace.'

The echo said nothing for a moment. He seemed confused.

'But I didn't choose to be kidnapped. If he calls me I have to go. There's no choice.'

'But he hasn't called you yet, has he?' Lotus watched him closely. 'Like you said, there is a connection between you two— you felt it. So maybe you should give Tom a chance to do what he must do.'

The echo said nothing. He realized his loyalties were being stretched to the limit.

'I don't understand why he wants to destroy Scarazand. Why is it so imp—'

Somewhere in the darkness there was a tinkling of glass.

'This one, is it?' rasped a gruff voice. 'No? Hellfire, blast and damnation. Try the next.'

The echo looked at Lotus and she pressed a finger to her lips.

'Hide,' she whispered

The echo did as he was told and Lotus silently tiptoed across to the small window overlooking the roof at the back. She listened. Something was thumping about out there . . .

'Eeny, meeny, miny, mo, where's she hiding, I don't bloody—'

'Oh!'

Lotus jumped back as an angry eye appeared the other side of the glass. With a tap the window swung open and the large, shaggy head of an eagle thrust itself through.

'Good evening, Miss Fancypants,' it growled. 'Having a nice little lie down, are ya?'

'H-h-hi. What a surprise. How are you?'

'None the better for seeing you.'

'Erm . . . what?'

The bird grunted savagely and tried to force itself in through the narrow gap. Unable to manage it, it ripped away the offending window frame with its beak and head-butted open the other window, then poured itself down into the attic. It looked about angrily.

'So this is where you're skulking when the Alamo's breached.'

Lotus did not understand.

'When Iron Ned's walking out the saloon.'

'What are you talking about?'

'The proverbial's hit the proverbial, *that's* what I'm talking about,' rasped the great raptor, shaking its mangy ruff. 'This is Little Bighorn, missy. Custer's last stand.'

Lotus may have been terrified, but she did her best to conceal it.

'If you spoke in English it might be a lot easier.'

The bird wheezed with anger. With one talon it thumped over a box, barged a chair out of the way and approached the girl menacingly.

'Fine, you want straight-talking I'll cut to the raw. I seem to remember telling you in no uncertain terms to look after young Scatterhorn.'

'I did—'

'And I seem to remember that if you didn't, there would be dire consequences. Namely, I would rip your head off.'

'Look, I've—'

'Don't you "look" me, missy,' it snarled, its long beak almost touching her neck. 'I meant what I said. I trusted you to look after him. How's that in plain English?'

Lotus held her ground. The only form of defence she had

ever known was attack. Folding her arms she stared at the bird haughtily.

'I don't know what you're talking about. I have looked after him.'

'Ah save yer breath! So what are you doing creeping around in a castle, pretending like you ain't here, when he's about to take part in the greatest battle there has ever been—or ever will be—hmm? How is it that Don Gervase Askary knows precisely who he is, and if those gorowhatsits don't get him someone else will, with his little box of poisons? Yes, Miss F-P, I—me—the cat's pyjamas, know all about it. Only apparently you don't.'

Lotus's pale face drained of all colour. She blinked uncertainly.

'But that's not true. It can't be.'

'Can't it? I speak the lingo remember? I parley with those who travel. Bad news travels dead fast.' The bird nodded towards the window. Lotus remembered the rooks sitting on the battlements . . . of course . . . they'd seen her, but—

'Hear this once cos I ain't repeatin' it. There's a big old crater opened up in the forests in Siberia, and them beetles have built a special causeway to connect it direct to Scarazand. The whole shaboodle's on a war footing. I never seen so many creepy-crawlers, battering rams, cannons, catapults, self-detonating ants . . . millions of them swarming on up there . . . and that's not to mention all the people and half people that live in that hell hole. Jails are emptied, hatcheries closed—everyone's getting ready for the last battle. Yes, that's what they're calling it, missy—*the last battle*! And guess who's going to be leading them out tomorrow morning at dawn? Guess who's going to be riding right at the head, next to that worm Askary himself?'

Lotus was too stunned to speak. She stared at the floor furiously: it was all so soon—too soon . . . but the moment had come and almost gone.

'We must go and get him out of there. Right now.'

'Correctamundo. 'Cept there ain't no "we" any more.'

The bird loomed up over her ferociously.

'But—'

'No buts. It's too late. I meant what I said, missy. You can turn into any creature you blinking well like—you're dead meat. The dingo's breakfast.'

'Tomorrow?'

The voice seemed to come straight out of the air. The bird twisted its neck round towards the chair beside the window. It could just make out a familiar shadow standing there in the darkness, his blond hair glowing like a halo.

'What is this?' The raptor glared back at Lotus. 'What is this, a bloody joke?'

Lotus shook her head. She cleared her throat.

'This . . . is Tom Scatterhorn's *echo*.'

The bird looked startled. Lotus motioned the boy to come out where the eagle could see him. He smiled nervously then came forward, not quite sure if the raptor was about to rip his head off.

'*This* is the boy who was supposed to be leading out that army. *This* is the boy who is prepared to defend his leader to the death.'

The eagle peered hard at the boy for a long time.

'Right,' it said at last. 'I get it. A copy-jobby thingamajig.'

'Yes.' Lotus smiled as politely as she could. 'Exactly that. Tom's echo.'

'But that still doesn't explain why you left him down in that hell hole—hmm?'

In a few brief sentences Lotus outlined all the events that had led them to this point. The bird listened in surly silence, occasionally muttering strange curses to itself.

'So instead of ripping each other to pieces,' she concluded, 'wouldn't it be more sensible if we all put our mutual dislikes aside and did everything we possibly can to rescue Tom?'

'I'm not taking you anywhere, missy.'

'No you're not. You'll be taking him, too. Both of us, together.'

Lotus's voice had risen back to its old commanding self and the bird didn't like the change of tone one little bit.

'Both of you?' The great bird swivelled in the echo's direction. 'What's he got to do with it?'

'He knows what Tom's thinking. They're connected. And if Tom dies—so will he.'

'Is that so?'

The boy was unsure what to say. He knew that Lotus was trying to bulldoze him into helping her, and because of that he instinctively wanted to say no . . . but he could not deny who he was, and who he always would be, beyond anything else . . . He was the echo of Tom Scatterhorn.

'You said something about poison?'

'A rumour. One of those rooks overheard some chat down there. It seems that a certain Dr Culexis and his mate Rainbird believe our Tom is an impostor. But Askary won't hear of it. So they have decided to take matters into their own hands.'

'How?'

The bird shrugged. The boy glanced at Lotus.

'What, you don't think they'll try and kill him?'

Lotus shrugged.

'Not directly. That might be difficult. Far better to exploit Tom's ignorance. Poison the Scaramoor.'

'The Scaramoor?'

'Why not? Didn't you say Culexis cares about it more than anything else? He knows Tom has never worn it before, so it's the perfect vehicle. Before Tom guesses anything's wrong he's strapped tight inside it and he can't get out. It's perfect.'

The echo sat in shocked silence. He realized that Lotus was right.

'But on such a day, in front of everyone . . . Culexis wouldn't dare, would he?'

Lotus regarded the boy coldly, her smooth, porcelain face nothing but a mask.

'In his position? I would. Taking the initiative: it shows great loyalty and devotion. Clever Dr Culexis kills the impostor secretly. He saves his master's life. He becomes indispensable.'

'But what about the battle?'

'What about it? Culexis is only interested in himself.'

The echo stared out of the window in confusion. The snow outside was glowing under a weak moon, making the ground seem luminous. If this was true, if something was about to happen to his original . . .

'Then I must help him, mustn't I? I must come with you. If you'll take me.'

Lotus walked up to the boy and smiled. There was a fire in his coal black eyes that she recognized.

'I was rather hoping you'd say that. Thank you. You've made the right decision.'

She put her hand on his shoulder. The echo pulled away in embarrassment.

'There's bound to be some old armour in this house,' he mumbled, slipping out into the corridor. 'Bound to be some, somewhere.'

The eagle stared at the girl, plainly not understanding.

'He's a good fighter. This is his fight. It's what he's been training all his life to do—defend his master against these gorogonas. That will help us much more than you think.'

'Fine. Bloody marvellous. Top hole,' rasped the great bird impatiently. 'Just rattle your blinking dags.'

Five minutes later two strange looking figures appear at the attic doorway.

'Oh here we go. No one mentioned fancy dress. Which one of you is King Arthur?'

'Very funny,' snapped Lotus. She strode into the room wearing an old steel breastplate and chain mail.

'Ha ha!'

The echo followed, clad in assorted parts of what might once have been a samurai suit of armour, with a long sword to match. The eagle thumped its talons on the floor, enjoying this hugely.

'What, so there's no helmet for me? No? Not even a pair of goggles? Cos I've got to look the part too, y'know. I ain't going underdressed. Not to a *proper* battle.'

'As a bird, I hardly think wearing goggles and a helmet is going to help you,' Lotus said, acidly.

'But what about all them flaming arrows?'

'They are the least of your worries.'

'And the clouds of poison gas?'

'Gorogonas are much worse than that.'

'Worse than them beetles that spit blobs of poisonous foam up my fundament?'

'Much, much worse.' The eagle stopped his mocking and peered at the girl uncertainly.

'Now look here, Miss F-P, what exactly are you suggesting?'

'According to August Catcher, gorogonas are different, and talking about it is just wasting the little time that we don't have. Rattle your dags?'

The bird snorted.

'And I thought I was daft. Git on then, yer pair of dragon slayers.'

CHAPTER 23

DEATH OF THE HERO?

It was dawn, and Tom Scatterhorn was standing on the balcony of the palace, fully dressed and holding the elaborate spiked helmet in his hand. For the last ten minutes he had been watching in grim fascination the large black hole that had appeared in the cave wall opposite. It seemed that all the inhabitants of Scarazand were desperately scrabbling up into it, and it was sucking them out into the labyrinth like a vast plughole. He had never seen so many beetles, and the cacophony of noise reverberating around the cave was deafening.

'All hail the Defender of Scarazand!'

Tom turned to find Don Gervase Askary marching towards him with a wide grin on his face.

'It's a perfect fit—no?' He passed an admiring glance at the gleaming black armour that encased Tom's body.

Tom said nothing. He noticed that unlike him, Don Gervase was wearing a sealskin coat, black boots, and a fur hat set at a jaunty angle. His only concession to the coming battle was a small revolver tucked into his pocket.

'You look like you're going skating.'

Don Gervase smiled. He was not going to let a little surliness from the impostor upset his mood.

'Maybe I shall. Perhaps tomorrow—after the battle.' He glanced up at the hole. 'As you probably guessed, that is the way up to that valley. Most of the army should be there by now. What a day this is going to be! I am expecting great things from you, boy. We all are.'

'Then you're making a big mistake.'

'Oh I don't think so. You will be fighting for your life, and if that doesn't motivate you, nothing will.'

Tom tried to ignore Don Gervase's unpleasant smile and spotted another figure appearing on the balcony.

'All ready to cast off, my lord. Ship shape and tickety boo.'

Ern Rainbird rolled towards them as if on the deck of a swaying ship. Unlike his master, Ern seemed to be taking no chances: he had swapped his blue beret and seaman's jumper for some sort of insect chainmail that covered him from head to foot. He had an axe slung over one shoulder and an ancient rucksack on his back.

'Ready for the action, sir?'

Tom stared back at Rainbird in his ridiculous costume in disgust.

'Young Scatterhorn is feeling very feisty this morning,' grinned Don Gervase, 'which is no bad thing before a battle.'

'You can say that again,' chuckled Ern, unable to take the smirk off his face. He followed silently as Don Gervase led the way to an ornate chariot at the end of the balcony and stepped aboard.

'Good luck, my lord,' said Rainbird with an elaborate bow.

'I'm expecting you to be following very close behind. And Culexis: where is he this morning?'

'Oh he had a bit of business to attend to last night . . . he'll be up directly.'

'Make very certain of that.'

Don Gervase clicked his fingers, and the sleek black and gold dragonfly beneath the chariot spread its wings and began to hum. The buzzing grew louder and the next instant they were airborne. There was a cheer below as thousands of airmen climbed into their cockpits and followed them out into the cave. Tom glanced back at the swarm of creatures lining up behind them. They were identical to those Satanflies that had ambushed him and Lotus in Scotland, only these were dressed in magnificent gold and black livery, with pennants streaming and gleaming armour—a vast, jostling insect cavalry, and he was riding at the very front. There was no escape now . . .

Into the black hole they swept, and on through the labyrinth beyond. Here Tom could see a solid tide of creatures and men, climbing in an unbroken line towards a small speck of light in the distance. The clatter of pincers and the muffled sounds of singing filled the darkness.

'You've staked everything on winning,' breathed Tom as they swept over the crawling armies towards the light. 'Will they be enough?'

'I have emptied Scarazand. Who knows?'

Tom tried to read the curious expression on Don Gervase's face. He seemed almost amused.

Soon they reached the circle of white light, which turned out to be a hole at the bottom of a vast crater. The rocky sides sloped steeply up in all directions, and teams of beetles and men worked frantically to keep the entrance clear of the choking carpet of mangled insects and boulders that were sliding down from the lip.

'So it's started already?'

'No no. This has nothing to do with Zumsteen. I thought we'd have a little light skirmishing to get us in the mood.'

Up they swept, over the heads of men and insects working their way up the steep sides with ladders and grappling hooks. A hail of rocks rained down on them.

'So you organized this just for us?'

'Of course. They don't know that—but we must have some fun today. Otherwise what would be the point?' Don Gervase waved at a terrified group of soldiers and half-breeds huddling behind an overhang. 'Heads down!'

They all stood up and instantly saluted the Glorious Leader.

'Heads *down*, you fools!'

An avalanche of stones crashed over the top them, sweeping them and their ladders away into the crater.

'Some people are born to die,' he chuckled. Tom stared at Don Gervase in disbelief: he really was crazy. On they flew, higher and higher towards the crater's rim. Up here, against almost impossible odds, clusters of massive, tank-like beetles had anchored themselves. Behind each one lines of half-breeds sheltered, waiting for gaps between the avalanches and then darting out, scrambling up the slopes and then throwing themselves upon the large glassy ants that were hurling down rocks from the crater's edge.

'As I said, this is just a little light entertainment,' rumbled Don Gervase as they swept over the fierce hand-to-hand fighting. 'To keep the stragglers occupied. The main army is already here.'

Tom looked out into the winter dawn and could see nothing more than an empty ocean of forests, stretching away in all directions. But as they sped down the crater's flank and turned towards the sun . . . the sight took Tom's breath away. Below the crater was a long, wide valley, dusted with snow. On it were arranged a vast chequerboard of brown squares, with what might have been huge fields of wheat behind, glittering in the misty morning light.

'Impressive—no?'

The dragonfly descended faster, and Tom could see that the fields of wheat were in fact living carpets of insects, horns and tusks and mandibles all moving in unison, and the chequerboard beyond was made up of half-breeds and soldiers, tens of thousands strong . . . Tom was starting to feel sick. He couldn't do this . . . the sounds of drumming grew louder. Suddenly a great cheer swept through the ranks.

'They've seen us.' Don Gervase grinned and raised his hand. 'Acknowledge them. Do it, boy.'

The roar was deafening as they swept over the pennants and banners snapping in the stiff breeze. Dizzily Tom raised his sword. The roar exploded all around.

'That's better. You're going to have to get used to this.'

At the rear of the great army, directly beneath the crater, rose nine towers forming a high stockade, and it was here they landed. The moment they touched the ground Don Gervase leapt out and a commander rushed up to greet him.

'Any signs yet?'

'Not yet, your grace,' he bowed. 'We are almost ready. Would you—'

'Indeed I would. Boy—' He indicated to Tom to follow and they marched across to the nearest tower. Up they went past floor after floor of gun crews readying themselves for battle and out onto a viewing platform at the top. Before them the might of Scarazand was arranged in perfect symmetry, like a military parade, defending the slopes of the crater. Beyond the sea of helmets and carapaces ran an empty stretch of ground several hundred metres wide, dusted with snow, and beyond that the steep slopes of the forest began. The armies stood waiting in noisy anticipation, facing the wall of dark trees beyond . . . Don Gervase clicked his fingers and instantly the commander handed him a long brass telescope. He trained it up into the trees hungrily.

'Hmm.' He checked his watch. 'What time do you make it?'

'Just gone seven, sir. Northern time.'

This was apparently not good news. Don Gervase snapped the telescope shut and frowned.

'Either they're late or we are early.'

'Unless we're in the wrong place.'

Don Gervase turned to Tom coldly.

'Just a joke.'

The Glorious Leader chose to ignore the insolent remark. Instead he handed Tom the telescope.

'Halfway up that slope you will find the hut where Nicholas

Zumsteen has been living. Above it, to the left, you will see a long low cliff. At its base are lines of white boulders dotted in the snow. They are not boulders.'

Tom pressed his eye to the telescope, but barely had he found the cliff when a great peal of thunder rumbled across the valley. Then came another, like metal sheets tearing at each other. Something was rolling down through the woods towards them, gathering pace as it descended, knocking down trees and bouncing off rocks . . .

'Ah, Caleb, so predictable.' Don Gervase turned to Tom with a broad grin on his face. 'He always used to start like this when we played as boys. The Queen's Gambit. Chess,' he grinned, enjoying Tom's confusion. 'Black's first move. Pawn forward two. Always.'

The object rolled out onto the plain, coming to a halt fifty metres from the nearest square.

Through the telescope Tom saw that it was a large oval-shaped pill the size of a car. The wind was beginning to blow lumps of snow off it to reveal a crystal-like surface beneath.

'So that is about to become . . . a gorogona?'

'Correct.' Don Gervase looked down at the legions of men and insects now silently watching the object. He was pleased that it seemed to have aroused their curiosity. He checked his watch once more. 'We have seven and a half minutes.'

'How do you know?'

'Ever since I discovered what Nicholas has been collecting I have made it my business to know everything about gorogonas. And the little egg you found in that pool yesterday was the final piece of the jigsaw. Thanks to you, boy, there is now not very much I don't know about them.'

Don Gervase smiled strangely. Tom was beginning to wonder if there was some great secret he had missed. Don Gervase was certainly behaving as if there was.

'You will take the cavalry on our right flank. Do not move until I give you the order. Go go.'

Tom hesitated. He saw the commander watching him.

'So I am not to be part of your bodyguard then?'

'I want the army to see what you can do first. I want you to inspire them. Because you will, won't you?'

He held out his hand for the telescope. Tom stared out at the legions of men and creatures beyond, waiting . . . what choice did he have?

Don Gervase smiled as he took back the telescope, and bent down to whisper in Tom's ear. 'Don't presume to let me down.'

The words slipped through his lips like smoke, and Tom was in no doubt what he meant. With a thundering heart Tom followed the commander back down the tower and across the stockade to the ramparts beyond. There a squadron of sleek black stag beetles stood waiting for him. Instantly a rider ran forward, leading a powerful black creature by its bridle, its head and flanks covered in armour to match his own.

'Feeling all right, my lord?'

It was Viola, the shaven-headed girl with the scarred face he had met yesterday.

'No. Not really.'

'It's the big one, isn't it? Doesn't get much bigger than this.

Here, let me help you with that.' Swiftly taking the magnificent helmet out of his hand she ran her glove around the
inside. 'Oh—you've forgotten your winter lining. Here, have
mine, I've got a spare.' Before Tom could say anything Viola
produced a black balaclava from her pocket and pulled it down
over Tom's head. His face suddenly felt sticky, and cold, too.

'What—'

'Any fool can be uncomfortable,' she interrupted, quickly
placing the magnificent helmet on Tom's head. The whole
squadron watched as she stood on tiptoes, tightening the
shoulder screws. 'That should feel a lot better. There we are.
All done.'

Holding his stirrup, she helped Tom up into the saddle. He
turned round to see the two boys who had recognized him from
the day before. They raised their swords in salute.

'Thanks,' said Tom, as Viola handed him his shield.

The girl smiled toothily.

'Believe me, sir, you've nothing to worry about, nothing at
all.'

'Haven't I?'

'Not if I can help it. We've always helped each other out in the
past, haven't we?'

She held Tom's eyes for a moment, then with the smallest of
smiles she slapped the beetle on the flanks. Dropping his visor,
Tom trotted down through the crowds leading his troops out
onto the right flank of the battlefield that now looked a little like
this:

'Magnificent sight, isn't it, your grace? Quite magnificent. What a day.'

Dr Culexis had climbed up to the platform and now waited obediently behind his master. Had Don Gervase turned round he would have noticed that instead of dressing for battle, his neat, clever henchman had affected the same casual jauntiness as himself, even down to the rather satisfied smirk on his face. But the Glorious Leader's eye was glued to his telescope. Dr Culexis gamely continued.

'A day when mettles will be tested: a day for every citizen of Scarazand to prove who they really are. A day of revelations—'

'Do shut up.'

Dr Culexis smiled and adjusted his fur hat. He could not contain his excitement.

'Where's Rainbird?'

'Down with the cavalry, my lord. Getting things set.'

Don Gervase grunted. He checked his watch.

'By my reckoning, five, four, three, two, one . . . and another, for luck.'

A loud crack split the silence.

'There.'

In the next second the crystal shell shattered onto the frozen earth. In its place lay a long lozenge shape, the sickly yellow colour of something long hidden from the sun. The gorogona shook a little, then began to unfold, unpeeling stickily to reveal grey armoured plates and coils of oily skin. Last of all, a pointed head rose up and blinked sleepily. It looked something like a cobra, some thirty metres long.

Dr Culexis sniggered.

'So it's just . . . just a snake?'

'Underestimate a gorogona at your peril, Culexis.'

The gorogona stared at the massed armies facing it. Stretching out the spiked hood behind its head like a parachute the creature suddenly screamed and spat, sending out a long jet of poison that splashed down harmlessly before the front lines. A ripple of laughter swept through the ranks. The half-breeds began to jeer and hurl insults back.

'How many of these gorogonas are there?'

'Four hundred, maybe five, hidden in those trees. Zumsteen collected two bags full.'

Dr Culexis stifled a chuckle. This was hardly going to be much of a battle. He had expected extraordinary insects . . . five hundred overgrown snakes against the might of Scarazand? What sort of a contest was that?

'It won't stay like this for long,' growled Don Gervase ominously. 'See how it is listening?'

The oily flanks of the great serpent were indeed vibrating, as if mimicking a slow, deep rhythm. The little doctor smiled sarcastically.

'I wonder what it can hear, my lord—the wind in the trees, perhaps?'

'The rhythm of our world. The heartbeat of Scarazand.'

The gorogona glared directly at the stockade, and then to the crater rising up behind them.

'That's it, my girl. That's the way in.'

Dr Culexis grinned awkwardly. How his Glorious Leader knew such things he could not guess, but he seemed to have a very peculiar attitude.

'And Zumsteen can actually *control* these serpents?'

'Of course not. Once she has sensed who we are and what we are protecting, she will come at us. Perhaps what she needs now is a little provocation.'

For a full minute Don Gervase kept his eye pressed to the telescope, watching the strange serpent as if under a microscope. He did not notice the restless grumblings of men and beasts below. From where he sat astride his mount Tom stared at the enormous beast in anticipation: like everyone else, he didn't think it looked too bad, and like everyone else he wondered why they weren't already attacking it—wasn't the plan to pick them off one by one? Shouldn't they get at it now, before—

WHOOSH!

A rocket seemed to have gone off in Tom's ear, and the next moment he was bolting out across the hard white ground. Swaying dangerously in the saddle he just managed to stay onboard, and grabbing the reins he hauled in.

'Stop!' he shouted. 'Stop!'

But the armoured beetle would not stop for anyone or anything . . . Tom pulled with all his might on one rein then the other, trying to turn it, but it made no difference, the insect's head seemed to be made of steel. Through the slits in his helmet Tom glimpsed lines of men flashing past, cheering and shaking their swords. And there was the gorogona, rearing up in his path . . . but he could smell smoke—where? He glanced back and gasped: he was dragging a burning wheel . . . someone had—

'What is that boy doing?' demanded Don Gervase.

'Perhaps it's some old cavalry tactic, my lord,' smirked Dr Culexis spotting a low grey helmet scuttling up through the ranks. 'Or perhaps Mr Rainbird has been up to his old tricks again. Setting fire to horses' tails is something of a family tradition.'

'What are you talking about?'

'My lord, there is something you should know,' Culexis began. 'That boy—'

A huge cheer interrupted Dr Culexis and he turned back to the battlefield. The gorogona, incensed that the beetle and rider should charge straight at it, squirmed out of the way and spat a stream of scalding poison. Tom just had time to raise his shield but the instant the poison splashed across the beetle the creature swerved in panic, sending Tom tumbling sideways to the ground. Dr Culexis smiled coolly. He began again.

'As I was saying, my lord. That boy, Tom Scatterhorn—'

'What about him,' growled Don Gervase, shaking the mesmerion from his cuff. His fingers began dancing across its surface. Dr Culexis watched them avidly.

'He is not who you think he is, my lord.'

'Isn't he?'

'No he absolutely isn't.'

Tom rolled over in a daze. Through the narrow slits of his helmet he could see yellowish coils sliding all around him. Then a blinding pain hit him in the head. He closed his eyes to find a thin red line on the horizon, stretching wider . . . 'GET UP!' screamed the voice. 'UP ON YOUR FEET AND FIGHT!'

Tom's face poured with sweat. He opened his eyes and rolled over. There, right in front of him, was the head of the gorogona. He could see its lazy grey eyes, its black tongue flickering inquisitively over his armour.

Don Gervase stared at the boy in amazement.

'Why isn't he moving? Defend yourself when I tell you to!'

But the terror of the moment concentrated Tom's mind. He ignored the screaming within. He knew exactly what he must do. Slowly his hands reached for his sword and drew it from his scabbard.

'My lord, the boy is not an echo. He is an impostor. An assassin . . .'

Don Gervase was not listening. His fingers stilled and he stood agog, watching the great snake hovering over the fallen boy. Had he been so wrong? This could not happen, this was not meant to happen at all, this was not—

Suddenly Tom leapt up. With both hands he thrust his sword deep into the gorogona's right eye and gouged it savagely. The creature screamed and reared, ripping the blade away and shaking its head in pain. Tom just had time to race back and grab his shield as the gorogona's wide hood flared, pulsed red then turned upon him. Black blood was pouring out of the deep hole where its eye had been. Instinctively Tom crouched low just as the poison blast hit him with all the force of a fire hydrant. Before he knew it he had somersaulted back ten metres across the ground. The shield had gone and the poison was igniting all around. In the next breath Tom was on his feet again and running straight towards the creature.

'What's he doing?' gasped Don Gervase. In a moment it was clear. Tom had spotted his sword lying on the ground and now it was in his hand. Through his narrow field of vision he could just make out the gorogona's great flanks twisting round towards him, and without thinking he plunged the sword deep into the serpent's side and held on. The armoured flesh slipped past his blade, opening up a long gash like a tear in a curtain. The gorogona screamed again and tried to squirm away but Tom managed to stay on his feet, moving with it, gripping his sword tightly with both hands . . .

'Look out!' screamed the half-breeds in the front line, banging on their shields trying to catch Tom's attention . . . . They could see the gorogona's head rising up behind him, bloody, split, hideous—

'Turn about, boy! About!'

Encased inside his helmet Tom was in another world. All he

could see was that wall of yellow flesh sliding past his sword. Sounds were muffled, distant—this was about his own survival, nothing else. Harder he pressed, deeper . . .

'WHOOSH!'

The flash was immense. In the next moment Tom had catapulted forward and lay in a crumpled heap on the ground. Again and again the gorogona blasted him with poison that blossomed into flame all around.

'Why doesn't he get up?' came a voice from the ranks.

'Come on, lad—trick it again! Get the other eye!'

'Don't let it do this to you!'

'Kill it!'

The chorus of shouts rose up louder but the boy lay still, curled up like a baby as the earth blazed all around him. Even the Scaramoor itself seemed to be on fire . . .

'So I thought it for the best, my lord,' concluded Dr Culexis. 'I was only thinking of your safety. And of course the security of Scarazand. And I suspect he is not acting alone.'

Don Gervase turned towards his henchman in blind fury.

'Even if his armour saves him out there, I guarantee he will not live another hour.'

'What did you say?'

Dr Culexis smiled in exasperation. His master had obviously not been listening to a word he said.

'*The Scaramoor*, my lord. It is dusted with bewilderbeetles. I made the preparation myself. And with the able assistance of Mr Rainbird the problem has now been solved.'

The Glorious Leader's head began to swim. There was a great gasp and he turned back to the gorogona. Something had happened to it: it was writhing drunkenly away from the boy, lurching uncertainly . . . with a violent shudder its head suddenly thumped to the ground. There was silence. For a moment.

'Look at that!'

The soldiers in the front line pointed to the long slit in the gorogona's flank. All along it streams of small black snakes began wriggling out. The creatures writhed around each other, congealing into a slippery sliding mass that expanded every second like some primitive creature, duplicating and spreading, wider and wider across the valley . . .

No one in the army moved now. They stood granite faced, staring at the spectacle unfolding before them. The first gorogona was dead, but already there were thousands more like her, and out of the forests behind more were coming, bouncing down the slopes . . .

'So this is it,' murmured Don Gervase, watching the gathering storm. 'This is how the world once was . . . before. A world devoured by worms.' There was a look of strange excitement on his face. He turned to Dr Culexis, who now stood very still behind him. 'A day when each man must prove his mettle, eh, Culexis?'

'Indeed, my—'

With one hand Don Gervase picked up the doctor by the throat and held him against the parapet. 'What exactly are you made of, Culexis? Tell me that?'

'I don't understand . . . my lord, I—'

'So you've poisoned his armour, have you?'

'I only thought to protect you—'

'Protect me? You are protecting no one but yourself, Culexis. But your ambition has run away with you this time.'

Dr Culexis could barely breathe. His lips began to turn blue as Don Gervase squeezed his glove tighter.

'Did you really think I didn't know who that boy was? What do you take me for—an idiot!'

Dr Culexis's eyes bulged.

'That boy has a purpose. That is why he is here. You will bring him back to me, alive, now—do you understand?'

'But supp—'

'Do it. If you want to live.'

Dr Culexis fell to the ground gasping.

'My lord, I think I'm hardly dressed for—'

'This is a battle, not the opera, Culexis. You should have thought of that. Now go.'

Dr Culexis rubbed his reddened neck painfully and scurried away. Don Gervase glanced over to where the commander stood at the corner of the platform.

'Begin.'

The man nodded swiftly and a second later the signal flew down the ranks . . . horns sounded, banners were raised, and then the drums began . . .

'A battle at the end of all things,' Don Gervase murmured, opening up his telescope. 'Betilda Marchmont was right about something.'

He scanned the trees in the distance. Where was his brother? Somewhere up in the branches, watching him, no doubt. Did he have any idea what he had brought into the world? Of course not—he was so naive . . . and the boy? Somewhere in the middle of that oily mess. Curled up in his scorched armour that was poisoning him from within. Don Gervase scowled furiously. The very thought of Culexis and Rainbird made him boil with rage— but he must be calm. Great leaders stay calm. Keep his head, when all around others are losing theirs. Something like that.

Seconds later the first squares began to advance, their leading edges solid walls of armoured wolfskidders the size of tanks, driven on by half-breeds with staves. Inside each square bombardier beetles ran at the heels of Skrolls carrying whips. The noise was tremendous.

'Fire incendiaries!'

Buckets of flaming oil began catapulting through the crisp air, splashing down into the writhing gorogonas. The snakes began to hiss and scream.

'Archers ho!'

A blizzard of needle sharp arrows shot over the heads of the front line, darkening the sky. Gorogonas were split open and pinned to the ground, but more began to rise up, turning to face the oncoming storm.

'Poisons away!'

From the flanks swarms of Satanflies zipped past, trailing lines of green and yellow gas. Flying fast and straight, they began dropping their deadly cargo into the silvery mass below. The killing smoke scurled and eddied about the valley.

'Charge!'

At the order the leading wolfskidders broke into an ungainly trot, keeping in line, and the driving half-breeds leapt up onto

DEATH OF THE HERO?

their flanks, yelling and beating on their shells like thunder. At the sound the gorogonas reared up as one, forming a single solid wall of flared hoods and glistening fangs . . . here and there red bombardier beetles broke loose and raced ahead, eager to be first into the fray . . . and like a wave hurling itself at a cliff, battle was joined.

What had been a wide empty space instantly become a thrashing mess of snakes and insects and men, moving of its own accord. Don Gervase watched from the safety of his tower, one moment staring into his telescope, the next spinning the mesmerion. He was trying to direct the battle, but it was impossible to see what was going on. Through the poison smoke and din he glimpsed men perishing, Satanflies snatched out of the sky, gorogonas cleaved in two, squares moving forward—more snakes arriving: what should he do? He didn't know. He felt strangely disconnected from it all. Suddenly and unexpectedly he found himself wishing Lotus was here at his side. Not because he missed her, obviously not—but because she was good at this: she led from the front, she had commanded his forces against the Chamber. Lotus relished pandemonium—he was not cut out for it. Murder was more his line: cold-blooded, premeditated killing: order—not chaos. All he really cared about at this moment was whether Betilda Marchmont had painted the truth, because if she had . . . Don Gervase glowered at the swirling chaos before him—it *was* exactly like that picture of hers . . . He needed that boy back, right now. Where was he? Out there somewhere, buried beneath the piles of dying and the dead, hidden amongst beetles and gorogonas and puddles of flaming oil, oblivious to it all . . .

CHAPTER 24

DAY OF THE SNAKES

'Gadzookarama,' whistled the eagle. 'There's a picture.'

Lotus climbed down from the great bird's back and the echo followed. For a moment they could do nothing more than just stare into the valley below. All night they had been searching the forests fruitlessly, and it was only when the dawn broke and the din of the battle began that they had found this hidden place. There, below the trees, stretched a wide valley dusted with snow. On it, a living carpet of gorogonas hurled themselves, wave after wave, against the massed ranks of Scarazand, who were defending the smooth slope that led up a large crater on the far side. The air was thick with arrows and insects, blooms of yellow gas and palls of black smoke.

'And Tommy Scatt's really in the middle of all that?' The great bird peered down into the thrashing, fighting tangle of creatures. 'How the hell are we going to find him?'

'My guess is he'll be right over there,' Lotus replied, pointing at the ring of black towers barely visible at the bottom of the slope 'Inside the stockade. It's the safest place. Probably right next to Don Gervase.'

The raptor squinted through the smoke towards the black towers. Gun flashes burst from every side, and surrounding it a steep rampart had been thrown up, from which archers were firing wave after wave of arrows . . .

'Listen, missy, I ain't a coward but I ain't stark staring mad, neither. There's no way I'll get you alive through that lot. Not a snowball's chance in hell.'

'But that's where he'll be.'

'Well I ain't takin' ya there. That's kamikaze.'

Lotus was furious but not surprised: she had half-suspected that the eagle might refuse. Even she had to admit it looked extremely dangerous.

'Plan B?'

'I'm thinking.'

'Look at this!' The echo had strayed down the track and stopped beside a shallow indentation in the cliff. 'I think I've found one.'

'Found what?'

'A gorogona?'

Forgetting their troubles the great bird and Lotus hurried to his side and peered into the shallow cave.

'Wow,' breathed Lotus, sweeping away the ice and dirt. 'So this is what they look like—before.'

Somewhere inside the clear cocoon was a yellowish shape coiled up tight in the clear liquid. The hide was vaguely metallic and there was a livid red mark on its side. It might have been a dragon, or a bomb—it was hard to tell.

'So how does an egg that Zumsteen collected on a beach turn into that?' demanded the eagle.

Lotus could not begin to understand. Fearlessly, she pressed her face towards the sleeping creature.

'All I know is that gorogonas are unlike anything else. That's what August Catcher told us, and maybe that is why Zumsteen chose them. They've been accidentally left over from some other age.'

'Now that's just marvellous,' rasped the eagle. 'So what you're saying is—Jeffery Joseph and Jehosophat!'

The next instant it had bounced up onto a rock. The boy and Lotus whipped round to see a large silver serpent staring at them through the trees. Its pale eyes peered at them vacantly.

'Don't move,' whispered Lotus. The gorogona slithered closer. She took a step forward and flexed her fingers.

'Lotus, I have an idea how to fight these things.'

'Tell me,' she hissed.

The echo carefully drew his sword.

'First you mustn't, you mustn't, you must—' Suddenly the boy was thrown onto his back, breathing fast.

'What?' Lotus turned round to see the echo's limbs shaking, his eyes rolling up . . .

'What's the matter?'

She dropped to his side. The boy was mumbling something incoherently: he seemed to be having a fit.

'Get out of it, yer nasty nasty!' spat the eagle, as the gorogona slithered closer still. 'Mush!'

The creature reared up like a cobra before them, its spiked hood flaring wide and pulsing. It opened its dripping mouth.

'I advise you to get back in the cave, Miss Fancypants. Before this gorowhatsit gets unpleasant!'

The boy opened his eyes and gripped Lotus's hand tightly. He was trying to tell her something.

'What is it?'

'There's one!'

The high shout came from somewhere above, and the next moment a flaming arrow slammed into the back of the gorogona's head. The serpent screamed and turned to find a patrol of armoured Satanflies swooping around the cliff towards it. On their backs rode soldiers armed with crossbows.

'Let's have it, lads! Quick!'

A volley of flaming arrows came down in quick succession, thudding into the serpent's hide and snapping on the rocks behind. The creature turned furiously and slithered back into the forest, trying to escape.

'After it, boys!'

Down they went, pursuing it through the trees, and a soldier with a couple of bombardier beetles dropped to the ground. Barely had the gorogona turned to defend itself from the insect's biting jaws than the soldier had boldly sliced it clean in two with his axe.

'Good going, mate,' rasped the bird approvingly. 'That's the way to do it!'

But even as the eagle spoke something seemed to happen to the two halves of the gorogona. The scaly flesh seemed to slide over the wounds and reform, each half with a new head . . . now there were two smaller gorogonas in the place of one. Puzzled, the man slashed again, slicing it in two, whereupon two more sprang up in its place, slithering apart and growing . . . more soldiers jumped down and joined in, but the more they cut the more they created, until they were knee deep in squirming creatures and locked in a vicious, desperate struggle . . .

Lotus edged back towards the cliff, too stunned to speak. Suddenly that writhing mass down in the valley made terrifying sense . . .

'Look.'

The boy behind her had come to his senses. He was crouching at the entrance to the cave with a lump of snowy earth in his glove. 'See this.'

In the palm of his hand wriggled a tiny grey worm, no bigger than a maggot. It was a gorogona, in miniature, complete in every way.

'Supposing they divide and divide and divide for ever, what then?'

Lotus sighed deeply.

'I don't know.' For the first time she seemed frightened, genuinely frightened. 'Zumsteen has no idea what he has brought back into the world. Not a clue.'

'Even all the billions of beetles in Scarazand are not going to be enough to stop these things,' murmured the boy. 'Do you think Don Gervase knows this?'

Lotus peered at the mysterious creature wriggling this way and that, growing every second.

'I wouldn't put it past him. Throwing all his forces into a battle that he suspects he can't win is just the sort of weird thing he would do.'

'But why? Why would he want his armies destroyed?'

The tiny snake was now the size of a small lizard, and its head was staring across the valley towards the crater. Its thin yellow skin seemed to be purring in a slow rhythm. 'Perhaps it's the Queen,' she wondered. 'Perhaps they can all sense her. Perhaps this battle is just an excuse to kill everything in Scarazand and replace it with something better.'

The echo smiled in disbelief.

'That's impossible. He wouldn't do that.'

'You don't know what he's capable of.'

'Right, I'm done with this loony stuff. I'm out,' barked the eagle, who was peering down at the tiny creature from his perch above. With one hop he bounced awkwardly to the ground, then lolloped off down the path at the base of the cliff.

'Where are you going?' called Lotus as he disappeared round the corner.

'I'm finding that boy and getting the hell out of this madhouse.'

'On foot?'

'Maybe. I'm warning you people, I ain't hangin' ab—'

The eagle skidded to an ungainly halt as a small crowd of goro-gonas slithered out of the trees in front of him.

'Now listen, fellas, I got no beef with you, I'm just the trans-port.' The silvery surfaced creatures squirmed around him, block-ing his exit. They stared emptily up at the great bird.

'There's absolutely no need for any nonsense. I'm just going to fly up there, out of your hair and—Euch!'

One gorogona opened its mouth wide and spat, hitting the eagle square in the face.

'That was neither nice nor necessary,' it rasped, angrily blinking away the poison. Others began to rear up, their hoods flaring.

'Fine, you don't like me. I'm not so keen on you myself but—'

A small barrage of stinging spit bounced off the rocks beside him.

'For Pete's sake!' The bird danced this way and that, turning in ungainly circles to avoid the stinging jets. 'I bet you're enjoying this aren't you, you little . . . BLOODY HELL FIRE!' yelled the great raptor, seeing its tail feathers begin to smoulder. Angrily it barged through its tormentors and clattered up into the air.

'Come back!' shouted Lotus as it soared above the trees.

'Why should I?' it roared.

'But you can't just leave us!'

'Just you watch me! I've had it with the bloody lot of you!'

'But what about Tom?'

The bird had already disappeared around the corner and out of sight. The gang of gorogonas gave chase, spitting poison in its general direction.

'Ha!' Lotus turned in bewildered fury. 'And I was the one who abandoned him. It was all my fault . . . it's a chicken.'

The boy stifled a smile.

'What's so funny?'

'Nothing. Just—'

'Just what?'

'It doesn't matter. Forget it.'

Lotus grunted and looked down into the woods below. The gorogonas had all gone now, they must have slithered down into the valley to join the main battle. The soldiers still lay where they fell.

'So what happened to you back there?'

'Erm . . . I'm not sure.' The boy seemed a little embarrassed. 'Something hit me.'

'Don Gervase?'

The boy shook his head.

'It wasn't a command. It was something else. Like I had fainted. And when I opened my eyes, there was a garden with a fountain, and a big house. There was an old camper van parked under the trees, and . . . ' The echo paused, struggling to remember. 'Two people by the door.'

Lotus studied the boy carefully, trying to understand what this might mean.

'Who were these people?'

'A man and a woman. They wanted me to go with them.'

'But obviously you didn't?'

He shrugged his shoulders awkwardly.

'Part of me wanted to. Because I recognized them. Somehow.'

Lotus said nothing for a moment. She stared at the battle raging in the valley, thinking hard.

'It's Tom, isn't it?' continued the boy. 'Something's happened to him. Something bad. Is he dying?'

Already Lotus was running down through the trees.

'Lotus, where are you going? Wait!'

But the girl kept running, picking up a crossbow and quiver from a dead soldier as she passed. The echo had no choice but to follow. He sprinted after her, struggling to catch up.

'So stupid,' she gasped between breaths. 'We should have forced that coward to fly through it. Take us to the stockade.'

The boy was panting so hard he could barely speak. The

battle seemed to be just below them now, he could hear the clang of armour and shouts clearly.

'But we can't fight our way across. You said it yourself. We'll never make it.'

Lotus grimaced. The echo was right. What to do? They needed help. They must advertise themselves somehow. Somehow get caught and then . . . Running out into a clearing she stopped and listened. Below the distant shouts she could hear a low rumble . . . wheels, hooves, jangling bridles . . . she glanced down the empty track ahead.

'Come here.'

The boy stood panting beside a tree.

'Why?'

'Here, quick!'

The echo had only known Lotus Askary for a short time but that was long enough to realize she rarely listened to anyone else's opinion and would not take no for an answer. Slowly he walked out into the clearing.

'Just stay there and don't move.'

'What are you doing?'

Already she had run away into the undergrowth and hidden behind a tree. Slinging the quiver over her shoulder she slipped an arrow into the crossbow and wound it back.

'Lotus?'

The rumbling came closer. Wheels thundered on the snow, and there was something else too, something swishing . . .

'What am I supposed to do?'

'Nothing. Don't move.'

The boy barely had time to grasp what Lotus was intending

before something thundered round the corner and her expression changed.

'Get down! Now!'

The echo flung himself to the ground, just as that same something swished through the air millimetres above his head. Angrily he scrambled to his feet to see a cavalryman in dark armour gallop past, towing a vicious scything contraption behind him. It was sheer good luck that he had ducked beneath the spinning blades in time. Then he turned again, only to find another black rider bearing down on him . . .

Thonk!

In the same instant the rider's body slumped forward, an arrow in his chest. He tipped off the side of his armoured beetle as it careered away through the trees. Lotus sidestepped quickly out onto the track, her crossbow already reloaded and levelled at the next rider galloping towards them.

'Hold up!'

The man raised his hand and skidded to a halt in the snow. A hundred black figures, maybe more, all mounted on heavily armoured insects, appeared behind him through the trees. Some were dragging scythes, some not, and the deep dents and gashes in their armour told its own story.

'Who are you?'

'You know who we are!' Lotus shouted back. The man at the front leapt off his mount and walked forward, his sword held out before him. Lotus kept her arrow levelled at his chest.

'My God . . . '

'Lotus Askary!'

Suddenly a cavalryman dug his spurs in hard and galloped

through the trees towards Lotus, raising his axe up to strike. Lotus neatly sidestepped her attacker then shot her arrow straight into the narrow joint between the insect's abdomen and thorax—slicing it clean in half. The rider was thrown tumbling into the snow.

'We are not enemies,' barked Lotus sharply, 'and I suggest you exercise more control over your men, captain, otherwise we will kill the lot of them. Is that understood?'

The captain bridled visibly, but he stared at the girl with interest: that haughty voice, that arrogant curl of her lip, it was some time since he had seen her . . . if it *was* her . . .

'You! Boy! Look at me!'

The echo shook the mop of blond hair out of his eyes and turned to face him. A murmur swept through the ranks.

'It's a trick, sir!'

'She's kidnapped him!'

'Don't trust them, sir!'

The captain approached cautiously, well aware that Lotus had already reloaded and had another arrow aimed at his throat. He had a nasty gash above one eye and did not look like someone to be trifled with.

'So you're not dead, then?'

'No.'

The echo's fierce black eyes held his.

'Why didn't you fight back?'

'He couldn't,' said Lotus, thinking on her feet. 'Culexis poisoned the Scaramoor. He tried to kill him.'

The captain did not seem as surprised by Culexis's treachery as he might. Maybe he suspected as much, maybe they all did . . .

'Is this true?' he growled.

The boy nodded. He seemed uncertain.

'So what the hell are you doing here with her?'

'I knew this was going to happen,' breezed Lotus. 'That's why I came back to rescue Tom and now we're going to settle his score—'

'Let him speak.'

The boy hesitated. He stared at the hostile ring of dark helmets encircling him through the trees. He had no idea how to lie . . .

'Answer the question.'

'You know we really don't have time for any of this.'

'With *respect*, miss, I'll not be taking any orders from a traitor,' the captain growled. He turned back to the boy and waited for him to speak.

'Lotus Askary is right,' said the echo awkwardly. 'It's true, Dr Culexis has poisoned the Scaramoor, and we are set on getting back to the stockade.. He can't be allowed to get away with it.' The boy did not seem very sure of himself, but the anger blazing in his eyes was real enough. 'Will you help us?'

The captain weighed this up in his mind.

'We have orders to find Nicholas Zumsteen. He has a small cabin up in these woods.'

'Not any longer, captain,' answered Lotus swiftly. 'The gorogonas have destroyed it. There's nothing left. We've just seen it for ourselves.'

The officer eyed her suspiciously.

'In that case, we'll hunt him down in these forests.'

'That is a complete waste of time,' she snorted. 'You could be searching for days, and anyway, he won't be here. The moment the gorogonas hatched they would have killed him just as soon as you or I. He can't control them—no one can. They are unlike anything you have ever seen in your life.'

The grizzled captain knew as much and disliked being reminded of it. But he disliked the girl's tone even more.

'So according to you, we should abandon the whole idea?'

'Yes. And if you are thinking of combing the woods for any stray gorogonas there's no point in that either,' Lotus added. 'You would just be making even more enemies for yourselves.'

With a wry smile the captain looked back down into the valley.

'Very well. But I can guarantee that it will be tasty down there. You may not get back alive. Are you all right with that, my lord?'

The echo nodded, his dark eyes holding the captain's like a magnet.

'If I don't try I'm going to die anyway,' he replied with brutal honesty. 'It's what I have to do.'

'Just as you say, my lord.' The officer turned to face his men. 'Company!' he bawled. 'Change of plan. You're all going to die after all!'

A chorus of grim laughter swept all around.

'We are to escort Tom Scatterhorn back to the stockade. He's returned from the dead to settle an old score—with Dr Culexis!'

There was a roar of approval from the riders.

'That's my old score,' hissed Lotus. 'So don't even think about it.'

'Fine,' he whispered.

'On my order at the edge of the trees. Diamond formation. Go to it!'

There was another burst of cheering, followed by the clatter of preparation. Girths were tightened, buckles fastened, harnesses adjusted . . . the captain turned back to the boy.

'You best ride with me, my lord,' he growled. 'And I'm not letting you go into battle dressed like that. You need some proper armour.'

'Could you find some for me, too?'

The officer might have believed the girl's story, but he had no time for her airs and graces.

'We can probably sort you out with something,' he muttered. 'But where you ride is up to you.'

'Apex?'

The captain shrugged as if he didn't care.

'Thank you,' she smiled, sensing this was a grudging privilege. 'You really don't believe we'll get through, do you?'

He laughed savagely, climbed back onto his mount and turned about.

'Shields, scythes, and luck were just enough to get us out here. Maybe the Defender of Scarazand and a maniac will be enough to get us back.' Digging in his spurs he trotted away down the hill.

CHAPTER 25

THE HOOLIGAN

'I hope we're not too late, old chum.'

'Hmm, what?'

'I think it may have already started. Doesn't that tell you some-thing?'

Sir Henry looked up from his booklet of tables and stared in the direction August was pointing. There, at the edge of the wide white plain on which they stood was a line of forested hills, and hanging over them was a pall of black smoke, rising and spreading like a vast thunderhead. The ominous sound of drumming and explosions boomed in the distance.

'It must be in that valley just below Nicholas's hut,' said Sir Henry, his eyes narrowing. 'I'm sure it was out that way.'

August harrumphed loudly and muffled himself against the wind.

'I suppose we'd better start walking. How far is it?'

'About five miles.'

'Very well, five miles it is.'

He began marching purposefully past the biplane in the direc-tion of the trees. 'Aren't you coming?'

'Wait, August. Listen.'

'Listen to what?'

'That.'

August stopped and turned back towards the long straight road on which they had landed. It sounded like the whine of an engine . . . it *was* the whine of an engine. A small headlight was approaching through the mist.

'Perfect,' muttered Sir Henry, stuffing the tables into his pocket and walking up to the edge of the road. Out of the gloom emerged the grey silhouette of a three-wheeled motorbike with a long wooden box at the back.

'I think this may challenge even your powers of persuasion,' said August, trudging back to join him.

'Hello!' said Sir Henry, waving cheerily as the driver slowed to a halt. 'Good morning.'

The driver stared at him suspiciously. He was a Mongolian, wrapped up in furs and scarves. He seemed very surprised to see them.

'We are stuck,' continued Sir Henry, indicating at the biplane. 'No more petrol. We wondered whether you could give us a lift as we would very much like to go over there.' Sir Henry pointed in the direction of the mysterious black cloud above the hills. 'Sooner rather than later, if possible. Would that be a terrible inconvenience?'

The man stared back at them keenly. Inside the wooden slatted compartment at the back an old shepherd and several sheep hid from the biting wind.

'Not sure he understands a word you're saying, old chap,' muttered August.

'We can offer you a thousand dollars,' said Sir Henry, trying again. He took a wad of money from his pocket and began to count.

'Dollars?' said the driver, in Russian, staring at the notes.

'That's right.' Sir Henry then repeated his offer in Russian, but the man did not seem very impressed. He pulled a bent cigarette out of his pocket and lit it inside his coat. He glanced up towards the hills.

'Why do you want to go up there?' he said in Russian. 'There is nothing but a mad Englishman's cabin up there.'

'Yes, I know. He's a friend of ours.' Sir Henry nodded at August. 'I was right. Zumsteen's hut is up there.'

The driver watched the notes.

'Four thousand.'

'What was that?' asked August.

'Too much. One thousand two hundred,' said Sir Henry in Russian, holding the man's sour gaze. He shook his head.

'Eight thousand.'

'Don't be ridiculous,' snorted Sir Henry. 'I'm not giving you more money than you earn in a year for a half hour detour.'

The man shrugged. He pointed at the sheep and the shepherd and began explaining something that to August sounded as if he was late for market, and the road where they wanted to go was no good, and it would break his motorbike, and this was his uncle, and he had a bad heart, and his sheep were sick too . . . it was quite a performance. When he had finished the driver stared down the empty road again.

'Eight thousand,' he repeated, in Russian.

'This is not going well, is it?' said August.

Sir Henry fumed.

'Never barter with a Siberian sheep farmer. Very well, my friend, if that's the way you want to play it.' Sir Henry put his money away. The driver smiled, assuming they had a deal.

'August, do you see that roll of twine behind Mr Contrary here?'

'I do.'

'I think the time has come to use it.'

'Isn't that a little drastic?'

'Like you said. We're extremely late.'

Suddenly Sir Henry pulled out an antiquated revolver and, cocking it, levelled it at the man's chest.

'Now get off your bike.'

The sight of the gun made the man panic. Throwing his arms up in the air he began shouting.

'Calm down, we're only going to tie you up. August, if you wouldn't mind.'

The man became even more agitated. And so did the shepherd. And so did the sheep.

The noise was tremendous.

'Very well then.'

Sir Henry fired once straight up into the air, whereupon the farmer leapt off the motorbike and sprinted away into the mist.

'Well I suppose it's better than tying the blighter up. Silly twit.'

The ancient shepherd immediately stood up in the back and began mumbling in Russian.

'What's he saying?'

'He's saying he likes English bandits very much.'

'Does he?'

'And he doesn't mind where we want to go. Just so long as we're nice to his sheep.'

August smiled in confusion.

'Just stay there, old fellow,' said Sir Henry in Russian.

The old man made many thanking gestures and sat down.

'But we can't bring him along too.'

'We can't very well leave him here, can we?' Sir Henry replied, swinging his leg over the motorbike and kick starting it. 'Anyway, he's refusing to get out. Climb aboard.'

Raising his eyebrows August sat pillion behind Sir Henry.

'You know you really are something of a hooligan, Henry, and frankly you always have been.'

'Thank you, August.'

'No I mean it.'

'I know you do. And I am. So there.'

Kicking the bike into gear, he revved hard then skidded away in the direction of the forest.

CHAPTER 26

THE FUTURE OF ALL THINGS

In less than ten minutes they were ready. Screened by the wall of trees, the hundred-strong column stood in diamond formation, just as their captain had instructed. Along each flank riders with chain mail and wide black chitin shields positioned themselves, while stationed at each corner stood powerful black beetles harnessed to those strange scything contraptions. Hidden at the very centre, in what might have been the safest place, the captain stood aboard a chariot with the echo at his side, now dressed in a cavalryman's blue-black armour.

'Remember, gentlemen, this is a phalanx. Shields are for *everyone*, particularly Mr Scatterhorn. Act as one, hold them high!'

A muffled murmur of approval drifted through the ranks, and the echo felt the furtive stares from all directions. These men were being ordered to protect him, probably even die for him in a matter of minutes . . . he was determined that he wouldn't let them down. Breath steamed from the soldiers' mouths and the beetles scratched the ground impatiently. They were anxious to get going, and so was he.

'Your shield is there, sir,' said the captain politely, indicating the long shape beside the wheel of the chariot. 'Are you ready?'

'Definitely,' said the boy, listening to the thunder of cannons beyond. He may not have had much practice at deception, but he knew how to fight, and this was his moment. Through the forest of armour and shields he saw Lotus, riding at the very apex. Now she was dressed in armour too, and wielding a pair of long wiry flails in each hand. She turned round to give him the thumbs up sign.

'Let's go.'

The captain dropped his face visor, and a musical tinkling rippled through the trees as everyone followed suit. The echo dropped his own and stared through its steel slits. He could hear nothing but the deafening thump of his heartbeat, drowning out that swirling chaos in the valley below . . .

'Forward!'

Somewhere to the left there was a shout, and the whole formation began to move, slowly at first, picking their way through the trees and out onto the hard ground. No one noticed that as the final scything beetle left the forest a tall man in a long black coat broke cover too, and running up behind it jumped up onto its back . . .

Once in the open the squadron broke into a brisk trot, the outriders bringing themselves up level to form a perfect diamond. Staying close to the edge of the trees, they followed the hillside until they reached the top of a gentle slope that ran down into the valley below. Another command and the diamond wheeled, and through his narrow slits the echo could see the raging battle dead ahead. On the far side of the valley floor he could just make out the towers of the stockade, and the slopes of the crater rising beyond. He braced himself against the chariot's rail . . . this was it.

The pace quickened, the insects breaking into a kind of looping canter. The riders jostled one another, keeping in tight formation, stirrup clanked stirrup, bridles jangled, and the swoo-swoo-swoo of the scythe blades began spinning faster . . .

'AVASTA!' screamed the captain, so loudly that it rang like a fire alarm inside the boy's helmet.

'AVASTA KA HAHN!' his men roared back, echoing the ancient war cry. Keeping formation the beetles broke into a ragged scurrying gallop, every rider lifting their shield ready. At the head Lotus stood up in her stirrups, whirling the flails above her head. There was no stopping now—they were bound together as one, borne on by the dread and excitement of the moment. On the plain ahead a shaft of low sunlight broke through the cloud and lit up the sea of slimy gorogonas . . . they seemed to stop for a moment, then turned to face the black diamond sweeping down the hill towards them . . .

'Flanks high!' roared the captain.

Instantly the long shields locked together as a wall. Volleys of poison fire began bouncing off them and splashing in through the gaps.

'Lock roof!'

The men in the centre raised their shields, and the echo slotted his own up into the waiting gap, completing the phalanx. The light was blotted out . . .

'Brace!' screamed the captain.

The soldiers tensed, they were galloping blind now . . . through the flying snow and gaps between the shields the echo could just glimpse a wall of gorogonas forming directly ahead, rising up like a squirming wave, blocking their path . . .

'Hold formation!' yelled the captain. 'Stay together and we'll live!'

The echo was sure he heard Lotus say something in reply, but it was lost in the thunder of the moment. Twenty strides, ten . . . the next second the diamond phalanx crunched into the gorogonas with such force that it was as if a giant pillow had exploded. The leading edge of serpents was literally pulverized into a fine mist, while the deadly spinning scythes cut a swathe through the rest, dividing the gorogonas faster than they could reform.

'Keep together, lads, tight formation!' bawled the captain as they rampaged blindly onwards. Cocooned inside his helmet, the echo had very little idea what was happening, except that the first wave had been broken, and when he dared to lower his shield a fraction he saw a sea of silvery serpents in full flight before them. Those that turned to fight were either crushed underfoot or demolished by Lotus—wielding her flails like smashing branches in a storm.

'I think your moment has come, sir,' shouted the captain, ripping away a couple of small gorogonas that had clamped themselves to his helmet. 'Show 'em you're still alive and we might prevail!'

The echo suddenly realized what was expected of him.

'Lift me up,' he commanded, and the captain hoisted him up onto his shoulders. Raising his visor the boy saw the whirlwind of the battle spread out all around: squares of half-breeds, swarms of insects and snakes writhing back and forth, locked in a mortal struggle.

'AVASTA!' he screamed, raising his sword aloft.

'AVASTA KA HAHN!' answered the riders around him, opening their shields and thrusting their swords into the air.

The cry echoed across the valley, and from all quarters of the battlefield the beleaguered half-breeds looked up to see a black phalanx stampeding towards them, carving a path through the sea of gorogonas like a magnificent armoured beast . . . there was a boy at its centre, his armour glinting in the pale sun, his sword held aloft . . . could it be, was it him? It must be . . .

'AVASTA KA HAHN!' The roars rang out as the half-breeds beat on their shields in unison . . . 'AVASTA KA HAHN!'

A spark of hope rushed through the ranks like bushfire . . . Tom Scatterhorn, their mascot, their hero—he was alive after all, and he was fighting . . . Like a god returning from the underworld he had conquered death somehow, and now he was back: to lead them against an ever-dividing enemy . . . They had a chance in this, a slim, slim chance . . .

Battle was joined, more ferociously than ever before. The ripple of excitement was even felt at the top of the stockade. Don Gervase hunted through the smoke and fire greedily, trying to see what was going on . . . and suddenly his telescope fell upon a girl riding at the head of the black phalanx. He gasped.

'Lotus?' It *was* Lotus, his daughter: wheeling her flails like an octopus, smashing at everything in her path, absolutely in her element . . . What was she doing here? Had she come to kill him? Or rescue Tom Scatterhorn? Possibly both . . . unless—

'My lord!' A breathless shout from down below. 'My lord, they've found him!'

Don Gervase put his head over the parapet to see Dr Culexis panting in the stockade.

'They have found the boy, my lord. Rainbird's bringing him in now.'

'Is he alive?'

Dr Culexis's face creased up painfully.

'I believe so. Just about.'

'I want him in here where I can see him. Alive or dead, it doesn't matter. Quickly man.'

Dr Culexis bowed low, struggling to understand his master's words. Alive, or dead?

Don Gervase could barely contain his excitement. He turned back to the chaos beyond—was it true? Yes it was! There—fifty metres beyond the ramparts was Rainbird, leading a small party of half-breeds bearing a stretcher. And on that stretcher lay Tom Scatterhorn, still wearing the Scaramoor, with a shield covering his body. Don Gervase watched as they dodged through the piles of dead insects, beating off attacks as they went: in a minute they would have him inside the stockade . . . Good, excellent, that was the lure, now all he could hope was that Lotus had not let her violent jealousy get the better of her . . . he scanned the tightly packed phalanx, the smoke, the flashing swords, the squirming snakes—there he was! The echo, right at the very heart of it, his black eyes flashing as he cut left and right . . . Don Gervase grinned wildly: everything was converging from all points of the compass, seemingly of its own accord. This was not what he had expected at all . . .

And Don Gervase Askary was not the only one to make a quick appraisal of the situation. On the other side of the valley, half hidden in the trees, Sir Henry Scatterhorn and August Catcher skidded to a halt on the stolen motorbike and stared at the battle raging below.

'To think Tom's lost in the middle of all that,' breathed August, watching the black phalanx career through the carpet of gorogonas. 'How on earth are we ever going to find him?'

Sir Henry scanned the chaos with his binoculars, then abruptly came to a halt. With a furrowed brow he handed them back to August.

'Look just to the left of those towers at the base of the crater.'

August anxiously did as he was told. There, in amongst the writhing snakes, the yellow smoke, the slashing swords . . .

'Not the stretcher?'

'Wounded, one presumes. Or worse. If it's him. Hate to say it, old boy, but you may have been right. Maybe we are too late.'

The two old friends sat in grim contemplation for a moment, lost in thought. From up here it was clear to see which way the battle was going. Don Gervase had arranged his armies in a wide arc defending the slope up to the crater. To the south and east, cliffs and high spurs prevented any ascent, which meant that the only way up into Scarazand was through his lines, and it was already starting to happen. One by one the squares of half-breeds and beetles were overwhelmed by the sheer numbers of their enemies and fell back in confusion towards the slope, only to find their path blocked by gorogonas that had raced to outflank them. Isolated from the main force, they were surrounded by the rising tide of snakes that then fell upon them from all sides. All across the valley floor squares of half-breeds and beetles were locked in desperate last-ditch battles, unable to get back to the shrinking perimeter around the crater.

'How long is Askary going to be able to keep this up?' growled Sir Henry.

August shrugged helplessly. He had never seen anything like this before.

'Until most of his forces are conveniently destroyed? It can't be long now, can it?'

Sir Henry grunted. He stared in silence at the heaps of dead littering the plain.

'I almost feel like giving them a hand. What on earth was Nicholas Zumsteen thinking of?'

'Quite,' murmured August. 'Because once those gorogonas get inside Scarazand and fall under the Queen's magnetic spell, and Askary realizes he can control them with that mesmerion ball of his . . . doesn't really bear thinking about, does it?'

Sir Henry shook his head savagely. August continued.

'Makes me half wonder whether that wasn't always Nicholas's intention, too. After all, he was the one who bought the mesmerion on Tithona in the first place, squirrelled it carefully away, then collected and bred all the gorogonas . . . perhaps we've seriously underestimated him. Perhaps he's not half as mad as we think.'

'Oh he is, old chap, they both are.' Sir Henry glowered across the chaos towards the stockade. 'Even more reason to get to that boy and finish the Queen off—come hell or high water. But the fact of the matter is we can't ride a tricycle into the middle of a battle.'

'And it's not only us.'

Sir Henry glanced back at the shepherd, still sitting with his sheep, listening to the yells and clang of armour. He smiled tooth-lessly.

'Then what we need is a disguise.'

'Precisely.'

August spotted the remains of a wolfskidder at the bottom of the slope, its carapace lying upturned like a giant bowl.

'A very large disguise.'

Sir Henry turned to his oldest friend and raised one sceptical eyebrow.

'And I'm the hooligan, am I?'

'It's rubbing off.'

In the same moment Sir Henry and August accelerated down the slope into the fray Dr Culexis turned away from his master. Given what had happened, he had hardly expected much praise for organizing the difficult and dangerous task of retrieving the boy; nevertheless a little more recognition might have been appropriate . . . but he had a strong sense that something had changed . . . In amongst the shouts and explosions beyond the stockade he heard a familiar battle cry, which could only mean one thing. Ignoring his duties, he quietly scurried up the steps of the nearest tower, climbing through the floors until he had reached the highest, to find a gun crew busy reloading their cannon with acid bombs. Dr Culexis silently approached the opening and stared out at the confusion beyond.

'Now there's a sight to warm the coldest heart,' muttered the gun captain, a wizened half-breed man with a hunchback and long thin hands. He was peering down a gun sight that was hanging from the roof. 'I told you he wouldn't abandon us.'

'Who are you talking about?'

The man shrank back a little to find the pale doctor standing beside him. Snatching away the spyglass Culexis pressed it to his eye. What he saw made the hairs on the back of his neck stand up.

'But . . . but how is that possible?'

'It's just like you said, sir. One champion. To lead us in one battle. A battle to end all battles. He's come back to save Scara—'

'SHUT UP!' screamed Dr Culexis, a blob of spittle flying out of the corner of his mouth. He looked again, and his face, already grey with cold, turned the colour of lichen. Not only was the echo out there, but Lotus Askary too, at the head of that black phalanx, bearing down on them through the sea of snakes . . . what was this, some sort of revenge mission? It was . . . she was going to attack the Glorious Leader. Instantly Culexis recognized his opportunity. He could win his favour back . . . he could be forgiven . . . but she must be destroyed, now. And that undeserving echo.

'You,' he barked at the gun crew carefully swinging their cannon towards the gorogonas beyond. 'You men, stop that!'

The half-breeds turned to face him grudgingly. Dr Culexis pointed at the phalanx rampaging towards them.

'That is your target. Fire on it.'

The gun crew looked at each other blankly. They did not appear to hear what he said.

'Can't you see, you idiots, that's Lotus Askary!'

'Beg pardon, sir, their ears is strapped,' said the gun captain, pointing at the strips of cloth that were bound tightly to their heads. 'But what about the boy?'

'He's turned against us.'

The gun captain shook his head; he would not believe it; indeed he could not.

'Sir, you are mistaken.'

Suddenly Dr Culexis grabbed him by the throat and pressed him against the wall.

'Do you want me to report you for refusing to do your duty? They're coming to kill us! It's a trick!'

'But how could—'

'DO IT!'

Dr Culexis's nostrils flared, his face incandescent with rage. The captain of the gun crew nodded nervously to his men. The barrel was swung round and the bomb aimer checked his sight. As he did so the gun captain lifted the half-breed's bound ear and whispered.

'Mount, not rider.'

'What did you say?'

'Just aimin' him, sir, just aimin' him!'

Culexis positioned himself directly behind the cannon.

'If that shot doesn't hit the girl—or the boy for that matter—you're both dead men, you understand?'

The bomb aimer nodded, and so did his captain—they understood exactly.

'Ready.'

'Fire!'

The echo was so busy fending off the gorogonas coiled around his helmet like hair that by the time he saw the bomb it was too late. Suddenly a red explosion burst just ahead of him, and the very next second the chariot upended and he was flying through the air. When he next opened his eyes he found himself lying on a mound of debris not far from the stockade, his armour drenched in smoking red acid . . . Was that an accident? But they'd meant to hit him, surely—

'Keep down,' whispered a voice. Before the boy had a chance to reply his head was pushed beneath a shield and a gorogona slithered over the top of it.

'Well, sir?'

Dr Culexis pressed his eye to the glass and sneered. The shot had struck the heart of the black phalanx—shattering the formation. The few riders that had survived now found themselves isolated and pursued by gangs of gorogonas intent on dragging them to the ground. But there was no sign of the girl. Or the boy, for that matter.

'You have earned yourself a reprieve. Reload.'

The gun crew glared at him mutinously. Nobody moved.

'That's right, you half-breed scum, *I* am commanding this gun now. Chop-chop!'

'Who took that shot!'

The booming voice echoed around the stockade.

'Which man took that shot! Show yourself!'

Dr Culexis nervously poked his head out of the platform to find Don Gervase scowling down at him.

'*You?* I thought I told you to bring in that stretcher—'

'It was not me, your grace,' he cringed, 'how could I possibly fire a cannon? I simply . . . that is to say the captain here thought he spotted someone.'

'Spotted who, Culexis?'

The neat little doctor's mind galloped wildly.

'Lotus Askary, my lord. I saw her myself. How she did it I don't—'

'Is she dead?'

'She won't be troubling us again, my lord!'

With a brazen wave Dr Culexis dipped out of sight.

Don Gervase returned to the chaos, fuming. He had been so busy watching the stretcher's dogged progress that the destruction of the phalanx took him completely by surprise. Of course this was bound to happen, someone was bound to recognize Lotus, and it would be Dr Culexis . . . But what about the boy? Don Gervase scanned the whirlwind of smoke and gorogonas that filled the hole where the phalanx had been . . . he could be anywhere down there—if he was even alive. Angrily Don Gervase shook the mersmerion from his cuff. The short winter's day was already coming to an end and he needed that boy inside the stockade right now, whether Lotus would bring him here or not . . .

'They think we're dead. That's good.'

The echo looked up from the debris to find the captain smiling down at him—his grizzled face running with blood.

'So that was deliberate?'

The captain nodded.

'They wouldn't do that unless they meant it. Smashed us up good and proper. Someone don't like you up there, evidently. And I've a fair idea who that might be, don't you?'

The echo nodded: Dr Culexis—of course. He had more reason to kill him than anyone else.

'I wouldn't hold much hope of getting inside now.'

The echo glanced over the ridge of debris towards the stockade some fifty metres away. The captain was right. Guns flashed from every tier, and all along the ramparts below waves of gorogonas were hurling themselves at lines of soldiers and Skrolls . . . there was no way through there, surely—

'Tom! Tom, where are you!'

The voice rose above the din of battle and the echo dared to stand up. There was Lotus Askary, running through the debris covered in dirt and blood. As soon as she saw him she raced over and threw herself down beside them.

'Did you see him?' she gasped.

The echo shook his head.

'Over there. He's on a stretcher. They're taking him in round the back.'

Lotus pointed through the flashing swords and smoke to where a gang of half-breeds were hauling a knight over the ramparts, savagely hacking away the gorogonas on every side. The boy turned pale: he recognized that armour, that helmet, the sword in the boy's hand . . .

'So the poison—'

'He's not gone yet,' growled Lotus. 'If he had, then so would you. Remember that.' Picking up a sword she thrust it into his hand. 'Come on. Before something worse happens.'

But no sooner had the boy taken it than he stopped dead. His eyes screwed tight shut and his fists closed.

'Are you all right?'

'I've got to go. Now.'

'Yes I know. We both have—'

'No you don't understand,' he said, fiercely pushing her away. 'I am not here for this.'

In an instant Lotus guessed what was happening. The echo was seeing the world through different eyes, and different things were true.

'He's spotted you, hasn't he? He knows we're here.'

She glanced up through the smoke at the stockade. Already the echo was racing straight for it without a thought for his own safety. The captain stared after him in confusion.

'Change of plan?'

Lotus hesitated. Was there any point in following the echo, who was now quite obviously under Don Gervase's command? What about Tom? She turned to the rampart. The stretcher had disappeared, he must be already inside the stockade. But if Don Gervase knew she was here . . . then so did Dr Culexis—

'The shot that destroyed us was deliberate, wasn't it?'

The captain nodded.

'I reckon he's lurking up there,' he nodded towards the closest tower and the cannon at the very top. 'That's the culprit.'

'All right.'

Lotus knew exactly what she intended to do. Crawling forward, she pulled a pair of flails out of a dead man's hand, then grabbed a shield, too.

'Do you need any help?'

'Do what you like,' she growled, buckling the flails round her wrists.

'Then I'm coming with you,' grunted the captain, dropping his visor. 'Let's get this over with.'

Hiding behind their shields they began weaving through the debris, covering half the distance to the stockade before they were spotted. Three large gorogonas slithered across their path and, rising up, twisted around each other to form a living tree. Their yellow hoods bloomed like flowers and their jaws opened, revealing a wall of dripping teeth . . .

'I do believe we're going to die,' gasped the captain, withdrawing behind his shield.

'Believe that and you will,' hissed Lotus, standing her ground. Out of the corner of her eye she noticed that the cannon in the closest tower was swinging around towards them . . .

'Charge it,' she whispered.

'Charge it?'

'Straight at it. Follow me. After three.' The cannon stopped moving. It was aiming straight at them.

'THREE!'

Together they hurled themselves at the tree of snakes and before they even connected with it the air seemed to explode. Where there had been silvery grey armour there was nothing but a mist of red-hot acid . . .

'KEEP RUNNING!' shouted Lotus, unaware that she was alone now. The rampart was only twenty metres away.

'Dammit! Can't you hit anything?'

Dr Culexis tore the spyglass away and kicked the wall hard. The gun crew kept their heads low as they rapidly recharged the acid cylinders and cranked up the winches once more.

'She was ever so fast, sir,' mumbled the gun captain. 'Sort of popped up, weasel-ish, y'know and then—'

'Don't you weasel-ish me, scumbag,' the doctor spat murderously. 'I know what you're doing—'

'But sir—'

'Is this man giving you gyp, doctor?'

There was Ern Rainbird, standing in the doorway. His chain mail was bloodied and his face was blackened with filth. His eyeballs seemed to be starting from his head.

'He is deliberately protecting Lotus Askary. Missing her, on purpose.'

'No, no . . . we—'

'Oh dear. That's not good.' Rainbird marched straight over and, picking up the gun captain by the scruff of the neck hurled him out over the ramparts into the sea of gorogonas. The half-breeds gasped in shock.

'Now then. Is it loaded?'

'Yessir,' came the hurried reply.

'Primed?'

'Yessir.'

Grabbing the handles of the gun Rainbird spun it round, deliberately aiming it at the gun crew themselves. They held up their hands in terror.

'You going to do as you're told this time, aren't you?'

The crew daren't move. They could barely nod.

'Right then.'

He dropped the barrel towards the ramparts beyond and hunted around for that girl. Where was she? Somewhere to the right a

great shout rang out, and through the smoke he glimpsed a flash
of silver and black. Rainbird swung the barrel round just in time
to see the echo leap over the rampart and throw himself onto the
back of a beetle. Urging it into a gallop the boy grabbed a passing
lance and raced straight down the line, making for the entrance to
the stockade. The girl must be with him—but where . . . where?

'Fire, Rainbird,' urged Culexis, seeing Rainbird track the boy
galloping past the debris.

'Can you see her?'

'It doesn't matter, kill him man. Now.'

Rainbird grimaced through the smoke.

'KILL HIM!'

Suddenly, and without quite knowing why, Ern Rainbird did
as he was told. But his aim was atrocious. The cannon recoiled,
and a bomb of red acid exploded directly into the imperial bodyguard, valiantly defending the rampart behind the galloping boy.
Rainbird staggered forward, his ears ringing, and looked down. It
was as if a dam had broken. Where there had been a wall of fighting men and insects there was now a hole, and through that hole
a tide of gorogonas was flowing. The wall was breached: he had
breached it. The shouts turned to screams of panic.

'You haven't reloaded.'

The gun crew stood dumbstruck, staring at the chaos below.

'Look what's happening!' shrieked Culexis, foam flying from
his mouth. 'Down there! They're coming in!'

The men did not need to be told again. In a mad rush they set
to work, and seconds later the gun was primed for action.

'Out of my way.'

The bomb aimer cowered as Dr Culexis took over the gun

himself and spun it on its axis so that it now faced inside the stockade. A wall of Skrolls had fallen back across the main entrance, battling to hold back the waves of gorogonas squirming all around them. In the centre of the stockade stood Don Gervase, frantically playing the mesmerion in his hand. To his right lay Tom Scatterhorn, still on his stretcher, oblivious. Suddenly a great serpent slithered through the rest and smashed over the ring of Skrolls. Rearing up, it approached Don Gervase and towered over him, its yellow hood flaring wildly.

'AVASTA!'

Don Gervase whipped round to see the echo galloping at full tilt straight at the gorogona. He gasped with excitement, was this it, the final play? The great serpent was about to unleash its venom but when it saw the boy it hesitated, and in that same second something caught Don Gervase's eye above . . . the muzzle of a cannon swivelling towards the rider . . .

'NO!' shouted Don Gervase in a panic. 'Don't fire! Don't fire!'

Dr Culexis's hand was frozen on the lever . . . what should he do?

In an instant the doctor made his decision: he aimed at the only person he could be certain of: Tom Scatterhorn, lying on his stretcher.

But it was already too late.

The second he pulled the lever the barrel lurched drunkenly to one side, spinning off its cradle and into the roof.

'That was a big mistake.'

Dr Culexis staggered back. Ern Rainbird dragged himself to his feet. They turned to face the opening behind them and froze in terror.

'Remember me? I'm your worst nightmare.'

Lotus Askary withdrew the flail from the cannon and began swishing the wires back and forth above her head like some strange deep-sea creature.

'But—'

With a flick she sent the wires slicing through the air like scythes, spinning around their necks. The two henchmen were dead before they hit the ground. Lotus barely noticed the towers collapsing beyond . . .

Down in the snowy stockade, the confusion of those last seconds lived long in the memories of those who saw it. For the echo, encased in his helmet, all he knew was what lay directly in front of him: the rest was a flickering dream, barely glimpsed. He had to protect the leader . . . he had to save him . . . the words hammered in his head, over and over . . . He galloped past the boy on the stretcher, lying unattended in the snow—he galloped past the Glorious Leader, ignoring his strange smile . . . his vision narrowed onto a small white patch of silvery hide in the neck of that huge swaying gorogona, its mouth hanging open above him . . . letting go of his reins he leant into his lance and buried it to the hilt in that column of soft white flesh . . . it juddered and snapped as he let go and grabbed the reins, pulling in so hard that his mount tipped onto its side and he was thrown from the saddle, spinning helplessly across the ground. Looking up, he glimpsed the gorogona collapsing backwards, screaming, then something red exploded behind him . . .

For Don Gervase Askary, the moment he had long anticipated
came so fast he was barely aware of it until it was over. It was not
quite what he had expected. Yes, the echo had come when asked,
though he had left it very late . . . and almost in the same second
someone fired a cannon directly into the base of one of the towers.
He watched as it wobbled, twisted, then slowly toppled sideways
into the next, which knocked into the next, and the next . . . on
it went around the stockade, each tower crashing down like giant
dominoes into the mass of gorogonas and men . . . it was the perfect end . . . with a wild laugh Don Gervase ran out through the
falling chaos to where his dragonfly chariot lay waiting. Leaping
aboard, he took up the reins and shook the creature to its feet . . .

'Stop!'

The next moment someone tackled him from behind, hauling him back onto the ground . . . Wriggling free, Don Gervase
Askary kicked his attacker viciously in the chest and urged the
dragonfly upwards. In an instant they were airborne. Don Gervase cast a curious glance back at the man sprawling in the snow.
He was dressed in a long black coat, with a hat pulled well down
over his ears . . .

'Nicholas? Is that you?'

Nicholas Zumsteen watched helplessly as his brother ascended
higher and scrambled to his feet.

'You can't win you know!' he shouted. 'You'll never beat them!
Nothing can!'

'I know! Aren't they magnificent!'

The dragonfly tilted up towards the crater leaving Zumsteen

dumbfounded, struggling to understand. Lying in the snow was Don Gervase's small black pistol. He picked it up and fired it wildly, but already the chariot was too high. The next moment the blast of a great horn rolled across the valley. The remains of those squares still fighting around their ragged colours turned to see a glistening river of snakes sweeping up the crater's flank. With the stockade fallen the battle had turned into a rout. There was nothing anyone could do to stop the gorogonas now.

Don Gervase stared down at the scene with grim satisfaction. Dusk was falling now, and there lay his once-mighty army of Scarazand, reduced to smouldering piles of debris stretching far out across the valley. It had been a high price to pay, but: this was the dawn of a new world. All he had to do was to wait for the gorogonas to descend into Scarazand and then, like everything else in thrall to the Queen's irresistible power, each and every one of them would be his. And gorogonas were far superior to mere beetles . . .

He smiled, and suddenly wished someone were there to congratulate him. He was on the cusp of a new and glorious chapter in his life. To think how low he had begun, and where he was going to now . . . and to think that his great plan had almost been derailed by a single thirteen-year-old boy . . . Don Gervase Askary's face cracked into a sneer: *almost*—yes this had been a curious charade—and one best forgotten. Without a backward glance Don Gervase descended into the crater. He did not notice the dark vee approaching in the western sky . . .

CHAPTER 27

TIME'S ARROW

So what had happened to that thirteen-year-old boy? Tom Scatterhorn's last waking memory was of jets of poison raining down on him as he lay on the frozen ground. Through the narrow grille in the Scaramoor he had seen the air suddenly ignite, then a thump from the gorogona's tail knocked him senseless. Unconscious, he never knew countless snakes had slithered over him, or that a heap of dead beetles had formed around him, or that a brave party of half-breed stretcher-bearers had battled their way out into the morass to recover his body. The next moment he opened his eyes the sky had darkened and he saw a rider colliding with a vast gorogona with such force that he was thrown spinning across the snow . . . there was an explosion of red above his head and suddenly the dark shadow towering over him began to wobble and collapse. A cannon and tackle tipped off a platform high above and fell straight towards him. And then the world went black again—

It might only have been for a second, but it felt like an eternity. When he awoke Tom found himself lying amid a pile of debris. There were shadows of men and snakes fighting all around.

Everything was silent—why was everything so silent? Sword . . . he must find his sword . . . he must defend himself. Trying to get up, he found he was pinned under a large beam that lay across his chest. But remarkably, he seemed to be in one piece. His armour seemed to have saved him. His armour . . .

'Tom?'

The voice swam up to him and Tom turned to see a shadow approaching.

'He's here! Over here!'

In a moment his helmet was off and Lotus was staring down at him, frantically searching for signs of life.

'Tom, can you hear me?'

Tom watched her groggily: why was she staring at him like that? Then she slapped him hard in the face. He blinked.

'You're alive!'

Another shadow staggered through the wreckage towards him. It was the rider.

'Quick. Help me.'

Together they heaved the beam off his chest and began wrestling with the leather straps.

'What's happening?'

'Your armour, we must get it off.'

'But—'

'Culexis poisoned it, he's trying to kill you. You're going to die.'

'No I'm not—'

'Yes you are. Don't argue. Turn him over,' she instructed the rider.

'Lotus it's OK—' Tom was thumped headfirst into the earth. He was rapidly recovering his senses. 'Lotus, it's—'

'Ignore him.'

Off came the leg grooves, the gauntlets, the elbows—

'Stop. Please. Ow,' he said, as she tore the feet away. 'I know Dr Culexis poisoned the armour.'

'What?'

'I know.'

Lotus stopped and rolled him back over again roughly.

'What do you mean you know?'

Tom sat up and lifted away the breastplate Lotus had just undone.

'You see?'

A thin white material, like spun silk, covered Tom's body. Dustings of black powder blew across its surface. Lotus suddenly felt very foolish.

'That's . . . but you idiot. Why didn't you tell us?'

'I am trying to.'

Lotus's anger could not disguise her relief. She smiled, then knocked him straight back to the ground.

'We thought you were going to die.'

'I can see that,' Tom said, now smiling himself. Sitting up, he looked across at the rider who had taken off his helmet. The boy's dark eyes watched him carefully.

'Hi.'

He held out his hand formally and Tom grasped it. Crackles of electricity passed between them.

'Thanks.'

'Thanks?' Lotus stared at them both. 'For what? Don't tell me you knew about this as well?'

The echo shook his head.

'He made lots of friends,' explained Tom. 'One of them realized what Culexis was up to and sent me a note. So I took a precaution, just in case.'

'Who was it?'

Tom thought back to the girl with the shaved head who had helped him put his helmet on: that fleeting look she had given him.

'I can't remember her name. But I think she knew you before you became famous. She gave me this.'

Tom slipped off the balaclava and handed it to his echo. The boy obviously recognized it straight away.

'Oh. Yes. Viola.' The echo nodded sheepishly. He wasn't about to explain any more. 'Well everyone hated Culexis, didn't they?'

Lotus stared at the two identical boys for a moment.

'What?' asked Tom.

'Nothing. It's just very strange seeing you together like this,' she smiled. 'Like two halves of the same person. Tom Scatterhorn: the thinker and the fighter.'

'Hell's bells—there he is!'

Suddenly the sky darkened as a racket of wings swooped and tore overhead. Instinctively Lotus and the echo ducked as a large flock of rooks descended noisily all around them. There was a loud crash as a cannon overturned and the next moment a familiar shape staggered out of the debris with purpose.

'Is he alive?' roared the ragged eagle.

'You're back?' Lotus stood up uncertainly. 'I thought you said—'

'Changed me mind, didn't I?' The raptor nosed past her and peered down at Tom. 'So you's definitely not dead?'

Tom nodded.

'Not even slightly? What about the poison?'

Pushing the armour aside, Tom stood up.

'I was tipped off. By his girlfriend.'

The great raptor looked from Tom to his echo and back, and if at that moment it could have smiled, it would. Instead it danced from one foot to the other, wriggling its neck violently.

'Dang it, Tom Scatterhorn, I'd almost given up on you! What with all these gorgonzolas and him and her and . . . never mind. We've got to get cracking, kiddo. Right this minute, as it happens.'

'What's happened?'

The eagle indicated the rooks perched all around.

'These blokes have just told me something peculiarly crucial. In fact I'm still in a state of shock.'

'What are you talking about?' demanded Lotus.

'The vent hole, missy. I've just found out where the blinking thing is!'

Lotus's jaw dropped in astonishment.

'And not only that, with a bit of advance preparation, I reckon you can sort out Askary and Scarazand for ever.'

Tom gasped.

'Me?'

'That's right, kiddo—you. But only you. Cos you're about to be there already. On that same night, in that *exact* place.'

Lotus and Tom stared at the eagle, trying to understand . . . and they were not alone. In amongst the wrecked towers crouched a man in a long black coat straining to hear the bird's harsh tones.

'I'm about to be there *already*?'

'Yep.'

'But you can't tell me where it is?'

'Nope. Indeed I have been particularly prevailed upon *not* to.'

The eagle indicated the stern-eyed rooks all around.

'And you're completely certain about this?' asked Lotus.

'What do you think we've bothered to come all the way back to this hell-hole for—a picnic?'

Tom looked at the motley eagle and the whole flock of rooks behind it. They looked extremely menacing, and in no mood to argue.

'There is one chance to end all this, kiddo—just one. It has to be you, and it has to be now. Are you game?'

'You know I am, only—'

'Good. Now get cracking and filch yerself some clobber, because it's going to be darn cold.'

'Darn cold?' persisted Lotus, wondering if she had guessed what the great bird meant. 'And it definitely can't be me, or even him?' She pointed at the echo.

'We have one golden rule when it comes to interfering with the past, Miss F-P, and that is—don't. But if you must, change as little as possible. That's the hard and fast of it. Otherwise everything goes out of kilter and you can't ever put it back. Believe me, no one but the original Tom Scatterhorn fits the bill. Now get up here, me old gullabong, before I grab yer by the pants.'

Tom ran back to the bird carrying whatever he had been able to scavenge from the battlefield: a thick green coat, an old pair of boots, a scarf, a beret . . .

'Good luck, then,' said Lotus watching him climb onto the eagle's back. 'I wish there was some way I could help you.'

Tom did not know what to say. His mind was in a blur.

Almost as soon as they had appeared the flock of birds lifted up and flew away, heading towards the rind of moon. Already the first stars were twinkling over the forest. Lotus stood watching them in silence, her mind racing with possibilities, and crouched inside the wreckage of a tower, Nicholas Zumsteen was having very similar thoughts. The eagle may have deliberately tried to be obscure, but he understood very well what it meant. The question was . . . he peered back up at the crater. Its flanks were now a solid sea of gorogonas, and there was still a fierce fight raging around the lip. Not that way. Jamming the pistol firmly into his belt he set off at a run across the battlefield . . .

'What now?' said the echo.

Lotus stared at the wreckage all around. Suddenly she felt completely deflated. The endgame was up there with Tom, far beyond her control. There was nothing more she could do . . . At that moment the sound of a motorbike rattled up the slope and a large brown carapace skidded to a halt beside the remains of the stockade. It seemed to be bleating unhappily. August Catcher crawled out from underneath it, followed by a breathless Sir Henry.

'Is he still alive? Is he?'

Lotus waved, wondering if this scene was about to be played out again.

'Great snakes!'

August leapt over the debris excitedly and stood beaming at the boy. An elaborate suit of armour lay in pieces at his feet.

'Let me guess, it's a very long story.'

'Very,' said Lotus. 'Because—'

'You're absolutely fine?'

The echo nodded sheepishly.

'Marvellous! Only we thought for a mo—'

'He's not who you think he is.'

August did not quite understand. Lotus pointed to the black vee formation flying fast into the clear evening sky.

'That's Tom up there. They're taking him back to Dragonport.'

'What? Why?'

'The bird has found the vent hole. Tom's got to get back to some particular evening when he might be able to destroy it. Most annoyingly it wouldn't say any more.'

By now Sir Henry had stridden purposefully up through the wreckage to join them.

'Problem?' he gasped, looking to Lotus then the echo in turn. August pointed towards the specks in the distance.

'They've beaten us to it, old bean.'

'No! But do they know exactly what's going to happen?'

Lotus shrugged petulantly. 'How should I know? No one tells me anything.'

'I don't see how they can,' said August. 'Not unless they've seen everything already, which I doubt. But it's too late to ask them now.'

Sir Henry stared up at the birds, barely scribbles against the pale sky.

'Dammit. Dammit dammit dammit.' With a heavy sigh he turned back to August, his noble face set as hard as granite. 'You know what it might mean.'

August shook his head grimly.

'Indeed. He has taken the boy's place. With all the consequences of that.'

'Why is everyone speaking in riddles?' said Lotus. 'I demand to be told what's happening. Tell me. Now.'

Sir Henry ignored Lotus's indignant stare and turned to the echo, thinking fast.

'Whose side are you on, old chap?'

The boy shifted uncomfortably.

'I'm . . . I guess I am with Tom, unless I get told otherwise.'

'Very good. That is very good.' Sir Henry collected his thoughts. He noticed the Scaramoor lying on the ground, and the clouds of airborne half-breeds still harrying the snakes with grenades and arrows . . .

'You see, it's possible—probable—that Tom is about to find himself in a great deal of danger. But there may be a way in which you can help him, only it will involve going against all your instincts. Would you be prepared to do that?'

The echo stared into Sir Henry's wrinkled, ancient face. He had never met this man before, but there was something about him he instinctively recognized and trusted.

'I could try. What is it?'

'So have they always known that the lightning was going to strike?'

'These boys? No way, kiddo. They just got the sniff it was going to happen tonight. And as for the vent hole actually being in Dragonport . . . strewth, what are the chances of that? I always thought Dragonport smelt daggy because it's a daggy sort of place, isn't it? I was stunned.'

Tom watched the tiny fires receding fast behind them and he had to admit he was stunned, too. When the echo had told him it was hidden in a tree, he never believed that the tree might be at Catcher Hall, August's own house, where *he* had lived . . .

'But I *have* always known you had something to do with the endgame. A lynchpin. Everyone knows that.' The eagle nodded at the black rooks flying all around. 'I tell ya, in the ways of the birds the name of Tom Scatterhorn is well known. You're dead famous.'

'Dead famous?'

'*Dead famous.* Not to say famously dead, or deadly famous, just y'know—famous, dang it.'

Launching into a swift dive they sped down the slenderest of moonbeams, the rooks taking the lead. One by one they darted ahead, sliding into the vortex of air like scraps of paper sucked into a tunnel. Tom closed his eyes . . . a heavy thud hammered in his ears, followed by a flash of blue, green . . . and then they were flying through a thick wet mist. Far below, a necklace of lanterns glowed.

'Is this right?' asked Tom, amazed that they had got here so quickly.

'I'm following them,' rasped the bird, its head barely visible in the gloom. 'This is their backyard. They know every shortcut there ever was.'

The rooks screeched out a high ululating call, then swept down towards the lights. The great bird answered once then slipped away in the other direction, rapidly descending until it bounced to a halt at the top of a narrow lane. Tom looked around and he recognized the view immediately. They were somewhere up near the gates of Catcher Hall. Below lay Dragonport, the frozen river, and the ice fair. Wide curtains of mist were blowing in off the estuary, erasing the houses and trees.

'Sorry I can't take you any closer, but they don't want me to arouse any suspicions. Not tonight, of all nights. We've got to pretend like it's all normal. Got a watch?'

Tom nodded. The raptor listened. A church bell was ringing somewhere.

'Ten o'clock,' it rasped. Tom reset his watch nervously and slipped it back onto his wrist. 'Now they reckon it's going to be bang on quarter to one, but I wouldn't trust a rook's timekeeping so best be early to make sure.'

'OK.'

'Now you're clear what you're gonna do?'

Tom nodded. He had been thinking about everything the eagle had told him and had come up with a plan.

'And you're sure you can remember where the key is?'

'If it's where it always used to be.'

'What about an axe?'

'There's one in the woodshed.'

'Right. But you're not to touch or change anything else. That's the cast iron rule when you go back. Got it?'

Tom nodded, shivering a little.

'Let's hope you ain't disturbed.'

'Might I be?'

The eagle grunted.

'There's a gamekeeper that lives down the bottom of the hill, but I doubt he'll be about. Not in this weather. And when you find the right tree, look for something up in the branches that opens and closes. It's like a flower, so them rooks said. Give the thing a damn good wallop—bust it right off if you can—then stand well clear.'

Tom suddenly felt very self-conscious in his tatty greatcoat, black beret and boots pilfered from the battlefield.

'Do I look all right?'

The great raptor watched the boy push the tangle of hair out of his eyes.

'You look like a bloody disgrace. So you'll do fine.'

Tom smiled nervously.

'Best get going then, kiddo. And just remember, lightning never strikes twice. No pressure.'

'Thanks.'

'Seriously, mate—finish it. Finish it tonight if you can. And you *can*. Just be yourself. What could be easier than that?'

With a determined smile Tom drew up his scarf against the wind and hurried in through the iron gates of Catcher Hall.

'We're all rootin' for ya.'

The boy did not look back. The eagle stood a while, watching until the slim shape had disappeared around the corner.

'Ah well.'

Shaking the snow off its feathers, the great raptor turned to see a small lantern bobbing up the lane. It was carried by a boy in a ragged jacket and top hat, whistling tunelessly as he picked his way up through the dirty snow. Silently the eagle slunk across into the shadows, and was about to retreat still further when the whistling stopped. The eagle froze, still as a statue. It shut its eyes and listened as the whistling began again and the footsteps crunched closer and closer. And then they stopped. The boy raised up his lantern and stared.

'No.'

Cautiously he stepped forward and peered at the eagle's scruffy head.

'It *is* a bleedin' bird.'

He poked it and jumped back. Nothing happened. He kicked one huge yellow talon. Nothing happened. The boy hesitated. Was it asleep? Maybe it wasn't a real bird at all. Feeling bolder, he reached out and stealthily grasped one of the delicate grey fan feathers around the eagle's neck. The instant he began to pull one angry yellow eye snapped open in front of his.

'AHH!'

With a frightened yelp the boy dropped his lantern and raced away down the hill.

'Dang it,' snorted the eagle. There was he lecturing Tom and already he'd gone and altered something. There was no way that young ruffian was coming back up here now. Maybe it didn't matter, but every little change had a consequence, even that folded scrap of newspaper the boy had left lying in the lane . . .

All too soon Tom Scatterhorn found himself staring up at the blazing lights of Catcher Hall. He took a deep breath; then another. He could barely believe that this was the very same night that he had arrived in the past almost three years ago, when he had fallen through that wicker basket under the stairs in the museum and found himself in the trunk upstairs in Catcher Hall. That was the beginning, he remembered it all so clearly now. He had stepped out onto the landing and met Mrs Cuddy the housekeeper standing holding a tray. Beside her stood Noah, her youngest son. They hadn't seemed at all surprised to see him. They thought he had got lost. They had sent him up to the attic, and when he opened the door there was August Catcher, busy stuffing a kingfisher. Somehow August had known he was coming too—in fact he was expected. August had been looking forward to meeting his new assistant . . .

Leaving the safety of the shadows, Tom boldly climbed the steps to the front door. He had never known why any of this should have been—it had all been part of the strange experience of falling back through time. But now he realized it was his opportunity. All he had to do was be himself—nothing more. Complete the circle. Lifting the heavy brass knocker Tom knocked loudly, twice. Footsteps echoed across the stone hallway. What about the black beret, should he leave it on or take it off? Hastily he stuffed it back in his pocket.

'Can I help you, boy?'

A stout, friendly-looking woman in a blue apron appeared, her dimpled cheeks as red as apples. It was the housekeeper: Mrs Cuddy. Tom swallowed hard. That singsong voice, it was just the same. Suddenly his head had gone blank.

'Erm . . . I've come about . . . the position.'

Mrs Cuddy peered at the blond scarecrow dressed in an odd greatcoat and scarf. She wondered if this was some sort of trick.

'We ain't got nothing to sell here.'

'I believe Mr August Catcher requires an assistant?'

'Oh, that! You's seen the paper, then?'

'That's right.'

'Silly me, I'd clean forgotten. Come in out of the weather, lad.' She bustled him inside. 'We don't normally get visitors this time o' night. I expect you got lost on the way up here, hmm?'

'That's it,' mumbled Tom, following her as she crossed the hall. Down they went towards the large kitchen at the back that Tom remembered so well from his days before. A couple of saucepans were bubbling away on the range and an odd collection of boots and stockings were hanging above it. The room was filled with the fuggy smell of gravy and wet clothes. It was rather comforting.

'This lad's come about the position,' said Mrs Cuddy bustling over to the kettle.

Tom turned towards the table and had to pinch himself to stop smiling: there was Noah and Abel, his older brother, drinking bowls of soup. Noah grinned at him cheerily as he sat down.

'What's yer name, boy?'

'Tom.'

'Tom what?'

'Tom Sc—' Tom stopped himself: no, *no*—don't do that. He had made that mistake too many times already. 'Just Tom will do.'

'Right Tom, I'll go and let Mr August know you're here. Abel, when you've finished will you put all them knives and forks away for me please?'

'Mam,' grunted Abel, glancing at the long line of silver cutlery he had just finished polishing at the end of the table. Mrs Cuddy picked up a large basket of sheets and approached the back stairs door.

'Be an angel and do the doors for me, Noah. Noah?'

'Comin.'

Noah slipped a large hunk of bread into his mouth and slid off the bench, giving Tom a good look as he went past.

'Bin down the fair then?'

Tom nodded. Noah eyed his strange clothes.

'You a skater?'

'Erm—kind of.'

'It's the midnight race tonight. What skates you got?'

'Noah, will you quit yackin' and open this door,' said his mother impatiently.

'I'm savin' for a new pair. Them red 'uns in Stannard's window. You seen 'em?'

'No.'

'Dead flashy they are. Proper—'

'Noah, you'll be getting a clip round the ear in a minute.'

The boy grinned, then opened the door for his mother and they disappeared up the back stairs.

Tom took a seat beside the stove, and watched Abel slowly blow on each spoonful of soup and chew his bread. In the corner, just beyond him, was the scullery door. Tom prayed the key to the woods was still hanging behind it as he remembered it used to be. But how was he going to get to it? He couldn't do anything with Abel sitting there.

'You a gyppo then?' said Abel, suspiciously.

Tom shook his head.

'No.'

Abel eyed Tom's filthy hands and face then glanced at the long line of silver on the table.

'Got recommendations?'

Again Tom shook his head.

'Cos Mr August don't just employ anyone.'

'I know.'

Abel grunted and went back to his soup. Slowly the minutes ticked by. Tom began to fidget. It was half past ten now, and Abel didn't seem to be in any hurry. He wasn't sure exactly what time it was when he had fallen back into this house from the museum, but he could hardly still be sitting down here when he was also up in August's workshop in the attic . . .

'Can I use the lavatory?'

'Lavatory?' Abel repeated, as if he had never heard the word. 'Bog's out the back.'

'Thanks.'

Tom gratefully jumped to his feet and walked boldly over to the scullery door, opening it and stepping inside.

'Not that way.'

Tom's hand searched in the darkness across the back of the door, his fingers closing around a heavy key . . .

'Oi!'

Slipping the key into his coat pocket Tom turned back to Abel and smiled.

'Sorry, I thought you meant, sorry . . . '

Abel shook his head in despair. He indicated the corridor.

'Thanks.'

Gratefully Tom raced along it: and then he stopped. You can't change anything, the eagle had insisted, and he knew it—tinkering with the past was forbidden, even the smallest change might have a consequence reaching far beyond . . . but Tom couldn't ignore this—it was a matter of life and death. He had to say something.

'Abel?'

The boy looked up from his soup.

'If August Catcher ever gives you enough money to buy a horse at the ice fair, don't whatever you do let Noah try it out. In fact, don't let him go anywhere near it, OK?'

Abel Cuddy glared at him as if he was mad.

'Just try to remember that. Please.'

There, he had said it. Away he ran, down through the warren of servants' passages until he found himself out in the kitchen garden. Keeping low, he scurried between the beds towards the high wall at the end, and with trembling fingers placed the key in the lock of the small wooden door. There was a loud squeak of protest, then the lock turned . . . Yes . . . Tom had half-wondered whether it might have seized up as he had never seen anyone come down here . . . Quietly closing it behind him, Tom knew that all he had to do now was . . . Axe. He'd forgotten the axe! The eagle had insisted . . . Tom cursed silently. He'd have to go back. It was in the woodshed next to the house. He'd run right past it. Carefully he opened the door again, but barely had he begun to retrace his steps when something emerged from the shadow of the woodshed. A stovepipe hat; then the owner of that hat, a burly man with a gun crooked over his arm, then three dogs, trotting at his heel. They must have seen him, how could they not? Tom's heart was beating so fast he could barely think. He'd have to use something else. Find something else to break it open with . . .

Before he knew it Tom was back in the wood with the door locked firmly behind him.

'It's nearish the middle, close to a broken-down shed, and it looks a bit like a hand . . . '

The eagle's instructions spun around Tom's head as he forced his way down into the thicket. How was he going to find the right tree in this? It could be anywhere, the whole place was a tangle of dead trees and brambles and it was so dark he could barely see his own hands. Tom pressed on blindly. Thick swirls of mist were sweeping up the hill towards him. Everything in this wood smelt rotten, sickly, dead . . .

Don't panic. Be patient. There's time. You'll find it.

But supposing he didn't?

Suddenly Tom heard a noise to the left. He froze, instantly, and listened. Above the roar of the trees there had been a clang. It sounded like someone had dropped something heavy . . . Forcing a path towards the sound, Tom suddenly found himself on the edge of an oval clearing. It was as unexpected as it was mysterious, a small patch of light in the darkness. What was this place? It felt ancient, strange . . . Tentatively Tom stepped out onto the frosty grass and listened. Was that the outline of a roof? The mist obscured it again. Maybe it was . . .

Thump. There it was again. Closer now. Like hammering . . . Ignoring his racing heart, Tom crept forward towards the sound. In the darkness beyond the clearing he could just make out the shape of a mighty tree standing on its own. It was like a bull elephant, so old and gnarled that heavy iron bands held its splitting trunk together. At its core, five massive dead branches reached up towards the sky like . . . Tom stared at it giddily. That was it! The

481

vent hole—he knew it—the hollow tree that had concealed the beetles' greatest secret for thousands of years; but that was where the noise was coming from. Someone was already up in there, hacking at it with an axe . . .

CHAPTER 28

THE LAST SECRET

'Hey!'

No answer. Whoever was up there obviously had the same idea as Tom . . . perhaps he could help; unless . . . a dark shape slithered down through the branches to the ground. Instinctively Tom drew back as the shadow strode purposefully towards him, axe in hand. The man was dressed in a long black coat and his wide peaked cap was pulled down low over his eyes. He had a nervous manner that Tom instantly recognized.

'Nicholas? Nicholas Zumsteen?'

Zumsteen froze and stared into the shadows. When he saw Tom he suddenly relaxed.

'You're late,' he grinned. 'I'd been wondering when you'd turn up.'

'So . . . you know?'

'Of course I do.'

'But how?'

'You weren't the only one out on the battlefield, Tom Scatterhorn. That ludicrous mishmash of an eagle may have thought it was being very clever at hiding the truth, but I made an educated guess, and now you are here, I see I was right. What is it, a bolt of lightning?'

'Erm . . .'

'Well it can't be long now,' said Zumsteen, listening to the thunder rolling in the distance. 'I've made a start and there are some more pieces of iron in that shed. It will take both of us to wedge it open properly.'

Zumsteen slipped inside the old doorway and began rummaging around. A moment later he reappeared with a collection of iron hoops that might have once held a barrel together.

'So you really want to destroy Scarazand?'

'I would have thought that was fairly obvious, wouldn't you?' he barked, carrying his load swiftly across the clearing. 'You've seen what my brother is capable of. He's fooled us all. Somehow he discovered that the gorogonas could be controlled by the Queen. Quite how he did it, I don't know—I can only assume that someone very close to him gave him one. And that is why he deliberately lost the battle.' Nicholas Zumsteen dumped his bundle at the base of the tree and strode back for the axe lying on the grass. 'So are you going to stand there like a lemon or give me a hand?'

Still Tom hesitated, he wasn't sure why: there was something in Zumsteen's attitude . . .

'I can't do this alone, Tom Scatterhorn,' he warned, sensing Tom's reluctance.

'But I thought—'

Suddenly Tom found a pistol pointing at his forehead. Zumsteen stared at him coldly.

'You were the one who gave him that gorogona, weren't you?'

Tom backed away, his hands raised high above his head.

'And the mesmerion, which I had carefully tracked down and hidden away in a place he would never find it.'

'That wasn't my faul—'

'Isn't it time you made amends for this catalogue of stupidity and did the right thing for once? I think I deserve that.'

Tom stared into Zumsteen's pale, nervous face. There was a strange glint of red in his eyes, a malevolent, burning anger . . . he brought the gun closer.

'Don't forget, Tom Scatterhorn, I have saved your life once already. You owe me a favour.'

'But why do I have—'

'Get up in that tree. Now.'

By now Tom knew something was wrong, and Zumsteen sensed it. His lips curled into a sneer.

'You don't trust me. You think I'm just like him, don't you?'

The next second there was a loud creak and the heart of the ancient oak opened up like a flower. A cloud of yellow gas bloomed forth, followed by the long silhouette of Don Gervase.

'Don't you dare go anywhere, boy.'

The moment Zumsteen turned his back Tom edged away into the shadows. There was a crash of branches and Don Gervase Askary strode confidently out into the clearing with a very pleased expression on his face.

'What a surprise! If it isn't my little brother, building a tree house.'

'Don't come any closer!' shouted Zumsteen, aiming his pistol.

Don Gervase ignored the threat.

'How predictable that once you realized how foolish you have been you would attempt to use this last secret in some way. But why tonight, I wonder? What is so special about December the fifteenth 1899?' He glanced at the snow on the ground, the gale roaring through the trees. 'A winter storm: hmm—intriguing: so what is it? A few fireworks from the ice fair, some dynamite stolen from the docks? No? Ah, I've got it—you've persuaded August Catcher to build you a bomb?'

Zumsteen's knuckle whitened on the grip of his pistol.

'Stay back, I said.'

A cold, mocking smile fixed on Don Gervase's face.

'Put it down, Caleb.'

With one finger he slowly and deliberately pushed the barrel away from his chest to the ground.

'That's better. We both know you won't use it. Because you never could shoot anyone in cold blood, could you? Never had the guts.'

For a full five seconds the two brothers glowered at each other, ignoring the thunder rolling overhead.

'What do you want?'

'The mesmerion,' growled Zumsteen. 'It belongs to me. Like everything else you've stolen.'

Don Gervase seemed to find this highly amusing.

'Oh Caleb, I'm disappointed. You're supposed to be my better half. *You* want to control Scarazand?'

Zumsteen grimaced.

'I won't ask you again.'

'And if I refuse? Well?'

Don Gervase waited, gloating as Zumsteen tried to think of an answer.

'What will you do then, little brother—summon a bolt of lightning?'

Suddenly Zumsteen smashed his pistol across Don Gervase's face, sending him staggering backwards. Don Gervase was shocked, and barely had he clutched at his bloodied nose than Zumsteen knocked him to the ground. They wrestled, violently tearing at each other's chest and face until Don Gervase lay pinned to the frosty earth with Zumsteen pressing one knee into his neck.

'Give me that ball,' he hissed. With both hands he lunged at the mesmerion that had slipped into his brother's palm. A thin steel feeler instantly slithered from Don Gervase's cuff and wrapped itself protectively around his fingers. 'Give it to me!'

Don Gervase could barely breathe, but somehow his thin lips split into a smirk.

'You'll never manage it, Caleb. You're too weak.'

Zumsteen ground his knee down harder, forcing him to choke.

'I think I could kill you even now.'

'You're insane, Dorian.'

'Am I?'

Zumsteen glanced to his right. There lay the axe . . . in a flash he stretched out and grabbed it. With one swift blow he brought it down on Don Gervase's wrist, cutting his hand clean off. Don Gervase stared at the stump of his arm and screamed, but already Zumsteen had ripped the mesmerion away and was racing for the tree.

Don Gervase writhed violently in the snow, his skin beginning to boil and blotch . . . the next second he screamed again and exploded out of his body into a vast black beetle. Sloughing off his ripped skin he turned and rushed after Nicholas Zumsteen . . .

'Get away from me!' Zumsteen shouted, leaping up into the branches and climbing as fast as he could. 'Stay back!'

But the beetle did not stay back. On it came, scrambling up through the tree at extraordinary speed. Reaching the vent hole first Zumsteen turned just in time to see the great stag's head emerging through the branches behind him . . . he knew he could not escape. Suddenly he too began to shake uncontrollably, his face swelling and boiling . . . Tom's eyes widened as the next moment Zumsteen's skin ripped apart and an identical beetle burst out, instantly locking horns with Don Gervase. Together they became one solid machine, slamming each other around the vent hole: down came dead branches and showers of twigs as they wrestled back and forth, until at last one beetle gained a foothold inside the lip of the chimney and dropped inside. In a series of violent jerks it began to pull the other down after it . . . Its adversary held on, held on, straining every sinew as it struggled to stay on its feet . . . but with a sudden stumble it lurched forwards and fell away out of sight . . .

Tom ran out into the clearing, barely able to breathe. They'd gone, both of them, back into Scarazand . . . Was that the end? A deep roll of thunder jolted him to his senses. He looked up. The trees overhead were roaring like a furnace. The time! He'd almost forgotten . . . frantically Tom checked his watch. It was 12.42 a.m. Three minutes. He had three minutes left. Or less . . .

There was a bark somewhere below. Then more, echoing up through the trees towards him, and footsteps too . . . Tom didn't want to hear any more. Grabbing the bloodied axe lying in the snow he raced up to the ancient tree and, sliding the handle into his belt, began hauling himself up through the branches . . . but barely had he left the ground before his hands began to burn . . .

'Ow,' he gasped. 'Ow!'

His skin felt as if it was on fire. That hurt . . . that *really* hurt . . . what was it? The palms of his hands were covered in something white and burning, like acid . . . it must be oozing out of the bark, the tree was attacking him . . . Tom shouted in pain and frustration. He had seen some gauntlets lying on the battlefield, if only—

'Come away out of there!'

Tom looked down. There was the gamekeeper, gun in hand, crashing up through the trees, his dogs yelping excitedly before him.

Ignore them. Ignore everything . . .

Hiding his hands in his sleeves as best he could Tom climbed fast, wriggling and squirming up through the branches till at last he reached the central hollow. From here the five great branches spread, and in the middle was a hole, its bark petals pushed back by three planks of wood . . . Covering his nose and mouth Tom dared to peer down into the chimney: far below was the dim outline of the Queen, her glistening pulpy flanks now swarming with what looked like black worms . . . gorogonas . . . Above her two black beetles circled, lunging at each other viciously. Tom's head swam—the booming was terrific, and the gas . . . he turned away, clenching his eyes tight shut as a yellow cloud bloomed out. When he looked back something was different . . . the hole, somehow it was smaller. It *was* smaller.

'No . . .'

In an instant Tom realized what was happening. The planks Zumsteen had wedged across the chimney to keep it open were not strong enough. One of them had been knocked askew by the two great beetles in their wild descent. Now the lid was slowly beginning to close itself once more, hiding the precious Queen, protecting her—

With a roar Tom took a wild swing at the rising petals with his axe—then another and another, not caring who heard the hollow clangs . . . but it was no use. Up they came, slowly, inexorably—

'STOP!'

A voice from somewhere inside the chimney . . . another bloom of gas bubbled up, followed by a head and shoulders . . .

'Tom! Are you up here?'

It was a boy in armour, his face bloodied and blackened . . . his echo.

'What's happening!' he panted.

'The lid,' gasped Tom. 'It's closing. I can't stop it . . . ' He glanced at his watch. The second hand was closing on twelve forty-four. No time left.

'We can hold it!' shouted his echo.

Throwing himself across the opening he braced his back against one side and jammed his legs across the other. With all his might he pushed and pushed . . . the petals slowed a little . . . in an instant Tom manoeuvred himself into a position opposite, a mirror image.

'Hard as you can,' gasped the boy, hearing the wood creak and buckle behind him. 'We can stop it! Push!'

Tom closed his eyes and thrust his legs out with all his might. His thighs burned and his lungs felt as if they were on fire . . . yes! They were holding it back, forcing it open wider, wider . . . but then—there was a deep groan somewhere inside, as if the tree had sensed their resistance: it began pushing up harder, faster, overpowering them, crushing the two boys together . . . Tom watched helplessly as his knees began to rise . . . he glanced at his watch . . . the second hand was sweeping past the bottom of the dial . . .

'How long?'

Tom shook his head desperately.

'We've got to get out.'

The echo grimaced and gritted his teeth, refusing to give in . . . their knees were almost touching—

'Come on!'

In an instant Tom swung himself up out of the hole. When he glanced back the Queen was no longer there. A black shape had blotted her out. Something was scrabbling fast up the chimney towards them. Don Gervase . . . he must have seen what they were doing . . . he must have realized . . .

'Quick!' yelled Tom, dragging his echo clear. A pair of serrated black mandibles shot out of the chimney followed by the head and mouth—

'Tom Scatterhorn!' roared the creature. 'You . . . '

But the petals closed up around its black body, wedging it tight. Tom panicked.

'He's jammed! He's stuck! He's going to save it!'

Without a thought the echo darted forward and thrust his sword deep into the beetle's shining mouth. The creature screamed and twisted, but still it didn't move . . . the boy leapt onto its head and stamped viciously, crushing its beady eyes, breaking its teeth, then he leant into his sword, forcing the point deeper into its brain . . . There was a loud scrape and the next moment the great beetle began sliding away down the chimney, taking the echo with it—

'NO!'

Tom gasped. His eyes widened. But he couldn't move. He daren't. One second. Two seconds. Three, four—

BANG!

A colossal explosion shattered the air. A hollow boom sounded somewhere far underground, and the walls of the chimney glowed hot like a candle. Tom opened his eyes to find himself somehow curled up like a baby against the bark. Some deep, primitive instinct had saved him. Crawling across to the chimney he stared open-mouthed at the scene below. The Queen was engulfed in a lazy ripple of green flame: there was a black hole in her head where the lightning had struck. Her veins were streams of yellow fire. Above her floated the silhouette of the boy, his armour glowing pink like a living jewel, and two black shapes—

'He did it . . . ' Tom wiped the sweat out of his eyes. 'He really did it . . . '

And then Tom's joy turned to terror as he realized what was about to happen . . . the death of the Queen . . . the sila scream . . . the end of the colony, the end of him . . . fiercely his heart began pounding in his chest, beating out every last second . . . there was so much more he wanted to do, to see, to be—

Too late . . .

He watched a fireball suddenly bloom and bubble in the chasm below, all angry orange and red: up it came—shrivelling the black beetles and bearing them and the boy roaring up the chimney towards him, flooding the air with a sound that seemed to shake the bones out of his body, shake the tree from the earth, shake the very air itself—

B-B-B-BOOM!

In the blink of a second the magnetic pulse rippled out into the sky and accelerated far, far out across the universe. Tom vaguely glimpsed the tower of flame, then something burst inside his head and he knew no more.

CHAPTER 29

HYACINTHS AND FLOOR POLISH

After a long, long time, two figures appeared in the clearing. The storm had passed now, and the wind blown itself out, too. Nothing moved but the moon and the stars, turning like clockwork towards the dawn.

'This is quite irreversible,' muttered August, staring at the place where the ancient tree had once stood. It looked as if it had been split in two by the blow of a mighty axe. Carefully the two friends picked their way through the fallen limbs to the great hole in the centre where the trunk had been.

'So that's what it looked like,' whispered Sir Henry, leaning over the edge and peering in. 'Almost unreal.'

August stared in quiet wonder at the chaos raging below.

'I wasn't convinced he'd really do it, you know. In fact I was half-hoping he wouldn't.'

'Shame on you, August. That boy was headstrong, if nothing else. It's a family trait.'

'I'd noticed.'

With a heavy sigh August mooched off into the debris. Now that it had actually happened he couldn't help feeling guilty.

It seemed such a waste of a young life . . . Stepping over a branch his eye was caught by something red poking out of the dirty snow.

'Good lord.'

It was a long thin hand, cut off at the wrist. A feeler was still wrapped around its fingers. August stared at it a moment, bewildered, then moved on. Not far away there was another curiosity, but this he recognized.

'You have got a lot to answer for,' he murmured, picking the mesmerion out of the snow and giving it a squeeze. Slipping the ball into his pocket, he was about to move on when he noticed something glinting close by in the moonlight: two somethings, in fact. Carefully August placed them in his palm and turned into the moonlight. At first glance they appeared to be a pair of beads, as black as coal and polished by fire. Only the melted red outlines of carapaces and shrivelled heads suggested that they might once have been some kind of beetle.

'August!'

Sir Henry's sharp tone cut through the stillness. He turned to see his friend kneeling on the far side of the clearing.

'I fear we may have been too hasty.'

'What? Who is it?'

Sir Henry did not reply. Hastily slipping his finds into his pocket August scrambled over, his heart full of dread. There lay Tom Scatterhorn, his face bloody and dark, dressed in a pair of old boots and a greatcoat. On the other side of a fallen branch lay his echo, his elaborate armour scorched and dented. His helmet had gone and a long streak of blood stretched across his face.

'But surely they're not alive? How can they be, after that?'

Sir Henry pressed his fingers to the neck of the echo: there was no pulse. Then he bent his head to Tom's chest. Was that the dimmest of heartbeats . . . a vague flutter of life?

'I can't be sure. I don't know.'

August wiped his brow uneasily.

'This is all our fault. We encouraged him knowing this would happen.'

'No, August. On the contrary, I seem to remember we were both very careful to warn him off.' They stared in silence at Tom's grey face. There was a strange expression on his lips—almost like a smile.

'I mean, of course we *wanted* him to destroy Scarazand, and yes, he did have some misguided notion that he had to sacrifice himself for the greater good, or whatever, but—' Sir Henry shrugged. 'Frankly, old chap—it was *his* decision. He knew that if the Queen died he too would perish. You told him as much yourself.'

August's expression hardened.

'But the fact remains that we used him. If we'd been a little braver we might have intervened ourselves. But we didn't dare—knowing that he would. For which he has paid dearly. Don't you think we owe him another chance?'

The anger in August's voice was unmistakable. Sir Henry watched him reach into his satchel and, after a brief rummage around, draw out a small blue bottle.

'Is that wise, old chap, bearing in mind who else is bound to have perished in all this?' August appeared not to have heard him. Ignoring Sir Henry's disapproving gaze he shook a small violet handkerchief out of his jacket pocket.

'I seem to remember you once held strong views about changing fate.'

'Fate has already changed, Henry, or are you suggesting we try and put this tree back together exactly as it was? What is the same here now?'

Sir Henry did not need reminding. Obviously August was right.

'Supposing it's too late?'

Tom had no idea how long he had been walking, it might have been hours, or seconds. When he looked up, he found himself standing outside a high wall covered in ivy. It was so high he couldn't see the top of it. He didn't know whether he was awake, or if this was a dream, but he could see an arched door set in wall before him, and knew that he had to go through that door. So he did, and Tom found himself in a garden. There were neatly cut lawns, a fountain, and a white path before him, leading up to a tall stone house framed by dark trees. Everything was as fake and flat as a stage set, even the spray of stars glittering beyond. I know this place, thought Tom. I have been here before, somehow. I know this place.

'Yes you do know this place,' answered a voice. 'You have been here before.'

Tom froze. Was that voice in his head? It seemed—

'August?'

He turned round to find a shadow leaning against a tree. The man moved out into the dappled moonlight.

'Hello,' he said.

Tom stared at August's shock of white hair, his shabby tweed suit. He seemed real, and yet Tom couldn't be so sure.

'Is this a dream?'

August Catcher's face, as wizened and crumpled as bark, smiled kindly.

'But I'm not . . . ' For some reason Tom did not want to say the word. 'What am I doing here?'

'I think you have come to retrieve that other part of your-self.'

'My echo?'

August nodded.

'He's not leaving without you. He can't. He's waiting for you up there.'

Tom looked up at the windows. He couldn't see anyone.

'And he is not alone, either.'

'What do you mean?'

Tom turned back to the tree but August had gone. Where he had stood there was nothing. Just a tree in the moonlight.

'August?'

The garden was empty. Nothing moved. A deafening silence imprisoned everything. Tom wondered if he had been talking to himself. Maybe he had . . .

Feeling very conspicuous he set off up the white gravel path towards the house. With each step the kicked stones hung like weightless planets, slowly spreading themselves back down to the ground. What was he doing in this place? On reaching the fountain he looked up at the windows again. This time he could see a pale face framed against the darkness on the top floor. The echo's cheeks were streaked with blood and he still wore that blackened suit of armour. Tom felt a shiver run down his spine. So he was waiting for me? But where must they go?

'Tom?'

A tall, rangy man was standing at the top of the steps. A dark-haired woman walked out of the house to join him. They stood together, side by side, smiling happily.

'Tom darling, where have you been? We've all been waiting for you.'

'Mum? Dad?'

They kept smiling, but did not come any closer.

'Look.' Sam Scatterhorn pointed across to where an old camper van was parked in the shadow of a cedar tree. 'We've got the old girl back up and running. How about that?'

Sam grinned and Poppy smiled too, her eyes full of love and tenderness.

'We made such a mess of everything, Tom. We should have told you right from the start. We should have trusted you. It was so stupid.' She paused. 'We've not been very good parents, I'm afraid.'

'But now we can be together,' smiled Sam. 'Will you come with us?'

Tom was aware that the fierce-eyed boy at the window was watching him intently.

'Where are we going?'

'Oh you know, around. Just like in the bad old days.' His dad winked. 'It's what you're here for, isn't it?'

In that moment Tom realized that it was, and he felt his heart was about to burst. He wanted nothing more than to race up the steps and throw himself into their arms . . . but the instant he moved forward something stopped him. Something fundamental, as if there was a glass wall between them.

'Tom?'

His mother's expression changed. She sensed something was wrong.

'What's that noise?'

'What's what noise, darling?'

Tom looked around him nervously. There was an engine throbbing somewhere, getting louder . . . in the sky—

'Can't you hear it?'

Tom's nose began to tingle. The garden was filling with the smell of chemicals and flowers, a heavy, choking scent, spreading, everywhere . . .

'What's the matter, Tom?'

He did not know, but before he could stop himself he was running away down the white gravel path.

'Tom!' called his mother. 'Tom, where are you going? Don't leave us!'

Sam and Poppy Scatterhorn stood on the steps watching their son race hard away from them. And as he ran, Tom's own heart began beating faster, faster, another drum catching up with that engine booming inside his head, until the two beats merged into one . . .

'Come back!'

The door in the ivy flung open before him and a spark of light danced out—

'Supposing it's too late,' whispered a voice.

Tom opened his eyes. Slowly the darkness began to clear. There were August Catcher and Sir Henry, smiling down at him. August held a small blue bottle in his hands.

'Well?'

'Still with us, old chap?'

Tom nodded groggily. The tree lay in shattered pieces all around. The moon still hung in the sky. It was all coming back. Carefully August wrapped up a small blue bottle in his violet handkerchief then slipped it back into his top pocket. Hyacinths, floor polish . . . that smell . . . *that* smell. Tom looked into August's ancient, kindly face, so lined that his eyes were nothing but bright dots. He said:

'Sometimes, it is worth changing things. Perhaps it was selfish of me, but I rather assumed you would like to do a bit more living. A lot more living, as it happens. I hope I wasn't wrong in that.'

Tom's head was swimming. Of course he wanted to live: how could he not? Who would choose to be dead rather than alive? Sitting up, he saw the echo lying on the ground beyond the branch, his armour glinting in the moonlight.

'But he's gone, hasn't he?'

Sir Henry nodded.

'Much better that there's only one Tom Scatterhorn from now on.'

'Because I saw him there, with . . . with—' A lump began to rise in his throat.

'Poppy and Sam?'

Tom nodded.

'What happened to them?'

August's bright eyes narrowed for a moment.

'Out on the battlefield, once the stockade fell and all those gorogonas broke loose—'

'They never stood a chance, old bean,' murmured Sir Henry, putting his hand on Tom's shoulder. 'Like all the others, I'm afraid.'

Tom said nothing. He stared at the ground. Of course, he understood this now, but even so . . .

'Did you want to join them?'

'A little.' Tom smiled bravely. 'But . . . not enough, I suppose. I'm glad you did it. Thank you.'

Sir Henry's angular face brimmed with admiration. He held out his hand.

'You're a very remarkable young man, Tom Scatterhorn. Perhaps you would like to see exactly what it is you have done.'

Taking Sir Henry's hand, Tom gingerly got to his feet, feeling very bruised indeed. Leaning on Sir Henry's arm he hobbled over to the rim of the hole.

'Now what does that remind you of?'

For a moment Tom stared down at the chaos in silence. Far below lay the Queen, now just a blackened smoking heap. All around her Scarazand was collapsing. Bridges, lumps of rock, mountains of pulp and racks of larvae were tumbling away into the chasm below. All around the cave walls countless gorogonas clung, desperately trying to escape the maelstrom, but one by one their safe havens broke off and plunged into the darkness. Even the labyrinth—the thicket of white pathways that stretched out in every direction—was starting to disintegrate . . .

'Plum duff.' Sir Henry's eyes glinted mischievously. 'Plum duff, you know. With brown sugar and ice cream. It's delicious. You mean to say you've never had it?'

'I think it's more of a cherry trifle,' said August. 'With a fistful of hundreds and thousands, and possibly some toasted almonds thrown in.'

For the first time in a long, long while Tom found himself smiling. Yes, it was just like looking down into a vast, swirling pudding. The scale was so enormous it was hard to believe this was actually real.

'So the gorogonas . . . '

'The sila scream would have killed most of them. And for the rest, without the labyrinth there is no way out of that chasm. Except up through this little chimney of course,' August winked.

Tom stood watching the collapsing world. It was a strange, bittersweet feeling, but only now did he realize that Scarazand had truly, finally gone. He was free, at last. Turning round, he looked to where the echo lay, his blackened armour glinting in the moonlight.

'You know, this only happened because of him. That beetle was caught in the chimney. If he hadn't jumped on its head, forced it down, the lightning would never—'

'Pah! He wouldn't have even been there were it not for you!' Sir Henry roared. 'Give yourself some credit, old chap. You are two sides of the same coin.'

'Precisely,' added August. 'You've done something truly remarkable here. Both of you. It's a triumph. Enjoy it,' he smiled, throwing an arm across his shoulder. 'That's better.'

'There is one more thing.'

'Is there?'

'It's quite important.'

August's eyes sparkled.

'When is it not? Fire away.'

'If Scarazand has been destroyed tonight, December fifteenth 1899, does that mean that from now on everything will be different?'

'From *now* on—yes, I think it does,' August replied. 'You are here, we are here, we have lived and we are not about to rewrite our own history. But what you have just done, Tom, is from this moment on create an alternative future—one in which Scarazand will not feature in any shape or form.'

'And that alternative future is fast upon us,' said Sir Henry, consulting his watch. 'In precisely two hours the sun will rise and I'll bet it won't be long before someone comes up to see where the lightning struck. At which point there is going to be one hell of a scene.'

'Quite,' agreed August. 'And I suppose it is vaguely possible that one of those tiny gorogonas might worm their way up here and escape. Which would be a shame,' he added, with considerable understatement.

Tom looked across at his echo lying in the debris.

'And there's him, too.'

'Quite. But there is—'

'*Was* a solution to that,' interrupted Sir Henry, catching August's eye.

'What do you mean?'

'Oh it's nothing,' blustered August. 'Just something that used to happen before. It's quite inappropriate now.'

Avoiding Tom's enquiring look they kept their eyes fixed on the maelstrom below.

'But I've got it,' said Sir Henry suddenly. 'At this moment, August, you are fast asleep up there in Catcher Hall.'

'Snoring more than likely,' he admitted. 'Go on.'

'Well supposing we disguise the hole with brambles, branches, mud, etcetera, etcetera—for now. Then tomorrow morning, when you sit down to breakfast and open your post, you find a letter addressed to you, in confidence, from me, describing everything that has happened here tonight, and advising you to take an immediate and secret course of action to seal this hole for ever.'

August gave a wry smile and rubbed his head.

'You forget, Henry, that at this moment in my life I am a serious taxidermist. My head is full of chemical equations, techniques for stuffing pythons and parakeets, I would never believe such an extraordinary story. I'd think you were pulling my leg. In fact I'd be certain of it.'

'Even if the evidence is right here in your own wood?'

'I doubt whether I'd even bother to come down to check. I never did before, did I?'

Sir Henry frowned. He had to admit this was a problem. August was, by his own admission, cynical, lazy, otherwordly . . .

'But you might, if—' Sir Henry grinned like a lion. 'Supposing that letter was not written by me. Supposing it was written by *you*—and addressed to you, in your own hand.'

August stared at the vent hole, thinking hard.

'A letter written to myself . . . *from* myself, in the future?'

Sir Henry's eyes narrowed.

'Exactly. And you might also suggest an alternative to that miserable pauper's grave while you're at it.'

August glanced down at the echo, then back to his old friend. His crumpled features split into a smile.

'I think that is inspired.'

'Good. Good good good. I hoped you might say that.'

CHAPTER 30

THE RETURN OF THE OTHER

It was the first of May, a Sunday, and very early in the morning, and it seemed as if the whole world had crawled out of the shadow of a long and bitter winter and was stretching itself out in the warm spring sunlight. The streets were empty, the sky was blue, there was barely a breath of wind: it was a beautiful day—but not everyone thought so. A rusty red motorbike and sidecar clattered around the corner into Museum Street, ridden by a small man with a dark expression on his face. Jos Scatterhorn had not slept well. He had been tormented by that nightmare again, the one where he'd spent his entire life stuck in a creaky old museum that was falling down and no one wanted to visit . . . only to wake up and find it was true.

'Come on,' he grunted, as the engine spluttered and coughed and finally died at the bottom of the hill. Jos heaved himself off the seat and thought about giving it a hearty kick, only to remember what had happened the last time he had done that. He had limped for a week. Instead, he flipped open the fuel tank lid and peered inside.

'Empty, I presume?' said Melba, his wife, who sat patiently in the sidecar reading a book.

'Someone's siphoned it off. It's been filched. It's—'

'Entirely predictable,' interrupted Melba. Sliding out of the sidecar she strode up the hill towards the museum. 'Come along, you silly man.'

Jos Scatterhorn harrumphed inside his helmet.

'Bleeding filchers.'

Hefting the bike onto its stand he scurried after her, wrestling his helmet free.

'I don't know why we keep bothering with this, Melba,' he puffed, 'it's Sunday! Who wants to spend a lovely sunny morning traipsing around a damp, cold, unpleasant—'

'There's always someone. Goths, ghouls, ghost-hunters, lost tourists—don't forget we've been voted the "spookiest place" in Dragonport ten years in a row. And frankly, have you got any better ideas?'

Jos Scatterhorn wheezed violently. He most certainly did. The tide was in, he could take *Sugarmouse*, his beloved fishing smack, out for a sail. Or there was the cup final this afternoon. Why, he would even consider chopping down that sea of nettles in the back garden rather than spend yet another—Jos was just about to place his key in the heavy lock when he noticed that the Museum's front door was ajar. It had not been forced. It was already open.

'But I locked it. Of course I locked it. When have I ever . . .'

'I'm starting to have serious doubts about your sanity, Jos Scatterhorn.'

Jos withered a little under Melba's stare. This could mean a great many things, most of which he didn't want to contemplate this early in the morning.

'Hello?'

He pushed the heavy door so that it swung in noisily on its hinges. Silence.

'Anyone there?'

Jos peered at the familiar parade of dusty cases and faded animals dissolving into the gloom. It was quiet as a grave. Steeling himself, he sidestepped a red fire bucket full of rainwater and rolled into the hall.

'Hello-o—'

'Good morning.'

A tall, elegant man in a tweed suit prowled out from behind a display case and fixed him with a quick eye. He had thick white whiskers and his skin was the colour of yellowed ivory. He seemed to be very, very old: but strangely alert.

'And who, pray, might you be?'

Jos Scatterhorn was momentarily taken aback. This was certainly not the hooded ruffian he was expecting.

'I might ask you the same question.'

'My name is Sir Henry Scatterhorn, and we have a package for Tom. Is he here?'

Jos scratched a non-existent hair on his head, wondering if he had heard correctly. 'Sorry, did you just say—'

'Sir Henry Scatterhorn. That's right. That's me.' Sir Henry concealed his impatience with a smile. 'Well? Is Tom here or not?'

Jos let out a little cough. This man, if it *was* this man—and Jos could not be entirely sure—was the founder of this museum. He must be at least a hundred and fifty years old.

'There is no one here of whom you speak.'

'You're a week early.'

Sir Henry spun round to see a thin woman with a medieval haircut emerge from the doorway. She was as spare and sharp as the man was ample and short.

'The Dragonport vampire convention is *next* Sunday. You'll have to come back. Though I like your costume. Sir Henry Scatterhorn—how apt.'

Sir Henry was mystified.

'Show us your fangs.'

'What?'

'Oh go on, open your mouth.'

'My mouth?'

'Well, you must have fangs. All vampires have fangs. What about a blood capsule? No? I suppose it might spoil the suit. Rented, I imagine.'

At that moment another elderly gentleman trotted down the stairs. He wore a blue tweed suit, thick as a blanket, and a shock of white hair stood upright on his head. He too was oddly nimble for one so old.

'August, apparently he's not here.'

'Not here? Oh dear.'

'And they think I'm a vampire.'

'A vampire? What kind of madhouse is this?'

Jos looked from one to the other in bewilderment. Not August as in *Catcher*?

'What this place needs is a new roof and a damn good sweep,' he said, running a thick line of dust off a case with his finger. 'Joseph Scatterhorn, I presume? Thought as much. Now there's a new exhibit up with the reptiles and it's turned out rather well, though I say it myself. Don't whatever you do tinker with it, or else there will be trouble. And be sure to tell the boy where it is when he arrives. It's a little surprise for him.'

'The boy—'

'He'll recognize it all right,' interrupted August, shuffling at speed towards the door. 'And I do think you should try a bit harder. This place is filthy, and it's damp, and filth and damp and taxidermy do not go together. A little jollification is required my friend, razzamatazz. Give it life! I did!'

With a chuckle August Catcher raised his hand and melted away into the light.

'Joseph *Scatterhorn*—eh?' Sir Henry looked Jos up and down and failed to see any family resemblance. It was like comparing a warthog with a cheetah. Then he glanced at the buckets of rain water, the filthy windows, the collapsing displays . . .

'But of course. How interesting. Obviously not. Never mind. Sorry to disappoint you, madam.'

With a grin Sir Henry turned and followed his companion out into the street. For several seconds Jos and Melba stood motionless, staring at the spring sunlight pouring in through the open door.

'Not the vampire convention, then?'

Melba was lost for words. She had spent the last thirty years padding about the deep gloom of the museum, and she stoically accepted that its mysterious atmosphere played tricks on the mind and occasionally moved things around like a conjuror. But meeting the founder, and the creator, in person—that just about topped it all.

'Supposing he *has* left something up there.'

'Don't, Jos. Just don't.'

A minute later they were up in the reptile gallery, peering into the small case that had been left on the table. Melba tapped the glass once, half-expecting it not to be there.

'Is it real?'

'Obviously it's real.'

'So obviously they were.'

By now Melba was also wishing she had never got out of bed: but this was not the end of it. A few minutes later a loud creak echoed across the gloomy hall and the front door opened once more.

'Uncle Jos? Melba? Hello?'

There was no answer.

A boy walked into the foyer and looked around. He was narrowly built and hungry looking, and his shock of blond hair lit up like a halo.

'Oh hi,' he said, smiling broadly when he spotted two shadows lurking at the top of the stairs. He held up a brown paper bag. 'Bacon sandwiches. I thought I'd surprise you.'

Jos knotted his eyebrows together into a hedge. This was prankstery gone too far.

'Looking for vampires, are you?'

'No.'

'Seen something you want to nick?'

'No—'

'Then who the blazes are you? "Tom", I suppose?'

The boy smiled awkwardly.

'Yes. Of course I am. Don't you recognize me?'

Jos and Melba carefully descended the stairs and approached the boy as if he was some dangerously unpredictable creature.

Like the other two visitors, he seemed quite real, but unlike them, there was something familiar about him . . .

'You say you've brought us sandwiches?'

'That's right. Please, help yourself.'

Jos glanced at the bag. He could smell the bacon.

'Very well, "Tom", I've no idea who the hell you are, but you're very kind, and I don't mind if I do.'

Pulling out a sandwich he unwrapped it and began munching noisily.

'I don't suppose your other name is *Scatterhorn*, is it?' asked Melba, taking one for herself. 'And this is a school project to re-trace your roots?'

Tom laughed nervously, wondering whether that was a joke.

'It's very popular these days. The world's obsessed with finding out who they are and where they came from.'

'Obsessed,' nodded Jos. 'Good sandwich, lad.'

'Excellent,' chimed Melba. 'Aren't you going to have one?'

Tom watched them sitting on the stairs, eating contentedly. He was rapidly beginning to wonder if their confusion was genuine.

'Erm . . . maybe.'

Trying to ignore his racing heart, Tom hurried out into the sunshine and turned back to face the museum. Above the great door were the two stone dragons, holding between them the stone tablet which read:

THE SCATTERHORN MUSEUM

FOUNDED 1906 BY SIR HENRY SCATTERHORN

BEQUEATHED TO THE PEOPLE OF DRAGONPORT

GOD SAVE THE KING

And that was it. His name was not there. He had not restored the museum, which meant . . . the bomb went off silently in Tom's head. It was just as August had told him it would be. This was a *new* future . . . it might look familiar, but it was a world in which he had taken no part, until the moment he had stepped into it an hour ago. He was not on any record, he might not even exist. He was no one.

A little while later Melba appeared at the doorway with a steaming cup of tea. The boy was still sitting on the sunlit steps. There was a lost look on his face.

'Here,' she said, handing it to him.

Tom took it gratefully and blew on the surface.

'Everything all right?'

'Yes. Thanks.'

'Sorry we were a little unfriendly earlier. The fact is we don't get many visitors these days, and this morning . . . we were in a slight state of shock, to put it mildly.' Melba paused. 'I must say I'm intrigued to know why you thought we were your aunt and uncle.'

Tom looked up into her angular, birdlike face. There was no point in trying to explain, she'd never understand.

'I didn't really . . . I was just . . . confused.'

'But you are doing a school project?'

'Yes.'

'And your name is Scatterhorn?'

Tom nodded.

'Tom Scatterhorn. Hmm. Well there aren't many of us about. But you do look very familiar.'

'Do I?'

'Indeed you do. I don't forget faces. Names, always, but faces—never. I've seen you before somewhere. Definitely.' She was about to dart back through the great door when she stopped suddenly and remembered. 'By the way, there was someone here earlier calling himself Sir Henry Scatterhorn. Said he was looking for you.'

'Oh?'

'And an August Catcher, too. Do you know them?'

'Erm . . . kind of. In a way.'

Melba wrinkled her nose thoughtfully: she could not possibly understand how this might be, but the news seemed to have instantly lifted the boy's spirits.

'They've left something for you upstairs. Maybe you should come in and have a look. It's up behind the bird galleries. Rather peculiar.'

Tom hurriedly gulped down the rest of his tea and stepped back into the brown darkness of the museum. He had no idea what they might have left for him, but as he walked past each dusty model and ancient specimen case, he couldn't help noticing that they were all as moth-eaten and unloved as the very first day he had arrived at the Museum in another lifetime. There was the mammoth, the dodo, the man-eating tiger, the porcupine . . . never before had he felt such a connection to all these tatty animals, and though it was painful to admit, he knew exactly why. Thanks to August Catcher, he was alive, but out of time, and so were they. He had become one of them. They were the same . . .

'Well if it isn't the hero himself.'

Tom was so lost in his daydreams that he hadn't noticed the

shadow standing behind the tree full of toucans at the top of the stairs. She was wearing a long grey coat and matching hat, and stood poised like a ballerina.

'Hi, Tom. Fancy meeting you here.'

Lotus Askary emerged from the darkness, her large, cat-like eyes glittering mischievously. Tom felt strangely happy to see her familiar face, though he couldn't help but wonder . . .

'Surprised to see me? Didn't think I'd survive?' She beamed at his confusion. 'I was never like the others, don't you remember? Kafka beetle: different breed. Never had that same instinct to protect the Queen. And as for being *here*, right now: I have only just arrived, like you have. How did you do it?'

'The trunk. In Catcher Hall.'

'Of course. I'd forgotten about that old connection.'

There was an awkward silence for a moment. Neither of them knew quite what to say.

'But congratulations. That was quite a stunt. You really did it, Tom.'

'It was a joint effort. It took both of us.'

'Myself and I, you mean.' Lotus looked at him and grinned. 'You're so funny. Even after all that you'll never be much good at blowing your own trumpet. And in answer to your next question, well I've come back to see you, of course, but also see what's changed around here, now that everything's so different.'

Tom smiled at her sarcasm.

'That might take you a while. This is the Scatterhorn Museum. Nothing changes.'

'Actually something has.' There was a strange smirk on Lotus's face that Tom couldn't immediately understand. 'Isn't there a new exhibit up in the reptile room? Jos Scatterhorn said so. Perhaps we should take a look together.'

Lotus led the way through the cases of chattering parrots, gangs of kookaburras and moth-eaten macaws into the small reptile room at the end. On the table in the centre stood a domed glass case, which at first glance contained a jungle scene. There were a couple of poison dart frogs, a stick insect or two, and in the middle sat a plump green chameleon, its tail and thumbs curled around a twig. It was staring mournfully at the reflection of the moon in a puddle.

Lotus pressed her face towards the glass.

'Oh!'

Suddenly an eyeball swivelled back to stare at her. Then the other swivelled in the opposite direction towards Tom. He gasped in amazement.

'Chameleons' eyes do that—don't they?'

Lotus nodded. She stared at the reptile for a moment and it stared back at her gloomily.

'And they're very peculiar eyeballs. Almost burnt.'

Lotus was right: August seemed to have used a pair of identical black beads, with red lines melted into the surface, that seemed to describe the shapes of—

'Wait . . . ' Tom gasped. 'Wait. That isn't . . . is that—'

'It must be. August must have found them in the debris of the tree. Shrivelled to nothing more than that.'

Lotus contemplated the chameleon with a look of deep satisfaction on her face. This was the real reason she had come back. To make quite certain they had both gone for ever. Here was the final proof.

'What about the moon?' said Tom, now realizing the true meaning of this little tableau. Lotus followed the mournful gaze of the chameleon down into the puddle. There, just below the water's dark surface, was the pale outline of a ball.

'It's the mesmerion, isn't it? It's got to be.'

Lotus's eyes sparkled: of course, Tom was right. She had not expected this, too.

'Just beyond their reach. For ever. August Catcher is a genius.'

Tom nodded in silent agreement. Of course August was a genius—but he had always known that.

'Actually he wasn't completely stupid himself.'

'Who?'

'Don Gervase Askary.'

'Lotus, he was insane.'

'Maybe a little insane—but he was also right about many things. He knew that the death of the Queen would do far more than just destroy Scarazand. That pulse rippled far, far out across the universe. There are bound to be others who heard it.'

'Which others?'

Lotus shrugged. 'Who knows? But we should be ready for them if they come, don't you think?'

A clever, knowing smile flickered briefly on her lips.

Then Tom noticed a single pale ball hanging from her bracelet. The light danced through it like quicksilver.

'What is that?'

'This?' Her fingers crossed its shining surface. 'Oh, it's just something I found. In a cave.' She winked. Lotus was not about to tell him any more than that. 'What are you going to do now?' she said, changing the subject.

Tom glanced at the dusty reptiles all around. He couldn't pretend this wasn't a question weighing heavily on his mind.

'I don't know. Everything feels a bit strange.'

Lotus's large, catlike eyes regarded him thoughtfully.

'Don't try to be ordinary, Tom. Don't try to fit in. You never will. Not now.'

'That's what I'm worried about. Who wants to be ordinary?'

'So don't be,' she grinned, staring at the boy with blond hair and dark eyes who looked strangely young, strangely old at the same time.

'I'm going to miss you, Tom Scatterhorn, and I never thought I'd say that.'

Tom never thought she would say that either. But Lotus was right, there was something unspoken between them now, a world of secrets that bound them together.

'I'll always know where to find you, won't I?'

'Maybe.'

'Maybe?' She laughed. 'Don't tell me you're bored with the Scatterhorn Museum already?' Lotus hesitated, and thought about saying something else—but she didn't. Instead she turned towards the door.

'Oh if you're looking for something that *is* completely different, go down to those woods below Catcher Hall. It's very impressive.'

With the briefest of smiles she was gone. Tom stood in the gloom, listening as her footsteps echoed down the stairs and out onto the street. He knew she had thought of asking him to go with her. But he also knew what his answer would have been.

The woods below Catcher Hall . . . of course, he had almost forgotten. The vent hole.

By the time Tom had made his way across Dragonport the sky was glowing golden and the sea was as smooth as milk.

'Echo Gardens', read the sign sticking out of a hedge. Feeling a surge of excitement building within him, Tom hurried along the warm pavement and entered through the pair of tall iron gates at the end. Where the wood had been there was now a small park, laid out with flowerbeds and neatly clipped grass. Dogs chased each other through the trees and families walked about, enjoying the warm spring evening. At the far end, framed against the dark trees, stood a bronze statue on a high plinth, burning red in the last rays of the sun. The shape was familiar . . . Tom quickened his pace, and before he knew it he was running past the benches and fountains—and the figure began to emerge . . . he was a tousle-haired boy dressed in an intricate suit of armour, bearing a sword in one hand and an extraordinary spiked and snarling helmet in the other. He stood alert, ready, on guard, his deep-set eyes gazing out across the estuary towards the sea beyond. All around his feet lay the debris of battle: shields, swords, armour, and heaps upon heaps of dead serpents, coiled everywhere . . .

Tom's heart was racing so fast he could barely read the elaborate gothic inscription beneath.

'𝕴 𝖉𝖎𝖘𝖈𝖔𝖛𝖊𝖗𝖊𝖉 𝖙𝖍𝖊 𝕸𝖚𝖘𝖊𝖚𝖒'𝖘 𝕾𝖊𝖈𝖗𝖊𝖙,
𝕬𝖓𝖉 𝖆 𝕳𝖎𝖉𝖉𝖊𝖓 𝖂𝖔𝖗𝖑𝖉, 𝖙𝖊𝖊𝖒𝖎𝖓𝖌 𝖆𝖓𝖉 𝖍𝖔𝖙,
𝕴𝖙𝖘 𝕻𝖗𝖎𝖓𝖈𝖊 𝖜𝖆𝖘 𝖒𝖞 𝕱𝖔𝖗𝖌𝖔𝖙𝖙𝖊𝖓 𝕰𝖈𝖍𝖔,
𝕬𝖓𝖉 𝖍𝖊 𝖕𝖊𝖗𝖎𝖘𝖍𝖊𝖉 𝖚𝖕𝖔𝖓 𝖙𝖍𝖎𝖘 𝖘𝖕𝖔𝖙.'

Tom stared down at the heavy stone slab on which the plinth

stood. That was it—the vent hole: right there. The lid on Scarazand. Not only had August read his own letter—he had obviously chosen to believe the whole story. And he had written his epitaph, too.

Small footsteps approached, and Tom turned to see a boy staring up at the statue beside him. He couldn't have been more than five years old, and he was wearing a red woolly hat.

'Who is he?' asked the boy.

Tom hesitated.

'It doesn't say. He doesn't have a name.'

'Is he a knight?'

'Kind of. He's an echo.'

The boy glanced at Tom mistrustfully. He had dark brown eyes and wisps of blond hair poked out from beneath his hat.

'Why does his armour look like a beetle?'

'That's a very special suit of armour. It's called the Scaramoor.'

The boy stared at the helmet a moment, then ran back to his mother who was pushing a pushchair up the hill. There was a little girl asleep inside.

'Who is it, Tommy?' she said.

'He's a knight. But he doesn't have a name. He's an echo.'

'Oh is he? Look at that spiky armour—and that helmet with antlers, isn't it amazing?'

'And the snakes. I bet he's killed them.'

'I bet he has.'

Tom retreated to a bench and watched as a blond, scruffy man sloped up the path to join them, his hands thrust deep in his pockets.

'Doesn't that remind you of someone?'

The man looked up at the statue and laughed.

'Maybe, in ten years' time.'

'What?' asked the boy.

'That could be you, Tommy,' said his mother. 'I know that look.' She stared up at the statue's proud, determined face. 'My forgotten echo . . . it's very peculiar. Perhaps he's a relation, Sam.'

'I doubt it. It's some fantasy figure, isn't it?'

'But wasn't there a Sir someone Scatterhorn who used to live in Dragonport?'

'Sir Henry Scatterhorn. Yes, he was quite a famous big-game hunter in his time. But Poppy, this obviously isn't him.'

Poppy stared up at the statue's familiar face once more.

'Funny though, isn't it? The resemblance.'

'But aren't we all supposed to have an identical twin, a doppelgänger, out there somewhere. Isn't that what they say?'

Poppy shrugged, taking one last look at the statue they drifted off through the trees.

'Actually Sir Henry Scatterhorn founded a little museum. I remember being taken to it once, years ago.'

'What was it like?'

'Very dark and very weird. Full of monkeys with stuffing falling out of their heads and toothless tigers—there was a very strange old couple running the place.'

'Maybe we should go and find it.'

'It can't be still open. It was about to fall down even then.'

'That's a shame. I bet Tommy would like to have seen it.'

522

They turned and waited as the boy came racing around the fountain towards them.

'Yes,' grinned Sam, holding out his hand. 'I'll bet he would.'

Tom sat rooted to the bench, watching as the young family moved down towards the iron gates and out of sight. So his parents *were* alive in this new future . . . of course, why shouldn't they be? But they weren't *his* parents, they were complete strangers, with another son, and a daughter too, and they would never know who he was . . .

'Captured the likeness most precisely. Those devious eyes, that scraggy nest of hair—it's you, kiddo. Down to a tee.'

Tom blinked out of his daydream to find that the park was empty. How long he had been sitting there he didn't know. The sun had set, the gates were locked and he had never even heard the eagle crash-landing in the trees behind him.

'Don't worry, mate, no one's listening,' rasped the bird, shaking out its feathers in the branches. 'Doesn't it feel strange seeing him up there like that?'

'Yes it does. Very.'

The eagle snorted.

'Like looking at your own gravestone, I imagine. Not many people have that pleasure.'

Dropping to the ground with an ungainly bounce, the raptor lolloped out towards the bench.

'So you pleased to be back?'

Tom took a deep breath. He stared up at the statue, now just a dark shape against the trees.

'Everything's finished,' he said quietly.

'You can say that again.'

'I'm not sure I belong here any more.' Suddenly Tom's eyes had filled with hot tears. He turned away in embarrassment, blinking hard. 'I should never have come back.'

The great bird stared out at the estuary, glowing gold in the distance. 'I know that feeling, kiddo. You's of this world, but not exactly in it. Both dead and alive at the same time. That's the gift and the curse that August Catcher has saddled us with. Welcome to immortality, mate.'

Tom felt the weight of these words bear down upon him and he shivered.

'But I don't want to be immortal. I didn't ask to be. I just . . . I don't know what I want to be.'

Tom stared into the thickening shadows and wiped his eyes. Suddenly he felt more alone than he had ever been in his life.

'Yeah, well maybe you're right. Maybe you don't belong here any more. You've done one hell of a lot, my old gullabong. More than most folks will ever do in their entire lives. Perhaps now is the time to start afresh, somewhere . . . completely different.'

The great bird squinted down towards the park gates to see a battered red Land Rover draw up outside. It was very old and a collection of jerry cans and tents were strapped to its roof. It looked as if it might have been about to set off for the North Pole—or Timbuktu, or possibly both.

'And I'll bet I'm not the only one who's reached that conclusion. I reckon they've just seen that little family, too.'

Tom followed the bird's gaze and watched August and Sir

Henry climb out and stand beside the locked park gates. They peered up into the shadows.

'Go with them, kiddo. They's where you really belong. Birds of a feather should stick together—specially folks like ourselves.'

Tom stood up, sparks dancing in his eyes. Suddenly he knew in his heart the eagle was right. That was where he belonged . . .

'But if I do, will I ever see you again?'

'Oh I think there's a fair chance of that,' replied the raptor with a wink. 'You know what I always say.'

'Does a frog have a waterproof bum?'

'Correctamundo.'

Tom was unable to stop smiling.

Bending down, the great ragged creature gave him a friendly rub, and Tom hugged it tight.

'Thanks. For everything. I really mean it.'

The eagle nodded, then nudged him gently away with its beak. Its fierce yellow eyes were shining.

'Now get out of here Tom Scatterhorn, before I chase ya.'

Tom turned, and with a wave he ran down through the darkening trees.

Photo credit: Chloë Stewart

Henry Chancellor has spent many years of his life making documentary films, which have taken him all over the world, meeting some very peculiar people in some very peculiar places. Some of these films have won awards. He has also written a couple of factual books: *Colditz: The Definitive History*, (based on his Channel Four series) and *James Bond: the Man and his World*. *The Forgotten Echo* is the final book in his Tom Scatterhorn trilogy. He lives in Suffolk with his wife, three children, dog, cat, and several other animals.

ACKNOWLEDGEMENTS

The Remarkable Adventures of Tom Scatterhorn have been so full of unexpected twists and turns that Tom had almost as many adventures in the different drafts of these books as he has in the stories that finally made it into print. Without the good advice and unerring faith of Liz Cross, my editor and publisher, I suspect Tom might still be lost in those thickets, even now. I also owe a huge debt of gratitude to Simon Trewin, whose enthusiasm saved the manuscript from languishing in a box somewhere and has supported me along the way. I would also like to thank Christopher Gibbs, Molly Dallas, and all at Oxford for producing such handsome books; Kate Williams, Tessa Girwan, and everyone who helpfully read the stories as they evolved, especially Hassan Amini, Charlotte Stewart, John Wrathall, Louis, Inigo, Esme. Last but not least I want to thank Chloë, who saw everything, read everything, and much, much more besides.

For more on the world of Tom Scatterhorn go to
www.henrychancellor.com